We've dug our holes and hallowed caves
Put goblin foes in shallow graves
This day our work is just begun
In the mines where silver rivers run

Beneath the stone the metal gleams
Torches shine on silver streams
Beyond the eyes of the spying sun
In the mines where silver rivers run

The hammers chime on Mithril pure
As dwarven mines in days of yore
A craftsman's work is never done
In the mines where silver rivers run

To dwarven gods we sing our praise
Put another orc in a shallow grave
We know our work has just begun
In the land where silver rivers run

FANTASY ADVENTURE

Streams of Silver

Book Two: The Icewind Dale Trilogy

R.A. Salvatore

Cover Art by
CLYDE CALDWELL

TSR, Inc.
PRODUCTS OF YOUR IMAGINATION™

STREAMS OF SILVER

This book is protected under the copyright laws of the United States of America. Any reproduction or other unauthorized use of the material or artwork contained herein is prohibited without the express written permission of TSR, Inc.

Distributed to the book trade in the United States by Random House, Inc. and in Canada by Random House of Canada, Ltd.

Distributed in the United Kingdom by TSR UK Ltd.

Distributed to the toy and hobby trade by regional distributors.

FORGOTTEN REALMS, PRODUCTS OF YOUR IMAGINATION, AD&D, and the TSR logo are trademarks owned by TSR, Inc.

First Printing, January 1989
Printed in the United States of America.
Library of Congress Catalog Card Number: 88-51721

9 8 7 6 5 4 3 2 1

ISBN: 0-88038-672-X
All characters in this book are fictitious. Any resemblance to actual persons, living or dead, is purely coincidental.

TSR, Inc.
P.O. Box 756
Lake Geneva,
WI 53147 U.S.A.

TSR Ltd.
120 Church End, Cherry Hinton
Cambridge CB1 3LB
United Kingdom

As with everything I do,
To my wife, Diane
And to the most important people
in our lives
Bryan, Geno, and Caitlin

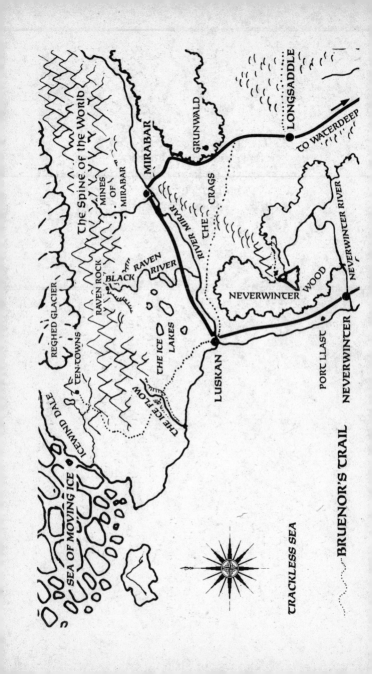

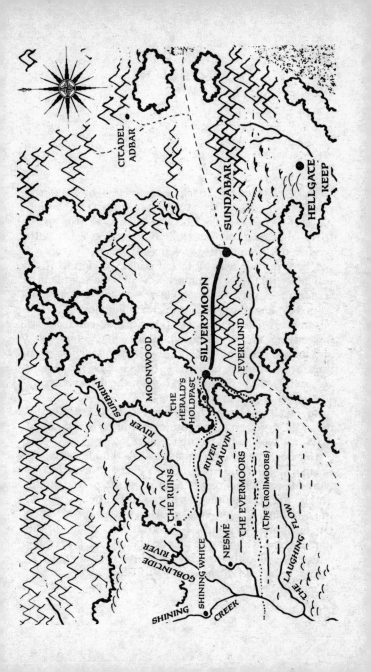

Prelude

On a dark throne in a dark place perched the dragon of shadow. Not a very large worm, but foulest of the foul, its mere presence, blackness; its talons, swords worn from a thousand thousand kills; its maw ever warm with the blood of victims; its black breath, despair.

A raven's coat was its tested scales, so rich in their blackness that they shimmered in colors, a scintillating facade of beauty for a soulless monster. Its minions named it Shimmergloom and paid it all honor.

Gathering its strength over the course of centuries, as dragons do, Shimmergloom kept its wings folded back and moved not at all, except to swallow a sacrifice or to punish an insolent underling. It had done its part to secure this place, routing the bulk of the dwarven army that stood to face its allies.

How well the dragon had eaten that day! The hides of dwarves were tough and muscled, but a razor-toothed maw was well suited to such a meal.

And now the dragon's many slaves did all the work, bringing it food and heeding to its every desire. The day would come when they would need the power of the dragon again, and Shimmergloom would be ready. The huge mound of plundered treasures beneath it fueled the dragon's strength, and in this respect, Shimmergloom was surpassed by none of its kind, possessing a hoard beyond the imagination of the richest kings.

And a host of loyal minions, willing slaves to the dragon of darkness.

* * * * *

The chill wind that gave Icewind Dale its name whistled across their ears, its incessant groan eliminating the casual conversation the four friends usually enjoyed. They moved west across the barren tundra, and the wind, as always, came from the east, behind them, quickening their already strong pace.

Their posture and the determined drive of their strides reflected the eagerness of a newly begun quest, but the set of each adventurer's face revealed a different perspective of the journey.

The dwarf, Bruenor Battlehammer, leaned forward from his waist, his stocky legs pumping mightily beneath him, and his pointed nose, poking out above the shag of his wagging red beard, led the way. He seemed set in stone, apart from his legs and beard, with his many-notched axe held firmly before him in his gnarled hands, his shield, emblazoned with the standard of the foaming mug, strapped tightly on the back of his overstuffed pack, and his head, adorned in a many-dented horned helm, never turning to either side. Neither did his eyes deviate from the path and rarely did they blink. Bruenor had initiated this journey to find the ancient homeland of Clan Battlehammer, and though he fully realized that the silvery halls of his childhood were hundreds of miles away, he stomped along with the fervor of one whose long-awaited goal is clearly in sight.

Beside Bruenor, the huge barbarian, too, was anxious. Wulfgar loped along smoothly, the great strides of his long legs easily matching the dwarf's rolling pace. There was a sense of urgency about him, like a spirited horse on a short rein. Fires hungry for adventure burned in his pale eyes as clearly as in Bruenor's, but unlike the dwarf, Wulfgar's gaze was not fixed upon the straight road before them. He was a young man out to view the wide world for the first time and he continually looked about, soaking up every sight and sensation that the landscape had to offer.

He had come along to aid his friends on their adventure, but he had come, as well, to expand the horizons of his own world. The entirety of his young life had been spent within the isolating natural boundaries of Icewind Dale, limiting his experiences to the ancient ways of his fellow barbarian tribesmen and the frontier peoples of Ten-Towns.

There was more out there, Wulfgar knew, and he was determined to grasp as much of it as he possibly could.

Less interested was Drizzt Do'Urden, the cloaked figure trotting easily beside Wulfgar. His floating gait showed him to be of elven heritage, but the shadows of his low-pulled cowl suggested something else. Drizzt was a drow, a black elf, denizen of the lightless underworld. He had spent several years on the surface, denying his heritage, yet had found that he could not escape the aversion to the sun inherent in his people.

And so he sunk low within the shadow of his cowl, his stride nonchalant, even resigned, this trip being merely a continuation of his existence, another adventure in a life-long string of adventures. Forsaking his people in the dark city of Menzoberranzan, Drizzt Do'Urden had willingly embarked upon the road of the nomad. He knew that he would never be truly accepted anywhere on the surface; perceptions of his people were too vile (and rightly so) for even the most tolerant of communities to take him in. The road was his home now; he was always traveling to avoid the inevitable heartache of being forced from a place that he might have come to love.

Ten-Towns had been a temporary sanctuary. The forlorn wilderness settlement housed a large proportion of rogues and outcasts and, though Drizzt wasn't openly welcomed, his hard-earned reputation as a guardian of the towns' borders had granted him a small measure of respect and tolerance from many of the settlers. Bruenor named him a true friend, though, and Drizzt had willingly set out beside the dwarf on the trek, despite his apprehension that once he moved out beyond the influence of his reputation, the treatment he received would be less than civil.

Every so often, Drizzt dropped back the dozen yards or so to check on the fourth member of the party. Huffing and puffing, Regis the halfling brought up the rear of the troupe (and not by choice) with a belly too round for the road and legs too short to match the pumping strides of the dwarf. Paying now for the months of luxury he had enjoyed in the palatial house in Bryn Shander, Regis cursed the turn of luck that had forced him to the road. His greatest love was comfort and he worked at perfecting the arts of eating and sleeping as diligently as a young lad with dreams of heroic deeds swung his first sword. His friends were truly surprised when he joined them on the road, but they were happy to have him along, and even Bruenor, so desperate to see his ancient homeland again, took care not to set the pace too far beyond Regis's ability to keep up.

Certainly Regis pushed himself to his physical limits, and without his customary complaining. Unlike his companions, though, whose eyes looked to the road up ahead, he kept glancing back over his shoulder, back toward Ten-Towns and the home he had so mysteriously abandoned to join in the journey.

Drizzt noted this with some concern.

Regis was running away from something.

The companions kept their westerly course for several days. To their south, the snow-capped peaks of the jagged mountains, the Spine of the World, paralleled their journey. This range marked the southern boundary to Icewind Dale and the companions kept an eye out for its end. When the westernmost peaks died away to flat ground, they would turn south, down the pass between the mountains and the sea, running out of the dale altogether and down the last hundred mile stretch to the coastal city of Luskan.

Out on the trail each morning before the sun rose at their backs, they continued running into the last pink lines of sunset, stopping to make camp at the very last opportunity before the chill wind took on its icy nighttime demeanor.

Then they were back on the trail again before dawn, each running within the solitude of his own perspectives and fears.

A silent journey, save the endless murmur of the eastern wind.

❧ BOOK 1: ❧

Searches

❧ 1 ❧

A Dagger at Their Backs

He kept his cloak pulled tightly about him, though little light seeped in through the curtained windows, for this was his existence, secretive and alone. The way of the assassin.

While other people went about their lives basking in the pleasures of the sunlight and the welcomed visibility of their neighbors, Artemis Entreri kept to the shadows, the dilated orbs of his eyes focused on the narrow path he must take to accomplish his latest mission.

He truly was a professional, possibly the finest in the entire realms at his dark craft, and when he sniffed out the trail of his prey, the victim never escaped. So the assassin was unbothered by the empty house that he found in Bryn Shander, the principal city of the ten settlements in the wasteland of Icewind Dale. Entreri had suspected that the halfling had slipped out of Ten-Towns. But no matter; if this was indeed the same half-ling that he had sought all the way from Calimport, a thousand miles and more to the south, he had made better progress than he ever could have hoped. His mark had no more than a two-week head start and the trail would be fresh indeed.

Entreri moved through the house silently and calmly, seeking hints of the halfling's life here that would give him the edge in their inevitable confrontation. Clutter greeted him in every room—the halfling had left in a hurry, probably aware that the assassin was closing in. Entreri considered this a good sign, further heightening his suspicions that this halfling, Regis, was the same Regis who had served the Pasha Pook those years ago in the distant southern city.

The assassin smiled evilly at the thought that the halfling knew he was being stalked, adding to the challenge of the hunt as Entreri pitted his stalking prowess against his intended victim's hiding ability. But the end result was predictable, Entreri knew, for a frightened person invariably made a fatal mistake.

The assassin found what he was looking for in a desk drawer in the master bedroom. Fleeing in haste, Regis had neglected to take precautions to conceal his true identity. Entreri held the small ring up before his gleaming eyes, studying the inscription that clearly identified Regis as a member of Pasha Pook's thieves' guild in Calimport. Entreri closed his fist about the signet, the evil smile widening across his face.

"I have found you, little thief," he laughed into the emptiness of the room. "Your fate is sealed. There is nowhere for you to run!"

His expression changed abruptly to one of alertness as the sound of a key in the palatial house's front door echoed up the hallway of the grand staircase. He dropped the ring into his belt pouch and slipped, as silent as death, to the shadows of the top posts of the stairway's heavy banister.

The large double doors swung open, and a man and a young woman stepped in from the porch ahead of two dwarves. Entreri knew the man, Cassius, the spokesman of Bryn Shander. This had been his home once, but he had relinquished it several months earlier to Regis, after the halfling's heroic actions in the town's battle against the evil wizard, Akar Kessell, and his goblin minions.

Entreri had seen the other human before, as well, though he hadn't yet discovered her connection to Regis. Beautiful women were a rarity in this remote setting, and this young woman was indeed the exception. Shiny auburn locks danced gaily about her shoulders, the intense sparkle of her dark blue eyes enough to bind any man hopelessly within their depths.

Her name, the assassin had learned, was Catti-brie. She lived with the dwarves in their valley north of the city, particularly with the leader of the dwarven clan, Bruenor, who had adopted her as his own a dozen years before when a goblin raid had left her orphaned.

This could prove a valuable meeting, Entreri mused. He cocked an ear through the banister poles to hear the discussion below.

"He's been gone but a week!" Catti-brie argued.

"A week with no word," snapped Cassius, obviously upset. "With my beautiful house empty and unguarded. Why, the front door was unlocked when I came by a few days ago!"

"Ye gave the house to Regis," Catti-brie reminded the man.

"Loaned!" Cassius roared, though in truth the house had indeed been a gift. The spokesman had quickly regretted turning over to Regis the key to this palace, the grandest house north of Mirabar. In retrospect, Cassius understood that he had been caught up in the fervor of that tremendous victory over the goblins, and he suspected that Regis had lifted his emotions even a step further by using the reputed hypnotic powers of the ruby pendant.

Like others who had been duped by the persuasive halfling, Cassius had come to a very different perspective on the events that had transpired, a perspective that painted Regis unfavorably.

"No matter the name ye call it," Catti-brie conceded, "ye should not be so hasty to decide that Regis has forsaken the house."

The spokesman's face reddened in fury. "Everything out today!" he demanded. "You have my list. I want all of the halfling's belongings out of my house! Any that remain when I return tommorrow shall become my own by the rights of possession! And I warn you, I shall be compensated dearly if any of my property is missing or damaged!" He turned on his heel and stormed out the doors.

"He's got his hair up about this one," chuckled Fender Mallot, one of the dwarves. "Never have I seen one whose friends swing from loyalty to hatred more than Regis!"

Catti-brie nodded in agreement of Fender's observation. She knew that Regis played with magical charms, and she figured that his paradoxical relationships with those around him were an unfortunate side effect of his dabblings.

"Do ye suppose he's off with Drizzt and Bruenor?" Fender asked. Up the stairs, Entreri shifted anxiously.

"Not to doubt," Catti-brie answered. "All winter they've been asking him to join in the quest for Mithril Hall, an' to be sure, Wulfgar's joining added to the pressure."

"Then the little one's halfway to Luskan, or more," reasoned Fender. "And Cassius is right in wantin' his house back."

"Then let us get to packing," said Catti-brie. "Cassius has enough o' his own without adding to the hoard from Regis's goods."

Entreri leaned back against the banister. The name of Mithril Hall was unknown to him, but he knew the way to Luskan well enough. He grinned again, wondering if he might catch them before they ever reached the port city.

First, though, he knew that there still might be some valuable information to be garnered here. Catti-brie and the dwarves set about the task of collecting the halfling's belongings, and as they moved from room to room, the black shadow of Artemis Entreri, as silent as death, hovered about them. They never suspected his presence, never would have guessed that the gentle ripple in the drapes was anything more than a draft flowing in from the edges of the window, or that the shadow behind a chair was disproportionately long.

He managed to stay close enough to hear nearly all of their conversation, and Catti-brie and the dwarves spoke of little else than the four adventurers and their journey to Mithril Hall. But Entreri learned little for his efforts. He already knew of the halfling's famed companions— everyone in Ten-Towns spoke of them often: of Drizzt Do'Urden, the renegade drow elf, who had forsaken his dark-skinned people in the bowels of the Realms and roamed the borders of Ten-Towns as a solitary guardian against the intrusions of the wilderness of Icewind Dale; of Bruenor Battlehammer, the rowdy leader of the dwarven clan that lived in the valley near Kelvin's Cairn; and most of all, of Wulfgar, the mighty barbarian, who was captured and raised to adulthood by Bruenor, returned with the savage tribes of the dale to defend Ten-Towns against the goblin army, then struck up a truce between all the peoples of Icewind Dale. A bargain that had salvaged, and promised to enrich, the lives of all involved.

"It seems that you have surrounded yourself with formidable allies, halfling," Entreri mused, leaning against the back of a large chair, as Catti-brie and the dwarves moved into an adjoining room. "Little help they will offer. You are mine!"

Catti-brie and the dwarves worked for about an hour, filling two large sacks, primarily with clothes. Catti-brie was astounded with the stock of possessions Regis had collected since his reputed heroics against Kessell and the goblins—mostly gifts from grateful citizens. Well aware of the halfling's love of comfort, she could not understand what had possessed him to run off down the road after the others. But what truly amazed her was that Regis hadn't hired porters to bring along at least a few of his belongings. And the more of his treasures that she discovered as she moved through the palace, the more this whole scenario of haste and impulse bothered her. It was too out of character for Regis. There had to be another factor, some missing element, that she hadn't yet weighed.

"Well, we got more'n we can carry, and most o' the stuff anyway!" declared Fender, hoisting a sack over his sturdy shoulder. "Leave the rest for Cassius to sort, I say!"

"I would no' give Cassius the pleasure of claiming any of the things," Catti-brie retorted. "There may yet be valued items to be found. Two of ye take the sacks back t'our rooms at the inn. I'll be finishing the work up here."

"Ah, yer too good to Cassius," Fender grumbled. "Bruenor had him marked right as a man taking too much pleasure in counting what he owns!"

"Be fair, Fender Mallot," Catti-brie retorted, though her agreeing smile belied any harshness in her tone. "Cassius served the towns well in the war and has been a fine leader for the people of Bryn Shander. Ye've seen as well as meself that Regis has a talent for putting up a cat's fur!"

Fender chuckled in agreement. "For all his ways of gettin' what he wants, the little one has left a row or two of ruffled victims!" He patted the other dwarf on the shoulder and they headed for the main door.

"Don't ye be late, girl," Fender called back to Catti-brie. "We're to the mines again. Tomorrow, no later!"

"Ye fret too much, Fender Mallot!" Catti-brie said, laughing.

Entreri considered the last exchange and again a smile widened across his face. He knew well the wake of magical charms. The "ruffled victims" that Fender had spoken of described exactly the people that Pasha Pook had duped back in Calimport. People charmed by the ruby pendant.

The double doors closed with a bang. Catti-brie was alone in the big house—or so she thought.

She was still pondering Regis's uncharacteristic disappearance. Her continued suspicions that something was wrong, that some piece of the puzzle was missing, began to foster within her the sense that something was wrong here in the house, as well.

Catti-brie suddenly became aware of every noise and shadow around her. The "click-click" of a pendulum clock. The rustle of papers on a desk in front of an open window. The swish of drapes. The scutterings of a mouse within the wooden walls.

Her eyes darted back to the drapes, still trembling slightly from their last movement. It could have been a draft through a crack in the window, but the alert woman suspected differently. Reflexively dropping to a crouch and reaching for the dagger on her hip, she started toward the open doorway a few feet to the side of the drapes.

Entreri had moved quickly. Suspecting that more could yet be learned from Catti-brie, and not willing to pass up the opportunity offered by the dwarves' departure, he had slipped into the most favorable position for an attack and now waited patiently atop the narrow perch of the open door, balanced as easily as a cat on a window sill. He listened for her approach, his dagger turning over casually in his hand.

Catti-brie sensed the danger as soon as she reached the doorway and saw the black form dropping to her side. But as quick as her reactions were, her own dagger was not halfway from its sheath before the thin fingers of a cool hand had clamped over her mouth, stifling a cry, and the razored edge of a jeweled dagger had creased a light line on her throat.

She was stunned and appalled. Never had she seen a man move so quickly, and the deadly precision of Entreri's strike unnerved her. A sudden tenseness in his muscles assured her that if she persisted in drawing her weapon, she would be dead long before she could use it. Releasing the hilt, she made no further move to resist.

The assassin's strength also surprised her as he easily lifted her to a chair. He was a small man, slender as an elf and barely as tall as she, but every muscle on his compact frame was toned to its finest fighting edge. His very presence exuded an aura of strength and an unshakable confidence. This, too, unnerved Catti-brie, because it wasn't the brash cockiness of an exuberant youngster, but the cool air of superiority of one who had seen a thousand fights and had never been bested.

Catti-brie's eyes never turned from Entreri's face as he quickly tied her to the chair. His angular features, striking cheekbones and a strong jaw line, were only sharpened by the straight cut of his raven black hair. The shadow of beard that darkened his face appeared as if no amount of shaving could ever lighten it. Far from unkempt, though, everything about the man spoke of control. Catti-brie might even have considered him handsome, except for his eyes.

Their gray showed no sparkle. Lifeless, devoid of any hint of compassion or humanity, they marked this man as an instrument of death and nothing more.

"What do ye want o' me?" Catti-brie asked when she mustered the nerve.

Entreri answered with a stinging slap across her face. "The ruby pendant!" he demanded suddenly. "Does the halfling still wear the ruby pendant?"

Catti-brie fought to stifle the tears welling in her eyes. She was disoriented and off guard and could not respond immediately to the man's question.

The jeweled dagger flashed before her eyes and slowly traced the circumference of her face.

"I have not much time," Entreri declared flatly. "You will tell me what I need to know. The longer it takes you to answer, the more pain you will feel."

His words were calm and spoken with honesty.

Catti-brie, toughened under Bruenor's own tutelage, found herself unnerved. She had faced and defeated goblins before, even a horrid troll once, but this collected killer terrified her. She tried to respond, but her trembling jaw would allow no words.

The dagger flashed again.

"Regis wears it!" Catti-brie shrieked, a tear tracing a solitary line down each of her cheeks.

Entreri nodded and smiled slightly. "He is with the dark elf, the dwarf, and the barbarian," he said matter-of-factly. "And they are on the road to Luskan. And from there, to a place called Mithril Hall. Tell me of Mithril Hall, dear girl." He scraped the blade on his own cheek, its fine edge poignantly clearing a small patch of beard. "Where does it lie?"

Catti-brie realized that her inability to answer would probably spell her end. "I—I know not," she stammered boldly, regaining a measure of the discipline that Bruenor had taught her, though her eyes never left the glint of the deadly blade.

"A pity," Entreri replied. "Such a pretty face. . . ."

"Please," Catti-brie said as calmly as she could with the dagger moving toward her. "Not a one knows! Not even Bruenor! To find it is his quest."

The blade stopped suddenly and Entreri turned his head to the side, eyes narrowed and all of his muscles taut and alert.

Catti-brie hadn't heard the turn of the door handle, but the deep voice of Fender Mallot echoing down the hall-way explained the assassin's actions.

"'Ere, where are ye, girl?"

Catti-brie tried to yell, "Run!" and her own life be damned, but Entreri's quick backhand dazed her and drove the word out as an indecipherable grunt.

Her head lolling to the side, she just managed to focus her vision as Fender and Grollo, battle-axes in hand, burst into the room. Entreri stood ready to meet them, jeweled dagger in one hand and a saber in the other.

For an instant, Catti-brie was filled with elation. The dwarves of Ten-Towns were an iron-fisted battalion of hardened warriors, with Fender's prowess in battle among the clan second only to Bruenor's.

Then she remembered who they faced, and despite their apparent advantage, her hopes were washed away by a wave of undeniable conclusions. She had witnessed the blur of the assassin's movements, the uncanny precision of his cuts.

Revulsion welling in her throat, she couldn't even gasp for the dwarves to flee.

Even had they known the depths of the horror in the man standing before them, Fender and Grollo would not have turned away. Outrage blinds a dwarven fighter from any regard for personal safety, and when these two saw their beloved Catti-brie bound to the chair, their charge at Entreri came by instinct.

Fueled by unbridled rage, their first attacks roared in with every ounce of strength they could call upon. Conversely, Entreri started slowly, finding a rhythm and allowing the sheer fluidity of his motions to build his momentum. At times he seemed barely able to parry or dodge the ferocious swipes. Some missed their mark by barely an inch, and the near hits spurred Fender and Grollo on even further.

But even with her friends pressing the attack, Catti-brie understood that they were in trouble. Entreri's hands seemed to talk to each other, so perfect was the complement of their movements as they positioned the jeweled dagger and saber. The synchronous shufflings of his feet kept him in complete balance throughout the melee. His was a dance of dodges, parries, and counter-slashes.

His was a dance of death.

Catti-brie had seen this before, the telltale methods of the finest swordsman in all of Icewind Dale. The comparison to Drizzt Do'Urden was inescapable; their grace and movements were so alike, with every part of their bodies working in harmony.

But they remained strikingly different, a polarity of morals that subtly altered the aura of the dance.

The drow ranger in battle was an instrument of beauty to behold, a perfect athlete pursuing his chosen course of righteousness with unsurpassed fervor. But Entreri was merely horrifying, a passionless murderer callously disposing of obstacles in his path.

The initial momentum of the dwarves' attack began to diminish now, and both Fender and Grollo wore a look of amazement that the floor was not yet red with their opponent's blood. But while their attacks were slowing, Entreri's momentum continued to build. His blades were a blur, each thrust followed by two others that left the dwarves rocking back on their heels.

Effortless, his movements. Endless, his energy.

Fender and Grollo maintained a solely defensive posture, but even with all of their efforts devoted to blocking, everyone in the room knew that it was only a matter of time before a killing blade slipped through.

Catti-brie didn't see the fatal cut, but she saw vividly the bright line of blood that appeared across Grollo's throat. The dwarf continued fighting for a few moments, oblivious to the cause of his inability to find his breath. Then, startled, Grollo dropped to his knees, grasping his throat, and gurgled into the blackness of death.

Fury spurred Fender beyond his exhaustion. His axe chopped and cut wildly, screaming for revenge.

Entreri toyed with him, actually carrying the charade so far as to slap him on the side of the head with the flat of the saber.

Outraged, insulted, and fully aware that he was overmatched, Fender launched himself into a final, suicidal, charge, hoping to bring the assassin down with him.

Entreri sidestepped the desperate lunge with an amused laugh, and ended the fight, driving the jeweled dagger deep into Fender's chest, and following through with a skull-splitting slash of the saber as the dwarf stumbled by.

Too horrified to cry, too horrified to scream, Catti-brie watched blankly as Entreri retrieved the dagger from Fender's chest. Certain of her own impending death, she closed her eyes as the dagger came toward her, felt its metal, hot from the dwarf's blood, flat on her throat.

And then the teasing scrape of its edge against her soft, vulnerable skin as Entreri slowly turned the blade over in his hand.

Tantalizing. The promise, the dance of death.

Then it was gone. Catti-brie opened her eyes just as the small blade went back into its scabbard on the assassin's hip. He had taken a step back from her.

"You see," he offered in simple explanation of his mercy, "I kill only those who stand to oppose me. Perhaps, then, three of your friends on the road to Luskan shall escape the blade. I want only the halfling."

Catti-brie refused to yield to the terror he evoked. She held her voice steady and promised coldly, "You underestimate them. They will fight you."

With calm confidence, Entreri replied, "Then they, too, shall die."

Catti-brie couldn't win in a contest of nerves with the dispassionate killer. Her only answer to him was her defiance. She spat at him, unafraid of the consequences.

He retorted with a single stinging backhand. Her eyes blurred in pain and welling tears, and Catti-brie slumped into blackness. But as she fell unconscious, she heard a few seconds longer, the cruel, passionless laughter fading away as the assassin moved from the house.

Tantalizing. The promise of death.

❧ 2 ❧

City of Sails

"Well, there she is, lad, the City of Sails," Bruenor said to Wulfgar as the two looked down upon Luskan from a small knoll a few miles north of the city.

Wulfgar took in the view with a profound sigh of admiration. Luskan housed more than fifteen thousand—small compared to the huge cities in the south and to its nearest neighbor, Waterdeep, a few hundred miles farther down the coast. But to the young barbarian, who had spent all of his eighteen years among nomadic tribes and the small villages of Ten-Towns, the fortified seaport seemed grand indeed.

A wall encompassed Luskan, with guard towers strategically spaced at varying intervals. Even from this distance, Wulfgar could make out the dark forms of many soldiers pacing the parapets, their spear tips shining in the new light of the day.

"Not a promising invitation," Wulfgar noted.

"Luskan does not readily welcome visitors," said Drizzt, who had come up behind his two friends. "They may open their gates for merchants, but ordinary travelers are usually turned away."

"Our first contact is there," growled Bruenor. "And I mean to get in!"

Drizzt nodded and did not press the argument. He had given Luskan a wide berth on his original journey to Ten-Towns. The city's inhabitants, primarily human, looked upon other races with disdain. Even surface elves and dwarves were often refused entry. Drizzt suspected that the guards would do more to a drow elf than simply put him out.

"Get the breakfast fire burning," Bruenor continued, his angry tones reflecting his determination that nothing would turn him from his course. "We're to break camp early, an' make the gates 'fore noon. Where's that blasted Rumblebelly?"

Drizzt looked back over his shoulder in the direction of the camp. "Asleep," he answered, though Bruenor's question was wholly rhetorical. Regis had been the first to bed and the last to awaken (and never without help) every day since the companions had set out from Ten-Towns.

"Well, give him a kick!" Bruenor ordered. He turned back to the camp, but Drizzt put a hand on his arm to stay him.

"Let the halfling sleep," the drow suggested. "Perhaps it would be better if we came to Luskan's gate in the less-revealing light of dusk."

Drizzt's request confused Bruenor for just a moment—until he looked more closely at the drow's sullen visage and recognized the trepidation in his eyes. The two had become so close in their years of friendship that Bruenor often forgot that Drizzt was an outcast. The farther they traveled from Ten-Towns, where Drizzt was known, the more he would be judged by the color of his skin and the reputation of his people.

"Aye, let 'im sleep," Bruenor conceded. "Maybe I could use a bit more, meself!"

They broke camp late that morning and set a leisurely pace, only to discover later that they had misjudged the distance to the city. It was well past sunset and into the early hours of darkness when they finally arrived at the city's north gate.

The structure was as unwelcoming as Luskan's reputation: a single iron-bound door set into the stone wall between two short, squared towers was tightly shut before them. A dozen fur-capped heads poked out from the parapet above the gate and the companions sensed many more eyes, and probably bows, trained upon them from the darkness atop the towers.

"Who are you who come to the gates of Luskan?" came a voice from the wall.

"Travelers from the north," answered Bruenor. "A weary band come all the way from Ten-Towns in Icewind Dale!"

"The gate closed at sunset," replied the voice. "Go away!"

"Son of a hairless gnoll," grumbled Bruenor under his breath. He slapped his axe across his hands as though he meant to chop the door down.

Drizzt put a calming hand on the dwarf's shoulder, his own sensitive ears recognizing the clear, distinctive click of a crossbow crank.

Then Regis unexpectedly took control of the situation. He straightened his pants, which had dropped below the bulge of his belly, and hooked his thumbs in his belt, trying to appear somewhat important. Throwing his shoulders back, he walked out in front of his companions.

"Your name, good sir?" he called to the soldier on the wall.

"I am the Nightkeeper of the North Gate. That is all you need to know!" came the gruff reply. "And who—"

"Regis, First Citizen of Bryn Shander. No doubt you have heard my name or seen my carvings."

The companions heard whispers up above, then a pause. "We have viewed the scrimshaw of a halfling from Ten-Towns. Are you he?"

"Hero of the goblin war and master scrimshander," Regis declared, bowing low. "The spokesmen of Ten-Towns will not be pleased to learn that I was turned into the night at the gate of our favored trading partner."

Again came the whispers, then a longer silence. Presently the four heard a grating sound behind the door, a portcullis being raised, knew Regis, and then the banging of the door's bolts being thrown. The halfling looked back over his shoulder at his surprised friends and smiled wryly.

"Diplomacy, my rough dwarven friend," he laughed.

The door opened just a crack and two men slipped out, unarmed but cautious. It was quite obvious that they were well protected from the wall. Grim-faced soldiers huddled along the parapets, monitoring every move the strangers made through the sights of crossbows.

"I am Jierdan," said the stockier of the two men, though it was difficult to judge his exact size because of the many layers of fur he wore.

"And I am the Nightkeeper," said the other. "Show me what you have brought to trade."

"Trade?" echoed Bruenor angrily. "Who said anything about trade?" He slapped his axe across his hands again, drawing nervous shufflings from above. "Does this look like the blade of a stinkin' merchant?"

Regis and Drizzt both moved to calm the dwarf, though Wulfgar, as tense as Bruenor, stayed off to the side, his huge arms crossed before him and his stern gaze boring into the impudent gatekeeper.

The two soldiers backed away defensively and the Nightkeeper spoke again, this time on the edge of fury. "First Citizen," he demanded of Regis, "why do you come to our door?"

Regis stepped in front of Bruenor and steadied himself squarely before the soldier. "Er . . . a preliminary scouting of the marketplace," he blurted out, trying to fabricate a story as he went along. "I have some especially fine carvings for market this season and I wanted to be certain that everything on this end, including the paying price for scrimshaw, shall be in place to handle the sale."

The two soldiers exchanged knowing smiles. "You have come a long way for such a purpose," the Nightkeeper whispered harshly. "Would you not have been better suited to simply come down with the caravan bearing the goods?"

Regis squirmed uncomfortably, realizing that these soldiers were far too experienced to fall for his ploy. Fighting his better judgement, he reached under his shirt for the ruby pendant, knowing that its hypnotic powers could convince the Nightkeeper to let them through, but dreading showing the stone at all and further opening the trail for the assassin that he knew wasn't far behind.

Jierdan started suddenly, however, as he noticed the figure standing beside Bruenor. Drizzt Do'Urden's cloak had shifted slightly, revealing the black skin of his face.

As if on cue, the Nightkeeper tensed as well and, following his companion's lead, quickly discerned the cause of Jierdan's sudden reaction. Reluctantly, the four adventurers dropped their hands to their weapons, ready for a fight they didn't want.

But Jierdan ended the tension as quickly as he had begun it, by bringing his arm across the chest of the Nightkeeper and addressing the drow openly. "Drizzt Do'Urden?" he asked calmly, seeking confirmation of the identity he had already guessed.

The drow nodded, surprised at the recognition.

"Your name, too, has come down to Luskan with the tales from Icewind Dale," Jierdan explained. "Pardon our surprise." He bowed low. "We do not see many of your race at our gates."

Drizzt nodded again, but did not answer, uncomfortable with this unusual attention. Never before had a gatekeeper bothered to ask him his name or his business. And the drow had quickly come to understand the advantage of avoiding gates altogether, silently slipping over a city's wall in the darkness and seeking the seedier side, where he might at least have a chance of standing unnoticed in the dark corners with the other rogues. Had his name and heroics brought him a measure of respect even this far from Ten-Towns?

Bruenor turned to Drizzt and winked, his own anger dissipated by the fact that his friend had finally been given his due from a stranger.

But Drizzt wasn't convinced. He didn't dare hope for

such a thing—it left him too vulnerable to feelings that he had fought hard to hide. He preferred to keep his suspicions and his guard as close to him as the dark cowl of his cloak. He cocked a curious ear as the two soldiers backed away to hold a private conversation.

"I care not of his name," he heard the Nightkeeper whisper at Jierdan. "No drow elf shall pass my gate!"

"You err," Jierdan retorted. "These are the heroes of Ten-Towns. The halfling is truly First Citizen of Bryn Shander, the drow a ranger with a deadly, but undeniably honorable, reputation, and the dwarf—note the foaming mug standard on his shield—is Bruenor Battlehammer, leader of his clan in the dale."

"And what of the giant barbarian?" asked the Nightkeeper, using a sarcastic tone in an attempt to sound unimpressed, though he was obviously a bit nervous. "What rogue might he be?"

Jierdan shrugged. "His great size, his youth, and a measure of control beyond his years. It seems unlikely to me that he should be here, but he might be the young king of the tribes that the tale-tellers have spoken of. We should not turn these travelers away; the consequences may be grave."

"What could Luskan possibly fear from the puny settlements in Icewind Dale?" the Nightkeeper balked.

"There are other trading ports," Jierdan retorted. "Not every battle is fought with a sword. The loss of Ten-Towns' scrimshaw would not be viewed favorably by our merchants, nor by the trading ships that put in each season."

The Nightkeeper scrutinized the four strangers again. He didn't trust them at all, despite his companion's grand claims, and he didn't want them in his city. But he knew, too, that if his suspicions were wrong and he did something to jeopardize the scrimshaw trade, his own future would be bleak. The soldiers of Luskan answered to the merchants, who were not quick to forgive errors that thinned their purses.

The Nightkeeper threw up his hands in defeat. "Go in, then," he told the companions. "Keep to the wall and make your way down to the docks. The last lane holds the Cutlass, and you'll be warm enough there!"

Drizzt studied the proud strides of his friends as they marched through the door, and he guessed that they had also overheard pieces of the conversation. Bruenor confirmed his suspicions when they had moved away from the guard towers, down the road along the wall.

"Here, elf," the dwarf snorted, nudging Drizzt and being obviously pleased. "So the word's gone beyond the dale and we're heared of even this far south. What have ye to say o' that?"

Drizzt shrugged again and Bruenor chuckled, assuming that his friend was merely embarrassed by the fame. Regis and Wulfgar, too, shared in Bruenor's mirth, the big man giving the drow a good-hearted slap on the back as he slipped to the lead of the troupe.

But Drizzt's discomfort stemmed from more than embarrassment. He had noted the grin on Jierdan's face as they had passed, a smile that went beyond admiration. And while he had no doubts that some tales of the battle with Akar Kessell's goblin army had reached the City of Sails, it struck Drizzt odd that a simple soldier knew so much about him and his friends, while the gatekeeper, solely responsible for determining who passed into the city, knew nothing.

Luskan's streets were tightly packed with two- and three-story buildings, a reflection of the desperation of the people there to huddle within the safety of the city's high wall, away from the ever-present dangers of the savage northland. An occasional tower, a guard post, perhaps, or a prominent citizen's or guild's way to show superiority, sprouted from the roofline. A wary city, Luskan survived, even flourished, in the dangerous frontier by holding fast to an attitude of alertness that often slipped over the line into paranoia. It was a city of shadows, and the four visitors this night keenly felt the curious and dangerous stares peeking out from every darkened hole as they made their way.

The docks harbored the roughest section of the city, where thieves, outlaws, and beggars abounded in their narrow alleys and shadowed crannies. A perpetual ground fog wafted in from the sea, blurring the already dim avenues into even more mysterious pathways.

Such was the lane the four friends found themselves turning down, the last lane before the piers themselves, a particularly decrepit run called Half-Moon Street. Regis, Drizzt, and Bruenor knew immediately that they had entered a collecting ground for vagabonds and ruffians, and each put a hand to his weapon. Wulfgar walked openly and without fear, although he, too, sensed the threatening atmosphere. Not understanding that the area was atypically foul, he was determined to approach his first experience with civilization with an open mind.

"There's the place," said Bruenor, indicating a small group, probably thieves, congregating before the doorway of a tavern. The weatherbeaten sign above the door named the place the Cutlass.

Regis swallowed hard, a frightening mixture of emotions welling within him. In his early days as a thief in Calimport, he had frequented many places like this, but his familiarity with the environment only added to his apprehension. The forbidden allure of business done in the shadows of a dangerous tavern, he knew, could be as deadly as the hidden knives of the rogues at every table. "You truly want to go in there?" he asked his friends squeamishly.

"No arguing from ye!" Bruenor snapped back. "Ye knew the road ahead when ye joined us in the dale. Don't ye be whining now!"

"You are well guarded," Drizzt put in to comfort Regis.

Overly proud in his inexperience, Wulfgar pressed the statement even further. "What cause would they have to do us harm? Surely we have done no wrong," he demanded. Then he proclaimed loudly to challenge the shadows,

"Fear not, little friend. My hammer shall sweep aside any who stand against us!"

"The pride o' youth," Bruenor grumbled as he, Regis, and Drizzt exchanged incredulous looks.

The atmosphere inside the Cutlass was in accord with the decay and rabble that marked the place outside. The tavern portion of the building was a single open room, with a long bar defensively positioned in the corner of the rear wall, directly across from the door. A staircase rose up from the side of the bar to the structure's second level, a staircase more often used by painted, over-perfumed women and their latest companions than by guests of the inn. Indeed, merchant sailors who put into Luskan usually came ashore only for brief periods of excitement and entertainment, returning to the safety of their vessels if they could manage it before the inevitable drunken sleep left them vulnerable.

More than anything else, though, the tavern at the Cutlass was a room of the senses, with myriad sounds and sights and smells. The aroma of alcohol, from strong ale and cheap wine to rarer and more powerful beverages, permeated every corner. A haze of smoke from exotic pipe-weeds, like the mist outside, blurred the harsh reality of the images into softer, dreamlike sensations.

Drizzt led the way to an empty table tucked beside the door, while Bruenor approached the bar to make arrangements for their stay. Wulfgar started after the dwarf, but Drizzt stopped him. "To the table," he explained. "You are too excited for such business; Bruenor can take care of it."

Wulfgar started to protest, but was cut short.

"Come on," Regis offered. "Sit with Drizzt and me. No one will bother a tough old dwarf, but a tiny halfling and a skinny elf might look like good sport to the brutes in here. We need your size and strength to deter such unwanted attention."

Wulfgar's chin firmed up at the compliment and he

strode boldly toward the table. Regis shot Drizzt a know-ing wink and turned to follow.

"Many lessons you will learn on this journey, young friend," Drizzt mumbled to Wulfgar, too softly for the barbarian to hear. "So far from your home."

Bruenor came back from the bar bearing four flagons of mead and grumbling under his breath. "We're to get our business finished soon," he said to Drizzt, "and get back on the road. The cost of a room in this orc-hole is open thievery!"

"The rooms were not meant to be taken for a whole night," Regis snickered.

But Bruenor's scowl remained. "Drink up," he told the drow. "Rat Alley is but a short walk, by the tellin's of the barmaid, and it might be that we can make contact yet this night."

Drizzt nodded and sipped the mead, not really wanting any of it, but hoping that a shared drink might relax the dwarf. The drow, too, was anxious to be gone from Luskan, fearful that his own identity—he kept his cowl pulled even tighter in the tavern's flickering torchlight—might bring them more trouble. He worried further for Wulfgar, young and proud, and out of his element. The barbarians of Icewind Dale, though merciless in battle, were undeniably honorable, basing their society's struc-ture entirely on strict and unbending codes. Drizzt feared that Wulfgar would fall easy prey to the false images and treachery of the city. On the road in the wild lands Wulfgar's hammer would keep him safe enough, but here he was likely to find himself in deceptive situa-tions involving disguised blades, where his mighty weap-on and battle-prowess offered little help.

Wulfgar downed his flagon in a single gulp, wiped his lips with zeal, and stood. "Let us be going," he said to Bruenor. "Who is it that we seek?"

"Sit yerself back down and shut yer mouth, boy," Bruenor scolded, glancing around to see if any unwant-ed attention had fallen upon them. "This night's work is for me and the drow. No place for a too-big fighter like yerself! Ye stay here with Rumblebelly an' keep yer mouth shut and yer back to the wall!"

Wulfgar slumped back in humiliation, but Drizzt was glad that Bruenor seemed to have come to similar conclusions about the young warrior. Once again, Regis saved a measure of Wulfgar's pride.

"You are not leaving with them!" he snapped at the barbarian. "I have no desire to go, but I would not dare to remain here alone. Let Drizzt and Bruenor have their fun in some cold, smelly alley. We'll stay here and enjoy a well-deserved evening of high entertainment!"

Drizzt slapped Regis's knee under the table in thanks and rose to leave. Bruenor quaffed his flagon and leaped from his chair.

"Let's be going, then," he said to the drow. And then to Wulfgar, "Keep care of the halfling, and beware the women! They're mean as starved rats, and the only thing they aim to bite at is your purse!"

Bruenor and Drizzt turned at the first empty alleyway beyond the Cutlass, the dwarf standing nervous guard at its entrance while Drizzt moved down a few steps into the darkness. Convinced that he was safely alone, Drizzt removed from his pouch a small onyx statuette, meticulously carved into the likeness of a hunting cat, and placed it on the ground before him.

"Guenhwyvar," he called softly. "Come, my shadow."

His beckon reached out across the planes, to the astral home of the entity of the panther. The great cat stirred from its sleep. Many months had passed since its master had called, and the cat was anxious to serve.

Guenhwyvar leaped out across the fabric of the planes, following a flicker of light that could only be the calling of the drow. Then the cat was in the alley with Drizzt, alert at once in the unfamiliar surroundings.

"We walk into a dangerous web, I fear," Drizzt explained. "I need eyes where my own cannot go."

Without delay and without a sound, Guenhwyvar sprang to a pile of rubble, to a broken porch landing, and up to the rooftops. Satisfied, and feeling much more secure now, Drizzt slipped back to the street where Bruenor waited.

"Well, where's that blasted cat?" Bruenor asked, a hint of relief in his voice that Guenhwyvar was actually not with the drow. Most dwarves are suspicious of magic, other than the magical enchantments placed upon weapons, and Bruenor had no love for the panther.

"Where we need him most," was the drow's answer. He started off down Half-Moon Street. "Fear not, mighty Bruenor, Guenhwyvar's eyes are upon us, even if ours cannot return their protective gaze!"

The dwarf glanced all around nervously, beads of sweat visible at the base of his horned helm. He had known Drizzt for several years, but had never gotten comfortable around the magical cat.

Drizzt hid his smile under his cowl.

Each lane, filled with piles of rubble and refuse, appeared the same, as they made their way along the docks. Bruenor eyed each shadowed niche with alert suspicion. His eyes were not as keen in the night as those of the drow, and if he had seen into the darkness as clearly as Drizzt, he might have clutched his axe handle even more tightly.

But the dwarf and drow weren't overly concerned. They were far from typical of the drunkards that usually stumbled into these parts at night, and not easy prey for thieves. The many notches on Bruenor's axe and the sway of the two scimitars on the drow's belt would serve as ample deterrent to most ruffians.

In the maze of streets and alleyways, it took them a long while to find Rat Alley. Just off the piers, it ran parallel to the sea, seemingly impassable through the thick fog. Long, low warehouses lined both its sides, and broken crates and boxes cluttered the alley, reducing the already narrow passage in many places to single-file breadth.

"Nice place to be walkin' down on a gloomy night," Bruenor stated flatly.

"Are you certain that this is the lane?" Drizzt asked, equally unenthused about the area before them.

"By the words o' the merchant in Ten-Towns, if one's alive that can get me the map, the one be Whisper. An' the place to find Whisper is Rat Alley—always Rat Alley."

"Then on with it," said Drizzt. "Foul business is best finished quickly."

Bruenor slowly led the way into the alley. The two had barely gone ten feet when the dwarf thought he heard the click of a crossbow. He stopped short and looked back at Drizzt. "They're on us," he whispered.

"In the boarded window above and to the right of us," Drizzt explained, his exceptional night vision and hearing having already discerned the sound's source. "A precaution, I hope. Perhaps a good sign that your contact is close."

"Never called a crossbow aimed at me head a good sign!" argued the dwarf. "But on, then, and keep yerself at the ready. This place reeks of danger!" He started again through the rubble.

A shuffle to their left told them that eyes were upon them from that way as well. But still they continued, understanding that they couldn't have expected any different a scenario when they had started out from the Cutlass. Rounding a final mound of broken planks, they saw a slender figure leaning against one of the alleyway's walls, cloak pulled tightly against the chill of the evening mist.

Drizzt leaned over Bruenor's shoulder. "May that be the one?" he whispered.

The dwarf shrugged, and said, "Who else?" He took one more step forward, planted his feet firmly, wide apart, and addressed the figure. "I be looking for a man named Whisper," he called. "Might that be yerself?"

"Yes, and no," came the reply. The figure turned

toward them, though the low-pulled cloak revealed little.

"What games do ye play?" Bruenor shot back.

"Whisper I am," replied the figure, letting the cloak slip back a little. "But for sure no man!"

They could see clearly now that the figure addressing them was indeed a woman, a dark and mysterious figure with long black hair and deeply set, darting eyes that showed experience and a profound understanding of survival on the street.

❧ 3 ❧

Night Life

The Cutlass grew busier as the night wore on. Merchant sailors crowded in from their ships and the locals were quick into position to feed upon them. Regis and Wulfgar remained at the side table, the barbarian wide-eyed with curiosity at the sights around him, and the halfling intent on cautious observation.

Regis recognized trouble in the form of a woman sauntering toward them. Not a young woman, and with the haggard appearance all too familiar on the dockside, but her gown, quite revealing in every place that a lady's gown should not be, hid all her physical flaws behind a barrage of suggestions. The look on Wulfgar's face, his chin nearly level with the table, Regis thought, confirmed the halfling's fears.

"Well met, big man," the woman purred, slipping comfortably into the chair next to the barbarian.

Wulfgar looked at Regis and nearly laughed out loud in disbelief and embarrassment.

"You are not from Luskan," the woman went on. "Nor do you bear the appearance of any merchants now docked in port. Where are you from?"

"The north," Wulfgar stammered. "The dale . . . Icewind."

Regis hadn't seen such boldness in a woman since his years in Calimport, and he felt that he should intervene. There was something wicked about such women, a perversion of pleasure that was too extraordinary. Forbidden fruit made easy. Regis suddenly found himself homesick for Calimport. Wulfgar would be no match for the wiles of this creature.

"We are poor travelers," Regis explained, emphasizing the "poor" in an effort to protect his friend. "Not a coin left, but with many miles to go."

Wulfgar looked curiously at his companion, not quite understanding the motive behind the lie.

The woman scrutinized Wulfgar once again and smacked her lips. "A pity," she groaned, and then asked Regis, "Not a coin?"

Regis shrugged helplessly.

"A pity it is," the woman repeated, and she rose to leave.

Wulfgar's face blushed a deep red as he began to comprehend the true motives behind the meeting.

Something stirred in Regis, as well. A longing for the old days, running in Calimport's bowery, tugged at his heart beyond his strength to resist. As the woman started past him, he grabbed her elbow. "Not a coin," he explained to her inquiring face, "but this." He pulled the ruby pendant out from under his coat and set it dangling at the end of its chain. The sparkles caught the woman's greedy eye at once and the magical gemstone sucked her into its hypnotic entrancement. She sat down again, this time in the chair closest to Regis, her eyes never leaving the depths of the wondrous, spinning ruby.

Only confusion prevented Wulfgar from erupting in outrage at the betrayal, the blur of thoughts and emotions in his mind showing themselves as no more than a blank stare.

Regis caught the barbarian's look, but shrugged it away with his typical penchant for dismissing negative emotions, such as guilt. Let the morrow's dawn expose his ploy for what it was; the conclusion did not diminish his ability to enjoy this night. "Luskan's night bears a chill wind," he said to the woman.

She put a hand on his arm. "We'll find you a warm bed, have no fear."

The halfling's smile nearly took in his ears.

Wulfgar had to catch himself from falling off of his chair.

Bruenor regained his composure quickly, not wanting to insult Whisper, or to let her know that his surprise in finding a woman gave her a bit of an advantage over him. She knew the truth, though, and her smile left Bruenor even more flustered. Selling information in a setting as dangerous as Luskan's dockside meant a constant dealing with murderers and thieves, and even within the structure of an intricate support network it was a job that demanded a hardened hide. Few who sought Whisper's services could hide their obvious surprise at finding a young and alluring woman practising such a trade.

Bruenor's respect for the informant did not diminish, though, despite his surprise, for the reputation Whisper had earned had come to him across hundreds of miles. She was still alive, and that fact alone told the dwarf that she was formidable.

Drizzt was considerably less taken aback by the discovery. In the dark cities of the drow elves, females normally held higher stations than males, and were often more deadly. Drizzt understood the advantage Whisper carried over male clients who tended to underestimate her in the male-dominated societies of the dangerous northland.

Anxious to get this business finished and get back on the road, the dwarf came straight to the purpose of the meeting. "I be needing a map," he said, "and been told that yerself was the one to get it."

"I possess many maps," the woman replied coolly.

"One of the north," Bruenor explained. "From the sea to the desert, and rightly naming the places in the ways o' what races live there!"

Whisper nodded. "The price shall be high, good dwarf," she said, her eyes glinting at the mere notion of gold.

Bruenor tossed her a small pouch of gems. "This should pay for yer trouble," he growled, never pleased to be relieved of money.

Whisper emptied the contents into her hand and scrutinized the rough stones. She nodded as she slipped them back into the pouch, aware of their considerable value.

"Hold!" Bruenor squawked as she began to tie the pouch to her belt. "Ye'll be taking none o' me stones till I be seeing the map!"

"Of course," the woman replied with a disarming smile. "Wait here. I shall return in a short while with the map you desire." She tossed the pouch back to Bruenor and spun about suddenly, her cloak snapping up and carrying a gust of the fog with it. In the flurry, there came a sudden flash, and the woman was gone.

Bruenor jumped back and grabbed at his axe handle. "What sorcerous treachery is this?" he cried.

Drizzt, unimpressed, put a hand on the dwarf's shoulder. "Calm, mighty dwarf," he said. "A minor trick and no more, masking her escape in the fog and the flash." He pointed toward a small pile of boards. "Into that sewer drain."

Bruenor followed the line of the drow's arm and relaxed. The lip of an open hole was barely visible, its grate leaning against the warehouse wall a few feet farther down the alley.

"Ye know these kind better than meself, elf," the dwarf stated, flustered at his lack of experience in handling the rogues of a city street. "Does she mean to bargain fair, or do we sit here, set up for her thievin' dogs to plunder?"

"No to both," answered Drizzt. "Whisper would not be alive if she collared clients for thieves. But I would hardly expect any arrangement she might strike with us to be a fair bargain."

Bruenor took note that Drizzt had slipped one of his scimitars free of its sheath as he spoke. "Not a trap, eh?" the dwarf asked again, indicating the readied weapon.

"By her people, no," Drizzt replied. "But the shadows conceal many other eyes."

More eyes than just Wulfgar's had fallen upon the half-ling and the woman.

The hardy rogues of Luskan's dockside often took great sport in tormenting creatures of less physical stat-ure, and halflings were among their favorite targets. This particular evening, a huge, overstuffed man with furry eyebrows and beard bristles that caught the foam from his ever-full mug dominated the conversation at the bar, boasting of impossible feats of strength and threatening everybody around him with a beating if the flow of ale slowed in the least.

All of the men gathered around him at the bar, men who knew him, or of him, nodded their heads in enthusi-astic agreement with his every word, propping him up on a pedestal of compliments to dispel their own fears of him. But the fat man's ego needed further sport, a new victim to cow, and as his gaze floated around the perime-ter of the tavern, it naturally fell upon Regis and his large, but obviously young friend. The spectacle of a halfling wooing the highest priced lady at the Cutlass presented an opportunity too tempting for the fat man to ignore.

"Here now, pretty lady," he slobbered, ale spouting with every word. "Think the likes of a half-a-man'll make the night for ye?" The crowd around the bar, anxious to keep in the fat man's high regard, exploded into over-zealous laughter.

The woman had dealt with this man before and she had seen others fall painfully before him. She tossed him a concerned look, but remained firmly tied to the pull of the ruby pendant. Regis, though, immediately looked away from the fat man, turning his attention to where he suspected the trouble most likely would begin—to the other side of the table and Wulfgar.

He found his worries justified. The proud barbarian's knuckles whitened from the grasp he had on the table, and the seething look in his eye told Regis that he was on the verge of exploding.

"Let the taunts pass!" Regis insisted. "This is not worth a moment of your time!"

Wulfgar didn't relax a bit, his glare never releasing his adversary. He could brush away the fat man's insults, even those cutting at Regis and the woman. But Wulfgar understood the motivation behind those insults. Through exploitation of his less-able friends, Wulfgar was being challenged by the bully. How many others had fallen victim to this hulking slob? he wondered. Perhaps it was time for the fat man to learn some humility.

Recognizing some potential for excitement, the grotesque bully came a few steps closer.

"There, move a bit, half-a-man," he demanded, waving Regis aside.

Regis took a quick inventory of the tavern's patrons. Surely there were many in here who might jump in for his cause against the fat man and his obnoxious cronies. There was even a member of the official city guard, a group held in high respect in every section of Luskan.

Regis interrupted his scan for a moment and looked at the soldier. How out of place the man seemed in a dog-infested spittoon like the Cutlass. More curious still, Regis knew the man as Jierdan, the soldier at the gate who had recognized Drizzt and had arranged for them to pass into the city just a couple of hours earlier.

The fat man came a step closer, and Regis didn't have time to ponder the implications.

Hands on hips, the huge blob stared down at him. Regis felt his heart pumping, the blood coursing through his veins, as it always did in this type of on-the-edge confrontation that had marked his days in Calimport. And now, like then, he had every intention of finding a way to run away.

But his confidence dissipated when he remembered his companion.

Less experienced, and Regis would be quick to say, "less wise!" Wulfgar would not let the challenge go unanswered. One spring of his long legs easily carried him over the table and placed him squarely between the fat man and Regis. He returned the fat man's ominous glare with equal intensity.

The fat man glanced to his friends at the bar, fully aware that his proud young opponent's distorted sense of honor would prevent a first strike. "Well, look ye here," he laughed, his lips turned back in drooling anticipation, "seems the young one has a thing to say."

He started slowly to turn back on Wulfgar, then lunged suddenly for the barbarian's throat, expecting that his change in tempo would catch Wulfgar by surprise.

But although he was inexperienced in the ways of taverns, Wulfgar understood battle. He had trained with Drizzt Do'Urden, an ever-alert warrior, and had toned his muscles to their sharpest fighting edge. Before the fat man's hands ever came near his throat, Wulfgar had snapped one of his own huge paws over his opponent's face and had driven the other into the fat man's groin.

His stunned opponent found himself rising into the air.

For a moment, onlookers were too amazed to react at all, except for Regis, who slapped a hand across his own disbelieving face and inconspicuously slid under the table.

The fat man outweighed three average men, but the barbarian brought him up easily over the top of his seven-foot frame, and even higher, to the full extension of his arms.

Howling in helpless rage, the fat man ordered his supporters to attack. Wulfgar watched patiently for the first move against him.

The whole crowd seemed to jump at once. Keeping his calm, the trained warrior searched out the tightest concentration, three men, and launched the human missile, noting their horrified expressions just before the waves of blubber rolled over them, blasting them backward. Then their combined momentum smashed an entire section of the bar from its supports, knocking the unfortunate innkeeper away and sending him crashing into the racks holding his finest wines.

Wulfgar's amusement was short-lived, for other ruffians were quickly upon him. He dug his heels in where he was, determined to keep his footing, and lashed out with his great fists, swatting his enemies aside, one by one, and sending them sprawling into the far corners of the room.

Fighting erupted all around the tavern. Men who could not have been spurred to action if a murder had been committed at their feet sprang upon each other with unbridled rage at the horrifying sight of spilled booze and a broken bar.

Few of the fat man's supporters were deterred by the general row, though. They rolled in on Wulfgar, wave after wave. He held his ground well, for none could delay him long enough for their reinforcements to get in. Still, the barbarian was being hit as often as he was connecting with his own blows. He took the punches stoically, blocking out the pain through sheer pride and his fighting tenacity that simply would not allow him to lose.

From his new seat under the table, Regis watched the action and sipped his drink. Even the barmaids were into it now, riding around on some unfortunate combatants' backs, using their nails to etch intricate designs into the men's faces. In fact, Regis soon discerned that the only other person in the tavern who wasn't in the fight, other than those who were already unconscious, was Jierdan. The soldier sat quietly in his chair, unconcerned with the brawling beside him and interested only, it seemed, in watching and measuring Wulfgar's prowess.

This, too, disturbed the halfling, but once again he found that he didn't have time to contemplate the soldier's unusual actions. Regis had known from the start that he would have to pull his giant friend out of this, and now his alert eyes had caught the expected flash of steel. A rogue in the line directly behind Wulfgar's latest opponents had drawn a blade.

"Damn!" Regis muttered, setting down his drink and pulling his mace from a fold in his cloak. Such business always left a foul taste in his mouth.

Wulfgar threw his two opponents aside, opening a path for the man with the knife. He charged forward, his eyes up and staring into those of the tall barbarian. He didn't even notice Regis dart out from between Wulfgar's long legs, the little mace poised to strike. It slammed into the man's knee, shattering the kneecap, and sent him sprawling forward, blade exposed, toward Wulfgar.

Wulfgar side-stepped the lunge at the last moment and clasped his hand over the hand of his assailant. Rolling with the momentum, the barbarian knocked aside the table and slammed into the wall. One squeeze crushed the assailant's fingers on the knife hilt, while at the same time Wulfgar engulfed the man's face with his free hand and hoisted him from the ground. Crying out to Tempus, the god of battle, the barbarian, enraged at the appearance of a weapon, slammed the man's head through the wooden planks of the wall and left him dangling, his feet fully a foot from the floor.

An impressive move, but it cost Wulfgar time. When he turned back toward the bar, he was buried under a flurry of fists and kicks from several attackers.

*　*　*　*　*

"Here she comes," Bruenor whispered to Drizzt when he saw Whisper returning, though the drow's heightened senses had told him of her coming long before the dwarf was aware of it. Whisper had only been gone a half-hour or so, but it seemed much longer to the two friends in the alley, dangerously open to the sights of the crossbowmen and other thugs they knew were nearby.

Whisper sauntered confidently up to them. "Here is the map you desire," she said to Bruenor, holding up a rolled parchment.

"A look, then," the dwarf demanded, starting forward.

The woman recoiled and dropped the parchment to

her side. "The price is higher," she stated flatly. "Ten times what you have already offered."

Bruenor's dangerous glare did not deter her. "No choice is left to you," she hissed. "You shall find no other who can deliver this unto you. Pay the price and be done with it!"

"A moment," Bruenor said with sudden calm. "Me friend has a say in this." He and Drizzt moved a step away.

"She has discovered who we are," the drow explained, though Bruenor had already come to the same conclusion. "And how much we can pay."

"Be it the map?" Bruenor asked.

Drizzt nodded. "She would have no reason to believe that she is in any danger, not down here. Have you the money?"

"Aye," said the dwarf, "but our road is long yet, and I fear we'll be needing what I've got and more."

"It is settled then," Drizzt replied. Bruenor recognized the fiery gleam that flared up in the drow's lavender eyes. "When first we met this woman, we struck a fair deal," he went on. "A deal we shall honor."

Bruenor understood and approved. He felt the tingle of anticipation start in his blood. He turned back on the woman and noticed at once that she now held a dagger at her side instead of the parchment. Apparently she understood the nature of the two adventurers she was dealing with.

Drizzt, also noticing the metallic glint, stepped back from Bruenor, trying to appear unmenacing to Whisper, though in reality, he wanted to get a better angle on some suspicious cracks that he had noticed in the wall—cracks that might be the edgings of a secret door.

Bruenor approached the woman with his empty arms outstretched. "If that be the price," he grumbled, "then we have no choice but to pay. But I'll be seein' the map first!"

Confident that she could put her dagger into the

dwarf's eye before either of his hands could get back to his belt for a weapon, Whisper relaxed and moved her empty hand to the parchment under her cloak.

But she underestimated her opponent.

Bruenor's stubby legs twitched, launching him up high enough to slam his helmet into the woman's face, splattering her nose and knocking her head into the wall. He went for the map, dropping the original purse of gems onto Whisper's limp form and muttering, "As we agreed."

Drizzt, too, had sprung into motion. As soon as the dwarf flinched, he had called upon the innate magic of his heritage to conjure a globe of darkness in front of the window harboring the crossbowmen. No bolts came through, but the angered shouts of the two archers echoed throughout the alley.

Then the cracks in the wall split open, as Drizzt had anticipated, and Whisper's second line of defense came rushing through. The drow was prepared, scimitars already in his hands. The blades flashed, blunt sides only, but with enough precision to disarm the burly rogue that stepped out. Then they came in again, slapping the man's face, and in the same fluidity of motion, Drizzt reversed the angle, slamming one pommel, and then the other, into the man's temples. By the time Bruenor had turned around with the map, the way was clear before them.

Bruenor examined the drow's handiwork with true admiration.

Then a crossbow quarrel ticked into the wall just an inch from his head.

"Time to go," Drizzt observed.

"The end'll be blocked, or I'm a bearded gnome," Bruenor said as they neared the exit to the alley. A growling roar in the building beside them, followed by terrified screams, brought them some comfort.

"Guenhwyvar," Drizzt stated as two cloaked men burst out into the street before them and fled without looking back.

"Sure that I'd forgotten all about that cat!" cried

Bruenor.

"Be glad that Guenhwyvar's memory is greater than your own," laughed Drizzt, and Bruenor, despite his feelings for the cat, laughed with him. They halted at the end of the alley and scouted the street. There were no signs of any trouble, though the heavy fog provided good cover for a possible ambush.

"Take it slow," Bruenor offered. "We'll draw less attention."

Drizzt would have agreed, but then a second quarrel, launched from somewhere down the alley, knocked into a wooden beam between them.

"Time to go!" Drizzt stated more decisively, though Bruenor needed no further encouragement, his little legs already pumping wildly as he sped off into the fog.

They made their way through the twists and turns of Luskan's rat maze, Drizzt gracefully gliding over any rubble barriers and Bruenor simply crashing through them. Presently, they grew confident that there was no pursuit, and they changed their pace to an easy glide.

The white of a smile showed through the dwarf's red beard as he kept a satisfied eye cocked over his shoulder. But when he turned back to view the road before him, he suddenly dove down to the side, scrambling to find his axe.

He had come face up with the magical cat.

Drizzt couldn't contain his laughter.

"Put the thing away!" Bruenor demanded.

"Manners, good dwarf," the drow shot back. "Remember that Guenhwyvar cleared our escape trail."

"Put it away!" Bruenor declared again, his axe swinging at the ready.

Drizzt stroked the powerful cat's muscled neck. "Do not heed his words, friend," he said to the cat. "He is a dwarf, and cannot appreciate the finer magics!"

"Bah!" Bruenor snarled, though he breathed a bit easier as Drizzt dismissed the cat and replaced the onyx statue in his pouch.

The two came upon Half-Moon Street a short while later, stopping in a final alley to look for any signs of ambush. They knew at once that there had been trouble, for several injured men stumbled, or were carried, past the alley's entrance.

Then they saw the Cutlass, and two familiar forms sitting on the street out in front.

"What're ye doin' out here?" Bruenor asked as they approached.

"Seems our big friend answers insults with punches," said Regis, who hadn't been touched in the fray. Wulfgar's face, though, was puffy and bruised, and he could barely open one eye. Dried blood, some of it his own, caked his fists and clothes.

Drizzt and Bruenor looked at each other, not too surprised.

"And our rooms?" Bruenor grumbled.

Regis shook his head. "I doubt it."

"And my coins?"

Again the halfling shook his head.

"Bah!" snorted Bruenor, and he stamped off toward the door of the Cutlass.

"I wouldn't . . . " Regis started, but then he shrugged and decided to let Bruenor find out for himself.

Bruenor's shock was complete when he opened the tavern door. Tables, glass, and unconscious patrons lay broken all about the floor. The innkeeper slumped over one part of the shattered bar, a barmaid wrapping his bloodied head in bandages. The man Wulfgar had implanted into the wall still hung limply by the back of his head, groaning softly, and Bruenor couldn't help but chuckle at the handiwork of the mighty barbarian. Every now and then, one of the barmaids, passing by the man as she cleaned, gave him a little push, taking amusement at his swaying.

"Good coins wasted," Bruenor surmised, and he walked back out the door before the innkeeper noticed him and set the barmaids upon him.

"Hell of a row!" he told Drizzt when he returned to his companions. "Everyone in on it?"

"All but one," Regis answered. "A soldier."

"A soldier of Luskan, down here?" asked Drizzt, surprised by the obvious inconsistency.

Regis nodded. "And even more curious," he continued, "it was the same guard, Jierdan, that let us into the city."

Drizzt and Bruenor exchanged concerned looks.

"We've killers at our backs, a busted inn before us, and a soldier paying us more mind than he should," said Bruenor.

"Time to go," Drizzt responded for the third time. Wulfgar looked at him incredulously. "How many men did you down tonight?" Drizzt asked him, putting the logical assumption of danger right out before him. "And how many of them would drool at the opportunity to put a blade in your back?"

"Besides," added Regis before Wulfgar could answer, "I've no desire to share a bed in an alley with a host of rats!"

"Then to the gate," said Bruenor.

Drizzt shook his head. "Not with a guard so interested in us. Over the wall, and let none know of our passing."

An hour later, they were trotting easily across the open grass, feeling the wind again beyond the break of Luskan's wall.

Regis summed up their thoughts, saying, "Our first night in our first city, and we've betrayed killers, fought down a host of ruffians, and caught the attention of the city guard. An auspicious beginning to our journey!"

"Aye, but we've got this!" cried Bruenor, fairly bursting with anticipation of finding his homeland now that the first obstacle, the map, had been overcome.

Little did he or his friends know, however, that the map he clutched so dearly detailed several deadly regions, one in particular that would test the four friends to their limits—and beyond.

❧ 4 ❧

The Conjuring

A landmark of wonder marked the very center of the City of Sails, a strange building that emanated a powerful aura of magic. Unlike any other structure in all the Forgotten Realms, the Hosttower of the Arcane seemed literally a tree of stone, boasting five tall spires, the largest being the central, and the other four, equally high, growing out of the main trunk with the graceful curving arc of an oak. Nowhere could any sign of the mason be seen; it was obvious to any knowledgeable viewer that magic, not physical labor, had produced this artwork.

The Archmage, undisputed Master of the Hosttower, resided in the central tower, while the other four housed the wizards closest in the line of succession. Each of these lesser towers, representing the four compass directions, dominated a different side of the trunk, and its respective wizard held responsibility for watching over and influencing the events in the direction he overlooked. Thus, the wizard west of the trunk spent his days looking out to sea, and to the merchant ships and pirates riding out on Luskan's harbor.

A conversation in the north spire would have interested the companions from Ten-Towns this day.

"You have done well, Jierdan," said Sydney, a younger, and lesser, mage in the Hosttower, though displaying enough potential to have gained an apprenticeship with one of the mightiest wizards in the guild. Not a pretty woman, Sydney cared little for physical appearances, instead devoting her energies to her unrelenting pursuit of power. She had spent most of her twenty-five years working toward one goal—the title of Wizard—and her determination and poise gave most around her little doubt about her ability to attain it.

Jierdan accepted the praise with a knowing nod, understanding the condescending manner in which it was offered. "I only performed as I was instructed," he replied under a facade of humility, tossing a glance to the frail-looking man in brown mottled robes who stood staring out of the room's sole window.

"Why would they come here?" the wizard whispered to himself. He turned to the others, and they recoiled instinctively from his gaze. He was Dendybar the Mottled, Master of the North Spire, and though he appeared weak from a distance, closer scrutiny revealed a power in the man mightier than bulging muscles. And his well-earned reputation for valuing life far less than the pursuit of knowledge intimidated most who came before him. "Did the travelers give any reason for coming here?"

"None that I would believe," Jierdan replied quietly. "The halfling spoke of scouting out the marketplace, but I—"

"Not likely," interrupted Dendybar, speaking more to himself than to the others. "Those four weigh more into their actions than simply a merchant expedition."

Sydney pressed Jierdan, seeking to keep her high favor with the Master of the North Spire. "Where are they now?" she demanded.

Jierdan didn't dare fight back against her in front of Dendybar. "On the docks . . . somewhere," he said, then shrugged.

"You do not know?" hissed the young mage.

"They were to stay at the Cutlass," Jierdan retorted. "But the fight put them out on the street."

"And you should have followed them!" Sydney scolded, dogging the soldier relentlessly.

"Even a soldier of the city would be a fool to travel

alone about the piers at night," Jierdan shot back. "It does not matter where they are right now. I have the gates and the piers watched. They cannot leave Luskan without my knowledge!"

"I want them found!" Sydney ordered, but then Dendybar silenced her.

"Leave the watch as it is," he told Jierdan. "They must not depart without *my* knowledge. You are dismissed. Come before me again when you have something to report."

Jierdan snapped to attention and turned to leave, casting one final glare at his competitor for the mottled wizard's favor as he passed. He was only a soldier, not a budding mage like Sydney, but in Luskan, where the Hosttower of the Arcane was the true, secretive force behind all of the power structures in the city, a soldier did well to find the favor of a wizard. Captains of the guard only attained their positions and privileges with the prior consent of the Hosttower.

"We cannot allow them to roam freely," argued Sydney when the door had closed behind the departing soldier.

"They shall bring no harm for now," replied Dendybar. "Even if the drow carries the artifact with him, it will take him years to understand its potential. Patience, my friend, I have ways of learning what we need to know. The pieces of this puzzle will fit together nicely before much longer."

"It pains me to think that such power is so close to our grasp," sighed the eager young mage. "And in the possession of a novice!"

"Patience," repeated the Master of the North Spire.

Sydney finished lighting the ring of candles that marked the perimeter of the special chamber and moved slowly toward the solitary brazier that stood on its iron tripod just outside the magic circle inscribed upon the floor. It disappointed her to know that once the brazier was also burning, she would be instructed to depart.

Savoring every moment in this rarely opened room, considered by many to be the finest conjuring chamber in all the northland, Sydney had many times begged to remain in attendance.

But Dendybar never let her stay, explaining that her inevitable inquiries would prove too much of a distraction. And when dealing with the nether worlds, distractions usually proved fatal.

Dendybar sat cross-legged within the magic circle, chanting himself into a deep meditative trance and not even aware of Sydney's actions as she completed the preparations. All of his senses looked inward, searching his own being to ensure that he was fully prepared for such a task. He had left only one window in his mind open to the outside, a fraction of his awareness hinging on a single cue: the bolt of the heavy door being snapped back into place after Sydney had departed.

His heavy eyelids cracked open, their narrow line of vision solely fixed upon the fires of the brazier. These flames would be the life of the summoned spirit, giving it a tangible form for the period Dendybar kept it locked to the material plane.

"*Ey vesus venerais dimin dou,*" the wizard began, chanting slowly at first, then building into a solid rhythm. Swept away by the insistent pull of the casting, as though the spell, once given a flicker of life, drove itself to the completion of its dweomer, Dendybar rolled on through the various inflections and arcane syllables with ease, the sweat on his face reflecting eagerness more than nerves.

The mottled wizard reveled in summoning, dominating the will of beings beyond the mortal world through the sheer insistence of his considerable mental strength. This room represented the pinnacle of his studies, the indisputable evidence of the vast boundaries of his powers.

This time he was targeting his favorite informant, a spirit that truly despised him, but could not refuse his

R. A. SALVATORE

call. Dendybar came to the climactic point in the casting, the naming. "Morkai," he called softly.

The brazier's flame brightened for just an instant.

"Morkai!" Dendybar shouted, tearing the spirit from its hold on the other world. The brazier puffed into a small fireball, then died into blackness, its flames transmuted into the image of a man standing before Dendybar.

The wizard's thin lips curled upward. How ironic, he thought, that the man he had arranged to murder would prove to be his most valuable source of information.

The specter of Morkai the Red stood resolute and proud, a fitting image of the mighty wizard he had once been. He had created this very room back in the days when he served the Hosttower in the role of Master of the North Spire. But then Dendybar and his cronies had conspired against him, using his trusted apprentice to drive a dagger into his heart, and thus opening the trail of succession for Dendybar himself to reach the coveted position in the spire.

That same act had set a second, perhaps more significant, chain of events into motion, for it was that same apprentice, Akar Kessell, who had eventually come to possess the Crystal Shard, the mighty artifact that Dendybar now believed in Drizzt Do'Urden's hands. The tales that had filtered down from Ten-Towns of Akar Kessell's final battle had named the dark elf as the warrior who had brought him down.

Dendybar could not know that the Crystal Shard now lay buried beneath a hundred tons of ice and rock on the mountain in Icewind Dale known as Kelvin's Cairn, lost in the avalanche that had killed Kessell. All that he knew of the tale was that Kessell, the puny apprentice, had nearly conquered all of Icewind Dale with the Crystal Shard and that Drizzt Do'Urden was the last to see Kessell alive.

Dendybar wrung his hands eagerly whenever he thought of the power that the relic would bring to a more learned wizard.

"Greetings, Morkai the Red," Dendybar laughed. "How polite of you to accept my invitation."

"I accept every opportunity to gaze upon you, Dendybar the Assassin," replied the specter. "I shall know you well when you ride Death's barge into the darkened realm. Then we shall be on even terms again. . . ."

"Silence!" Dendybar commanded. Though he would not admit the truth to himself, the mottled wizard greatly feared the day when he would have to face the mighty Morkai again. "I have brought you here for a purpose," he told the specter. "I have no time for your empty threats."

"Then tell me the service I am to perform," hissed the specter, "and let me be gone. Your presence offends me."

Dendybar fumed, but did not continue the argument. Time worked against a wizard in a spell of summoning, for it drained him to hold a spirit on the material plane, and each second that passed weakened him a little bit more. The greatest danger in this type of spell was that the conjuror would attempt to hold control for too long, until he found himself too weak to control the entity he had summoned.

"A simple answer is all that I require from you this day, Morkai," Dendybar said, carefully selecting each word as he went. Morkai noted the caution and suspected that Dendybar was hiding something.

"Then what is the question?" the specter pressed.

Dendybar held to his cautious pace, considering every word before he spoke it. He did not want Morkai to get any hint of his motives in seeking the drow, for the specter would surely pass the information across the planes. Many powerful beings, perhaps even the spirit of Morkai himself, would go after such a powerful relic if they had any idea of the shard's whereabouts.

"Four travelers, one a drow elf, came to Luskan from Icewind Dale this day," the mottled wizard explained. "What business do they have in the city? Why are they here?"

Morkai scrutinized his nemesis, trying to find the reason for the question. "That is a query better asked of your city guard," he replied. "Surely the guests stated their business upon entering the gate."

"But I have asked you!" Dendybar screamed, exploding suddenly in rage. Morkai was stalling, and each passing second now took its toll on the mottled wizard. The essence of Morkai had lost little power in death, and he fought stubbornly against the spell's binding dweomer. Dendybar snapped open a parchment before him.

"I have a dozen of these penned already," he warned.

Morkai recoiled. He understood the nature of the writing, a scroll that revealed the true name of his very being. And once read, stripping the veil of secrecy from the name and laying bare the privacy of his soul, Dendybar would invoke the true power of the scroll, using off-key inflections of tone to distort Morkai's name and disrupt the harmony of his spirit, thus racking him to the core of his being.

"How long shall I search for your answers?" Morkai asked.

Dendybar smiled at his victory, though the drain on him continued to heighten. "Two hours," he replied without delay, having carefully decided the length of the search before the summoning, choosing a time limit that would give Morkai enough opportunity to find some answers, but not long enough to allow the spirit to learn more than he should.

Morkai smiled, guessing the motives behind the decision. He snapped backward suddenly and was gone in a puff of smoke, the flames that had sustained his form relegated back to their brazier to await his return.

Dendybar's relief was immediate. Although he still had to concentrate to keep the gate to the planes in place, the pull against his will and the drain on his power lessened considerably when the spirit had gone. Morkai's will power had nearly broken him during their encounter, and Dendybar shook his head in disbelief that the old master could reach out from the grave so mightily. A shudder ran up his spine as he pondered his wisdom in plotting against one so powerful. Every time he summoned Morkai, he was reminded that his own day of reckoning would surely come.

Morkai had little trouble in learning about the four adventurers. In fact, the specter already knew much about them. He had taken a great interest in Ten-Towns during his reign as Master of the North Spire, and his curiosity had not died with his body. Even now, he often looked in on the doings in Icewind Dale, and anyone who concerned himself with Ten-Towns in recent months knew something of the four heroes.

Morkai's continued interest in the world he had left behind was not an uncommon trait in the spirit world. Death altered the ambitions of the soul, replacing the love of material or social gains with an eternal hunger for knowledge. Some spirits had looked down upon the Realms for centuries untold, simply collecting information and watching the living go about their lives. Perhaps it was envy for the physical sensations they could no longer feel. But whatever the reason, the wealth of knowledge in a single spirit often outweighed the collected works in all of the libraries in the Realms combined.

Morkai learned much in the two hours Dendybar had alotted him. His turn now came to choose his words carefully. He was compelled to satisfy the summoner's request, but he intended to answer in as cryptic and ambiguous a manner as he possibly could.

Dendybar's eyes glinted when he saw the brazier's flames begin their telltale dance once again. Had it been two hours already? he wondered, for his rest seemed much shorter, and he felt that he had not fully recovered from his first encounter with the specter. He could not refute the dance of the flames, though. He straightened himself and tucked his ankles in closer, tightening and securing his cross-legged, meditative position.

The ball of fire puffed in its climactic throes and Morkai appeared before him. The specter stood back obediently, not offering any information until Dendybar specifically asked for it. The complete story behind the visit of the four friends to Luskan remained sketchy to Morkai, but he had learned much of their quest, and more than he wanted Dendybar to find out about. He still hadn't discerned the true intentions behind the mottled wizard's inquiries, but felt certain that Dendybar was up to no good, whatever his goals.

"What is the purpose of the visit?" Dendybar demanded, angry at Morkai's stalling tactics.

"You yourself have summoned me," Morkai responded slyly. "I am compelled to appear."

"No games!" growled the mottled wizard. He glared at the specter, fingering the scroll of torment in open threat. Notorious for answering literally, beings from other planes often flustered their conjurors by distorting the connotative meaning of a question's exact wording.

Dendybar smiled in concession to the specter's simple logic and clarified the question. "What is the purpose of the visit to Luskan by the four travelers from Icewind Dale?"

"Varied reasons," Morkai replied. "One has come in search of the homeland of his father, and his father before him."

"The drow?" Dendybar asked, trying to find some way to link his suspicions that Drizzt planned to return to the underworld of his birth with the Crystal Shard. Perhaps an uprising by the dark elves, using the power of the shard? "Is it the drow who seeks his homeland?"

"Nay," replied the specter, pleased that Dendybar had fallen off on a tangent, delaying the more specific, and more dangerous line of questioning. The passing minutes would soon begin to dissipate Dendybar's hold upon the specter, and Morkai hoped that he could find a way to get free of the mottled wizard before revealing too much about Bruenor's company. "Drizzt Do'Urden has forsaken his homeland altogether. He shall never return to the bowels of the world, and certainly not with his dearest friends in tow!"

"Then who?"

"Another of the four flees from danger at his back," Morkai offered, twisting the line of inquiry.

"Who seeks his homeland?" Dendybar demanded more emphatically.

"The dwarf, Bruenor Battlehammer," replied Morkai, compelled to obey. "He seeks his birthplace, Mithril Hall, and his friends have joined in his quest. Why does this interest you? The companions have no connection to Luskan, and pose no threat to the Hosttower."

"I did not summon you here to answer your questions!" Dendybar scolded. "Now tell me who is running from danger. And what is the danger?"

"Behold," the specter instructed. With a wave of his hand, Morkai imparted an image upon the mind of the mottled wizard, a picture of a black-cloaked rider wildly charging across the tundra. The horse's bridle was white with lather, but the rider pressed the beast onward relentlessly.

"The halfling flees from this man," Morkai explained, "though the rider's purpose remains a mystery to me." Telling Dendybar even this much angered the specter, but Morkai could not yet resist the commands of his nemesis. He felt the bonds of the wizard's will loosening, though, and suspected that the summoning neared its end.

Dendybar paused to consider the information.

Nothing of what Morkai had told him gave any direct link to the Crystal Shard, but he had learned, at least, that the four friends did not mean to stay in Luskan for very long. And he had discovered a potential ally, a further source of information. The black-cloaked rider must be mighty indeed to have set the halfling's formidable troupe fleeing down the road.

Dendybar was beginning to formulate his next moves, when a sudden insistent pull of Morkai's stubborn resistance broke his concentration. Enraged, he shot a threatening glare back at the specter and began unrolling the parchment. "Impudent!" he growled, and though he could have stretched out his hold on the specter a bit longer if he had put his energies into a battle of wills, he started reciting the scroll.

Morkai recoiled, though he had consciously provoked Dendybar to this point. The specter could accept the racking, for it signaled the end of the inquisition. And Morkai was glad that Dendybar hadn't forced him to reveal the events even farther from Luskan, back in the dale just beyond the borders of Ten-Towns.

As Dendybar's recitations twanged discordantly on the harmony of his soul, Morkai removed the focal point of his concentration across hundreds of miles, back to the image of the merchant caravan now one day out from Bremen, the closest of the Ten Towns, and to the image of the brave young woman who had joined up with the traders. The specter took comfort in the knowledge that she had, for a while at least, escaped the probings of the mottled wizard.

Not that Morkai was altruistic; he had never been accused of an abundance of that trait. He simply took great satisfaction in hindering in any way he could the knave who had arranged his murder.

*   *   *   *   *

Catti-brie's red-brown locks tossed about her shoulders. She sat high up on the lead wagon of the merchant caravan that had set out from Ten-Towns on the previous day, bound for Luskan. Unbothered by the chill breeze, she kept her eyes on the road ahead, searching for some sign that the assassin had passed that way. She had relayed information about Entreri to Cassius, and he would pass it along to the dwarves. Catti-brie wondered now if she had been justified in sneaking away with the merchant caravan before Clan Battlehammer could organize its own chase.

But only she had seen the assassin at work. She knew well that if the dwarves went after him in a frontal assault, their caution wiped away in their lust of revenge for Fender and Grollo, many more of the clan would die.

Selfishly, perhaps, Catti-brie had determined that the assassin was her own business. He had unnerved her, had stripped away years of training and discipline and reduced her to the quivering semblance of a frightened child. But she was a young woman now, no more a girl. She had to personally respond to that emotional humiliation, or the scars from it would haunt her to her grave, forever paralyzing her along her path to discover her true potential in life.

She would find her friends in Luskan and warn them of the danger at their backs, and then together they would take care of Artemis Entreri.

"We make a strong pace," the lead driver assured her, sympathetic to her desire for haste.

Catti-brie did not look at him; her eyes rooted on the flat horizon before her. "Me heart tells me 'tisn't strong enough," she lamented.

The driver looked at her curiously, but had learned better than to press her on the point. She had made it clear to them from the start that her business was private. And being the adopted daughter of Bruenor Battlehammer, and reputedly a fine fighter in her own right, the merchants had counted themselves lucky to have her along and had respected her desire for privacy. Besides, as one of the drivers had so eloquently argued during their informal meeting before the journey, "The notion of staring at an ox's ass for near to three-hunnerd miles makes the thought o' having that girl along for company sit well with me!"

They had even moved up their departure date to accommodate her.

"Do not worry, Catti-brie," the driver assured her, "we'll get you there!"

Catti-brie shook her blowing hair out of her face and looked into the sun as it set on the horizon before her. "But can it be in time?" she asked softly and rhetorically, knowing that her whisper would break apart in the wind as soon as it passed her lips.

♣ 5 ♣

The Crags

Drizzt took the lead as the four companions jogged along the banks of the river Mirar, putting as much ground between themselves and Luskan as possible. Although they hadn't slept in many hours, their encounters in the City of Sails had sent a burst of adrenaline through their veins and none of them was weary.

Something magical hung in the air that night, a crispy tingling that would have made the most exhausted traveler lament closing his eyes to it. The river, rushing swiftly and high from the spring melt, sparkled in the evening glow, its whitecaps catching the starlight and throwing it back into the air in a spray of bejeweled droplets.

Normally cautious, the friends could not help but let their guard down. They felt no danger lurking near, felt nothing but the sharp, refreshing chill of the spring night and the mysterious pull of the heavens. Bruenor lost himself in dreams of Mithril Hall; Regis in memories of Calimport; even Wulfgar, so despondent about his ill-fated encounter with civilization, felt his spirits soar. He thought of similar nights on the open tundra, when he had dreamed of what lay beyond the horizons of his world. Now, out beyond those horizons, Wulfgar found only one element missing. To his surprise, and against the adventuring instincts that denied such comfortable thoughts, he wished that Catti-brie, the woman he had grown to cherish, was with him now to share the beauty of this night.

If the others had not been so preoccupied with their

own enjoyment of the evening, they would have noticed an extra bounce in Drizzt Do'Urden's graceful step as well. To the drow, these magical nights, when the heavenly dome reached down below the horizon, bolstered his confidence in the most important and difficult decision he had ever made, the choice to forsake his people and his homeland. No stars sparkled above Menzoberranzan, the dark city of the black elves. No unexplainable allure tugged at the heartstrings from the cold stone of the immense cavern's lightless ceiling.

"How much my people have lost by walking in darkness," Drizzt whispered into the night. The pull of the mysteries of the endless sky carried the joy of his spirit beyond its normal boundaries and opened his mind to the unanswerable questions of the multiverse. He was an elf, and though his skin was black, there remained in his soul a semblance of the harmonic joy of his surface cousins. He wondered how general these feelings truly ran among his people. Did they remain in the hearts of all drow? Or had eons of sublimation extinguished the spiritual flames? To Drizzt's reckoning, perhaps the greatest loss that his people had suffered when they retreated to the depths of the world was the loss of the ability to ponder the spirituality of existence simply for the sake of thought.

The crystalline sheen of the Mirar gradually dulled as the lightening dawn dimmed the stars. It came as an unspoken disappointment to the friends as they set their camp in a sheltered spot near the banks of the river.

"Be knowin' that nights like that are few," Bruenor observed as the first ray of light crept over the eastern horizon. A glimmer edged his eye, a hint of the wondrous fantasizing that the normally practical dwarf rarely enjoyed.

Drizzt noted the dwarf's dreamy glow and thought of the nights that he and Bruenor had spent on Bruenor's Climb, their special meeting place, back in the dwarf's valley in Ten-Towns. "Too few," he agreed.

With a resigned sigh, they set to work, Drizzt and Wulfgar starting breakfast while Bruenor and Regis examined the map they had obtained in Luskan.

For all of his grumbling and teasing about the halfling, Bruenor had pressured him to come along for a very definite reason, aside from their friendship, and though the dwarf had masked his emotions well, he was truly overjoyed when Regis had come up huffing and puffing on the road out of Ten-Towns in a last-minute plea to join the quest.

Regis knew the land south of the Spine of the World better than any of them. Bruenor himself hadn't been out of Icewind Dale in nearly two centuries, and then he had been just an unbearded dwarf-child. Wulfgar had never left the dale, and Drizzt's only trek across the world's surface had been a nighttime adventure, skipping from shadow to shadow and avoiding many of the places the companions would need to search out, if they were ever to find Mithril Hall.

Regis ran his fingers across the map, excitedly recalling to Bruenor his experiences in each of the places listed, particularly Mirabar, the mining city of great wealth to the north, and Waterdeep, true to its name as the City of Splendors, down the coast to the south.

Bruenor slipped his finger across the map, studying the physical features of the terrain. "Mirabar'd be more to me liking," he said at length, tapping the mark of the city tucked within the southern slopes of the Spine of the World. "Mithril Hall's in mountains, that much I know, and not aside the sea."

Regis considered the dwarf's observations for just a moment, then plunked his finger down on yet another spot, by the scale of the map a hundred miles and more inland from Luskan. "Longsaddle," he said. "Halfway to Silverymoon, and halfway between Mirabar and Waterdeep. A good place to search out our course."

"A city?" Bruenor asked, for the mark on the map was no more than a small black dot.

"A village," Regis corrected. "There are not many people there, but a family of wizards, the Harpells, have lived there for many years and know the northland as well as any. They would be happy to help us."

Bruenor scratched his chin and nodded. "A fair hike. What might we be seeing along the way?"

"The crags," Regis admitted, a bit disheartened as he remembered the place. "Wild and orc-filled. I wish we had another road, but Longsaddle still seems the best choice."

"All roads in the north hold danger," Bruenor reminded him.

They continued their scrutiny of the map, Regis recalling more and more as they went. A series of unusual and unidentified markings—three in particular, running in an almost straight line due east of Luskan to the river network south of Lurkwood—caught Bruenor's eye.

"Ancestral mounds," Regis explained. "Holy places of the Uthgardt."

"Uthgardt?"

"Barbarians," answered Regis grimly. "Like those in the dale. More wise to the ways of civilization, perhaps, but no less fierce. Their separate tribes are all about the northland, wandering the wilds."

Bruenor groaned in understanding of the halfling's dismay, all too familiar himself with the savage ways and fighting prowess of barbarians. Orcs would prove much less formidable foes.

By the time the two had finished their discussion, Drizzt was stretching out in the cool shade of a tree overhanging the river and Wulfgar was halfway through his third helping of breakfast.

"Yer jaw still dances for food, I see!" Bruenor called as he noted the meager portions left on the skillet.

"A night filled with adventure," Wulfgar replied gaily, and his friends were glad to observe that the brawl had apparently left no scars upon his attitude. "A fine meal and a fine sleep, and I shall be ready for the road once more!"

"Well don't ye get too comfortable yet!" Bruenor ordered. "Ye've a third of a watch to keep this day!"

Regis looked about, perplexed, always quick to recognize an increase in his workload. "A third?" he asked. "Why not a fourth?"

"The elf's eyes are for the night," Bruenor explained. "Let him be ready to find our way when the day's flown."

"And where is our way?" Drizzt asked from his mossy bed. "Have you come to a decision for our next destination?"

"Longsaddle," Regis replied. "Two hundred miles east and south, around Neverwinter Wood and across the crags."

"The name is unknown to me," Drizzt replied.

"Home of the Harpells," Regis explained. "A family of wizards reknowned for their good-natured hospitality. I spent some time there on my way to Ten-Towns."

Wulfgar balked at the idea. The barbarians of Icewind Dale despised wizards, considering the black arts a power employed only by cowards. "I have no desire to view this place," he stated flatly.

"Who asked ye?" growled Bruenor, and Wulfgar found himself backing down from his resolve, like a son refusing to hold a stubborn argument in the face of a scolding by his father.

"You will enjoy Longsaddle," Regis assured him. "The Harpells have truly earned their hospitable reputation, and the wonders of Longsaddle will show you a side of magic you never expected. They will even accept . . . " He found his hand involuntarily pointing to Drizzt, and he cut short the statement in embarrassment.

But the stoic drow just smiled. "Fear not, my friend," he consoled Regis. "Your words ring of truth, and I have come to accept my station in your world." He paused and looked individually into each uncomfortable stare that was upon him. "I know my friends, and I dismiss my enemies," he stated with a finality that dismissed their worries.

"With a blade, ye do," Bruenor added with a soft chuckle, though Drizzt's keen ears caught the whisper.

"If I must," the drow agreed, smiling. Then he rolled over to get some sleep, fully trusting in his friends' abilities to keep him safe.

They passed a lazy day in the shade beside the river. Late in the afternoon, Drizzt and Bruenor ate a meal and discussed their course, leaving Wulfgar and Regis soundly asleep, at least until they had eaten their own fill.

"We'll stay with the river for a night more," Bruenor said. "Then southeast across the open ground. That'd clear us of the wood and lay open a straight path 'fore us."

"Perhaps it would be better if we traveled only by night for a few days," Drizzt suggested. "We know not what eyes follow us out of the City of Sails."

"Agreed," replied Bruenor. "Let's be off, then. A long road before us, and a longer one after that!"

"Too long," murmured Regis, opening a lazy eye.

Bruenor shot him a dangerous glare. He was nervous about this trek and about bringing his friends on a dangerous road, and in an emotional defense, he took all complaints about the adventure personally.

"To walk, I mean," Regis quickly explained. "There are farmhouses in this area, so there must be some horses about."

"Horses'd bring too a high price in these parts," replied Bruenor.

"Maybe . . . " said the halfling slyly, and his friends could easily guess what he was thinking. Their frowns reflected a general disapproval.

"The crags stand before us!" Regis argued. "Horses might outrun orcs, but without them, we shall surely fight for every mile of our hike! Besides, it would only be a loan. We could return the beasts when we were through with them."

Drizzt and Bruenor did not approve of the halfling's

proposed trickery, but could not refute his logic. Horses would certainly aid them at this point of the journey.

"Wake the boy," Bruenor growled.

"And about my plan?" asked Regis.

"We'll make the choice when we find the opportunity!"

Regis was contented, confident that his friends would opt for the horses. He ate his fill, then scraped together the supper's meager remnants and went to wake Wulfgar.

They were on the trail again soon after, and a short time after that, they saw the lights of a small settlement in the distance.

"Take us there," Bruenor told Drizzt. "Mighten be that Rumblebelly's plan's worth a try."

Wulfgar, having missed the conversation at the camp, didn't understand, but offered no argument, or even questioned the dwarf. After the disaster at the Cutlass, he had resigned himself to a more passive role on the trip, letting the other three decide which trails they were to take. He would follow without complaint, keeping his hammer ready for when it became needed.

They moved inland away from the river for a few miles, then came upon several farms clustered together inside a stout wooden fence.

"There are dogs about," Drizzt noted, sensing them with his exceptional hearing.

"Then Rumblebelly goes in alone," said Bruenor.

Wulfgar's face twisted in confusion, especially since the halfling's look indicated that he wasn't thrilled with the idea. "That I cannot allow," the barbarian spouted. "If any among us needs protection, it is the little one. I'll not hide here in the dark while he walks alone into danger!"

"He goes in alone," Bruenor said again. "We're here for no fight, boy. Rumblebelly's to get us some horses."

Regis smiled helplessly, caught fully in the trap that Bruenor had clearly set for him. Bruenor would allow him to appropriate the horses, as Regis had insisted, but

with the grudging permission came a measure of responsibility and bravery on his part. It was the dwarf's way of
absolving himself of involvement in the trickery.

Wulfgar remained steadfast in his determination to
stand by the halfling, but Regis knew that the young warrior might inadvertently cause him problems in such del-
icate negotiations. "You stay with the others," he
explained to the barbarian. "I can handle this deal alone."

Mustering up his nerve, he pulled his belt over the
hang of his belly and strode off toward the small settlement.

The threatening snarls of several dogs greeted him as
he approached the fence's gate. He considered turning
back—the ruby pendant probably wouldn't do him much
good against vicious dogs—but then he saw the silhouette of a man leave one of the farmhouses and start his
way.

"What do you want?" the farmer demanded, standing
defiantly on the other side of the gate and clutching an
antique pole arm, probably passed down through his
family's generations.

"I am but a weary traveler," Regis started to explain,
trying to appear as pitiful as he could. It was a tale the
farmer had heard far too often.

"Go away!" he ordered.

"But—"

"Get you gone!"

Over a ridge some distance away, the three companions watched the confrontation, though only Drizzt
viewed the scene in the dim light well enough to understand what was happening. The drow could see the
tenseness in the farmer by the way he gripped the hal-
berd, and could judge the deep resolve in the man's
demands by the unbending scowl upon his face.

But then Regis pulled something out from under his
jacket, and the farmer relaxed his grip upon the weapon
almost immediately. A moment later, the gate swung
open and Regis walked in.

The friends waited anxiously for several grueling hours with no further sign of Regis. They considered confronting the farmers themselves, worried that some foul treachery had befallen the halfling. Then finally, with the moon well past its peak, Regis emerged from the gate, leading two horses and two ponies. The farmers and their families waved good-bye to him as he left, making him promise to stop and visit if he ever passed their way again.

"Amazing," laughed Drizzt. Bruenor and Wulfgar just shook their heads in disbelief.

For the first time since he had entered the settlement, Regis pondered that his delay might have caused his friends some distress. The farmer had insisted that he join in for supper before they sat down to discuss whatever business he had come about, and since Regis had to be polite (and since he had only eaten one supper that day) he agreed, though he kept the meal as short as possible and politely declined when offered his fourth helping. Getting the horses proved easy enough after that. All he had to do was promise to leave them with the wizards in Longsaddle when he and his friends moved on from there.

Regis felt certain that his friends could not stay mad at him for very long. He had kept them waiting and worrying for half the night, but his endeavor would save them many days on a dangerous road. After an hour or two of feeling the wind rushing past them as they rode, they would forget any anger they held for him, he knew. Even if they didn't so easily forgive, a good meal was always worth a little inconvenience to Regis.

Drizzt purposely kept the party moving more to the east than the southeast. He found no landmarks on Bruenor's map that would let him approximate the straight course to Longsaddle. If he tried the direct route and missed the mark, no matter how slightly, they would come upon the main road from the northern city of

Mirabar not knowing whether to turn north or south. By going directly east, the drow was assured that they would hit the road to the north of Longsaddle. His path would add a few miles, but perhaps save them several days of backtracking.

Their ride was clear and easy for the next day and night, and after that, Bruenor decided that they were far enough from Luskan to assume a more normal traveling schedule. "We can go by day, now," he announced early in the afternoon of their second day with the horses.

"I prefer the night," Drizzt said. He had just awakened and was brushing down his slender, well-muscled black stallion.

"Not me," argued Regis. "Nights are for sleeping, and the horses are all but blind to holes and rocks that could lame them up."

"The best for both then," offered Wulfgar, stretching the last sleep out of his bones. "We can leave after the sun peaks, keeping it behind us for Drizzt, and ride long into the night."

"Good thinking, lad," laughed Bruenor. "Seems to be after noon now, in fact. On the horses, then! Time's for going!"

"You might have held your thoughts to yourself until after supper!" Regis grumbled at Wulfgar, reluctantly hoisting the saddle onto the back of the little white pony.

Wulfgar moved to help his struggling friend. "But we would have lost half a day's ride," he replied.

"A pity that would have been," Regis retorted.

That day, the fourth since they had left Luskan, the companions came upon the crags, a narrow stretch of broken mounds and rolling hills. A rough, untamed beauty defined the place, an overpowering sense of wilderness that gave every traveler here a feeling of conquest, that he might be the first to gaze upon any particular spot. And, as was always the case in the wilds, with the adventurous excitement came a degree of danger. They had barely entered the first dell in the up-and-down terrain when Drizzt spotted tracks that he knew well: the trampling march of an orc band.

"Less than a day old," he told his concerned companions.

"How many?" asked Bruenor.

Drizzt shrugged. "A dozen at least, maybe twice that number."

"We'll keep to our path," the dwarf suggested. "They're in front of us, and that's better'n behind."

When sunset came, marking the halfway point of that day's journey, the companions took a short break, letting the horses graze in a small meadow.

The orc trail was still before them, but Wulfgar, taking up the rear of the troupe had his sights trained behind.

"We are being followed," he said to his friends' inquiring faces.

"Orcs?" Regis asked.

The barbarian shook his head. "None like I have ever seen. By my reckoning, our pursuit is cunning and cautious."

"Might be that the orcs here are more wise to the ways of goodly folk than be the orcs of the dale," said Bruenor, but he suspected something other than orcs, and he didn't have to look at Regis to know that the halfling shared his concerns. The first map marking that Regis had identified as an ancestral mound could not be far from their present position.

"Back to the horses," Drizzt suggested. "A hard ride might do much to improve our position."

"Go till after moonset," Bruenor agreed. "And stop when ye've found a place we can hold against attack. I've a feeling we're to see some fighting 'fore the dawn finds us!"

They encountered no tangible signs during the ride, which took them nearly across the span of the crags. Even the orc trail faded off to the north, leaving the path before them apparently clear. Wulfgar was certain, though, that he caught several sounds behind them, and movements along the periphery of his vision.

Drizzt would have liked to continue until the crags were fully behind them, but in the harsh terrain, the horses had reached the limit of their endurance. He pulled up into a small copse of fir trees set on top of a small rise, fully suspecting, like the others, that unfriendly eyes were watching them from more than one direction.

Drizzt was up one of the trees before the others had even dismounted. They tethered the horses close together and set themselves around the beasts. Even Regis would find no sleep, for, though he trusted Drizzt's night vision, his blood had already begun pumping in anticipation of what was to come.

Bruenor, a veteran of a hundred fights, felt secure enough in his battle prowess. He propped himself calmly against a tree, his many-notched axe across his chest, one hand firmly in place upon its handle.

Wulfgar, though, made other preparations. He began by gathering together broken sticks and branches and sharpening their points. Seeking every advantage, he set them in strategic positions around the area to provide the best layout for his stand, using their deadly points to cut down the routes of approach for his attackers. Other sticks he cunningly concealed in angles that would trip up and stick the orcs before they ever reached him.

Regis, the most nervous of all, watched it all and noted the differences in his friends' tactics. He felt that there was little he could do to prepare himself for such a fight, and he sought only to keep himself far enough out of the way so as not to hinder the efforts of his friends. Perhaps the opportunity would arise for him to make a surprise strike, but he didn't even consider such possibilities at this point. Bravery came to the halfling spontaneously. It was certainly nothing he ever planned.

With all of their diversions and preparations deflecting their nervous anticipation, it came as almost a relief when, barely an hour later, their anxiety became reality. Drizzt whispered down to them that there was movement on the fields below the copse.

"How many?" Bruenor called back.

"Four to one against us, and maybe more," Drizzt replied.

The dwarf turned to Wulfgar. "Ye ready, boy?"

Wulfgar slapped his hammer out before him. "Four against one?" he laughed. Bruenor liked the young warrior's confidence, though the dwarf realized that the odds might actually prove more lopsided, since Regis wouldn't likely be out in the open fighting.

"Let 'em in, or hit them out in the field?" Bruenor asked Drizzt.

"Let them in," the drow replied. "Their stealthy approach shows me that they believe surprise is with them."

"And a turned surprise is better'n a first blow from afar," Bruenor finished. "Do what ye can with yer bow when it's started, elf. We'll be waitin' fer ye!"

Wulfgar imagined the fire seething in the drow's lavender eyes, a deadly gleam that always belied Drizzt's outward calm before a battle. The barbarian took comfort, for the drow's lust for battle outweighed even his own, and he had never seen the whirring scimitars outdone by any foe. He slapped his hammer again and crouched in a hole beside the roots of one of the trees.

Bruenor slipped between the bulky bodies of two of the horses, pulling his feet up into a stirrup on each, and Regis, after he had stuffed the bedrolls to give the appearance of sleeping bodies, scooted under the low-hanging boughs of one of the trees.

The orcs approached the camp in a ring, obviously looking for an easy strike. Drizzt smiled in hope as he noted the gaps in their ring, open flanks that would prevent quick support to any isolated group. The whole band would hit the perimeter of the copse together, and Wulfgar, closest to the edge, would most likely launch the first strike.

The orcs crept in, one group slipping toward the horses, another toward the bedrolls. Four of them passed Wulfgar, but he waited a second longer, allowing the others to get close enough to the horses for Bruenor to strike.

Then the time for hiding had ended.

Wulfgar sprang from his concealment, Aegis-fang, his magical warhammer, already in motion. "Tempus!" he cried to his god of battle, and his first blow crashed in, swatting two of the orcs to the ground.

The other group rushed to get the horses free and out of the camp, hoping to cut off any escape route.

But were greeted by the snarling dwarf and his ringing axe!

As the surprised orcs leaped into the saddles, Bruenor clove one down the middle, and took a second one's head clean from its shoulders before the remaining two even knew that they had been attacked.

Drizzt picked as targets the orcs closest to the groups under attack, delaying the support against his friends for as long as possible. His bowstring twanged, once, twice, and a third time, and a like number of orcs fell to the earth, their eyes closed and their hands helplessly clenched upon the shafts of the killing arrows.

The surprise strikes had cut deeply into the ranks of their enemies, and now the drow pulled his scimitars and dropped from his perch, confident that he and his companions could finish the rest off quickly. His smile was short-lived, though, for as he descended, he noticed more movement in the field.

Drizzt had come down in the middle of three creatures, his blades in motion before his feet had even touched the ground. The orcs were not totally surprised—one had seen the drow dropping—but Drizzt had them off balance and swinging around to bring their weapons to bear.

With the drow's lightninglike strikes, any delay at all

meant certain death, and Drizzt was the only one in the jumble of bodies under control. His scimitars slashed and thrust into orcan flesh with killing precision.

Wulfgar's fortunes were equally bright. He faced two of the creatures, and though they were vicious fighters, they could not match the giant barbarian's power. One got its crude weapon up in time to block Wulfgar's swing, but Aegis-fang blasted through the defense, shattering the weapon and then the unfortunate orc's skull without even slowing for the effort.

Bruenor fell into trouble first. His initial attacks went off perfectly, leaving him with only two standing opponents—odds that the dwarf liked. But in the excitement, the horses reared and bolted, tearing their tethers free from the branches. Bruenor tumbled to the ground, and before he could recover, was clipped in the head by the hoof of his own pony. One of the orcs was similarly thrown down, but the last one landed free of the commotion and rushed to finish off the stunned dwarf as the horses cleared the area.

Luckily, one of those spontaneous moments of bravery came over Regis at that moment. He slipped out from under the tree, falling in silently behind the orc. It was tall for an orc, and even on the tips of his toes, Regis did not like the angle of a strike at its head. Shrugging resignedly, the halfling reversed his strategy.

Before the orc could even begin to strike at Bruenor, the halfling's mace came up between its knees and higher, driving into its groin and lifting it clear off the ground. The howling victim grasped at its injury, its eyes lolling about aimlessly, and dropped to the ground with no further ambitions for battle.

It had all happened in an instant, but victory was not yet won. Another six orcs poured into the fray, two cutting off Drizzt's attempt to get to Regis and Bruenor, three more going to the aid of their lone companion facing the giant barbarian. And one, creeping along the same line Regis had taken, closed on the unsuspecting halfling.

At the same moment Regis made out the drow's warning call, a club slammed between his shoulder blades, blasting the wind from his lungs and tossing him to the ground.

Wulfgar was pressed on all four sides, and despite his boasts before the battle, he found that he didn't care for the situation. He concentrated on parrying, hoping that the drow could get to him before his defenses broke down.

He was too badly outnumbered.

An orcan blade cut into a rib, another clipped his arm.

Drizzt knew that he could defeat the two he now faced, but doubted that it would be in time for him to help his barbarian friend. Or the halfling. And there were still reinforcements on the field.

Regis rolled onto his back to lay right beside Bruenor, and the dwarf's groaning told him that the fight was over for both of them. Then the orc was above him, its club raised above its head, and an evil smile spread wide upon its ugly face. Regis closed his eyes, having no desire to watch the descent of the blow that would kill him.

Then he heard the sound of impact . . . above him.

Startled, he opened his eyes. A hatchet was embedded into his attacker's chest. The orc looked down at it, stunned. The club dropped harmlessly behind the orc, and it, too, fell backward, quite dead.

Regis didn't understand. "Wulfgar?" he asked into the air.

A huge form, nearly as large as Wulfgar's, sprang over him and pounced upon the orc, savagely tearing the hatchet free. He was human, and wearing the furs of a barbarian, but unlike the tribes of Icewind Dale, this man's hair was black.

"Oh, no," Regis groaned, remembering his own warnings to Bruenor about the Uthgardt barbarians. The man had saved his life, but knowing the savage reputation, Regis doubted that a friendship would grow out of the encounter. He started to sit up, wanting to express his sincere thanks and dispel any unfriendly notions the barbarian might have about him. He even considered using the ruby pendant to evoke some friendly feelings.

But the big man, noting the movement, spun suddenly and kicked him in the face.

And Regis fell backward into blackness.

❧ 6 ❧

Sky Ponies

Black-haired barbarians, screaming in the frenzy of battle, burst into the copse. Drizzt realized at once that these burly warriors were the forms he had seen moving behind the orcan ranks on the field, but he wasn't yet certain of their allegiance.

Whatever their ties, their arrival struck terror into the remaining orcs. The two fighting Drizzt lost all heart for the battle, a sudden shift in their posture revealing their desire to break off the confrontation and flee. Drizzt obliged, assured that they wouldn't get far anyway, and sensing that he, too, would be wise to slip from sight.

The orcs fled, but their pursuers soon caught them in another battle just beyond the trees. Less obvious in his flight, Drizzt slipped unnoticed back up the tree where he had left his bow.

Wulfgar could not so easily sublimate his battle lust. With two of his friends down, his thirst for orcan blood was insatiable, and the new group of men that had joined the fight cried out to Tempus, his own god of battle, with a fervor that the young warrior could not ignore. Distracted by the sudden developments, the ring of orcs around Wulfgar let up for just a moment, and he struck hard.

One orc looked away, and Aegis-fang tore its face off before its eyes returned to the fight at hand. Wulfgar bore through the gap in the ring, jostling a second orc as he passed. As it stumbled in its attempt to turn and realign its defense, the mighty barbarian chopped it down. The two remaining turned and fled, but Wulfgar was right behind. He launched his hammer, blasting one from life, and sprang upon the other, bearing it to the ground beneath him and then crushing the life from it with his bare hands.

When he was finished, when he had heard the final crack of neckbone, Wulfgar remembered his predicament and his friends. He sprang up and backed away, his back against the trees.

The black-haired barbarians kept their distance, respectful of his prowess, and Wulfgar could not be sure of their intentions. He scanned around for his friends. Regis and Bruenor lay side by side near where the horses had been tethered; he could not tell if they were alive or dead. There was no sign of Drizzt, but a fight continued beyond the other edge of the trees.

The warriors fanned out in a wide semi-circle around him, cutting off any routes of escape. But they stopped their positioning suddenly, for Aegis-fang had magically returned to Wulfgar's grasp.

He could not win against so many, but the thought did not dismay him. He would die fighting, as a true warrior, and his death would be remembered. If the black-haired barbarians came at him, many, he knew, would not return to their families. He dug his heels in and clasped the warhammer tightly. "Let us be done with it," he growled into the night.

"Hold!" came a soft, but imperative whisper from above. Wulfgar recognized Drizzt's voice at once and relaxed his grip. "Keep to your honor, but know that more lives are at stake than your own!"

Wulfgar understood then that Regis and Bruenor were probably still alive. He dropped Aegis-fang to the ground and called out to the warriors, "Well met."

They did not reply, but one of them, nearly as tall and heavily muscled as Wulfgar, broke rank and closed in to stand before him. The stranger wore a single braid in his long hair, running down the side of his face and over his shoulder. His cheeks were painted white in the image of wings. The hardness of his frame and disciplined set of his face reflected a life in the harsh wilderness, and were it not for the raven color of his hair, Wulfgar would have thought him to be of one of the tribes of Icewind Dale.

The dark-haired man similarly recognized Wulfgar, but better versed in the overall structures of the societies in the northland, was not so perplexed by their similarities. "You are of the dale," he said in a broken form of the common tongue. "Beyond the mountains, where the cold wind blows."

Wulfgar nodded. "I am Wulfgar, son of Beornegar, of the Tribe of the Elk. We share gods, for I, too, call to Tempus for strength and courage."

The dark-haired man looked around at the fallen orcs. "The god answers your call, warrior of the dale."

Wulfgar's jaw lifted in pride. "We share hatred for the orcs, as well," he continued, "but I know nothing of you or your people."

"You shall learn," the dark-haired man replied. He held out his hand and indicated the warhammer. Wulfgar straightened firmly, having no intentions of surrendering, no matter the odds. The dark-haired man looked to the side, drawing Wulfgar's eyes with his own. Two warriors had picked up Bruenor and Regis and slung them over their backs, while others had recaptured the horses and were leading them in.

"The weapon," the dark-haired man demanded. "You are in our land without our say, Wulfgar, son of Beornegar. The price of that crime is death. Shall you watch our judgement over your small friends?"

The younger Wulfgar would have struck then, damning them all in a blaze of glorious fury. But Wulfgar had learned much from his new friends, Drizzt in particular. He knew that Aegis-fang would return to his call, and he knew, too, that Drizzt would not abandon them. This was not the time to fight.

He even let them bind his hands, an act of dishonor

that no warrior of the Tribe of the Elk would ever allow. But Wulfgar had faith in Drizzt. His hands would be freed again. Then he would have the last word.

By the time they reached the barbarian camp, both Regis and Bruenor had regained consciousness and were bound and walking beside their barbarian friend. Dried blood crusted Bruenor's hair and he had lost his helm, but his dwarven toughness had carried him through another encounter that should have finished him.

They crested a rise and came upon the perimeter of a ring of tents and blazing campfires. Whooping their war cries to Tempus, the returning war party roused the camp, tossing severed orc heads into the ring to announce their glorious arrival. The fervor inside the camp soon matched the level of the entering war party, and the three prisoners were pushed in first, to be greeted by a score of howling barbarians.

"What do they eat?" Bruenor asked, more in sarcasm than concern.

"Whatever it is, feed them quickly," Regis replied, drawing a clap on the back of his head and a warning to be silent from the guard behind him.

The prisoners and horses were herded into the center of the camp and the tribe encircled them in a victory dance, kicking orc heads around in the dust and singing out, in a language unknown to the companions, their praise to Tempus and to Uthgar, their ancestral hero, for the success this night.

It went on for nearly an hour, and then, all at once, it ended and every face in the ring turned to the closed flap of a large and decorated tent.

The silence held for a long moment before the flap swung open. Out jumped an ancient man, as slender as a tent pole, but showing more energy than his obvious years would indicate. His face painted in the same markings as the warriors, though more elaborately, he wore a patch with a huge green gemstone sewn upon it over one eye. His robe was the purest white, its sleeves showing as feathered wings whenever he flapped his arms out to the side. He danced and twirled through the ranks of the warriors, and each held his breath, recoiling until he had passed.

"Chief?" Bruenor whispered.

"Shaman," corrected Wulfgar, more knowledgeable in the ways of tribal life. The respect the warriors showed this man came from a fear beyond what a mortal enemy, even a chieftain, could impart.

The shaman spun and leaped, landing right before the three prisoners. He looked at Bruenor and Regis for just a moment, then turned his full attention upon Wulfgar.

"I am Valric High Eye," he screeched suddenly. "Priest of the followers of the Sky Ponies! The children of Uthgar!"

"Uthgar!" echoed the warriors, clapping their hatchets against their wooden shields.

Wulfgar waited for the commotion to die away, then presented himself. "I am Wulfgar, son of Beornegar, of the Tribe of the Elk."

"And I'm Bruenor—" began the dwarf.

"Silence!" Valric shouted at him, trembling with rage. "I care nothing for you!"

Bruenor closed his mouth and entertained dreams concerning his axe and Valric's head.

"We meant no harm, nor trespass," Wulfgar began, but Valric put his hand up, cutting him short.

"Your purpose does not interest me," he explained calmly, but his excitement resurged at once. "Tempus has delivered you unto us, that is all! A worthy warrior?" He looked around at his own men and their response showed eagerness for the coming challenge.

"How many did you claim?" he asked Wulfgar.

"Seven fell before me," the young barbarian replied proudly.

Valric nodded in approval. "Tall and strong," he commented. "Let us discover if Tempus is with you. Let us judge if you are worthy to run with the Sky Ponies!"

Shouts started at once and two warriors rushed over to unbind Wulfgar. A third, the leader of the war party who had spoken to Wulfgar at the copse of trees, tossed down his hatchet and shield and stormed into the ring.

Drizzt waited in his tree until the last of the war party had given up the search for the rider of the fourth horse and departed. Then the drow moved quickly, gathering together some of the dropped items: the dwarf's axe and Regis's mace. He had to pause and steady himself when he found Bruenor's helm, though, blood-stained and newly dented, and with one of its horns broken away. Had his friend survived?

He shoved the broken helm into his sack and slipped out after the troupe, keeping a cautious distance.

Relief flooded through him when he came upon the camp and spotted his three friends, Bruenor standing calmly between Wulfgar and Regis. Satisfied, Drizzt put aside his emotions and all thoughts of the previous encounter, narrowing his vision to the situation before him, formulating a plan of attack that would free his friends.

The dark-haired man held his open hands out to Wulfgar, inviting his blond counterpart to clasp them. Wulfgar had never seen this particular challenge before, but it was not so different from the tests of strength that his own people practised.

"Your feet do not move!" instructed Valric. "This is the challenge of strength! Let Tempus show us your worth!"

Wulfgar's firm visage didn't reveal a hint of his confidence that he could defeat any man at such a test. He brought his hands up level with those of his opponent.

The man grabbed at them angrily, snarling at the large foreigner. Almost immediately, before Wulfgar had even straightened his grip or set his feet, the shaman screamed out to begin, and the dark-haired man drove his hands forward, bending Wulfgar's back over his wrists. Shouting erupted from every corner of the encampment; the dark-haired man roared and pushed with all his strength, but as soon as the moment of surprise had passed, Wulfgar fought back.

The iron-corded muscles in Wulfgar's neck and shoulders snapped taut and his huge arms reddened with the forced surge of blood into their veins. Tempus had blessed him truly; even his mighty opponent could only gape in amazement at the spectacle of his power. Wulfgar looked him straight in the eye and matched the snarl with a determined glare that foretold the inevitable victory. Then the son of Beornegar drove forward, stopping the dark-haired man's initial momentum and forcing his own hands back into a more normal angle with his wrists. Once he had regained parity, Wulfgar realized that one sudden push would put his opponent into the same disadvantage that he had just escaped. From there, the dark-haired man would have little chance of holding on.

But Wulfgar wasn't anxious to end this contest. He didn't want to humiliate his opponent—that would breed only an enemy—and even more importantly, he knew that Drizzt was about. The longer he could keep the contest going, and the eyes of every member of the tribe fixed upon him, the longer Drizzt would have to put some plan into motion.

The two men held there for many seconds, and Wulfgar couldn't help but smile when he noticed a dark shape slip in among the horses, behind the enthralled guards at the other end of the camp. Whether it was his imagination, he could not tell, but he thought that he saw two points of lavender flame staring out at him from the darkness. A few seconds more, he decided, though he knew that he was taking a chance by not finishing the challenge. The shaman could declare a draw if they held for too long.

But then it was over. The veins and sinews in Wulfgar's

arms bulged and his shoulders lifted even higher. "Tempus!" he growled, praising the god for yet another victory, and then with a sudden, ferocious explosion of power, he drove the dark-haired man to his knees. All around, the camp went silent, even the shaman being stricken speechless by the display.

Two guards moved tentatively to Wulfgar's side.

The beaten warrior pulled himself to his feet and stood facing Wulfgar. No hints of anger marred his face, just honest admiration, for the Sky Ponies were an honorable people.

"We would welcome you," Valric said. "You have defeated Torlin, son of Jerek Wolf-slayer, Chieftain of the Sky Ponies. Never before has Torlin been bested!"

"What of my friends?" Wulfgar asked.

"I care nothing for them!" Valric snapped back. "The dwarf will be set free on a trail leading from our land. We have no quarrel with him or his kind, nor do we desire any dealings with them!"

The shaman eyed Wulfgar slyly. "The other is a weakling," he stated. "He shall serve as your passage to the tribe, your sacrifice to the winged horse."

Wulfgar did not immediately respond. They had tested his strength, and now were testing his loyalties. The Sky Ponies had paid him their highest honor in offering him a place in their tribe, but only on condition that he show his allegiance beyond any doubt. Wulfgar thought of his own people, and the way they had lived for so many centuries on the tundra. Even in this day, many of the barbarians of Icewind Dale would have accepted the terms and killed Regis, considering the life of a halfling a small price for such an honor. This was the disillusionment of Wulfgar's existence with his people, the facet of their moral code that had proved unacceptable to his personal standards.

"No," he replied to Valric without blinking.

"He is a weakling!" Valric reasoned. "Only the strong deserve life!"

"His fate is not mine to decide," Wulfgar replied. "Nor yours."

Valric motioned to the two guards and they immediately rebound Wulfgar's hands.

"A loss for our people," Torlin said to Wulfgar. "You would have received a place of honor among us."

Wulfgar didn't answer, holding Torlin's stare for a long moment, sharing respect and also the mutual understanding that their codes were too different for such a joining. In a shared fantasy that could not be, both imagined fighting beside the other, felling orcs by the score and inspiring the bards to a new legend.

It was time for Drizzt to strike. The drow had paused by the horses to view the outcome of the contest and also to better measure his enemies. He planned his attack for effect more than for damage, wanting to put on a grand show to cow a tribe of fearless warriors long enough for his friends to break free of the ring.

No doubt, the barbarians had heard of the dark elves. And no doubt, the tales they had heard were terrifying.

Silently, Drizzt tied the two ponies behind the horses, then mounted the horses, a foot in one stirrup on each. Rising between them, he stood tall and threw back the cowl of his cloak. The dangerous glow in his lavender eyes sparkling wildly, he bolted the mounts into the ring, scattering the stunned barbarians closest to him.

Howls of rage rose up from the surprised tribesmen, the tone of the shouts shifting to one of terror when they viewed the black skin. Torlin and Valric turned to face the oncoming menace, though even they did not know how to deal with a legend personified.

And Drizzt had a trick ready for them. With a wave of his black hand, purple flames spouted from Torlin and Valric's skin, not burning, but casting both the superstitious tribesmen into a horrified frenzy. Torlin dropped to his knees, clasping his arms in disbelief, while the highstrung shaman dove to the ground and began rolling in the dirt.

Wulfgar took his cue. Another surge of power through his arms snapped the leather bonds at his wrists. He continued the momentum of his hands, swinging them upward, catching both of the guards beside him squarely in the face and dropping them to their backs.

Bruenor also understood his part. He stomped heavily onto the instep of the lone barbarian standing between him and Regis, and when the man crouched to grasp his pained foot, Bruenor butted him in the head. The man tumbled as easily as Whisper had back in Rat Alley in Luskan.

"Huh, works as well without the helmet!" Bruenor marveled.

"Only for a dwarf's head!" Regis remarked as Wulfgar grabbed both of them by the back of their collars and hoisted them easily onto the ponies.

He was up then, too, beside Drizzt, and they charged through the other side of the camp. It had all happened too quickly for any of the barbarians to ready a weapon or form any kind of defense.

Drizzt wheeled his horse behind the ponies to protect the rear. "Ride!" he yelled to his friends, slapping their mounts on the rump with the flat of his scimitars. The other three shouted in victory as though their escape was complete, but Drizzt knew that this had been the easy part. The dawn was fast approaching, and in this up-and-down, unfamiliar terrain, the native barbarians could easily catch them.

The companions charged into the silence of pre-dawn, picking the straightest and easiest path to gain as much ground as possible. Drizzt still kept an eye behind them, expecting the tribesmen to be fast on their trail. But the commotion in the camp had died away almost immediately after the escape, and the drow saw no signs of pursuit.

Now only a single call could be heard, the rhythmic singing of Valric in a tongue that none of the travelers understood. The look of dread on Wulfgar's face made all of them pause. "The powers of a shaman," the barbarian explained.

Back in the camp, Valric stood alone with Torlin inside the ring of his people, chanting and dancing through the ultimate ritual of his station, summoning the power of his tribe's Spiritual Beast. The appearance of the drow elf had completely unnerved the shaman. He stopped any pursuit before it had even begun and ran to his tent for the sacred leather satchel needed for the ritual, deciding that the spirit of the winged horse, the Pegasus, should deal with these intruders.

Valric targeted Torlin as the recipient of the spirit's form, and the son of Jerek awaited the possession with stoic dignity, hating the act, for it stripped him of his identity, but resigned to absolute obedience to his shaman.

From the moment it began, however, Valric knew that in his excitement, he had overstepped the urgency of the summoning.

Torlin shrieked and dropped to the ground, writhing in agony. A gray cloud surrounded him, its swirling vapors molding with his form, reshaping his features. His face puffed and twisted, and suddenly spurted outward into the semblance of a horse's head. His torso, as well, transmuted into something not human. Valric had meant only to impart some of the strengths of the spirit of the Pegasus in Torlin, but the entity itself had come, possessing the man wholly and bending his body into its own likeness.

Torlin was consumed.

In his place loomed the ghostly form of the winged horse. All in the tribe fell to their knees before it, even Valric, who could not face the image of the Spiritual Beast. But the Pegasus knew the shaman's thoughts and understood its children's needs. Smoke fumed from the spirit's nostrils and it rose into the air in pursuit of the escaping intruders.

The friends had settled their mounts into a more comfortable, though still swift, pace. Free of their bonds, with the dawn breaking before them and no apparent pursuit behind them, they had eased up a bit. Bruenor fiddled with his helmet, trying to push the latest dent out far enough for him to get the thing back on his head. Even Wulfgar, so shaken a short time before when he had heard the chanting of the shaman, began to relax.

Only Drizzt, ever wary, was not so easily convinced of their escape. And it was the drow who first sensed the approach of danger.

In the dark cities, the black elves often dealt with otherworldly beings, and over the many centuries they had bred into their race a sensitivity for the magical emanations of such creatures. Drizzt stopped his horse suddenly and wheeled about.

"What do ye hear?" Bruenor asked him.

"I hear nothing," Drizzt answered, his eyes darting about for some sign. "But something is there."

Before they could respond, the gray cloud rushed down from the sky and was upon them. Their horses bucked and reared in uncontrollable terror and in the confusion none of the friends could sort out what was happening. The Pegasus then formed right in front of Regis and the halfling felt a deathly chill penetrate his bones. He screamed and dropped from his mount.

Bruenor, riding beside Regis, charged the ghostly form fearlessly. But his descending axe found only a cloud of smoke where the apparition had been. Then, just as suddenly, the ghost was back, and Bruenor, too, felt the icy cold of its touch. Tougher than the halfling, he managed to hold to his pony.

"What?" he cried out vainly to Drizzt and Wulfgar.

Aegis-fang whistled past him and continued on at the target. But the Pegasus was only smoke again and the magical warhammer passed unhindered through the swirling cloud.

In an instant, the spirit was back, swooping down upon

Bruenor. The dwarf's pony spun down to the ground in a frantic effort to scramble away from the thing.

"You cannot hit it!" Drizzt called after Wulfgar, who went rushing to the dwarf's aid. "It does not exist fully on this plane!"

Wulfgar's mighty legs locked his terrified horse straight and he struck as soon as Aegis-fang returned to his hands.

But again he found only smoke before his blow.

"Then how?" he yelled to Drizzt, his eyes darting around to spot the first signs of the reforming spirit.

Drizzt searched his mind for answers. Regis was still down, lying pale and unmoving on the field, and Bruenor, though he had not been too badly injured in his pony's fall, appeared dazed and shivering from the chill of unearthly cold. Drizzt grasped at a desperate plan. He pulled the onyx statue of the panther from his pouch and called for Guenhwyvar.

The ghost returned, attacking with renewed fury. It descended upon Bruenor first, mantling the dwarf with its cold wings. "Damn ye back to the Abyss!" Bruenor roared in brave defiance.

Rushing in, Wulfgar lost all sight of the dwarf, except for the head of his axe bursting harmlessly through the smoke.

Then the barbarian's mount halted in its tracks, refusing, against all efforts, to move any closer to the unnatural beast. Wulfgar leaped from his saddle and charged in, crashing right through the cloud before the ghost could reform, his momentum carrying both him and Bruenor out the other side of the smoky mantle. They rolled away and looked back, only to find that the ghost had disappeared altogether again.

Bruenor's eyelids drooped heavily and his skin held a ghastly hue of blue, and for the first time in his life, his indomitable spirit had no gumption for the fight. Wulfgar, too, had suffered the icy touch in his pass through the ghost, but he was still more than ready for another round with the thing.

"We can't fight it!" Bruenor gasped through his chattering teeth. "Here for a strike, it is, but gone when we hit back!"

Wulfgar shook his head defiantly. "There is a way!" he demanded, though he had to concede the dwarf's point. "But my hammer cannot destroy clouds!"

Guenhwyvar appeared beside its master and crouched low, seeking the nemesis that threatened the drow.

Drizzt understood the cat's intentions. "No!" he commanded. "Not here." The drow had recalled something that Guenhwyvar had done several months earlier. To save Regis from the falling stone of a crumbling tower, Guenhwyvar had taken the halfling on a journey through the planes of existence. Drizzt grabbed onto the panther's thick coat.

"Take me to the land of the ghost," he instructed. "To its own plane, where my weapons will bite deeply into its substantial being."

The ghost appeared again as Drizzt and the cat faded into their own cloud.

"Keep swinging!" Bruenor told his companion. "Keep it as smoke so's it can't get at ye!"

"Drizzt and the cat have gone!" Wulfgar cried.

"To the land of the ghost," Bruenor explained.

It took Drizzt a long moment to set his bearings. He had come into a place of different realities, a dimension where everything, even his own skin, assumed the same hue of gray, objects being distinguishable only by a thin waver of black that outlined them. His depth perception was useless, for there were no shadings, and no discernible light sources to use as a guide. And he found no footing, nothing tangible beneath him, nor could he even know which way was up or down. Such concepts didn't seem to fit here.

He did make out the shifting outlines of the Pegasus as it jumped between planes, never fully in one place or the other. He tried to approach it and found propulsion to be an act of the mind, his body automatically following the instructions of his will. He stopped before the shifting lines, his magical scimitar poised to strike when the target fully appeared.

Then the outline of the Pegasus was complete and Drizzt plunged his blade into the black waver that marked its form. The line shifted and bent, and the outline of the scimitar shivered as well, for here even the properties of the steel blade took on a different composition. But the steel proved the stronger and the scimitar resumed its curved edge and punctured the line of the ghost. There came a sudden tingling in the grayness, as though Drizzt's cut had disturbed the equilibrium of the plane, and the ghost's line trembled in a shiver of agony.

Wulfgar saw the smoke cloud puff suddenly, almost reforming into the ghost shape. "Drizzt!" he called out to Bruenor. "He has met the ghost on even terms!"

"Get ye ready, then!" Bruenor replied anxiously, though he knew that his own part in the fight had ended. "The drow might bring it back to ye long enough for a hit!" Bruenor clutched at his sides, trying to hug the deathly cold out of his bones, and stumbled over to the halfling's unmoving form.

The ghost turned on Drizzt, but the scimitar struck again. And Guenhwyvar jumped into the fray, the cat's great claws tearing into the black outline of its enemy. The Pegasus reeled away from them, understanding that it held no advantage against foes on its own plane. Its only recourse was a retreat back to the material plane.

Where Wulfgar waited.

As soon as the cloud resumed its shape, Aegis-fang hammered into it. Wulfgar felt a solid strike for just a moment, and knew that he had hit his mark. Then the smoke blew away before him.

The ghost was back with Drizzt and Guenhwyvar, again facing their relentless stabs and rakes. It shifted back again, and Wulfgar struck quickly. Trapped with no retreat, the ghost took hits from both planes. Every time it materialized before Drizzt, the drow noted that its outline came thinner and less resistant to his thrusts. And every time the cloud reformed before Wulfgar, its density had diminished. The friends had won, and Drizzt watched in satisfaction as the essence of the Pegasus slipped free of the material form and floated away through the grayness.

"Take me home," the weary drow instructed Guenhwyvar. A moment later, he was back on the field beside Bruenor and Regis.

"He'll live," Bruenor stated flatly at Drizzt's inquiring look. "More to faintin' than to dying'd be me guess."

A short distance away, Wulfgar, too, was hunched over a form, broken and twisted and caught in a transformation somewhere between man and beast. "Torlin, son of Jerek," Wulfgar explained. He lifted his gaze back toward the barbarian camp. "Valric has done this. The blood of Torlin soils his hands!"

"Torlin's own choice, perhaps?" Drizzt offered.

"Never!" Wulfgar insisted. "When we met in challenge, my eyes looked upon honor. He was a warrior. He would never have allowed this!" He stepped away from the corpse, letting its mutilated remains emphasize the horror of the possession. In the frozen pose of death, Torlin's face had retained half the features of a man, and half of the equine ghost.

"He was the son of their chieftain," Wulfgar explained. "He could not refuse the demands of the shaman."

"He was brave to accept such a fate," Drizzt remarked.

"Son of their chieftain?" snorted Bruenor. "Seems we've put even more enemies on the road behind us! They'll be looking to settle this score."

"As will I!" Wulfgar proclaimed. "His blood is yours to carry, Valric High Eye!" he shouted into the distance, his calls echoing around the mounds of the crags. Wulfgar looked back to his friends, rage seething in his features, as he declared grimly, "I shall avenge Torlin's dishonor."

Bruenor nodded his approval at the barbarian's dedication to his principles.

"An honorable task," Drizzt agreed, holding his blade out to the east, toward Longsaddle, the next stop along their journey. "But one for another day."

❧ 7 ❧

Dagger and Staff

Entreri stood on a hill a few miles outside the City of Sails, his campfire burning low behind him. Regis and friends had used this same spot for their last stop before they entered Luskan and, in fact, the assassin's fire burned in the very same pit. This was no coincidence, though. Entreri had mimicked every move the halfling's party had made since he had picked up their trail just south of the Spine of the World. He would move as they moved, shadowing their marches in an effort to better understand their actions.

Now, unlike the party before him, Entreri's eyes were not on the city wall, nor toward Luskan at all. Several campfires had sprung up in the night to the north, on the road back to Ten-Towns. It wasn't the first time those lights had appeared behind him, and the assassin sensed that he, too, was being followed. He had slowed his frantic pace, figuring that he could easily make up the ground while the companions went about their business in Luskan. He wanted to secure his own back from any danger before concentrating on snaring the halfling. Entreri had even left telltale signs of his passing, baiting his pursuers in closer.

He kicked the embers of the fire low and climbed back into the saddle, deciding it better to meet a sword face to face than to take a dagger in the back.

Into the night he rode, confident in the darkness. This was his time, where every shadow added to the advantage of one who lived in shadows.

He tethered his mount before midnight, close enough to the campfires to finish the trek on foot. He realized now that this was a merchant caravan; not an uncommon thing on the road to Luskan at this time of year. But his sense of danger nagged at him. Many years of experience had honed his instinct for survival and he knew better than to ignore it.

He crept in, seeking the easiest way into the circle of wagons. Merchants always lined many sentries around the perimeter of their camps, and even the pull-horses presented a problem, for the merchants kept them tied close beside their harnesses.

Still, the assassin would not waste his ride. He had come this far and meant to find out the purpose of those who followed him. Slithering on his belly, he made his way to the perimeter and began circling the camp underneath the defensive ring. Too silently for even wary ears to hear, he passed two guards playing at bones. Then he went under and between the horses, the beasts lowering their ears in fear, but remaining quiet.

Halfway around the circle, he was nearly convinced that this was an ordinary merchant caravan, and was just about to slip back into the night when he heard a familiar female voice.

"Ye said ye saw a spot o' light in the distance."

Entreri stopped, for he knew the speaker.

"Yeah, over there," a man replied.

Entreri slipped up between the next two wagons and peeked over the side. The speakers stood a short distance from him, behind the next wagon, peering into the night in the direction of his camp. Both were dressed for battle, the woman wearing her sword comfortably.

"I have underestimated you," Entreri whispered to himself as he viewed Catti-brie. His jeweled dagger was already in his hand. "A mistake I shan't repeat," he added, then crouched low and searched for a path to his target.

"Ye been good to me, for bringing me so fast," Catti-brie said. "I'm owing to ye, as Regis and the others'll be."

"Then tell me," the man urged. "What causes such urgency?"

Catti-brie struggled with the memories of the assassin. She hadn't yet come to terms with her terror that day in the halfling's house, and knew that she wouldn't until she had avenged the deaths of the two dwarven friends and resolved her own humiliation. Her lips tightened and she did not reply.

"As you wish," the man conceded. "Your reasons justify the run, we do not doubt. If we seem to pry, it only shows our desire to help you however we may."

Catti-brie turned to him, a smile of sincere appreciation on her face. Enough had been said, and the two stood and stared at the empty horizon in silence.

Silent, too, was the approach of death.

Entreri slipped out from under the wagon and rose suddenly between them, one hand outstretched to each. He grasped Catti-brie's neck tightly enough to prevent her scream, and he silenced the man forever with his blade.

Looking across the breadth of Entreri's shoulders, Catti-brie saw the horrific expression locked onto her companion's face, but she couldn't understand why he hadn't cried out, for his mouth was not covered.

Entreri shifted back a bit and she knew. Only the jeweled dagger's hilt was visible, its crosspiece flat against the underside of the man's chin. The slender blade had found the man's brain before he ever realized the danger.

Entreri used the weapon's handle to guide his victim quietly to the ground, then jerked it free.

Again the woman found herself paralyzed before the horror of Entreri. She felt that she should wrench away and shout out to the camp, even though he would surely kill her. Or draw her sword and at least try to fight back. But she watched helplessly as Entreri slipped her own dagger from her belt and, pulling her low with him, replaced it in the man's fatal wound.

Then he took her sword and pushed her down under the wagon and out beyond the camp's perimeter.

Why can't I call out? she asked herself again and again, for the assassin, confident of the level of terror, didn't even hold her as they slipped deeper into the night. He knew, and she had to admit to herself, that she would not give up her life so easily.

Finally, when they were a safe distance from the camp, he spun her around to face him—and the dagger. "Follow me?" he asked, laughing at her. "What could you hope to gain?"

She did not answer, but found some of her strength returning.

Entreri sensed it, too. "If you call out, I shall kill you," he declared flatly. "And then, by my word, I shall return to the merchants and kill them all as well!"

She believed him.

"I often travel with the merchants," she lied, holding the quiver in her voice. "It is one of the duties of my rank as a soldier of Ten-Towns."

Entreri laughed at her again. Then he looked into the distance, his features assuming an introspective tilt. "Perhaps this will play to my advantage," he said rhetorically, the beginnings of a plan formulating in his mind.

Catti-brie studied him, worried that he had found some way to turn her excursion into harm for her friends.

"I'll not kill you—not yet," he said to her. "When we find the halfling, his friends will not defend him. Because of you."

"I'll do nothing to aid ye!" Catti-brie spat. "Nothing!"

"Precisely," Entreri hissed. "You shall do nothing. Not with a blade at your neck—" he brought the weapon up to her throat in a morbid tease— "scratching at your smooth skin. When I am done with my business, brave girl, I shall move on, and you shall be left with your shame and your guilt. And your answers to the merchants who believe you murdered their companion!" In truth, Entreri didn't believe for a moment that his simple trick with Catti-brie's dagger would fool the merchants. It was merely a psychological weapon aimed at the young woman, designed to instill yet another doubt and worry into her jumble of emotions.

Catti-brie did not reply to the assassin's statements with any sign of emotion. No, she told herself, it won't be like that!

But deep inside, she wondered if her determination only masked her fear, her own belief that she would be held again by the horror of Entreri's presence, and that the scene would unfold exactly as he had predicted.

Jierdan found the campsite with little difficulty. Dendybar had used his magic to track the mysterious rider all the way from the mountains and had pointed the soldier in the right direction.

Tensed and his sword drawn, Jierdan moved in. The place was deserted, but it had not been that way for long. Even from a few feet away, the soldier from Luskan could feel the dying warmth of the campfire. Crouching low to mask his silhouette against the line of the horizon, he crept toward a pack and blanket off to the side of the fire.

Entreri rode his mount back into camp slowly, expecting that what he had left might have drawn some visitors. Catti-brie sat in front of him, securely bound and gagged, though she fully believed, to her own disgust, that her own terror made the bonds unnecessary.

The wary assassin realized that someone had entered the camp, before he had ever gotten near the place. He slid from his saddle, taking his prisoner with him. "A nervous steed," he explained to Catti-brie, taking obvious pleasure in the grim warning as he tied her to the horse's rear legs. "If you struggle, he will kick the life from you."

Then Entreri was gone, blending into the night as though he were an extension of its darkness.

Jierdan dropped the pack back to the ground, frustrated, for its contents were merely standard traveling gear and revealed nothing about the owner. The soldier was a veteran of many campaigns and had bested man and orc alike a hundred times, but he was nervous now, sensing something unusual, and deadly, about the rider. A man with the courage to ride alone on the brutal course from Icewind Dale to Luskan was no novice to the ways of battle.

Jierdan was startled, then, but not too surprised, when the tip of a blade came to rest suddenly in the vulnerable hollow on the back of his neck, just below the base of his skull. He neither moved nor spoke, hoping that the rider would ask for some explanation before driving the weapon home.

Entreri could see that his pack had been searched, but he recognized the furred uniform and knew that this man was no thief. "We are beyond the borders of your city," he said, holding his knife steady. "What business have you in my camp, soldier of Luskan?"

"I am Jierdan of the north gate," he replied. "I have come to meet a rider from Icewind Dale."

"What rider?"

"You."

Entreri was perplexed and uncomfortable with the soldier's response. Who had sent this man, and how had he known where to look? The assassin's first thoughts centered on Regis's party. Perhaps the halfling had arranged for some help from the city guard. Entreri slipped his knife back into its sheath, certain that he could retrieve it in time to foil any attack.

Jierdan understood the calm confidence of the act as well, and any thoughts that he might have had for striking at this man flew from him. "My master desires your audience," he said, thinking it wise to explain himself more completely. "A meeting to your mutual benefit."

"Your master?" asked Entreri.

"A citizen of high standing," Jierdan explained. "He has heard of your coming and believes that he may help with your quest."

"What does he know of my business?" Entreri snapped, angered that someone had dared to spy on him. But he was relieved, too, for the involvement of some other power structure within the city explained much, and possibly eliminated the logical assumption that the halfling was behind this meeting.

Jierdan shrugged. "I am merely his courier. But I, too, can be of assistance to you. At the gate."

"Damn the gate," Entreri snarled. "I'll take the wall easily enough. It is a more direct route to the places I seek."

"Even so, I know of those places, and of the people who control them."

The knife leaped back out, cutting in and stopping just before Jierdan's throat. "You know much, but you explain little. You play dangerous games, soldier of Luskan."

Jierdan didn't blink. "Four heroes from Ten-Towns came into Luskan five days ago: a dwarf, a halfling, a barbarian, and a black elf." Even Artemis Entreri couldn't hide a hint of excitement at the confirmation of his suspicions, and Jierdan noted the signs. "Their exact location escapes me, but I know the area where they are hiding. Are you interested?"

The knife returned again to its sheath. "Wait here," Entreri instructed. "I have a companion who shall travel with us."

"My master said that you rode alone," Jierdan queried.

Entreri's vile grin sent a shiver through the soldier's spine. "I acquired her," he explained. "She is mine and that is all that you ever need to know."

Jierdan didn't press the point. His sigh of relief was audible when Entreri had disappeared from sight.

Catti-brie rode to Luskan untied and ungagged, but Entreri's hold upon her was no less binding. His warning to her when he had retrieved her in the field had been succinct and undeniable. "A foolish move," he had said, "and you die. And you die with the knowledge that the dwarf, Bruenor, shall suffer for your insolence."

The assassin had told Jierdan no more about her, and the soldier didn't ask, though the woman intrigued him more than a little. Dendybar would get the answers, Jierdan knew.

They moved into the city later that morning, under the suspicious eye of the Daykeeper of the North Gate. It had cost Jierdan a week's pay to bribe them through, and the soldier knew he would owe even more when he returned that night, for the original deal with the Daykeeper allowed the passage of one outsider; nothing had been said about the woman. But if Jierdan's actions brought him Dendybar's favor, then they would be well worth the price.

According to the city code, the three gave up their horses at the stable just inside the wall, and Jierdan led Entreri and Catti-brie through the streets of the City of Sails, past the sleepy-eyed merchants and vendors who had been out since before dawn and into the very heart of the city.

The assassin was not surprised an hour later when they came upon a long grove of thick pine trees. He had suspected that Jierdan was somehow connected to this place. They passed through a break in the line and stood before the tallest structure in the city, the Hosttower of the Arcane.

"Who is your master?" Entreri asked bluntly.

Jierdan chuckled, his nerve bolstered by the sight of Dendybar's tower. "You shall meet him soon enough."

"I shall know now," Entreri growled. "Or our meeting is ended. I am in the city, soldier, and I do not require your assistance any longer."

"I could have the guards expel you," Jierdan shot back. "Or worse!"

But Entreri had the last word. "They would never find the remains of your body," he promised, the cold certainty of his tone draining the blood from Jierdan's face.

Catti-brie noted the exchange with more than a passing concern for the soldier, wondering if the time might soon come when she could exploit the untrusting nature of her captors to her own advantage.

"I serve Dendybar the Mottled, Master of the North Spire," Jierdan declared, drawing further strength from the mention of his powerful mentor's name.

Entreri had heard the name before. The Hosttower was a common topic of the whisperings all around Luskan and the surrounding countryside, and the name of Dendybar the Mottled came up often in conversation, describing the wizard as an ambitious power seeker in the tower, and hinting at a dark and sinister side of the man that allowed him to get what he wanted. He was dangerous, but potentially a powerful ally. Entreri was pleased. "Take me to him now," he told Jierdan. "Let us discover if we have business or no."

Sydney was waiting to escort them from the entry-room of the Hosttower. Offering no introduction, and asking for none, she led them through the twisting passages and secret doors to the audience hall of Dendybar the Mottled. The wizard waited there in grand style, wearing his finest robes and with a fabulous luncheon set before him.

"Greetings, rider," Dendybar said after the necessary, yet uncomfortable, moments of silence when each of the parties sized up the other. "I am Dendybar the Mottled, as you are already aware. Will you and your lovely companion partake of my table?"

His raspy voice grated on Catti-brie's nerves, and though she hadn't eaten since the supper the day before, she had no appetite for this man's hospitality.

Entreri shoved her forward. "Eat," he commanded.

She knew that Entreri was testing both her and the wizards. But it was time for her to test Entreri as well. "No," she answered, looking him straight in the eye.

His backhand knocked her to the floor. Jierdan and

Sydney started reflexively, but seeing no help forthcoming from Dendybar, quickly stopped and settled back to watch. Catti-brie moved away from the killer and remained in a defensive crouch.

Dendybar smiled at the assassin. "You have answered some of my questions about the girl," he said with an amused smile. "What purpose does she serve?"

"I have my reasons," was all that Entreri replied.

"Of course. And might I learn your name?"

Entreri's expression did not change.

"You seek the four companions from Ten-Towns, I know," Dendybar continued, having no desire to bandy the issue. "I seek them, as well, but for different reasons, I am sure."

"You know nothing of my reasons," Entreri replied.

"Nor do I care," laughed the wizard. "We can help each other to our separate goals. That is all that interests me."

"I ask for no help."

Dendybar laughed again. "They are a mighty force, rider. You underestimate them."

"Perhaps," replied Entreri. "But you have asked my purpose, yet have not offered your own. What business does the Hosttower have with travelers from Ten-Towns?"

"Fairly asked," answered Dendybar. "But I should wait until we have formalized an agreement before rendering an answer."

"Then I shan't sleep well for worry," Entreri spat.

Again the wizard laughed. "You may change your mind before this is finished," he said. "For now I offer a sign of good faith. The companions are in the city. Dockside. They were to stay in the Cutlass. Do you know it?"

Entreri nodded, now very interested in the wizard's words.

"But we have lost them in the alleyways of the western city," Dendybar explained, shooting a glare at Jierdan that made the soldier shift uneasily.

"And what is the price of this information?" Entreri

asked.

"None," replied the wizard. "Telling you helps my own cause. You will get what you want; what I desire will remain for me."

Entreri smiled, understanding that Dendybar intended to use him as a hound to sniff out the prey.

"My apprentice will show you out," Dendybar said, motioning to Sydney.

Entreri turned to leave, pausing to meet the gaze of Jierdan. "Ware my path, soldier," the assassin warned. "Vultures eat after the cat has feasted!"

"When he has shown me to the drow, I'll have his head," Jierdan growled when they had gone.

"You shall keep clear of that one," Dendybar instructed.

Jierdan looked at him, puzzled. "Surely you want him watched."

"Surely," agreed Dendybar. "But by Sydney, not you. Keep your anger," Dendybar said to him, noting the outraged scowl. "I preserve your life. Your pride is great, indeed, and you have earned the right. But this one is beyond your prowess, my friend. His blade would have you before you ever knew he was there."

Outside, Entreri led Catti-brie away from the Hosttower without a word, silently replaying and reviewing the meeting, for he knew that he had not seen the last of Dendybar and his cohorts.

Catti-brie was glad of the silence, too, engulfed in her own contemplations. Why would a wizard of the Hosttower be looking for Bruenor and the others? Revenge for Akar Kessell, the mad wizard that her friends had helped defeat before the last winter? She looked back to the treelike structure, and to the killer at her side, amazed and horrified at the attention her friends had brought upon themselves.

Then she looked into her own heart, reviving her spirit and her courage. Drizzt, Bruenor, Wulfgar, and Regis were going to need her help before this was all over. She must not fail them.

❧ BOOK 2: ❧
Allies

❧ 8 ❧

To the Peril
of Low-Flying Birds

The companions broke out of the twists and dips of the crags later in the afternoon, to their absolute relief. It had taken them some time to round up their mounts after the encounter with the Pegasus, particularly the halfling's pony, which had bolted early in the fight when Regis had gone down. In truth, the pony would not be ridden again, anyway; it was too skittish and Regis was in no condition to ride. But Drizzt had insisted that both horses and both ponies be found, reminding his companions of their responsibility to the farmers, especially considering the way they had appropriated the beasts.

Regis now sat before Wulfgar on the barbarian's stallion, leading the way with his pony tied behind and Drizzt and Bruenor a short distance back, guarding the rear. Wulfgar kept his great arms close around the halfling, his protective hold secure enough to allow Regis some much-needed sleep.

"Keep the setting sun at our backs," Drizzt instructed the barbarian.

Wulfgar called out his acknowledgement and looked back to confirm his bearings.

"Rumblebelly couldn't find a safer place in all the Realms," Bruenor remarked to the drow.

Drizzt smiled. "Wulfgar has done well."

"Aye," the dwarf agreed, obviously pleased. "Although I be wondering how much longer I can keep to callin' him a boy! Ye should have seen the Cutlass, elf," the dwarf chuckled. "A boatload of pirates who'd been seeing naught but the sea for a year and a day couldn't've done more wrecking!"

"When we left the dale, I worried if Wulfgar was ready for the many societies of this wide world," replied Drizzt. "Now I worry that the world may not be ready for him. You should be proud."

"Ye've had as much a hand in him as meself," said Bruenor. "He's me boy, elf, surer'n if I'd sired him meself. Not a thought to his own fears on the field back there. Ne'er have I viewed such courage in a human as when ye'd gone to the other plane. He waited—he hoped, I tell ye!—for the wretched beast to come back so he could get a good swing in to avenge the hurt to meself and the half-ling."

Drizzt enjoyed this rare moment of vulnerability from the dwarf. A few times before, he had seen Bruenor drop his callous facade, back on the climb in Icewind Dale when the dwarf thought of Mithril Hall and the wondrous memories of his childhood.

"Aye, I'm proud," Bruenor continued. "And I'm finding meself willing to follow his lead and trust in his choices."

Drizzt could only agree, having come to the same conclusions many months before, when Wulfgar had united the peoples of Icewind Dale, barbarian and Ten-Towner alike, in a common defense against the harsh tundra winter. He still worried about bringing the young warrior into situations like the dockside of Luskan, for he knew that many of the finest persons in the Realms had paid dearly for their first encounters with the guilds and underground power structures of a city, and that Wulfgar's deep compassion and unwavering code of honor could be manipulated against him.

But on the road, in the wild, Drizzt knew that he would never find a more valuable companion.

They encountered no further problems that day or night, and the next morning came upon the main road, the trading route from Waterdeep to Mirabar and passing Longsaddle on the way. No landmarks stood out to guide them, as Drizzt had anticipated, but because of his plan in keeping more to the east than the straight line southeast, their direction from here was clearly south.

Regis seemed much better this day and was anxious to see Longsaddle. He alone of the group had been to the home of the magic-using Harpell family and he looked forward to viewing the strange, and often outrageous, place again.

His excited chatting only heightened Wulfgar's trepidations, though, for the barbarian's distrust of the dark arts ran deep. Among Wulfgar's people, wizards were viewed as cowards and evil tricksters.

"How long must we remain in this place?" he asked Bruenor and Drizzt, who, with the crags safely behind them, had come up to ride beside him on the wide road.

"Until we get some answers," Bruenor answered. "Or until we figure a better place to go." Wulfgar had to be satisfied with the answer.

Soon they passed some of the outlying farms, drawing curious stares from the men in the fields who leaned on their hoes and rakes to study the party. Shortly after the first of these encounters, they were met on the road by five armed men called Longriders, representing the outer watch of the town.

"Greetings, travelers," said one politely. "Might we ask your intentions in these parts?"

"Ye might . . . " started Bruenor, but Drizzt stopped his sarcastic remark with an outstretched hand.

"We have come to see the Harpells," Regis replied. "Our business does not concern your town, though we seek the wise counsel of the family in the mansion."

"Well met, then," answered the Longrider. "The hill of the Ivy Mansion is just a few miles farther down the road, before Longsaddle proper." He stopped suddenly, noticing the drow. "We could escort you if you desire," he offered, clearing his throat in an effort to politely hide his gawking at the black elf.

"It is not necessary," said Drizzt. "I assure you that we

can find the way, and that we mean no ill toward any of the people of Longsaddle."

"Very well." The Longrider stepped his mount aside and the companions continued on.

"Keep to the road, though," he called after them. "Some of the farmers get anxious about people near the boundaries of their land."

"They are kindly folk," Regis explained to his companions as they moved down the road, "and they trust in their wizards."

"Kindly, but wary," Drizzt retorted, motioning to a distant field where the silhouette of a mounted man was barely visible on the far tree line. "We are being watched."

"But not bothered," said Bruenor. "And that's more than we can say about anywhere we've been yet!"

The hill of the Ivy Mansion comprised a small hillock sporting three buildings, two that resembled the low, wooden design of farmhouses. The third, though, was unlike anything the four companions had ever seen. Its walls turned at sharp angles every few feet, creating niches within niches, and dozens and dozens of spires sprouted from its many-angled roof, no two alike. A thousand windows were visible from this direction alone, some huge, others no bigger than an arrow slit.

No one design, no overall architectural plan or style, could be found here. The Harpells' mansion was a collage of independent ideas and experiments in magical creation. But there was truly a beauty within the chaos, a sense of freedom that defied the term "structure" and carried with it a feeling of welcome.

A rail fence surrounded the hillock and the four friends approached curiously, if not excitedly. There was no gate, just an opening and the road continuing through. Seated on a stool inside the fence, staring blankly at the sky, was a fat, bearded man in a carmine robe.

He noticed their arrival with a start. "Who are you and what do you want?" he demanded bluntly, angered at the interruption of his meditation.

"Weary travelers," replied Regis, "come to seek the wisdom of the reknowned Harpells."

The man seemed unimpressed. "And?" he prompted.

Regis turned helplessly to Drizzt and Bruenor, but they could only answer him with shrugs of their own, not understanding what more was required of them. Bruenor started to move his pony out in front to reiterate the group's intentions when another robed man came shuffling out of the mansion to join the first.

He had a few quiet words with the fat mage, then turned to the road. "Greetings," he offered the companions. "Excuse poor Regweld, here—" he patted the fat mage's shoulder— "for he has had an incredible run of bad luck with some experimenting—not that things will not turn out, mind you. They just might take some time.

"Regweld is really a fine wizard," he continued, patting the shoulder again. "And his ideas for crossbreeding a horse and a frog are not without merit; never mind the explosion! Alchemy shops can be replaced!"

The friends sat atop their mounts, biting back their amazement at the rambling discourse. "Why, think of the advantages for crossing rivers!" the robed man cried. "But enough of that. I am Harkle. How might I assist you?"

"Harkle Harpell?" Regis snickered. The man bowed.

"Bruenor of Icewind Dale, I be," Bruenor proclaimed when he had found his voice. "Me friends and meself have come hundreds of miles seeking the words of the wizards of Longsaddle. . . . " He noticed that Harkle, distracted by the drow, wasn't paying any attention to him. Drizzt had let his cowl slip back purposely to judge the reaction of the reputedly learned men of Longsaddle. The Longrider back on the road had been surprised, but not outraged, and Drizzt had to learn if the town in general would be more tolerant of his heritage.

"Fantastic," muttered Harkle. "Simply unbelievable!" Regweld, too, had now noticed the black elf and seemed interested for the first time since the party had arrived.

"Are we to be allowed passage?" Drizzt asked.

"Oh, yes, please do come in," replied Harkle, trying unsuccessfully to mask his excitement for the sake of etiquette.

Striding his horse out in front, Wulfgar started them up the road.

"Not that way," said Harkle. "Not the road; of course, it is not really a road. Or it is, but you cannot get through."

Wulfgar stopped his mount. "Be done with your foolery, wizard!" he demanded angrily, his years of distrust for practitioners of the magic arts boiling over in his frustration. "May we enter, or not?"

"There is no foolery, I assure you," said Harkle, hoping to keep the meeting amiable. But Regweld cut in.

"One of those," the fat mage said accusingly, rising from his stool.

Wulfgar glared at him curiously.

"A barbarian," Regweld explained. "A warrior trained to hate that which he cannot comprehend. Go ahead, warrior, take that big hammer off of your back."

Wulfgar hesitated, seeing his own unreasonable anger, and looked to his friends for support. He didn't want to spoil Bruenor's plans for the sake of his own pettiness.

"Go ahead," Regweld insisted, moving to the center of the road. "Take up your hammer and throw it at me. Satisfy your heartfelt desire to expose the foolery of a wizard! And strike one down in the process! A bargain if ever I heard one!" He pointed to his chin. "Right here," he chided.

"Regweld," sighed Harkle, shaking his head. "Please oblige him, warrior. Bring a smile to his downcast face."

Wulfgar looked once more to his friends, but again they had no answers. Regweld settled it for him.

"Bastard son of a caribou."

Aegis-fang was out and twirling through the air before the fat mage had finished the insult, bearing straight in on its mark. Regweld didn't flinch, and just before Aegis-fang would have crossed over the fence line, it smacked into something invisible, but as tangible as stone. Resounding like a ceremonial gong, the transparent wall shuddered and waves rolled out along it, visible to the astounded onlookers as mere distortions of the images behind the wall. The friends noticed for the first time that the rail fencing was not real, rather a painting on the surface of the transparent wall.

Aegis-fang dropped to the dust, as though all power had been drained from it, taking a long moment to reappear in Wulfgar's grasp.

Regweld's laughter was more of victory than of humor, but Harkle shook his head. "Always at the expense of others," he scolded. "You had no right to do that."

"He's better for the lesson," Regweld retorted. "Humility is also a valuable commodity for a fighter."

Regis had bitten his lip for as long as he could. He had known about the invisible wall all along, and now his laughter burst out. Drizzt and Bruenor could not help but follow the halfling's lead, and even Wulfgar, after he had recovered from the shock, smirked at his own "foolery."

Of course, Harkle had no choice but to stop his scolding and join in. "Do come in," he begged the friends. "The third post is real; you can find the gate there. But first, dismount and unsaddle your horses."

Wulfgar's suspicions came back suddenly, his scowl burying the smile. "Explain," he requested of Harkle.

"Do it!" Regis ordered, "or you shall find a bigger surprise than the last one."

Drizzt and Bruenor had already slipped from their saddles, intrigued, but not the least bit fearful of the hospitable Harkle Harpell. Wulfgar threw his arms out helplessly and followed, pulling the gear from the roan and leading the beast, and Regis's pony, after the others.

Regis found the entrance easily and swung it open for his friends. They came in without fear, but were suddenly assailed by blinding flashes of light.

When their eyes cleared again, they found that the horses and ponies had been reduced to the size of cats!

"What?" blurted Bruenor, but Regis was laughing again and Harkle acted as though nothing unusual had happened.

"Pick them up and come along," he instructed. "It is nearly time to sup, and the meal at The Fuzzy Quarterstaff is particularly delicious this night!"

He led them around the side of the weird mansion to a bridge crossing the center of the hillock. Bruenor and Wulfgar felt ridiculous carrying their mounts, but Drizzt accepted it with a smile and Regis thoroughly enjoyed the whole outrageous spectacle, having learned on his first visit that Longsaddle was a place to be taken lightly, appreciating the idiosyncrasies and unique ways of the Harpells purely for the sake of amusement.

The high-arcing bridge before them, Regis knew, would serve as yet another example. Though its span across the small stream was not great, it was apparently unsupported, and its narrow planks were completely unadorned, even without handrails.

Another robed Harpell, this one incredibly old, sat on a stool, his chin in his hand, mumbling to himself and seemingly taking no notice of the strangers whatsoever.

When Wulfgar, in the front beside Harkle, neared the bank of the stream, he jumped back, gasping and stuttering. Regis snickered, knowing what the big man had seen, and Drizzt and Bruenor soon understood.

The stream flowed UP the side of the hill, then vanished just before the top, though the companions could hear that water was indeed rushing along before them. Then the stream reappeared over the hill's crest, flowing down the other side.

The old man sprang up suddenly and rushed over to Wulfgar. "What can it mean?" he cried desperately. "How can it be?" He banged on the barbarian's massive chest in frustration.

Wulfgar looked around for an escape, not wanting to

even grab the old man in restraint for fear of breaking his frail form. Just as abruptly as he had come, the old man dashed back to the stool and resumed his silent pose.

"Alas, poor Chardin," Harkle said somberly. "He was mighty in his day. It was he who turned the stream up the hill. But near a score of years now he has been obsessed with finding the secret of the invisibility under the bridge."

"Why is the stream so different from the wall?" wondered Drizzt. "Certainly this dweomer is not unknown among the wizard community."

"Ah, but there is a difference," Harkle was quick to reply, excited at finding someone outside the Ivy Mansion apparently interested in their works. "An invisible object is not so rare, but a field of invisibility . . . " He swept his hand to the stream. "Anything that enters the river there takes on the property," he explained. "But only for as long as it remains in the field. And to a person in the enchanted area—I know because I have done this test myself—everything beyond the field is unseen, though the water and fish within appear normal. It defies our knowledge of the properties of invisibility and may actually reflect a tear into the fabric of a wholly unknown plane of existence!" He saw that his excitement had gone beyond the comprehension or interest of the drow's companions some time ago, so he calmed himself and politely changed the subject.

"The housing for your horses is in that building," he said, pointing to one of the low, wooden structures. "The underbridge will get you there. I must attend to another matter now. Perhaps we can meet later in the tavern."

Wulfgar, not completely understanding Harkle's directions, stepped lightly onto the first wooden planks of the bridge, and was promptly thrown backward by some unseen force.

"I said the *under*bridge," cried Harkle, pointing under the bridge. "You cannot cross the river this way by the overbridge; that is used for the way back! Stops any arguments in crossing," he explained.

Wulfgar had his doubts about a bridge he could not see, but he didn't want to appear cowardly before his friends and the wizard. He moved beside the bridge's ascending arc and gingerly moved his foot out under the wooden structure, feeling for the invisible crossing. There was only the air, and the unseen rush of water just below his foot, and he hesitated.

"Go on," coaxed Harkle.

Wulfgar plunged ahead, setting himself for a fall into the water. But to his absolute surprise, he did not fall down.

He fell up!

"Whoa!" the barbarian cried out as he thunked into the bottom of the bridge, headfirst. He lay there for a long moment, unable to get his bearings, flat on his back against the bottom of the bridge, looking down instead of up.

"You see!" screeched the wizard. "The *underbridge!*"

Drizzt moved next, leaping into the enchanted area with an easy tumble, and landing lightly on his feet beside his friend.

"Are you all right?" he asked.

"The road, my friend," groaned Wulfgar. "I long for the road, and the orcs. It is safer."

Drizzt helped him struggle to his feet, for the barbarian's mind argued every inch of the way against standing upside-down under a bridge, with an invisible stream rushing above his head.

Bruenor, too, had his reservations, but a taunt from the halfling moved him along, and soon the companions rolled back onto the grass of the natural world on the other bank of the stream. Two buildings stood before them, and they moved to the smaller, the one Harkle had indicated.

A blue-robed woman met them at the door. "Four?" she asked rhetorically. "You really should have sent word ahead."

"Harkle sent us," Regis explained. "We are not from these lands. Forgive our ignorance of your customs."

"Very well, then," huffed the woman. "Come along in. We are actually unusually unbusy for this time of the year. I am sure that I have room for your horses." She led them into the structure's main room, a square chamber. All four walls were lined, floor to ceiling, with small cages, just big enough for a cat-sized horse to stretch its legs. Many were occupied, their nameplates indicating that they were reserved for particular members of the Harpell clan, but the woman found four empty ones all together and put the companions' horses inside.

"You may get them whenever you desire," she explained, handing each of them a key to the cage of his particular mount. She paused when she got to Drizzt, studying his handsome features. "Who have we here?" she asked, not losing her calm monotone. "I had not heard of your arrival, but I am sure that many will desire an audience with you before you go! We have never seen one of your kind."

Drizzt nodded and did not reply, growing increasingly uncomfortable with this new type of attention. Somehow it seemed to degrade him even more than the threats of ignorant peasants. He understood the curiosity, though, and figured that he owed the wizards a few hours of conversation, at least.

The Fuzzy Quarterstaff, on the back side of the Ivy Mansion, filled a circular chamber. The bar sat in the middle, like the hub of a wheel, and inside its wide perimeter was another room, an enclosed kitchen area. A hairy man with huge arms and a bald head wiped his rag endlessly along the shiny surface of the bar, more to pass the time than to clean any spills.

Off to the rear, on a raised stage, musical instruments played themselves, guided by the jerking gyrations of a white-haired, wand-wielding wizard in black pants and a black waistcoat. Whenever the instruments hit a crescendo, the wizard pointed his wand and snapped the fingers of his free hand, and a burst of colored sparks erupted from each of the four corners of the stage.

The companions took a table within sight of the entertaining wizard. They had their pick of location, for as far as they could tell, they were the only patrons in the room. The tables, too, were circular, made of fine wood and sporting a many-faceted, huge green gemstone on a silver pedestal as a centerpiece.

"A stranger place I never heared of," grumbled Bruenor, uncomfortable since the underbridge, but resigned to the necessity of speaking with the Harpells.

"Nor I," said the barbarian. "And may we leave it soon."

"You are both stuck in the small chambers of your minds," Regis scolded. "This is a place to enjoy—and you know that no danger lurks here." He winked as his gaze fell upon Wulfgar. "Nothing serious, anyway."

"Longsaddle offers us a much needed rest," Drizzt added. "Here, we can lay the course of our next trek in safety and take back to the road refreshed. It was two weeks from the dale to Luskan, and nearly another to here, without reprieve. Weariness draws away the edge and takes the advantage from a skilled warrior." He looked particularly at Wulfgar as he finished the thought. "A tired man will make mistakes. And mistakes in the wild are, more often than not, fatal."

"So let us relax and enjoy the hospitality of the Harpells," said Regis.

"Agreed," said Bruenor, glancing around, "but just a short rest. And where in the nine hells might the barmaid be, or do ye have to get to it yerself for food and drink?"

"If you want something, then just ask," came a voice from the center of the table. Wulfgar and Bruenor both leaped to their feet, on guard. Drizzt noted the flare of light within the green gem and studied the object, immediately guessing the setup. He looked back over his shoulder at the barkeep, who stood beside a similar gemstone.

"A scrying device," the drow explained to his friends, though they, by now, had come to the same understanding and felt very foolish standing in the middle of an empty tavern with their weapons in their hands.

Regis had his head down, his shoulders rolling with his sobs of laughter.

"Bah! Ye knew all along!" Bruenor growled at him. "Ye've been takin' a bit of fun at our cost, Rumblebelly," the dwarf warned. "For meself, I'm wondering how much longer our road holds room for ye."

Regis looked up at the glare of his dwarven friend, matching it suddenly with a firm stare of his own. "We have walked and ridden more than four hundred miles together!" he retorted. "Through cold winds and orc raids, brawls and battles with ghosts. Allow me my pleasure for a short while, good dwarf. If you and Wulfgar would loosen the straps of your packs and see this place for what it is, you might find an equal share of laughter yourself!"

Wulfgar did smile. Then, all at once, he jerked back his head and roared, throwing away all of his anger and prejudice, so that he might take the halfling's advice and view Longsaddle with an open mind. Even the musical wizard stopped his playing to observe the spectacle of the barbarian's soul-cleansing scream.

And when he had finished, Wulfgar laughed. Not an amused chuckle, but a thunderous roll of laughter that flowed up from his belly and exploded out his wide-thrown mouth.

"Ale!" Bruenor called into the gemstone. Almost immediately, a floating disk of blue light slipped over the bar, bearing to them enough strong ale to last the night. A few minutes later, all traces of the tensions of the road had flown, and they toasted and quaffed their mugs with enthusiasm.

Only Drizzt kept his reserve, sipping his drink and staying alert to his surroundings. He felt no direct danger here, but he wanted to keep control against the wizards' inevitable probing.

Shortly, the Harpells and their friends began to make a steady stream into The Fuzzy Quarterstaff. The companions were the only newcomers in town this night, and all of the diners pulled their tables close by, trading stories of the road and toasts of lasting friendship over fine meals, and later, beside a warm hearth. Many, led by Harkle, concerned themselves with Drizzt and their interest in the dark cities of his people, and he had few reservations about answering their questions.

Then came the probing about the journey that had brought the companions so far. Bruenor actually initiated it, jumping up onto his table and proclaiming, "Mithril Hall, home of me fathers, ye shall be mine again!"

Drizzt grew concerned. Judging by the inquisitive reaction of the gathering, the name of Bruenor's ancient homeland was known here, at least in legend. The drow didn't fear any malicious actions by the Harpells, but he simply did not want the purpose of the adventure following, and possibly even preceding, him and his friends on the next leg of the journey. Others might well be interested in learning the location of an ancient dwarven stronghold, a place referred to in tales as, "the mines where silver rivers run."

Drizzt took Harkle aside. "The night grows long. Are there rooms available in the village beyond?"

"Nonsense," huffed Harkle. "You are my guests and shall remain here. The rooms have already been prepared."

"And the price for all of this?"

Harkle pushed Drizzt's purse away. "The price in the Ivy Mansion is a good tale or two, and bringing some interest into our existence. You and your friends have paid for a year and more!"

"Our thanks," replied Drizzt. "I think that it is time for my companions to rest. We have had a long ride, with much more before us."

"Concerning the road before you," said Harkle. "I have arranged for a meeting with DelRoy, the eldest of the Harpells now in Longsaddle. He, more than any of us, might be able to help steer your way."

"Very good," said Regis, leaning over to hear the conversation.

"This meeting holds a small price," Harkle told Drizzt. "DelRoy desires a private audience with you. He has sought knowledge of the drow for many years, but little is available to us."

"Agreed," replied Drizzt. "Now, it is time for us to find our beds."

"I shall show you the way."

"What time are we to meet with DelRoy?" asked Regis.

"Morning," replied Harkle.

Regis laughed, then leaned over to the other side of the table where Bruenor sat holding a mug motionless in his gnarled hands, his eyes unblinking. Regis gave the dwarf a little shove and Bruenor toppled, thudding into the floor without even a groan of protest. "Evening would be better," the halfling remarked, pointing across the room to another table.

Wulfgar was underneath it.

Harkle looked at Drizzt. "Evening," he agreed. "I shall speak to DelRoy."

The four friends spent the next day recuperating and enjoying the endless marvels of the Ivy Mansion. Drizzt was called away early for a meeting with DelRoy, while the others were guided by Harkle on a tour through the great house, passing through a dozen alchemy shops, scrying rooms, meditation chambers, and several secured rooms specifically designed for conjuring otherworldly beings. A statue of one Matherly Harpell was of particular interest, since the statue was actually the wizard himself. An unsuccessful mix of potions had left him stoned, literally.

Then there was Bidderdoo, the family dog, who had

once been Harkle's second cousin—again, a bad potion mix.

Harkle kept no secrets from his guests, recounting the history of his clan, its achievements, and its often disastrous failures. And he told them of the lands around Longsaddle, of the Uthgardt barbarians, the Sky Ponies, they had encountered, and of other tribes they might yet meet along their way.

Bruenor was glad that their relaxation carried a measure of valuable information. His goal pressed in on him every minute of every day, and when he spent any time without making any gains toward Mithril Hall, even if he simply needed to rest, he felt pangs of guilt. "Ye have to want it with all yer heart," he often scolded himself.

But Harkle had provided him with an important orientation to this land that would no doubt aid his cause in the days ahead, and he was satisfied when he sat down for supper at The Fuzzy Quarterstaff. Drizzt rejoined them there, sullen and quiet, and he wouldn't say much when questioned about his discussion with DelRoy.

"Think to the meeting ahead," was the drow's answer to Bruenor's probing. "DelRoy is very old and learned. He may prove to be our best hope of ever finding the road to Mithril Hall."

Bruenor was indeed thinking to the meeting ahead.

And Drizzt sat back quietly throughout the meal, considering the tales and the images of his homeland that he had imparted to DelRoy, remembering the unique beauty of Menzoberranzan.

And the malicious hearts that had despoiled it.

A short time later, Harkle took Drizzt, Bruenor, and Wulfgar to see the old mage—Regis had begged out of the meeting in lieu of another party at the tavern. They met DelRoy in a small, torchlit, and shadowy chamber, the flickerings of light heightening the mystery in the aged wizard's face. Bruenor and Wulfgar came at once to agree with Drizzt's observations of DelRoy, for decades of experience and untold adventures were etched visibly into the features of his leathery brown skin. His body was failing him now, they could see, but the sheen of his pale eyes told of inner life and left little doubt about the sharp edge of his mind.

Bruenor spread his map out on the room's circular table, beside the books and scrolls that DelRoy had brought. The old mage studied it carefully for a few seconds, tracing the line that had brought the companions to Longsaddle. "What do you recall of the ancient halls, dwarf?" he asked. "Landmarks or neighboring peoples?"

Bruenor shook his head. "The pictures in me head show the deep halls and workplaces, the ringing sound of iron on the anvil. The flight of me clan started in mountains; that's all I know."

"The northland is a wide country," Harkle remarked. "Many long ranges could harbor such a stronghold."

"That is why Mithril Hall, for all of its reputed wealth, has never been found," replied DelRoy.

"And thus our dilemma," said Drizzt. "Deciding where to even begin to look."

"Ah, but you have already begun," answered DelRoy. "You have chosen well to come inland; most of the legends of Mithril Hall stem from the lands east of here, even farther from the coast. It seems likely that your goal lies between Longsaddle and the great desert, though north or south, I cannot guess. You have done well."

Drizzt nodded and broke off the conversation as the old mage fell back into his silent examination of Bruenor's map, marking strategic points and referring often to the stack of books he had piled beside the table. Bruenor hovered beside DelRoy, anxious for any advice or revelations that might be forthcoming. Dwarves were patient folk, though, a trait that allowed their crafting to outshine the work of the other races, and Bruenor kept his calm as best he could, not wanting to press the wizard.

Some time later, when DelRoy was satisfied that his sorting of all the pertinent information was complete, he spoke again. "Where would you go next," he asked Bruenor, "if no advice were offered here?"

The dwarf looked back to his map, Drizzt peering over his shoulder, and traced a line east with his stubby finger. He looked to Drizzt for consent when he had reached a certain point that they had discussed earlier on the road. The drow nodded. "Citadel Adbar," Bruenor declared, tapping his finger on the map.

"The dwarven stronghold," said DelRoy, not too surprised. "A fine choice. King Harbromm and his dwarves may be able to aid you greatly. They have been there, in the Mithril Mountains, for centuries uncounted. Certainly Adbar was old even in the days when the hammers of Mithril Hall rang out in dwarven song."

"Is Citadel Adbar your advice to us, then?" Drizzt asked.

"It is your own choice, but as good a destination as I can offer," replied DelRoy. "But the way is long, five weeks at the least if all goes well. And on the east road beyond Sundabar, that is unlikely. Still, you may get there before the first colds of winter, though I doubt that you would be able to take Harbromm's information and resume your journey before the next spring."

"Then the choice seems clear," declared Bruenor. "To Adbar!"

"There is more you should know," said DelRoy. "And this is the true advice that I shall give to you: Do not be blinded to the possibilities along the road by the hopeful vision at the road's end. Your course so far has followed straight runs, first from Icewind Dale to Luskan, then from Luskan to here. There is little, other than monsters, along either of those roads to give a rider cause to turn aside. But on the journey to Adbar, you shall pass Silverymoon, city of wisdom and legacy, and the Lady Alustriel, and the Vault of Sages, as fine a library as exists in all the northland. Many in that fair city may be able to offer more aid to your quest than I, or even than King Harbromm.

"And beyond Silverymoon you shall find Sundabar, itself an ancient dwarven stronghold, where Helm, reknowned dwarf-friend, rules. His ties to your race run deep, Bruenor, tracing back many generations. Ties, perhaps, even to your own people."

"Possibilities!" beamed Harkle.

"We shall heed your wise advice, DelRoy," said Drizzt.

"Aye," agreed the dwarf, his spirits high. "When we left the dale, I had no idea beyond Luskan. Me hopes were to follow a road of guesses, expectin' half and more to be nothing of value. The halfling was wise in guiding us to this spot, for we've found a trail of clues! And clues to lead to more clues!" He looked around at the excited group, Drizzt, Harkle, and DelRoy, and then noticed Wulfgar, still sitting quietly in his chair, his huge arms crossed on his chest, watching without any apparent emotion. "What of yerself, boy?" Bruenor demanded. "Have ye a notion to share?"

Wulfgar leaned forward, resting his elbows on the table. "Neither my quest, nor my land," he explained. "I follow you, confident in any path you choose.

"And I am glad of your mirth and excitement," he added quietly.

Bruenor took the explanation as complete, and turned back to DelRoy and Harkle for some specific information on the road ahead. Drizzt, though, unconvinced of the sincerity of Wulfgar's last statement, let his gaze linger on the young barbarian, noting the expression in his eyes as he watched Bruenor.

Sorrow?

They spent two more restful days in the Ivy Mansion, though Drizzt was hounded constantly by curious Harpells who wanted more information about his rarely seen race. He took the questions politely, understanding their good intentions, and answered as best he could. When Harkle came to escort them out on the fifth morning, they were refreshed and ready to get on with their business. Harkle promised to arrange for the return of the horses to their rightful owners, saying that it was the least he could do for the strangers who had brought so much interest to the town.

But in truth, the friends had benefited more for the stay. DelRoy and Harkle had given them valuable information and, perhaps even more importantly, had restored their hope in the quest. Bruenor was up and about before dawn that last morning, his adrenaline pumping at the thought of returning to the road now that he had somewhere to go.

They moved out from the mansion throwing many good-byes and lamenting looks over their shoulders, even from Wulfgar, who had come in so steadfast in his antipathy toward wizards.

They crossed the overbridge, saying farewell to Chardin, who was too lost in his meditations of the stream to even notice, and soon discovered that the structure beside the miniature stable was an experimental farm. "It will change the face of the world!" Harkle assured them as he veered them toward the building for a closer look. Drizzt guessed his meaning even before they entered, as soon as he heard the high-pitched bleating and cricketlike chirping. Like the stable, the farm was one room, though part of it had no roof and was actually a field within walls. Cat-sized cows and sheep mulled about, while chickens the size of field mice dodged around the animals' tiny feet.

"Of course, this is the first season and we have not seen results yet," explained Harkle, "but we expect a high yield considering the small amount of resources involved."

"Efficiency," laughed Regis. "Less feed, less space, and you can blow them back up when you want to eat them!"

"Precisely!" said Harkle.

They next went to the stable, where Harkle picked out fine mounts for them, two horses and two ponies. These were gifts, Harkle explained, only to be returned at the companions' leisure. "It's the least we could do to aid such a noble quest," Harkle said with a low bow to stop any protests from Bruenor and Drizzt.

The road meandered, continuing on down the back of the hill. Harkle stood for a moment scratching his chin, a puzzled expression on his face. "The sixth post," he told himself, "but to the left or the right?"

A man working on a ladder (another amusing curiosity—to see a ladder rise up above the phony rails of the fence and come to rest in mid-air against the top of the invisible wall) came to their aid. "Forgot again?" he chuckled at Harkle. "He pointed to the railing off to one side. "Sixth post to your left!"

Harkle shrugged away his embarrassment and moved on.

The companions watched the workman curiously as they passed from the hill, their mounts still tucked under their arms. He had a bucket and some rags and was rubbing several reddish-brown spots from the invisible wall.

"Low-flying birds," Harkle explained apologetically. "But have no fear, Regweld is working on the problem even as we speak.

"Now we have come to the end of our meeting, though many years shall pass before you are forgotten in the Ivy Mansion! The road takes you right through the village of Longsaddle. You can restock your supplies there—it has all been arranged."

"Me deepest regards to yerself and yer kin," said Bruenor, bowing low. "Suren Longsaddle has been a bright spot on a bleary road!" The others were quick to agree.

"Farewell then, Companions of the Hall," sighed Harkle. "The Harpells expect to see a small token when you at last find Mithril Hall and start the ancient forges burning again!"

"A king's treasure!" Bruenor assured him as they moved away.

They were back on the road beyond Longsaddle's borders before noon, their mounts trotting along easily with fully stuffed packs.

"Well, which do ye prefer, elf," Bruenor asked later that day, "the jabs of a mad soldier's spear, or the pokings of a wonderin' wizard's nose?"

Drizzt chuckled defensively as he thought about the question. Longsaddle had been so different from anywhere he had ever been, and yet, so much the same. In either case, his color singled him out as an oddity, and it wasn't so much the hostility of his usual treatment that bothered him, as the embarrassing reminders that he would ever be different.

Only Wulfgar, riding beside him, caught his mumbled reply.

"The road."

9

There Is No Honor

"Why do you approach the city before the light of dawn?" the Nightkeeper of the North Gate asked the emissary for the merchant caravan that had pulled up outside Luskan's wall. Jierdan, in his post beside the Nightkeeper, watched with special interest, certain that this troupe had come from Ten-Towns.

"We would not impose upon the regulations of the city if our business were not urgent," answered the spokesman. "We have not rested for two days." Another man emerged from the cluster of wagons, a body limp across his shoulders.

"Murdered on the road," explained the spokesman. "And another of the party taken. Catti-brie, daughter of Bruenor Battlehammer himself!"

"A dwarf-maid?" Jierdan blurted out, suspecting otherwise, but masking his excitement for fear that it might implicate him.

"Nay, no dwarf. A woman," lamented the spokesman. "Fairest in all the dale, maybe in all the north. The dwarf took her in as an orphaned child and claimed her as his own."

"Orcs?" asked the Nightkeeper, more concerned with potential hazards on the road than with the fate of a single woman.

"This was not the work of orcs," replied the spokesman. "Stealth and cunning took Catti-brie from us and killed the driver. We did not even discover the foul deed until the next morn."

Jierdan needed no further information, not even a more complete description of Catti-brie, to put the pieces together. Her connection to Bruenor explained Entreri's interest in her. Jierdan looked to the eastern horizon and the first rays of the coming dawn, anxious to be cleared of his duties on the wall so that he could go report his findings to Dendybar. This little piece of news should help to alleviate the mottled wizard's anger at him for losing the drow's trail on the docks.

"He has not found them?" Dendybar hissed at Sydney.

"He has found nothing but a cold trail," the younger mage replied. "If they are on the docks yet, they are well disguised."

Dendybar paused to consider his apprentice's report. Something was out of place with this scenario. Four distinctive characters simply could not have vanished. "Have you learned anything of the assassin, then, or of his companion?"

"The vagabonds in the alleys fear him. Even the ruffians give him a respectfully wide berth."

"So our friend is known among the bowel-dwellers," Dendybar mused.

"A hired killer, I would guess," reasoned Sydney. "Probably from the south—Waterdeep, perhaps, though we should have heard more of him if that were the case. Perhaps even farther south, from the lands beyond our vision."

"Interesting," replied Dendybar, trying to formulate some theory to satisfy all the variables. "And the girl?"

Sydney shrugged. "I do not believe that she follows him willingly, though she has made no move to be free of him. And when you saw him in Morkai's vision, he was riding alone."

"He acquired her," came an unexpected reply from the doorway. Jierdan entered the room.

"What? Unannounced?" sneered Dendybar.

"I have news—it could not wait," Jierdan replied boldly.

"Have they left the city?" Sydney prompted, voicing her suspicions to heighten the anger she read on the mottled wizard's pallid face. Sydney well understood the dangers and the difficulties of the docks, and almost pitied Jierdan for incurring the wrath of the merciless Dendybar in a situation beyond his control. But Jierdan remained her competition for the mottled wizard's favor, and she wouldn't let sympathy stand in the way of her ambitions.

"No," Jierdan snapped at her. "My news does not concern the drow's party." He looked back to Dendybar. "A caravan arrived in Luskan today—in search of the woman."

"Who is she?" asked Dendybar, suddenly very interested and forgetting his anger at the intrusion.

"The adopted daughter of Bruenor Battlehammer," Jierdan replied. "Cat—"

"Catti-brie! Of course!" hissed Dendybar, himself familiar with most of the prominent people in Ten-Towns. "I should have guessed!" He turned to Sydney. "My respect for our mysterious rider grows each day. Find him and bring him back to me!"

Sydney nodded, though she feared that Dendybar's request would prove more difficult than the mottled wizard believed, probably even beyond her skills altogether.

She spent that night, until the early hours of the following morning, searching the alleyways and meeting places of the dockside area. But even using her contacts on the docks and all the magical tricks at her disposal, she found no sign of Entreri and Catti-brie, and no one willing or able to pass along any information that might help her in her search.

Tired and frustrated, she returned to the Hosttower the next day, passing the corridor to Dendybar's room, even though he had ordered her to report to him directly upon her return. Sydney was in no mood to listen to the mottled wizard's ranting about her failure.

She entered her small room, just off the main trunk of the Hosttower on the northern branch, below the rooms of the Master of the North Spire, and bolted the doors, further sealing them against unwelcomed intrusion with a magical spell.

She had barely fallen into her bed when the surface of her coveted scrying mirror began to swirl and glow. "Damn you, Dendybar," she growled, assuming that the disturbance was her master's doing. Dragging her weary body to the mirror, she stared deeply into it, attuning her mind to the swirl to bring the image clearer. It was not Dendybar that she faced, to her relief, but a wizard from a distant town, a would-be suitor that the passionless Sydney kept dangling by a thread of hope so that she could manipulate him as she needed.

"Greetings, fair Sydney," the mage said. "I pray I did not disturb your sleep, but I have exciting news!"

Normally, Sydney would have tactfully listened to the mage, feigned interest in the story, and politely excused herself from the encounter. But now, with Dendybar's pressing demands lying squarely across her shoulders, she had no patience for distractions. "This is not the time!" she snapped.

The mage, so caught up in his own news, seemed not to notice her definitive tone. "The most marvelous thing has happened in our town," he rambled.

"Harkle!" Sydney cried to break his babbling momentum.

The mage halted, crestfallen. "But, Sydney," he said.

"Another time," she insisted.

"But how often in this day does one actually see and speak with a drow elf?" Harkle persisted.

"I cannot—" Sydney stopped short, digesting Harkle's last words. "A drow elf?" she stammered.

"Yes," Harkle beamed proudly, thrilled that his news had apparently impressed his beloved Sydney. "Drizzt Do'Urden, by name. He left Longsaddle just two days ago. I would have told you earlier, but the mansion has just been astir about the whole thing!"

"Tell me more, dear Harkle," Sydney purred enticingly. "Do tell me everything."

* * * * *

"I am in need of information."

Whisper froze at the sound of the unexpected voice, guessing the speaker immediately. She knew that he was in town, and knew, too, that he was the only one who could have slipped through her defenses to get into her secret chambers.

"Information," Entreri said again, moving out from the shadows behind a dressing screen.

Whisper slid the jar of healing unguent into her pocket and took a good measure of the man. Rumors spoke of him as the deadliest of assassins, and she, all too familiar with killers, knew at once that the rumors rang with truth. She sensed Entreri's power, and the easy coordination of his movements. "Men do not come to my room uninvited," she warned bravely.

Entreri moved to a better vantage point to study the bold woman. He had heard of her as well, a survivor of the rough streets, beautiful and deadly. But apparently Whisper had lost an encounter. Her nose was broken and disjointed, splayed across her cheek.

Whisper understood the scrutiny. She squared her shoulders and threw her head back proudly. "An unfortunate accident," she hissed.

"It is not my concern," Entreri came back. "I have come for information."

Whisper turned away to go about her routine, trying to appear unbothered. "My price is high," she said coolly.

She turned back to Entreri, the intense but frighteningly calm look on his face telling her beyond doubt that her life would be the only reward for cooperation.

"I seek four companions," said Entreri. "A dwarf, a drow, a young man, and a halfling."

Whisper was unused to such situations. No crossbows

supported her now, no bodyguards waited for her signal behind a nearby secret door. She tried to remain calm, but Entreri knew the depth of her fear. She chuckled and pointed to her broken nose. "I have met your dwarf, and your drow, Artemis Entreri." She emphasized his name as she spoke it, hoping that her recognition would put him back on the defensive.

"Where are they?" Entreri asked, still in control. "And what did they request of you?"

Whisper shrugged. "If they remain in Luskan, I do not know where. Most probably they are gone; the dwarf has a map of the northland."

Entreri considered the words. "Your reputation speaks more highly of you," he said sarcastically. "You accept such a wound and let them slip through your grasp?"

Whispers eyes narrowed in anger. "I choose my fights carefully," she hissed. "The four are too dangerous for actions of frivolous vengeance. Let them go where they will. I want no business with them again."

Entreri's calm visage sagged a bit. He had already been to the Cutlass and heard of Wulfgar's exploits. And now this. A woman like Whisper was not easily cowed. Perhaps he should indeed re-evaluate the strength of his opponents.

"Fearless is the dwarf," Whisper offered, sensing his dismay and taking pleasure in furthering his discomfort. "And ware the drow, Artemis Entreri," she hissed pointedly, attempting to relegate him to a similar level of respect for the companions with the grimness of her tone. "He walks in shadows that we cannot see, and strikes from the darkness. He conjures a demon in the form of a great cat and—"

Entreri turned and started away, having no intention of allowing Whisper to gain any more of an advantage.

Reveling in her victory, Whisper couldn't resist the temptation to throw one final dart. "Men do not come to my room uninvited," she said again. Entreri passed into an adjoining room and Whisper heard the door to the alley close.

"I choose my fights carefully," she whispered to the emptiness of the room, regaining a measure of her pride with the threat.

She turned back to a small dressing table and took out the jar of unguent, quite pleased with herself. She examined her wound in the table's mirror. Not too bad. The salve would erase it as it had erased so many scars from the trials of her profession.

She understood her stupidity when she saw the shadow slip past her reflection in the mirror, and felt the brush of air at her back. Her business allowed no tolerance for errors, and offered no second chance. For the first and last time in her life, Whisper had let her pride rise above her judgment.

A final groan escaped her as the jeweled dagger sunk deeply into her back.

"I, too, choose my fights with care," Entreri whispered into her ear.

The next morning found Entreri outside a place he did not want to enter: the Hosttower of the Arcane. He knew that he was running out of options. Convinced now that the companions had long since left Luskan, the assassin needed some magical assistance to heat up the trail again. It had taken him nearly two years to sniff out the halfling in Ten-Towns, and his patience was wearing thin.

Catti-brie reluctantly but obediently at his side, he approached the structure, and was promptly escorted to Dendybar's audience hall, where the mottled wizard and Sydney waited to greet him.

"They have left the city," Entreri said bluntly, before any exchange of greetings.

Dendybar smiled to show Entreri that he had the upper hand this time. "As long as a week ago," he replied calmly.

"And you know where they are," Entreri reasoned.

Dendybar nodded, the smile still curling into his hollow cheeks.

The assassin didn't enjoy the game. He spent a long moment measuring his counterpart, searching for some hint of the wizard's intentions. Dendybar did likewise, still very much interested in an alliance with the formidable killer—but only on favorable terms.

"The price of the information?" Entreri asked.

"I do not even know your name," was Dendybar's reply.

Fair enough, the assassin thought. He bowed low. "Artemis Entreri," he said, confident enough to speak truthfully.

"And why do you seek the companions, carrying the dwarf's daughter in tow?" Dendybar pressed, playing his hand out to give the cocky assassin something to worry about.

"That is my own care," hissed Entreri, the narrowing of his eyes the only indication that Dendybar's knowledge had perturbed him.

"It is mine, as well, if we are to be allies in this!" shouted Dendybar, rising to stand tall and ominous and intimidate Entreri.

The assassin, though, cared little for the wizard's continuing antics, too engrossed in assessing the value of such an alliance. "I ask nothing of your business with them," Entreri replied at length. "Tell me only which one of the four it concerns."

It was Dendybar's turn to ponder. He wanted Entreri in his court, if for no other reason than he feared having the assassin working against him. And he liked the notion that he would not have to disclose anything about the artifact that he sought to this very dangerous man. "The drow has something of mine, or knowledge of where I can find it," he said. "I want it back."

"And the halfling is mine," Entreri demanded. "Where are they?"

Dendybar motioned to Sydney. "They have passed through Longsaddle," she said. "And are headed to Silverymoon, more than two weeks to the east."

The names were unknown to Catti-brie, but she was glad that her friends had a good lead. She needed time to sort out a plan, though she wondered how effective she could be surrounded by such powerful captors.

"And what do you propose?" Entreri asked.

"An alliance," replied Dendybar.

"But I have the information I need," Entreri laughed. "What do I gain in an alliance with you?"

"My powers can get you to them, and can aid in defeating them. They are not a weak force. Consider it of mutual benefit."

"You and I on the road? You seem more fitted to a book and a desk, wizard."

Dendybar locked an unblinking glare on the arrogant assassin. "I assure you that I can get wherever I desire more effectively than you ever could imagine," he growled. He let go of his anger quickly, though, being more interested in completing business. "But I shall remain here. Sydney will go in my stead, and Jierdan, the soldier, will be her escort."

Entreri did not like the idea of traveling with Jierdan, but he decided not to press the point. It might be interesting, and helpful, in sharing the hunt with the Hosttower of the Arcane. He agreed to the terms.

"And what of her?" Sydney asked, pointing to Catti-brie.

"She goes with me," Entreri was quick to answer.

"Of course," agreed Dendybar. "No purpose in wasting such a valuable hostage."

"We are three against five," Sydney reasoned. "If things do not work out as easily as the two of you seem to expect, the girl may prove to be our downfall."

"She goes!" demanded Entreri.

Dendybar had the solution already worked out. He turned a wry smile at Sydney. "Take Bok," he chuckled.

Sydney's face drooped at the suggestion, as though Dendybar's command had stolen her desire for the hunt.

Entreri wasn't sure if he liked this new development or

not.

Sensing the assassin's discomfort, Dendybar motioned Sydney to a curtained closet at the side of the room. "Bok," she called softly when she got there, the hint of a tremble in her voice.

It stepped through the curtain. Fully eight feet tall and three wide at the shoulders, the monster strode stiffly to the woman's side. A huge man, it seemed, and indeed the wizard had used pieces of human bodies for many of its parts. Bok was bigger and more square than any man living, nearly the size of a giant, and had been magically empowered with strength beyond the measures of the natural world.

"A golem," Dendybar proudly explained. "My own creation. Bok could kill us all right now. Even your fell blade would be of little use against it, Artemis Entreri."

The assassin wasn't so convinced, but he could not completely mask his intimidation. Dendybar had obviously tipped the scales of their partnership in his own favor, but Entreri knew that if he backed away from the bargain now he would be aligning the mottled wizard and his minions against him, and in direct competition with him for the dwarf's party. Furthermore, it would take him weeks, perhaps even months to catch the travelers by normal means and he did not doubt that Dendybar could get there faster.

Catti-brie shared the same uncomfortable thoughts. She had no desire to travel with the gruesome monster, but she wondered what carnage she would find when she finally caught up to Bruenor and the others if Entreri decided to break away from the alliance.

"Fear not," Dendybar comforted. "Bok is harmless, incapable of any independent thought, for, you see, Bok has no mind. The golem answers to my commands, or to Sydney's, and would walk into a fire to be consumed if we merely asked it to do so!"

"I have business to finish in the city," Entreri said, not doubting Dendybar's words and having little desire to hear any more about the golem. "When do we depart?"

"Night would be best," reasoned Dendybar. "Come back to the green outside the Hosttower when the sun is down. We shall meet there and get you on your way."

Alone in his chamber, save for Bok, Dendybar stroked the golem's muscled shoulders with deep affection. Bok was his hidden trump, his protection against the resistance of the companions, or the treachery of Artemis Entreri. But Dendybar did not part with the monster easily, for it played a powerful role, as well, in protecting him from would-be successors in the Hosttower. Dendybar had subtly but definitely passed along the warning to other wizards that any of them striking against him would have to deal with Bok, even if Dendybar were dead.

But the road ahead might be long, and the Master of the North Spire could not forsake his duties and expect to hold his title. Especially not with the Archmage just looking for any excuse to be rid of him, understanding the dangers of Dendybar's outspoken aspirations to the central tower.

"Nothing can stop you, my pet," Dendybar told the monster. In truth, he was simply reaffirming his own fears about his choice to send the inexperienced mage in his stead. He didn't doubt her loyalty, nor Jierdan's, but Entreri and the heroes from Icewind Dale were not to be taken lightly.

"I have given you the hunting power," Dendybar explained, as he tossed the scroll tube and the now-useless parchment to the floor. "The drow is your purpose and you can now sense his presence from any distance. Find him! Do not return to me without Drizzt Do'Urden!"

A guttural roar issued from Bok's blue lips, the only sound the unthinking instrument was capable of uttering.

Entreri and Catti-brie found the wizard's party already assembled when they arrived at the Hosttower later that night.

Jierdan stood alone, off to the side, apparently none too thrilled about partaking in the adventure, but having little choice. The soldier feared the golem, and had no love, or trust, for Entreri. He feared Dendybar more, though, and his uneasiness about the potential dangers on the road did not measure up against the certain dangers he would face at the hands of the mottled wizard if he refused to go.

Sydney broke away from Bok and Dendybar and walked across the way to meet her companions. "Greetings," she offered, more interested in appeasement now than competition with her formidable partner. "Dendybar prepares our mounts. The ride to Silverymoon shall be swift indeed!"

Entreri and Catti-brie looked to the mottled wizard. Bok stood beside him, holding an unrolled parchment out in view while Dendybar poured a smoky liquid from a beaker over a white feather and chanted the runes of the spell.

A mist grew at the wizard's feet, swirling and thickening into something with a definite shape. Dendybar left it to its transformation and moved to repeat the ritual a short way off. By the time the first magical horse had appeared, the wizard was creating the fourth and final one.

Entreri raised his brow. "Four?" he asked Sydney. "We are now five."

"Bok could not ride," she replied, amused at the notion. "It will run." She turned and headed back toward Dendybar, leaving Entreri with the thought.

"Of course," Entreri muttered to himself, somehow less thrilled than ever about the presence of the unnatural thing.

But Catti-brie had begun to view things a bit differently. Dendybar had obviously sent Bok along more to gain an advantage over Entreri than to ensure victory over her friends. Entreri must have known it, too.

Without realizing it, the wizard had set up just the type of nervous environment that Catti-brie hoped for, a tense situation that she might find a way to exploit.

❧ 10 ❧

Bonds of Reputation

The sun beamed brightly on the morning of the first day out from Longsaddle. The companions, refreshed by their visit with the Harpells, rode at a strong pace, but still managed to enjoy the clear weather and the clear road. The land was flat and unmarked, not a tree or hill anywhere near.

"Three days to Nesme, maybe four," Regis told them.

"More to three if the weather holds," said Wulfgar.

Drizzt shifted under his cowl. However pleasant the morning might seem to them, he knew they were still in the wilds. Three days could prove to be a long ride indeed.

"What do ye know of this place, Nesme?" Bruenor asked Regis.

"Just what Harkle told us," Regis replied. "A fair-sized city, trading folk. But a careful place. I have never been there, but tales of the brave people living on the edge of the Evermoors reach far across the northland."

"I am intrigued by the Evermoors," said Wulfgar. "Harkle would say little of the place, just shake his head and shiver whenever I asked of it."

"Not to doubt, a place with a name beyond truth," Bruenor said, laughing, unimpressed by reputations. "Could it be worse than the dale?"

Regis shrugged, not fully convinced by the dwarf's argument. "The tales of the Trollmoors, for that is the name given to those lands, may be exaggerated, but they are always foreboding. Every city in the north salutes the bravery of the people of Nesme for keeping the trading route along the Surbrin open in the face of such trials."

Bruenor laughed again. "Might it be that the tales be coming from Nesme, to paint them stronger than what they are?"

Regis did not argue.

By the time they broke for lunch, a high haze veiled the sunshine. Away to the north, a black line of clouds had appeared, rushing their way. Drizzt had expected as much. In the wild, even the weather proved an enemy.

That afternoon the squall line rolled over them, carrying sheets of rain and hailstones that clinked off of Bruenor's dented helm. Sudden cuts of lightning sliced the darkened sky and the thunder nearly knocked them from their mounts. But they plodded on through the deepening mud.

"This is the true test of the road!" Drizzt yelled to them through the howling wind. "Many more travelers are defeated by storms than by orcs, because they do not anticipate the dangers when they begin their journey!"

"Bah! A summer rain is all!" Bruenor snorted defiantly.

As if in prideful reply, a lightning bolt exploded just a few yards to the side of the riders. The horses jumped and kicked. Bruenor's pony went down, stumbling split-legged into the mud and nearly crushing the stunned dwarf in its scramble.

His own mount out of control, Regis managed to dive from the saddle and roll away.

Bruenor got to his knees and wiped the mud from his eyes, cursing all the while. "Damn!" he spat, studying the pony's movements. "The thing's lame!"

Wulfgar steadied his own horse and tried to start after Regis's bolting pony, but the hailstones, driven by the wind, pelted him, blinded him, and stung his horse, and again he found himself fighting to hold his seat.

Another lightning bolt thundered in. And another.

Drizzt, whispering softly and covering his horse's head

with his cloak to calm it, moved slowly beside the dwarf.

"Lame!" Bruenor shouted again, although Drizzt could barely hear him.

Drizzt only shook his head helplessly and pointed to Bruenor's axe.

More lightning came, and another blast of wind. Drizzt rolled to the side of his mount to shield himself, aware that he could not keep the beast calm much longer.

The hailstones began to come larger, striking with the force of slung bullets.

Drizzt's terrified horse jerked him to the ground and bucked away, trying to flee beyond the reach of the punishing storm.

Drizzt was up quickly beside Bruenor, but any emergency plans the two might have had were immediately deterred, for then Wulfgar stumbled back toward them.

He was walking—barely—leaning against the wind's push, using it to hold him upright. His eyes seemed droopy, his jaw twitched, and blood mixed with the rain on his cheek. He looked at his friends blankly, as if he had no comprehension of what had happened to him.

Then he fell, face down, into the mud at their feet.

A shrill whistle cut through the blunt wall of wind, a singular point of hope against the storm's mounting power. Drizzt's keen ears caught it as he and Bruenor hoisted their young friend's face from the muck. So far away the whistle seemed, but Drizzt understood how storms could distort one's perceptions.

"What?" Bruenor asked of the noise, noticing the drow's sudden reaction, for Bruenor had not heard the call.

"Regis!" Drizzt answered. He started dragging Wulfgar in the direction of the whistle, Bruenor following his lead. They didn't have time to discern if the young man was even alive.

The quick-thinking halfling saved them that day. Fully aware of the killing potential of squalls rolling down from the Spine of the World, Regis had crawled around in search of some shelter in the empty land. He stumbled across a hole in the side of a small ridge, an old wolf den perhaps, empty now.

Following the beacon of his whistles, Drizzt and Bruenor soon found him.

"It'll fill with the rain and we'll be drowned!" Bruenor yelled, but he helped Drizzt drag Wulfgar inside and prop him up against the rear wall of the cave, then took his place beside his friends as they worked to build a barrier of dirt and their remaining packs against the feared flood.

A groan from Wulfgar sent Regis scurrying to his side. "He's alive!" the halfling proclaimed. "And his wounds don't seem too bad!"

"Tougher'n a badger in a corner," Bruenor remarked.

Soon they had their den tolerable, if not comfortable, and even Bruenor stopped his complaining.

"The true test of the road," Drizzt said again to Regis, trying to cheer up his thoroughly miserable friend as they sat in the mud and rode out the night, the incessant booming of the thunder and pounding of the hail a constant reminder of the small margin of safety.

In reply, Regis poured a stream of water out of his boot.

"How many miles do ye reckon we made?" Bruenor grumbled at Drizzt.

"Ten, perhaps," the drow answered.

"Two weeks to Nesme, at this rate!" Bruenor muttered, folding his arms across his chest.

"The storm will pass," Drizzt offered hopefully, but the dwarf was no longer listening.

The next day began without rain, though thick gray clouds hung low in the sky. Wulfgar was fine by morning, but he still did not understand what had happened to him. Bruenor insisted that they start out at once, though Regis would have preferred that they remain in their hole until they were certain the storm had passed.

"Most of the provisions are lost," Drizzt reminded the halfling. "You might not find another meal beyond a pittance of dried bread until we reach Nesme."

Regis was the first one out of the hole.

Unbearable humidity and muddy ground kept the pace slow, and the friends soon found their knees aching from the constant twisting and sloshing. Their sodden clothes clung to them uncomfortably and weighed on their every step.

They came upon Wulfgar's horse, a burned and smoking form half-buried in the mud. "Lightning," Regis observed.

The three looked at their barbarian friend, amazed that he could have survived such a hit. Wulfgar, too, stared in shock, realizing what had dropped him from his mount in the night.

"Tougher'n a badger!" Bruenor hailed again to Drizzt.

Sunshine teasingly found a crack in the overcast now and then. The sunlight was nothing substantial, though, and by noon, the day had actually grown darker. Distant thunder foretold a dismal afternoon.

The storm had already spent its killing might, but that night they found no shelter beyond their wet clothes, and whenever the crackle of lightning lit up the sky, four hunched forms could be seen sitting in the mud, their heads downcast as they accepted their fate in helpless resignation.

For two more days they lumbered on through the rain and wind, having little choice and nowhere to go but forward. Wulfgar proved to be the savior of the party's morale at this low time. He scooped Regis up from the sodden ground, tossing the halfling easily onto his back, and explaining that he needed the extra weight for balance. By sparing the halfling's pride this way, the barbarian even managed to convince the surly dwarf to ride for a short time. And always, Wulfgar was indomitable. "A blessing, I tell you," he kept crying at the gray heavens. "The storm keeps the insects—and the orcs—out of our faces! And how many months shall it be before we want for water?"

He worked hard to keep their spirits high. At one point, he watched the lightning closely, timing the delay between the flash and the ensuing thunder. As they neared the blackened skeleton of a long-dead tree, the lightning flashed and Wulfgar pulled his trick. Yelling "Tempus!" he heaved his warhammer so that it smashed into, and leveled, the trunk at precisely the moment the thunder exploded around them. His amused friends looked back to him only to find him standing proud, arms and eyes uplifted to the gods as though they had personally answered his call.

Drizzt, accepting this whole ordeal with his customary stoicism, silently applauded his young friend and knew again, even more than before, that they had made a wise decision in bringing him along. The drow understood that his own duty in these rough times was to continue his role as sentry, keeping his diligent guard despite the barbarian's proclamation of safety.

Finally, the storm was blown away by the same brisk wind that had ushered it in. The bright sunshine and clear blue skies of the subsequent dawn lightened the companions' mood immeasurably and allowed them to think again of what lay ahead.

Especially Bruenor. The dwarf leaned forward in his pressing march, just as he had when they had first begun their journey back in Icewind Dale.

Red beard wagging with the intensity of his pumping stride, Bruenor found his narrow focus once again. He fell back into the dreams of his homeland, seeing the flickering shadows of the torchlight against the silver-streamed walls and the wondrous artifacts of his people's meticulous labors. His heightened concentration on Mithril Hall over the last few months had sparked clearer, and new, memories in him, and on the road now he remembered, for the first time in more than a century, the Hall of Dumathoin.

The dwarves of Mithril Hall had made a fine living in the trade of their crafted items, but they always kept their very finest pieces, and the most precious gifts bestowed upon them from outsiders, to themselves. In a large and decorated chamber that opened wide the eyes of every visitor, the legacy of Bruenor's ancestors sat in open display, serving as inspiration for the clan's future artists.

Bruenor chuckled softly at the memory of the wondrous hall and the marvelous pieces, mostly weapons and armor. He looked at Wulfgar striding beside him, and at the mighty warhammer he had crafted the year before. Aegis-fang might have hung in the Hall of Dumathoin if Bruenor's clan still ruled Mithril Hall, sealing Bruenor's immortality in the legacy of his people.

But watching Wulfgar handling the hammer, swinging it as easily as he would swing his own arm, Bruenor had no regrets.

The next day brought more good news. Shortly after they broke camp, the friends discovered that they had traveled farther than they had anticipated during the trials of the storm, for as they marched, the landscape around them went through subtle but definite transformations. Where before the ground had been sparsely overgrown with thin patches of scraggly weeds, a virtual sea of mud under the torrent of rain, they now found lush grasses and scattered copses of tall elms. Cresting a final ridge confirmed their suspicions, for before them lay the Dessarin Valley. A few miles ahead, swollen from the spring melt and the recent storm, and clearly visible from their high perch, the arm of the great river rolled steadily along its southbound trek.

The long winter dominated this land, but when they finally bloomed, the plants here made up for their short season with a vibrancy unmatched in all the world. Rich colors of spring surrounded the friends as they made their way down the slope to the river. The carpet of grass was so thick that they took off their boots and walked barefoot through the spongy softness. The vitality here was truly obvious, and contagious.

"Ye should see the halls," Bruenor remarked on sudden impulse. "Veins of purest mithril wider than yer hand! Streams of silver, they be, and bested in beauty only by what a dwarf's hand makes of 'em."

"The want of such a sight keeps our path running straight through the hardships," Drizzt replied.

"Bah!" Bruenor snorted good-heartedly. "Ye're here because I tricked ye into being here, elf. Ye had run outa reasons for holding back me adventure anymore!"

Wulfgar had to chuckle. He had been in on the deception that had duped Drizzt into agreeing to make this journey. After the great battle in Ten-Towns with Akar Kessell, Bruenor had feigned mortal injury, and on his apparent deathbed had begged the drow to journey with him to his ancient homeland. Thinking the dwarf about to expire, Drizzt could not refuse.

"And yerself!" Bruenor roared at Wulfgar. "I see why ye've come, even if ye're skull's too thick for ye to know!"

"Pray tell me," Wulfgar replied with a smile.

"Ye're running! But ye can't get away!" the dwarf cried. Wulfgar's mirth shifted to confusion.

"The girl's spooked him, elf," Bruenor explained to Drizzt. "Catti-brie's caught him in a net his muscles can-no' break!"

Wulfgar laughed along with Bruenor's blunt conclusions, taking no offense. But in the images triggered by Bruenor's allusions to Catti-brie, memories of a sunset view on the face of Kelvin's Cairn, or of hours spent talking on the rise of rocks called Bruenor's Climb, the young barbarian found a disturbing element of truth in the dwarf's observations.

"And what of Regis?" Drizzt asked Bruenor. "Have you discerned his motive for coming along? Might it be his love of ankle-deep mud that sucks his little legs in to the knees?"

Bruenor stopped laughing and studied the halfling's

reaction to the drow's questions. "Nay, I have not," he replied seriously after a few unrevealing moments. "This alone I know: If Rumblebelly chooses the road, it means only that the mud and the orcs measure up better than what he's leaving behind." Bruenor kept his eyes upon his little friend, again seeking some revelations in the halfling's response.

Regis kept his head bowed, watching his furry feet, visible below the diminishing roll of his belly for the first times in many months, as they plowed through the thick waves of green. The assassin, Entreri, was a world away, he thought. And he had no intention of dwelling on a danger that had been avoided.

A few miles up the bank they came upon the first major fork in the river, where the Surbrin, from the northeast, emptied into the main flow of the northern arm of the great river network.

The friends looked for a way to cross the larger river, the Dessarin, and get into the small valley between it and the Surbrin. Nesme, their next, and final stopover before Silverymoon, was farther up the Surbrin, and though the city was actually on the east bank of the river, the friends, taking the advice of Harkle Harpell, had decided to travel up the west bank and avoid the lurking dangers of the Evermoors.

They crossed the Dessarin without too much trouble, thanks to the incredible agility of the drow, who ran out over the river along an overhanging tree limb and leaped to a similar perch on the branch of a tree on the opposite bank. Soon after, they were all easily plodding along the Surbrin, enjoying the sunshine, the warm breeze, and the endless song of the river. Drizzt even managed to fell a deer with his bow, promising a fine supper of venison and restocked packs for the road ahead.

They camped right down by the water, under starshine for the first time in four nights, sitting around a fire and listening to Bruenor's tales of the silvery halls and the wonders they would find at the end of their road.

The serenity of the night did not carry over into the morning, though, for the friends were awakened by the sounds of battle. Wulfgar immediately scrambled up a nearby tree to learn who the combatants were.

"Riders!" he yelled, leaping and drawing out his warhammer even before he hit the ground. "Some are down! They do battle with monsters I do not know!" He was off and running to the north, Bruenor on his heels, and Drizzt circling to their flank down along the river. Less enthusiastic, Regis hung back, pulling out his small mace but hardly preparing for open battle.

Wulfgar was first on the scene. Seven riders were still up, trying vainly to maneuver their mounts into some form of a defensive line. The creatures they battled were quick and had no fear of running under stamping legs to trip up the horses. The monsters were only about three feet high, with arms twice that length. They resembled little trees, though undeniably animated, running about wildly, whacking with their clublike arms or, as another unfortunate rider discovered just as Wulfgar entered the fray, winding their pliable limbs around their foes to pull them from their mounts.

Wulfgar barreled between two creatures, knocking them aside, and bore down on the one that had just taken down the rider. The barbarian underestimated the monsters, though, for their rootlike toes found balance quickly and their long arms caught him from behind before he had gone two steps, grappling him on either side and stopping him in his tracks.

Bruenor charged in right behind. The dwarf's axe chopped through one of the monsters, splitting it down the middle like firewood, and then cut in wickedly on the other, sending a great chunk of its torso flying away.

Drizzt came up even with the battle, anxious but tempered, as always, by the overruling sensibility that had kept him alive through hundreds of encounters. He moved down to the side, below the drop of the bank, where he discovered a ramshackle bridge of logs spanning the Surbrin. The monsters had built it, Drizzt knew; apparently they weren't unthinking beasts.

Drizzt peered over the bank. The riders had rallied around the unexpected reinforcements, but one right before him had been wrapped by a monster and was being dragged from his horse. Seeing the treelike nature of their weird foes, Drizzt understood why the riders all wielded axes, and wondered how effective his slender scimitars would prove.

But he had to act. Springing from his concealment, he thrust both his scimitars at the creature. They nicked into the mark, having no more effect than if Drizzt had stabbed a tree.

Even so, the drow's attempt had saved the rider. The monster clubbed its victim one last time to keep him dazed, then released its hold to face Drizzt. Thinking quickly, the drow went to an alternate attack, using his ineffective blades to parry the clubbing limbs. Then, as the creature rushed in on him, he dove at its feet, uprooting it, and rolled it back over him toward the riverbank. He poked his scimitars into the barklike skin and pushed off, sending the monster tumbling toward the Surbrin. It caught a hold before it went into the water, but Drizzt was on it again. A flurry of well-placed kicks put the monster into the flow and the river carried it away.

The rider, by this time, had regained his seat and his wits. He stepped his horse to the bank to thank his rescuer.

Then he saw the black skin.

"Drow!" he screamed, and his axeblade cut down.

Drizzt was caught off guard. His keen reflexes got one blade up enough to deflect the edge of the axe, but the flat of the weapon struck his head and sent him reeling. He dove with the momentum of the hit and rolled, trying to put as much ground between himself and the rider as he could, realizing that the man would kill him before he could recover.

"Wulfgar!" Regis screamed from his own concealment a short way back on the bank. The barbarian finished off one of the monsters with a thunderous smack that sent cracks all along its length, and turned just as the rider was bringing his horse about to get at Drizzt.

Wulfgar roared in rage and bolted from his own fight, grabbing the horse's bridle while it was still in its turn and heaving with all his strength. Horse and rider toppled to the ground. The horse was up again at once, shaking its head and nervously trotting about, but the rider stayed down, his leg crushed under his mount's weight in the fall.

The remaining five riders worked in unison now, charging into groups of monsters and scattering them. Bruenor's wicked axe cut away, the dwarf all the while singing a woodchopper's song that he had learned as a boy.

"Go split the wood for the fire, me son,
Heat up the kettle and the meal's begun!"

he sang out as he methodically cut down one monster after another.

Wulfgar defensively straddled Drizzt's form, his mighty hammer shattering, with a single strike, any of the monsters that ventured too near.

The rout was on, and in seconds the few surviving creatures scampered in terror across the bridge over the Surbrin.

Three riders were down and dead, a fourth leaned heavily against his horse, nearly overcome by his wounds, and the one Wulfgar had dropped had fainted away for his agony. But the five remaining astride did not go to their wounded. They formed a semi-circle around Wulfgar and Drizzt, who was just now getting back to his feet, and kept the two pinned against the riverbank with axes ready.

"This is how ye welcome yer rescuers?" Bruenor barked at them, slapping aside one horse so that he could join his friends. "Me bet's that the same folk don't come to yer aid twice!"

"Foul company you keep, dwarf!" one of the riders retorted.

"Your friend would be dead if it were not for that foul company!" Wulfgar replied, indicating the rider lying off to the side. "And he repays the drow with a blade!"

"We are the Riders of Nesme," the rider explained. "Our lot is to die on the field, protecting our kin. We accept this fate willingly."

"Step yer horse one more foot and ye'll get yer wish," Bruenor warned.

"But you judge us unfairly," Wulfgar argued. "Nesme is our destination. We come in peace and friendship."

"You'll not get in—not with him!" spat the rider. "The ways of the foul drow elves are known to all. You ask us to welcome him?"

"Bah, yer a fool and so's yer mother," Bruenor growled.

"Ware your words, dwarf," the rider warned. "We are five to three, and mounted."

"Try yer threat, then," Bruenor shot back. "The buzzards won't get much eatin' with those dancing trees." He ran his finger along the edge of his axe. "Let's give 'em something better to peck at."

Wulfgar swung Aegis-fang easily, back and forth at the end of one arm. Drizzt made no move toward his weapons, and his steady calm was perhaps the most unnerving action of all to the riders.

Their speaker seemed less cocksure after the failure of his threat, but he held to a facade of advantage. "But we are not ungrateful for your assistance. We shall allow you to walk away. Be gone and never return to our lands."

"We go where we choose," snarled Bruenor.

"And we choose not to fight," Drizzt added. "It is not our purpose, nor our desire, to lay injury to you or to your town, Riders of Nesme. We shall pass, keeping our own business to ourselves and leaving yours to you."

"You shan't go anywhere near my town, black elf!"

another rider cried. "You may cut us down on the field, but there are a hundred more behind us, and thrice that behind them! Now be gone!" His companions seemed to regain their courage at his bold words, their horses stepping nervously at the sudden tensing of the bridles.

"We have our course," Wulfgar insisted.

"Damn 'em!" Bruenor roared suddenly. "I've seen too much of this band already! Damn their town. May the river wash it away!" He turned to his friends. "They do us a favor. A day and more we'll save by going straight through to Silverymoon, instead of around with the river."

"Straight through?" questioned Drizzt. "The Evermoors?"

"Can it be worse than the dale?" Bruenor replied. He spun back on the riders. "Keep yer town, and yer heads, for now," he said. "We're to cross the bridge here and be rid of yerselves and all of Nesme!"

"Fouler things than bog blokes roam the Trollmoors, foolish dwarf," the rider replied with a grin. "We have come to destroy this bridge. It will be burned behind you."

Bruenor nodded and returned the grin.

"Keep your course to the east," the rider warned. "Word will go out to all the riders. If you are sighted near Nesme, you will be killed."

"Take your vile friend and be gone," another rider taunted, "before my axe bathes in the blood of a black elf! Although I would then have to throw the tainted weapon away!" All the riders joined in the ensuing laughter.

Drizzt hadn't even heard it. He was concentrating on a rider in the back of the group, a quiet one who could use his obscurity in the conversation to gain an unnoticed advantage. The rider had slipped a bow off of his shoulder and was inching his hand, ever so slowly, toward his quiver.

Bruenor was done talking. He and Wulfgar turned away from the riders and started to the bridge. "Come on, elf," he said to Drizzt as he passed. "Me sleep'll come better when we're far away from these orc-sired dogs."

But Drizzt had one more message to send before he would turn his back on the riders. In one blinding movement, he spun the bow from his back, pulled an arrow from his quiver, and sent it whistling through the air. It knocked into the would-be bowman's leather cap, parting his hair down the middle, and stuck in a tree immediately behind, its shaft quivering a clear warning.

"Your misguided insults, I accept, even expect," Drizzt explained to the horrified horsemen. "But I'll brook no attempts to injure my friends, and I will defend myself. Be warned, and only once warned: If you make another move against us, you will die." He turned abruptly and moved down to the bridge without looking back.

The stunned riders certainly had no intention of hindering the drow's party any further. The would-be bowman hadn't even looked for his cap.

Drizzt smiled at the irony of his inability to clear himself of the legends of his heritage. Though he was shunned and threatened on the one hand, the mysterious aura surrounding the black elves also gave him a bluff powerful enough to dissuade most potential enemies.

Regis joined them at the bridge, bouncing a small rock in his hand. "Had them lined up," he explained of his impromptu weapon. He flicked the stone into the river. "If it began, I would have had the first shot."

"If it began," Bruenor corrected, "ye'd have soiled the hole ye hid in!"

Wulfgar considered the rider's warning of their path. "Trollmoors," he echoed somberly, looking up the slope across the way to the blasted land before them. Harkle had told them of the place. The burned-out land and bottomless bogs. The trolls and even worse horrors that had no names.

"Save us a day and more!" Bruenor repeated stubbornly.

Wulfgar wasn't convinced.

* * * * *

"You are dismissed," Dendybar told the specter.

As the flames reformed in the brazier, stripping him of his material form, Morkai considered this second meeting. How often would Dendybar be calling upon him? he wondered. The mottled wizard had not yet fully recovered from their last encounter, but had dared to summon him again so soon. Dendybar's business with the dwarf's party must be urgent indeed! That assumption only made Morkai despise his role as the mottled wizard's spy even more.

Alone in the room again, Dendybar stretched out from his meditative position and grinned wickedly as he considered the image Morkai had shown him. The companions had lost their mounts and were marching into the foulest area in all the North. Another day or so would put his own party, flying on the hooves of his magical steeds, even with them, though thirty miles to the north.

Sydney would get to Silverymoon long before the drow.

❧ 11 ❧

Silverymoon

The ride from Luskan was swift indeed. Entreri and his cohorts appeared to any curious onlookers as no more than a shimmering blur in the night wind. The magical mounts left no trail of their passing, and no living creature could have overtaken them. The golem, as always, lumbered tirelessly behind with great stiff-legged strides.

So smooth and easy were the seats atop Dendybar's conjured steeds that the party was able to keep up its run past the dawn and throughout the entire next day with only short rests for food. Thus, when they set their camp after the sunset of the first full day on the road, they had already put the crags behind them.

Catti-brie fought an inner battle that first day. She had no doubt that Entreri and the new alliance would overtake Bruenor. As the situation stood now, Catti-brie would be only a detriment to her friends, a pawn for Entreri to play at his convenience.

She could do little to remedy the problem, unless she found some way to diminish, if not overcome, the grip of terror that the assassin held on her. That first day she spent in concentration, blocking out her surroundings as much as she could and searching her inner spirit for the strength and courage she would need.

Bruenor had given her many tools over the years to wage such a battle, skills of discipline and self-confidence that had seen her through many difficult situations. On the second day of the ride, then, more confident and comfortable with her situation, Catti-brie was able to focus on her captors. Most interesting were the glares that Jierdan and Entreri shot each other. The proud soldier had obviously not forgotten the humiliation he had suffered the night of their first meeting on the field outside of Luskan. Entreri, keenly aware of the grudge, even fueling it in his willingness to bring the issue to confrontation, kept an untrusting eye on the man.

This growing rivalry may prove to be her most promising—perhaps her only—hope of escaping, Catti-brie thought. She conceded that Bok was an indestructible, mindless destroying machine, beyond any manipulation she might try to lay upon it, and she learned quickly that Sydney offered nothing.

Catti-brie had tried to engage the young mage in conversation that second day, but Sydney's focus was too narrow for any diversions. She would be neither sidetracked nor persuaded from her obsession in any way. She didn't even acknowledge Catti-brie's greeting when they sat down for their midday meal. And when Catti-brie pestered her further, Sydney instructed Entreri to "keep the whore away."

Even in the failed attempt, though, the aloof mage had aided Catti-brie in a way that neither of them could foresee. Sydney's open contempt and insults came as a slap in Catti-brie's face and instilled in her another tool that would help to overcome the paralysis of her terror: anger.

They passed the halfway point of their journey on the second day, the landscape rolling surrealistically by them as they sped along, and camped in the small hills northeast of Nesme, with the city of Luskan now fully two hundred miles behind them.

Campfires twinkled in the distance, a patrol from Nesme, Sydney theorized.

"We should go there and learn what we may," Entreri suggested, anxious for news of his target.

"You and I," Sydney agreed. "We can get there and back before half the night is through."

Entreri looked at Catti-brie. "What of her?" he asked the mage. "I would not leave her with Jierdan."

"You think that the soldier would take advantage of the girl?" Sydney replied. "I assure you that he is honorable."

"That is not my concern," Entreri smirked. "I fear not for the daughter of Bruenor Battlehammer. She would dispose of your honorable soldier and be gone into the night before we ever returned."

Catti-brie didn't welcome the compliment. She understood that Entreri's comment was more of an insult to Jierdan, who was off gathering firewood, than any recognition of her own prowess, but the assassin's unexpected respect for her would make her task doubly difficult. She didn't want Entreri thinking of her as dangerous, even resourceful, for that would keep him too alert for her to move.

Sydney looked to Bok. "I go," she told the golem, purposely loud enough for Catti-brie to easily hear. "If the prisoner tries to flee, run her down and kill her!" She shot Entreri an evil grin. "Are you content?"

He returned her smile and swung his arm out in the direction of the distant camp.

Jierdan returned then, and Sydney told him of their plans. The soldier didn't seem overjoyed to have Sydney and Entreri running off together, though he said nothing to dissuade the mage. Catti-brie watched him closely and knew the truth. Being left alone with her and the golem didn't bother him, she surmised, but he feared any budding friendship between his two road-mates. Catti-brie understood and even expected this, for Jierdan was in the weakest position of the three—subservient to Sydney and afraid of Entreri. An alliance between those two, perhaps even a pact excluding Dendybar and the Hosttower altogether, would at the least put him out, and more probably spell his end.

"Suren the nature of their dark business works against them," Catti-brie whispered as Sydney and Entreri left the camp, speaking the words aloud to reinforce her growing confidence.

"I could help ye with that," she offered to Jierdan as he worked to complete the campsite.

The soldier glared at her. "Help?" he scoffed. "I should make you do all of it by yourself."

"Yer anger is known to me," Catti-brie countered sympathetically. "I meself have suffered at Entreri's foul hands."

Her pity enraged the proud soldier. He rushed at her threateningly, but she held her composure and did not flinch. "This work is below yer station."

Jierdan stopped suddenly, his anger diffused by his intrigue at the compliment. An obvious ploy, but to Jierdan's wounded ego, the young woman's respect came as too welcome to be ignored.

"What could you know of my station?" he asked.

"I know ye are a soldier of Luskan," Catti-brie replied. "Of a group that's feared throughout all the northland. Ye should not do the grovel work while the mage and the shadow-chaser are off playing in the night."

"You're making trouble!" Jierdan growled, but he paused to consider the point. "You set the camp," he ordered at length, regaining a measure of his own self-respect by displaying his superiority over her. Catti-brie didn't mind, though. She went about the work at once, playing her subservient role without complaint. A plan began to take definite shape in her mind now, and this phase demanded that she make an ally among her enemies, or at least put herself in a position to plant the seeds of jealousy in Jierdan's mind.

She listened, satisfied, as the soldier moved away, muttering under his breath.

Before Entreri and Sydney even got close enough for a good view of the encampment, ritualistic chanting told them that this was no caravan from Nesme. They inched in more cautiously to confirm their suspicions.

Long-haired barbarians, dark and tall, and dressed in

ceremonial feathered garb, danced a circle around a wooden griffon totem.

"Uthgardt," Sydney explained. "The Griffon tribe. We are near to Shining White, their ancestral mound." She edged away from the glow of the camp. "Come," she whispered. "We will learn nothing of value here."

Entreri followed her back toward their own campsite. "Should we ride now?" he asked when they were safely away. "Gain more distance from the barbarians?"

"Unnecessary," Sydney replied. "The Uthgardt will dance the night through. All the tribe partakes of the ritual; I doubt that they even have sentries posted."

"You know much about them," the assassin remarked in an accusing tone, a hint to his sudden suspicions that there might be some ulterior plot controlling the events around them.

"I prepared myself for this journey," Sydney countered. "The Uthgardt keep few secrets; their ways are generally known and documented. Travelers in the northland would do well to understand these people."

"I am fortunate to have such a learned road companion," Entreri said, bowing in sarcastic apology.

Sydney, her eyes straight ahead, did not respond.

But Entreri would not let the conversation die so easily. There was method in his leading line of suspicions. He had consciously chosen this time to play out his hand and reveal his distrust even before they had learned the nature of the encampment. For the first time the two were alone, without Catti-brie or Jierdan to complicate the confrontation, and Entreri meant to put an end to his concerns, or put an end to the mage.

"When am I to die?" he asked bluntly.

Sydney didn't miss a step. "When the fates decree it, as with us all."

"Let me ask the question a different way," Entreri continued, grabbing her by the arm and turning her to face him. "When are you instructed to try to kill me?

"Why else would Dendybar have sent the golem?"

Entreri reasoned. "The wizard puts no store in pacts and honor. He does what he must to accomplish his goals in the most expedient way, and then eliminates those he no longer needs. When my value to you is ended, I am to be slain. A task you may find more difficult than you presume."

"You are perceptive," Sydney replied coolly. "You have judged Dendybar's character well. He would have killed you simply to avoid any possible complications. But you have not considered my own role in this. On my insistence, Dendybar put the decision of your fate into my hands." She paused a moment to let Entreri weigh her words. He could easily kill her right now, they both knew that, so the candor of her calm admission of a plot to murder him halted any immediate actions and forced him to hear her out.

"I am convinced that we seek different ends to our confrontation with the dwarf's party," Sydney explained, "and thus I have no intention of destroying a present, and potentially future, ally."

In spite of his ever-suspicious nature, Entreri fully understood the logic in her line of reasoning. He recognized many of his own characteristics in Sydney. Ruthless, she let nothing get in the way of her chosen path, but she did not stray from that path for any diversion, no matter how strong her feelings. He released her arm. "But the golem travels with us," he said absently, turning into the empty night. "Does Dendybar believe that we will need it to defeat the dwarf and his companions?"

"My master leaves little to chance," Sydney answered. "Bok was sent to seal Dendybar's claim on that which he desires. Protection against unexpected trouble from the companions. And against you."

Entreri carried her line of thinking a step farther. "The object the wizard desires must be powerful indeed," he reasoned.

Sydney nodded.

"Tempting for a younger mage, perhaps."

"What do you imply?" Sydney demanded, angry that Entreri would question her loyalty to Dendybar.

The assassin's assured smile made her squirm uncomfortably. "The golem's purpose is to protect Dendybar against unexpected trouble . . . from you."

Sydney stammered but could not find the words to reply. She hadn't considered that possibility. She tried logically to dismiss Entreri's outlandish conclusion, but the assassin's next remark clouded her ability to think.

"Simply to avoid any possible complications," he said grimly, echoing her earlier words.

The logic of his assumptions slapped her in the face. How could she think herself above Dendybar's malicious plotting? The revelation sent shivers through her, but she had no intention of searching for the answer with Entreri standing next to her. "We must trust in each other," she said to him. "We must understand that we both benefit from the alliance, and that it costs neither of us anything."

"Send the golem away then," Entreri replied.

An alarm went off in Sydney's mind. Was Entreri trying to instill doubt in her merely to gain an advantage in their relationship?

"We do not need the thing," he said. "We have the girl. And even if the companions refuse our demands, we have the strength to take what we want." He returned the mage's suspicious look. "You speak of trust?"

Sydney did not reply, and started again for their camp. Perhaps she should send Bok away. The act would satisfy Entreri's doubts about her, though it certainly would give him the upper hand against her if any trouble did come to pass. But dismissing the golem might also answer some of the even more disturbing questions that weighed upon her, the questions about Dendybar.

The next day was the quietest, and the most productive, of the ride. Sydney fought with her turmoil about the reasons for the golem's presence. She had come to the conclusion that she should send Bok away, if for no better reason than to prove to herself her master's trust.

Entreri watched the telltale signs of her struggle with interest, knowing that he had weakened the bond between Sydney and Dendybar enough to strengthen his own position with the young mage. Now he simply had to wait and watch for his next chance to realign his companions.

Likewise, Catti-brie kept her eye out for more opportunities to cultivate the seeds she had planted in Jierdan's thoughts. The snarls that she saw the soldier hide from Entreri, and from Sydney, told her that her plan was off to a grand start.

They made Silverymoon shortly after noon on the following day. If Entreri had any doubts left about his decision to join the Hosttower's party, they were dismissed when he considered the enormity of their accomplishment. With the tireless magical steeds, they had covered nearly five hundred miles in four days. And in the effortless ride, the absolute ease in guiding their mounts, they were hardly worn when they arrived in the foothills of the mountains just west of the enchanted city.

"The river Rauvin," Jierdan, at the front of the party, called back to them. "And a guard post."

"Pass it by," Entreri replied.

"No," Sydney said. "These are the guides across the Moonbridge. They will let us pass, and their aid will make our journey into the city much easier."

Entreri looked back to Bok, lumbering up the trail behind them. "All of us?" he asked incredulously.

Sydney hadn't forgotten the golem. "Bok," she said when the golem had caught up to them, "you are no longer needed. Return to Dendybar and tell him that all goes well."

Catti-brie's eyes lit up at the thought of sending the monster back, and Jierdan, startled, looked back with growing anxiety. Watching him, Catti-brie saw another advantage to this unexpected turn. By dismissing the golem, Sydney gave more credence to the fears of an alliance between Sydney and Entreri that Catti-brie had planted upon the soldier.

The golem did not move.

"I said go!" Sydney demanded. She saw Entreri's unsurprised stare from the corner of her eye. "Damn you," she whispered to herself. Still, Bok did not move.

"You are indeed perceptive," she snarled at Entreri.

"Remain here, then," she hissed at the golem. "We shall stay in the city for several days." She slipped down from her seat and stomped away, humbled by the assassin's wry smile at her back.

"What of the mounts?" Jierdan asked.

"They were created to get us to Silverymoon, no more," Sydney replied, and even as the four walked away down the path, the shimmering lights that were the horses faded into a soft blue glow, then were gone altogether.

They had little trouble getting through the guard post, especially when Sydney identified herself as a representative of the Hosttower of the Arcane. Unlike most cities in the hostile northland, bordering on paranoia in their fears of outsiders, Silverymoon did not keep itself hemmed within foreboding walls and lines of wary soldiers. The people of this city looked upon visitors as an enhancement to their culture, not as a threat to their way of life.

One of the Knights of Silver, the guardsmen at the post on the Rauvin, led the four travelers to the entrance of the Moonbridge, an arcing, invisible structure that spanned the river before the main gate of the city. The strangers crossed tentatively, uncomfortable for the lack of visible material under their feet. But soon enough they found themselves strolling down the meandering roadways of the magical city. Their pace unconsciously slowed, caught under the infectious laziness, the relaxed, contemplative atmosphere that dissipated even Entreri's narrow-visioned intensity.

Tall, twisting towers and strangely shaped structures

greeted them at every turn. No single architectural style dominated Silverymoon, unless it was the freedom of a builder to exercise his or her personal creativity without fear of judgement or scorn. The result was a city of endless splendors, not rich in counted treasures, as were Waterdeep and Mirabar, its two mightiest neighbors, but unrivaled in aesthetic beauty. A throwback to the earliest days of the Realms, when elves and dwarves and humans had enough room to roam under the sun and stars without fear of crossing some invisible borderline of a hostile kingdom, Silverymoon existed in open defiance of the conquerors and tyrants of the world, a place where no one held claim over another.

People of all the good races walked freely here and without fear, down every road and alleyway on the darkest of nights, and if the travelers passed by someone and were not greeted with a welcoming word, it was only because the person was too profoundly engaged in meditative contemplation.

"The dwarf's party is less than a week out of Longsaddle," Sydney mentioned as they moved through the city. "We may have several days of wait."

"Where do we go?" Entreri asked, feeling out of place. The values that obviously took precedence in Silverymoon were unlike those of any city he had ever encountered, and were completely foreign to his own perceptions of the greedy, lusting world.

"Countless inns line the streets," Sydney answered. "Guests are plentiful here, and are welcomed openly."

"Then our task in finding the companions, once they arrive, shall prove difficult indeed," Jierdan groaned.

"Not so," Sydney replied wryly. "The dwarf comes to Silverymoon in search of information. Soon after they arrive, Bruenor and his friends will make their way to the Vault of Sages, the most reknowned library in all the north."

Entreri squinted his eyes, and said, "And we will be there to greet them."

❧ 12 ❧

The Trollmoors

This was a land of blackened earth and misted bogs, where decay and an imposing sensation of peril over-ruled even the sunniest of skies. The landscape climbed and dropped continually, and the crest of each rise, mounted in hopes of an end to the place by any traveler here, brought only despair and more of the same unchanging scenes.

The brave Riders of Nesme ventured into the moors each spring to set long lines of fires and drive the monsters of the hostile land far from the borders of their town. The season was late and several weeks had passed since the last burning, but even now the low dells lay heavy with smoke and the waves of heat from the great fires still shimmered in the air around the thickest of the charred piles of wood.

Bruenor had led his friends into the Trollmoors in stubborn defiance of the riders, and was determined to pound his way through to Silverymoon. But after only the first day's travel, even he began to doubt the decision. The place demanded a constant state of alertness, and each copse of burned-out trees they passed made them pause, the black, leafless stumps and fallen logs bearing an uncomfortable resemblance to bog blokes. More than once, the spongy ground beneath their feet suddenly became a deep pit of mud, and only the quick reactions of a nearby companion kept them from finding out how deep any of the pits actually were.

A continual breeze blew across the moors, fueled by

the contrasting patches of hot ground and cool bogs, and carrying an odor more foul than the smoke and soot of the fires, a sickly sweet smell disturbingly familiar to Drizzt Do'Urden—the stench of trolls.

This was their domain, and all the rumors about the Evermoors the companions had heard, and had laughed away in the comfort of The Fuzzy Quarterstaff, could not have prepared them for the reality that suddenly descended upon them when they entered the place.

Bruenor had estimated that their party could clear the moors in five days if they kept a strong pace. That first day, they actually covered the necessary distance, but the dwarf had not foreseen the continual backtracking they would have to do to avoid the bogs. While they had marched for more than twenty miles that day, they were less than ten from where they started into the moors.

Still, they encountered no trolls, nor any other kind of fiend, and they set their camp that night under a guise of quiet optimism.

"Ye'll keep to the guard?" Bruenor asked Drizzt, aware that the drow alone had the heightened senses they would need to survive the night.

Drizzt nodded. "The night through," he replied, and Bruenor didn't argue. The dwarf knew that none of them would get any sleep that night, whether on guard, or not.

Darkness came suddenly and completely. Bruenor, Regis, and Wulfgar couldn't see their own hands if they held them inches from their faces. With the blackness came the sounds of an awakening nightmare. Sucking, sloshing footsteps closed in all about them. Smoke mixed with the nighttime fog and rolled in around the trunks of the leafless trees. The wind did not increase, but the intensity of its foul stench did, and it carried now the groans of the tormented spirits of the moors' wretched dwellers.

"Gather your gear," Drizzt whispered to his friends.

"What do ye see, then?" Bruenor asked softly.

"Nothing directly," came the reply. "But I feel them about, as do you all. We cannot let them find us sitting. We must move among them to keep them from gathering about us."

"My legs ache," complained Regis. "And my feet have swelled. I don't even know if I can get my boots back on!"

"Help him, boy," Bruenor told Wulfgar. "The elf's right. We'll carry ye if we must, Rumblebelly, but we're not staying!"

Drizzt took the lead, and at times he had to hold Bruenor's hand behind him, and so on down the line to Wulfgar in the rear, to keep his companions from stumbling from the path he had picked.

They could all sense the dark shapes moving around them, smell the foulness of the wretched trolls. Clearly viewing the host gathering about them, Drizzt alone understood just how precarious their position was, and he pulled his friends as fast as he could.

Luck was with them, for the moon came up then, transforming the fog into a ghostly silver blanket, and revealing to all the friends the pressing danger. Now with the movement visible on every side, the friends ran.

Lanky, lurching forms loomed up in the mist beside them, clawed fingers stretching out to snag at them as they rushed past. Wulfgar moved up to Drizzt's side, swatting the trolls aside with great sweeps of Aegis-fang, while the drow concentrated on keeping them going in the right direction.

For hours they ran, and still the trolls came on. Beyond all feelings of exhaustion, past the ache, and then the numbness in their limbs, the friends ran with the knowledge of the certain horrible death that would befall them if they faltered for even a second, their fear overruling their bodies' cries of defeat. Even Regis, too fat and soft, and with legs too short for the road, matched the pace and pushed those before him to greater speeds.

Drizzt understood the futility of their course. Wulfgar's hammer invariably slowed, and they all stumbled more and more with each minute that passed. The night had many hours more, and even the dawn did not guarantee an end to the pursuit. How many miles could they run? When would they turn down a path that ended in a bottomless bog, with a hundred trolls at their backs?

Drizzt changed his strategy. No longer seeking only to flee, he began looking for a defensible piece of ground. He spied a small mound, ten feet high perhaps, with a steep, almost sheer, grade on the three sides he could see from his angle. A solitary sapling grew up its face. He pointed the place out to Wulfgar, who understood the plan immediately and veered in. Two trolls loomed up to block their way, but Wulfgar, snarling in rage, charged to meet them. Aegis-fang slammed down in furious succession again and again, and the other three companions were able to slip behind the barbarian and make it to the mound.

Wulfgar spun away and rushed to join them, the stubborn trolls close in pursuit and now joined by a long line of their wretched kin.

Surprisingly nimble, even despite his belly, Regis scampered up the tree to the top of the mound. Bruenor, though, not built for such climbing, struggled for every inch.

"Help him!" Drizzt, his back to the tree and scimitars readied, cried to Wulfgar. "Then you get up! I shall hold them."

Wulfgar's breath came in labored gasps, and a line of bright blood was etched across his forehead. He stumbled into the tree and started up behind the dwarf. Roots pulled away under their combined weight, and they seemed to lose an inch for every one they gained. Finally, Regis was able to clasp Bruenor's hand and help him over the top, and Wulfgar, with the way clear before him, moved to join them. With their own immediate safety assured, they looked back in concern for their friend.

Drizzt battled three of the monsters, and more piled in

behind. Wulfgar considered dropping back from his perch halfway up the tree and dying at the drow's side, but Drizzt, periodically looking back over his shoulder to check his friends' progress, noted the barbarian's hesitation and read his mind. "Go!" he shouted. "Your delay does not help!"

Wulfgar had to pause and consider the source of the command. His trust of, and respect for, Drizzt overcame his instinctive desire to rush back into the fray, and he grudgingly pulled himself up to join Regis and Bruenor on the small plateau.

Trolls moved to flank the drow, their filthy claws reaching out at him from every side. He heard his friends, all three, imploring him to break away and join them, but knew that the monsters had already slipped in behind to cut off his retreat.

A smile widened across his face. The light in his eyes flared.

He rushed into the main host of trolls, away from the unattainable mound and his horrified friends.

The three companions had little time to dwell on the drow's fortunes, however, for they soon found themselves assailed from every side as the trolls came relentlessly on, scratching to get at them.

Each friend stood to defend his own side. Luckily, the climb up the back of the mound proved even steeper, at some places inverted, and the trolls could not effectively get at them from behind.

Wulfgar was most deadly, knocking a troll from the mound's side with each smack of his mighty hammer. But before he could even catch his breath, another had taken its place.

Regis, slapping with his little mace, was less effective. He banged with all his strength on fingers, elbows, even heads as the trolls edged in closer, but he could not dislodge the clutching monsters from their perch. Invariably, as each one crested the mound, either Wulfgar or Bruenor had to twist away from his own fight and swat the beast away.

They knew that the first time they failed with a single stroke, they would find a troll up and ready beside them on the top of the mound.

Disaster struck after only a few minutes. Bruenor spun to aid Regis as yet another monster pulled its torso over the top. The dwarf's axe cut in cleanly.

Too cleanly. It sliced into the troll's neck and drove right through, beheading the beast. But though the head flew from the mound, the body kept coming. Regis fell back, too horrified to react.

"Wulfgar!" Bruenor cried out.

The barbarian spun, not slowing long enough to gape at the headless foe, and slammed Aegis-fang into the thing's chest, blasting it from the mound.

Two more hands grabbed at the lip. From Wulfgar's side, another troll had crawled more than halfway over the crest. And behind them, where Bruenor had been, a third was up and straddling the helpless halfling.

They didn't know where to start. The mound was lost. Wulfgar even considered leaping down into the throng below to die as a true warrior by killing as many of his enemies as he could, and also so that he would not have to watch as his two friends were torn to pieces.

But suddenly, the troll above the halfling struggled with its balance, as though something was pulling it from behind. One of its legs buckled and then it fell backward into the night.

Drizzt Do'Urden pulled his blade from the thing's calf as it went over him, then deftly rolled to the top of the mound, regaining his feet right beside the startled halfling. His cloak streamed in tatters, and lines of blood darkened his clothing in many places.

But he still wore his smile, and the fire in his lavender eyes told his friends that he was far from finished. He darted by the gaping dwarf and barbarian and hacked at the next troll, quickly dispatching it from the side.

"How?" Bruenor asked, gawking, though he knew as

he rushed back to Regis that no answer would be forthcoming from the busy drow.

Drizzt's daring move down below had gained him an advantage over his enemies. Trolls were twice his size, and those behind the ones he fought had no idea that he was coming through. He knew that he had done little lasting damage to the beasts—the stab wounds he drove in as he passed would quickly heal, and the limbs he severed would grow back—but the daring maneuver gained him the time he needed to clear the rushing horde and circle out into the darkness. Once free in the black night, he had picked his path back to the mound, cutting through the distracted trolls with the same blazing intensity. His agility alone had saved him when he got to the base, for he virtually ran up the mound's side, even over the back of a climbing troll, too quickly for the surprised monsters to grasp him.

The defense of the mound solidified now. With Bruenor's wicked axe, Wulfgar's pounding hammer, and Drizzt's whirring scimitars each holding a side, the climbing trolls had no easy route to the top. Regis stayed in the middle of the small plateau, alternately darting in to help his friends whenever a troll got too close to gaining a hold.

Still the trolls came on, the throng below growing with every minute. The friends understood clearly the inevitable outcome of this encounter. The only chance lay in breaking the gathering of monsters below to give them a route of escape, but they were too engaged in simply beating back their latest opponents to search for the solution.

Except for Regis.

It happened almost by accident. A writhing arm, severed by one of Drizzt's blades, crawled into the center of their defenses. Regis, utterly revolted, whacked at the thing wildly with his mace. "It won't die!" he screamed as the thing kept wriggling and grabbing at the little weapon. "It won't die! Someone hit it! Someone cut it! Someone burn it!"

The other three were too busy to react to the halfling's desperate pleas, but Regis's last statement, cried out in dismay, brought an idea into his own head. He jumped upon the writhing limb, pinning it down for a moment while he fumbled in his pack for his tinderbox and flint.

His shaking hands could hardly strike the stone, but the tiniest spark did its killing work. The troll arm ignited and crackled into a crisp ball. Not about to miss the opportunity before him, Regis scooped up the fiery limb and ran over to Bruenor. He held back the dwarf's axe, telling Bruenor to let his latest opponent get above the line of the ridge.

When the troll hoisted itself up, Regis put the fire in its face. The head virtually exploded into flame and, screaming in agony, the troll dropped from the mound bringing the killing fire to its own companions.

Trolls did not fear the blade or the hammer. Wounds inflicted by these weapons healed quickly, and even a severed head would soon grow back. Such encounters actually helped propagate the wretched species, for a troll would regrow a severed arm, and a severed arm would regrow another troll! More than one hunting cat or wolf had feasted upon a troll carcass only to bring its own horrible demise when a new monster grew in its belly.

But even trolls were not completely without fear. Fire was their bane, and the trolls of Evermoor were more than familiar with it. Burns could not regenerate and a troll killed by flames was dead forever. Almost as if it were purposely in the gods' design, fire clung to a troll's dry skin as readily as to dry kindling.

The monsters on Bruenor's side of the mound fled away or fell in charred lumps. Bruenor patted the halfling on the back as he observed the welcomed spectacle, hope returning to his weary eyes.

"Wood," reasoned Regis. "We need wood."

Bruenor slipped his pack off his back. "Ye'll get yer

wood, Rumblebelly," he laughed, pointing at the sapling running up the side of the mound before him. "And there's oil in me pouch!" He ran across to Wulfgar. "The tree, boy! Help the halfling," was the only explanation he gave as he moved in front of the barbarian.

As soon as Wulfgar turned around and saw Regis fumbling with a flask of oil, he understood his part in the plan. No trolls as yet had returned to that side of the mound, and the stench of the burned flesh at the base was nearly overwhelming. With a single heave, the muscled barbarian tore the sapling from its roots and brought it up to Regis. Then he went back and relieved the dwarf, allowing Bruenor to put his axe to use in slicing up the wood.

Soon flaming missiles lit the sky all about the mound and fell into the troll horde with killing sparks popping all about. Regis ran to the lip of the mound with another flask of oil and sprinkled it down on the closest trolls, sending them into a terrified frenzy. The rout was on, and between the stampede and the quick spread of flames, the area below the mound was cleared in minutes, and not another movement did the friends see for the few remaining hours of the night, save the pitiful writhing of the mass of limbs, and the twitchings of burned torsos. Fascinated, Drizzt wondered how long the things would survive with their cauterized wounds that would not regenerate.

As exhausted as they were, none of the companions managed any sleep that night. With the breaking of dawn, and no sign of trolls around them, though the filthy smoke hung heavily in the air, Drizzt insisted that they move along.

They left their fortress and walked, because they had no other choice, and because they refused to yield where others might have faltered. They encountered nothing immediately, but could sense the eyes of the moors upon them still, a hushed silence that foretold disaster.

Later that morning, as they plodded along on the

mossy turf, Wulfgar stopped suddenly and heaved Aegis-fang into a small copse of blackened trees. The bog bloke, for that is what the barbarian's target truly was, crossed its arms defensively before it, but the magical warhammer hit with enough power to split the monster down the middle. Its frightened companions, nearly a dozen, fled their similar positions and disappeared into the moors.

"How could you know?" Regis asked, for he was certain that the barbarian had barely considered the clump of trees.

Wulfgar shook his head, honestly not knowing what had compelled him. Drizzt and Bruenor both understood, and approved. They were all operating on instinct now, their exhaustion rendering their minds long past the point of consistent, rational thought. Wulfgar's reflexes remained at their level of fine precision. He might have caught a flicker of movement out of the corner of his eye, so minuscule that his conscious mind hadn't even registered it. But his instinct for survival had reacted. The dwarf and the drow looked to each other for confirmation, not too surprised this time at the barbarian's continued show of maturity as a warrior.

The day became unbearably hot, adding to their discomfort. All they wanted to do was fall down and let their weariness overcome them.

But Drizzt pulled them onward, searching for another defensible spot, though he doubted that he could find one as well-designed as the last. Still, they had enough oil remaining to get them through another night if they could hold a small line long enough to put the flames to their best advantage. Any hillock, perhaps even a copse of trees, would suffice.

What they found instead was another bog, this one stretching as far as they could see in every direction, miles perhaps. "We could turn to the north," Drizzt suggested to Bruenor. "We may have come far enough east by now to break clear of the moors beyond the influence of Nesme."

"The night'll catch us along the bank," Bruenor observed grimly.

"We could cross," Wulfgar suggested.

"Trolls take to water?" Bruenor asked Drizzt, intrigued by the possibilities. The drow shrugged.

"Worth a try, then!" Bruenor proclaimed.

"Gather some logs," instructed Drizzt. "Take no time to bind them together—we can do that out on the water, if we must."

Floating the logs as buoys by their sides, they slipped out into the cold, still waters of the huge bog.

Though they weren't thrilled with the sucking, muddy sensation that pulled at them with each step, Drizzt and Wulfgar found that they could walk in many places, propelling the makeshift raft steadily along. Regis and Bruenor, too short for the water, lay across the logs. Eventually they grew more comfortable with the eerie hush of the bog, and accepted the water route as a quiet rest.

The return to reality was rude indeed.

The water around them exploded, and three troll-like forms hit them in sudden ambush. Regis, nearly asleep across his log, was thrown off it and into the water. Wulfgar took a hit in the chest before he could ready Aegis-fang, but he was no halfling, and even the considerable strength of the monster could not move him backward. The one that rose before the ever-alert drow found two scimitars at work on its face before its head even cleared the water.

The battle proved as fast and furious as its abrupt beginning. Enraged by the continued demands of the relentless moors, the friends reacted to the assault with a counterattack of unmatched fury. The drow's troll was sliced apart before it even stood straight, and Bruenor had enough time to prepare himself to get at the monster that had dropped Regis.

Wulfgar's troll, though it landed a second blow behind

the first, was hit with a savage flurry that it could not have expected. Not an intelligent creature, its limited reasoning and battle experience led it to believe that its foe should not have remained standing and ready to retaliate after it had squarely landed two heavy blows.

Its realization, though, served as little comfort as Aegis-fang pummeled the monster back under the surface.

Regis bobbed back to the surface then and slung an arm over the log. One side of his face was bright with a welt and a painful-looking scrape.

"What were they?" Wulfgar asked the drow.

"Some manner of troll," Drizzt reasoned, still stabbing at the unmoving form lying under the water before him.

Wulfgar and Bruenor understood the reason for his continued attacks. In sudden fright, they took up whacking at the forms lying beside them, hoping to mutilate the corpses enough so that they might be miles gone before the things rose to life once again.

Beneath the bog's surface, in the swirlless solitude of the dark waters, the severe thumping of axe and hammer disturbed the slumber of other denizens. One in particular had slept away a decade and more, unbothered by any of the potential dangers that lurked nearby, safe in its knowledge of supremacy.

Dazed and drained from the hit he had taken, as if the unexpected ambush had bent his spirit beyond its breaking point, Regis slumped helplessly over the log and wondered if he had any fight left in him. He didn't notice when the log began to drift slightly in the hot moors' breeze. It hooked around the exposed roots of a small line of trees and floated free into the lily-pad-covered waters of a quiet lagoon.

Regis stretched out lazily, only half aware of the change in his surroundings. He could still hear the conversation of his friends faintly in the background.

He cursed his carelessness and struggled against the stubborn hold of his lethargy, though, when the water began to churn before him. A purplish, leathery form broke the surface, and then he saw the huge circular maw with its cruel rows of daggerlike teeth.

Regis, up now, did not cry out or react in any way, fascinated by the specter of his own death looming before him.

A giant worm.

"I thought the water would offer us some protection from the foul things, at least," Wulfgar groaned, giving one final smack at the troll corpse that lay submerged beside him.

"At least the moving's easier," Bruenor put in. "Get the logs together, and let's move along. No figuring how many kin these three have stalking the area."

"I have no desire to stay and count," replied Wulfgar. He looked around, puzzled, and asked, "Where is Regis?"

It was the first time in the confusion of the fight that any of them noticed that the halfling had floated off. Bruenor started to call out, but Drizzt slapped a hand across his mouth.

"Listen," he said.

The dwarf and Wulfgar held very still and listened in the direction that the drow was now intently staring. After a moment of adjustment, they heard the halfling's quivering voice.

" . . . really is a beautiful stone," they heard, and knew at once that Regis was using the pendant to get himself out of trouble.

The seriousness of the situation came clear immediately, for Drizzt had sorted out the blur of images that he saw through a line of trees, perhaps a hundred feet to the west. "Worm!" he whispered to his companions. "Huge beyond anything I have ever seen!" He indicated a tall tree to Wulfgar, then started on a flanking course around to the south, pulling the onyx statue out of his pack as he went, and calling for Guenhwyvar. They would need all the help they could get with this beast.

Dipping low in the water, Wulfgar eased his way up to the tree line and started shinning up a tree, the scene now clear before him. Bruenor followed him, but slipped between the trees, going even deeper into the bog, and came into position on the other side.

"There are more, too," Regis bargained in a louder voice, hoping that his friends would hear and rescue him. He kept the hypnotizing ruby spinning on its chain. He didn't think for a moment that the primitive monster understood him, but it seemed perplexed enough by the gem's sparkles to refrain from gobbling him up, at least for the present. In truth, the magic of the ruby did little against the creature. Giant worms had no minds to speak of, and charms had no effect on them at all. But the huge worm, not really hungry and mesmerized by the dance of the light, allowed Regis to play through his game.

Drizzt came into position farther down the tree line, his bow now in hand, while Guenhwyvar stealthily slipped even farther around to the monster's rear. Drizzt could see Wulfgar poised, high in the tree above Regis and ready to leap into action. The drow couldn't see Bruenor, but he knew that the crafty dwarf would find a way to be effective.

Finally the worm tired of its game with the halfling and his spinning gem. A sudden sucking of air sizzled with acidic drool.

Recognizing the danger, Drizzt acted first, conjuring a globe of darkness around the halfling's log. Regis, at first, thought the sudden blackness signified the end of his life, but when the cold water hit his face and then swallowed him up as he rolled limply from the log, he understood.

The globe confused the monster for a moment, but the beast spat a stream of its killing acid anyway, the wicked stuff sizzling as it hit the water and setting the log ablaze.

Wulfgar sprang from his high perch, launching himself through the air fearlessly and screaming, "Tempus!" his legs flung wide, but his arm cocked with the war-hammer fully under control and ready to strike.

The worm lolled its head to the side to move away from the barbarian, but it didn't react quite fast enough. Aegis-fang crunched through the side of its face, tearing through the purplish hide and twisting the outer rim of its maw, snapping through teeth and bone. Wulfgar had given all that he possibly could in that one mighty blow, and he could not imagine the enormity of his success as he slapped belly-first into the cold water, beneath the drow's darkness.

Enraged by pain and suddenly more injured than it had ever been, the great worm issued a roar that split trees asunder and sent creatures of the moors scurrying for cover miles away. It rolled an arch along its fifty-foot length, up and down, in a continual splash that sent bursts of water high into the air.

Drizzt opened up, his fourth arrow nocked and ready before the first even reached its mark. The worm roared again in agony and spun on the drow, releasing a second stream of acid.

But the agile elf was gone long before the acid sizzled into the water where he had been standing.

Bruenor, meanwhile, had completely gone under the water, blindly stumbling toward the beast. Nearly ground into the mud by the worm's frenzied gyrations, he came up just behind the curl of the monster. The breadth of its massive torso measured fully twice his height, but the dwarf didn't hesitate, smacking his axe against the tough hide.

Guenhwyvar then sprang upon the monster's back and ran up its length, finding a perch on its head. The cat's clawed paws dug into the worm's eyes before it even had time to react to the new attackers.

Drizzt plucked away, his quiver nearly empty and a dozen feathered shafts protruding from the worm's maw and head. The beast decided to concentrate on

Bruenor next, his vicious axe inflicting the most severe wounds. But before it could roll over onto the dwarf, Wulfgar emerged from the darkness and heaved his warhammer. Aegis-fang thudded into the maw again and the weakened bone cracked apart. Acidic blobs of blood and bone hissed into the bog and the worm roared a third time in agony and protest.

The friends did not relent. The drow's arrows stung home in a continuous line. The cat's claws raked deeper and deeper into the flesh. The dwarf's axe chopped and hacked, sending pieces of hide floating away. And Wulfgar pounded away.

The giant worm reeled. It could not retaliate. In the wave of dizzying darkness that fast descended upon it, it was too busy merely holding to its stubborn balance. Its maw was broken wide open and one eye was out. The relentless beating of the dwarf and barbarian had blasted through its protective hide, and Bruenor growled in savage pleasure when his axe at last sank deep into exposed flesh.

A sudden spasm from the monster sent Guenhwyvar flying into the bog and knocked Bruenor and Wulfgar away. The friends didn't even try to get back, aware that their task was completed. The worm trembled and twitched in its last efforts of life.

Then it toppled into the bog in a sleep that would outlast any it had ever known—the endless sleep of death.

❧ 13 ❧

The Last Run

The dissipating globe of darkness found Regis once again clinging to his log, which was now little more than a black cinder, and shaking his head. "We are beyond ourselves," he sighed. "We cannot make it through."

"Faith, Rumblebelly," Bruenor comforted, sloshing through the water to join the halfling. "Tales we be making, for telling to our children's children, and for others to tell when we're no more!"

"You mean today, then?" Regis snipped. "Or perhaps we'll live this day and be no more tomorrow."

Bruenor laughed and grabbed hold of the log. "Not yet, me friend," he assured Regis with an adventurous smile. "Not till me business is done!"

Drizzt, moving to retrieve his arrows, noted how heavily Wulfgar leaned upon the worm's body. From a distance, he thought that the young barbarian was simply exhausted, but when he drew near, he began to suspect something more serious. Wulfgar clearly favored one leg in his pose, as though it, or perhaps his lower back, had been injured.

When Wulfgar saw the drow's concerned look, he straightened stoically. "Let us move on," he suggested, moving away toward Bruenor and Regis and doing his best to hide a limp.

Drizzt didn't question him about it. The young man was made of stuff as hard as the tundra in midwinter, and too altruistic and proud to admit an injury when nothing could be gained by the admission. His friends couldn't stop to wait for him to heal, and they certainly couldn't carry him, so he would grimace away the pain and plod on.

But Wulfgar truly was injured. When he splashed into the water after his fall from the tree, he had wickedly twisted his back. In the heat of the battle, his adrenaline pumping, he hadn't felt the wrenching pain. But now each step came hard.

Drizzt saw it as clearly as he saw the despair upon Regis's normally cheerful face, and as clearly as the exhaustion that kept the dwarf's axe swinging low, despite Bruenor's optimistic boasting. He looked all about at the moors, which seemed to stretch forever in every direction, and wondered for the first time if he and his companions had indeed gone beyond themselves.

Guenhwyvar hadn't been injured in the battle, just a bit shaken up, but Drizzt, recognizing the cat's limited range of movement in the bog, sent it back to its own plane. He would have liked to keep the wary panther at their point. But the water was too deep for the cat, and the only way Guenhwyvar could have kept moving would have been by springing from tree to tree. Drizzt knew it wouldn't work; he and his friends would have to go on alone.

Reaching deep within themselves to reinforce their resolve, the companions kept to their work, the drow inspecting the worm's head to salvage any of the score of arrows that he had fired, knowing all too well that he would probably need them again before they saw the end of the moors, while the other three retrieved the rest of the logs and provisions.

Soon after, the friends drifted through the bog with as little physical effort as they could manage, fighting every minute to keep their minds alert to the dangerous surroundings. With the heat of the day, though—the hottest one yet—and the gentle rocking of the logs on the quiet water, all but Drizzt dropped off, one by one, to sleep.

The drow kept the makeshift raft moving, and remained vigilant; they couldn't afford any delay, or any lapses. Luckily, the water opened up beyond the lagoon, and there were few obstructions for Drizzt to deal with. The bog became a great blur to him after a while, his tired eyes recording little detail, just general outlines and any sudden movements in the reeds.

He was a warrior, though, with lightning reflexes and uncanny discipline. The water trolls hit again, and the tiny flicker of consciousness that Drizzt Do'Urden had remaining summoned him back to reality in time to deny the monsters' advantage of surprise.

Wulfgar, and Bruenor, too, sprang from their slumber at the instant of his call, weapons in hand. Only two trolls rose to meet them this time and the three dispatched them in a few short seconds.

Regis slept through the whole affair.

The cool night came, mercifully dissipating the waves of heat. Bruenor made the decision to keep moving, two of them up and pushing at all times, and two of them at rest.

"Regis cannot push," Drizzt reasoned. "He is too short for the bog."

"Then let him sit and keep guard while I push," Wulfgar offered stoically. "I need no help."

"Then the two of ye take the first shift," said Bruenor. "Rumblebelly's slept the whole day away. He should be good for an hour or two!"

Drizzt climbed up on the logs for the first time that day and put his head down on his pack. He did not close his eyes, though. Bruenor's plan of working in turns sounded fair, but impractical. In the black night, only he could guide them and keep any kind of lookout for approaching danger. More than a few times while Wulfgar and Regis took their shift, the drow lifted his head and gave the halfling some insight about their surroundings and some advice about their best direction.

There would be no sleep for Drizzt again this night. He

vowed to rest in the morning, but when dawn at last broke, he found the trees and reeds again hunched in around them. The anxiety of the moors itself closed upon them, as though it were a single, sentient being watching over them and plotting against their passage.

The wide water actually proved of benefit to the companions. The ride on its glassy surface was easier than hiking, and despite the crouching perils, they encountered nothing hostile after their second rout of the water trolls. When their path finally returned to blackened land after days and nights of gliding, they suspected that they might have covered most of the distance to the other side of the Evermoors. Sending Regis up the tallest tree they could find, for the halfling was the only one light enough to get to the highest branches (especially since the journey had all but dissipated the roundness of his belly), their hopes were confirmed. Far on the eastern horizon, but no more than a day or two away, Regis saw trees—not the small copses of birch or the moss-covered swamp trees of the moors, but a thick forest of oak and elm.

They moved forward with a renewed spring in their step, despite their exhaustion. They walked upon solid ground again, and knew that they would have to camp one more time with the hordes of wandering trolls lurking near, but they now also carried the knowledge that the ordeal of the Evermoors was almost at an end. They had no intention of letting its foul inhabitants defeat them on this last leg of the journey.

"We should end our trek this day," Drizzt suggested, though the sun was more than an hour from the western horizon. The drow had already sensed the gathering presence, as the trolls awakened from their daytime rest and caught the strange scents of the visitors to the moors. "We must pick our campsite carefully. The moors have not yet freed us of their grasp."

"We'll lose an hour and more," Bruenor stated, more to open up the negative side of the plan than to argue. The dwarf remembered the horrible battle at the mound all too well, and had no desire to repeat that colossal effort.

"We shall gain the time back tomorrow," reasoned Drizzt. "Our need at present is to stay alive."

Wulfgar wholly agreed. "The smell of the foul beasts grows stronger each step," he said, "from every side. We cannot run away from them. So let us fight."

"But on our own terms," Drizzt added.

"Over there," Regis suggested, pointing to a heavily overgrown ridge off to their left.

"Too open," said Bruenor. "Trolls'd climb it as easily as we, and too many at a time for us to stop them!"

"Not while it's burning," Regis countered with a sneaky smile, and his companions came to agree with the simple logic.

They spent the rest of the daylight preparing their defenses. Wulfgar and Bruenor carried in as much dead wood as they could find, placing it in strategic lines to lengthen the diameter of the targeted area, while Regis cleared a firebreak at the top of the ridge and Drizzt kept a cautious lookout. Their defense plan was simple: let the trolls come at them, then set the entire ridge outside their camp ablaze.

Drizzt alone recognized the weakness of the plan, though he had nothing better to offer. He had fought trolls before they had ever come to these moors, and he understood the stubbornness of the wretched beasts. When the flames of their ambush finally died away— long before the dawning of the new day—he and his friends would be wide open to the remaining trolls. They could only hope that the carnage of the fires would dissuade any further enemies.

Wulfgar and Bruenor would have liked to do more, the memories of the mound too vivid for them to be satisfied with any defenses constructed against the moors. But when dusk came, it brought hungry eyes upon them. They joined Regis and Drizzt at the camp on top of the ridge and crouched low in anxious wait.

An hour passed, seeming like ten to the friends, and the night deepened.

"Where are they?" Bruenor demanded, his axe slapping nervously against his hand, belying uncharacteristic impatience from the veteran fighter.

"Why don't they come on?" Regis agreed, his anxiety bordering on panic.

"Be patient and be glad," Drizzt offered. "The more of the night we put behind us before we do battle, the better our chance to see the dawn. They may not have yet found us."

"More like they be gathering to rush us all at once," Bruenor said grimly.

"That is good," said Wulfgar, comfortably crouched and peering into the gloom. "Let the fire taste as much of the foul blood as it may!"

Drizzt took note of the settling effect the big man's strength and resolve had upon Regis and Bruenor. The dwarf's axe stopped its nervous bounce and came to rest calmly at Bruenor's side, poised for the task ahead. Even Regis, the most reluctant warrior, took up his small mace with a snarl, his knuckles whitening under his grip.

Another long hour passed.

The delay did not at all ease the companions' guard. They knew that danger was very near now—they could smell the stench gathering in the mist and darkness beyond their view.

"Strike up the torches," Drizzt told Regis.

"We'll bring the beasts upon us from miles around!" Bruenor argued.

"They have found us already," answered Drizzt, pointing down the ridge, though the trolls he saw shuffling in the darkness were beyond the limited night vision of his friends. "The sight of the torches may keep them back and grant us more time."

As he spoke, however, the first troll ambled up the ridge. Bruenor and Wulfgar waited in their crouch until the monster was nearly upon them, then sprang out with sudden fury, axe and warhammer leading the way in a brutal flurry of well-placed blows. The monster went down at once.

Regis had one of the torches lit. He threw it to Wulfgar and the barbarian set the writhing body of the fallen troll ablaze. Two other trolls that had come to the bottom of the ridge rushed back into the mist at the sight of the hated flames.

"Ah, ye pulled the trick too soon!" Bruenor groaned. "We're naught to catch a one with the torches in plain sight!"

"If the torches keep them back, then the fires have served us well," Drizzt insisted, though he knew better than to hope for such an occurrence.

Suddenly, as if the very moors had spit their venom at them, a huge host of trolls lined the entire base of the ridge. They came on tentatively, not thrilled by the presence of fire. But they came on relentlessly, stalking up the hill with drooling desire.

"Patience," Drizzt told his companions, sensing their eagerness. "Keep them behind the firebreak, but let as many as will get within the rings of kindling."

Wulfgar rushed out to the edge of the ring, waving his torch menacingly.

Bruenor stood back up, his last two flasks of oil in his hands, oil-soaked rags hanging from their spouts, and a wild smile across his face. "Season's a bit green for burning," he said to Drizzt with a wink. "Might need a little help in getting the thing going!"

Trolls swarmed on the ridge all around them, the slavering horde coming on determinedly, their ranks swelling with each step.

Drizzt moved first. Torch in hand, he ran to the kindling and set it burning. Wulfgar and Regis joined in right behind, putting as many fires as they could between them and the advancing trolls. Bruenor threw his torch over the first ranks of the monsters, hoping to get them in the middle of two blazes, then heaved his oil flasks into the most heavily concentrated groups.

Flames leaped up into the night sky, lightening the immediate area, but deepening the blackness beyond their influence. Crowded in so tightly, the trolls could not easily turn and flee, and the fire, as if it understood this, descended upon them methodically.

When one began to burn, its frenzied dance spread the light even farther down the ridge line.

All across the vast moors, creatures stopped their nightly actions and took notice of the growing pillar of flame and the wind-carried shrieks of dying trolls.

Huddled close at the top of the ridge, the companions found themselves nearly overcome by the great heat. But the fire peaked quickly with its feast of volatile troll flesh, and started to diminish, leaving a revulsive stench in the air and yet another blackened scar of carnage on the Evermoors.

The companions readied more torches for their flight from the ridge. Many trolls stood to do battle, even after the fire, and the friends could not hope to hold their ground with the fuel of their fires consumed. At Drizzt's insistence, they awaited the first clear escape route down the eastern side of the ridge, and when it opened, they charged into the night, bursting through the initial groups of unsuspecting trolls with a sudden assault that scattered the monsters and left several burning.

Into the night they ran, blindly rushing through mud and bramble, hoping that luck alone would keep them from being sucked in by some bottomless bog. So complete was their surprise at the ridge that for many minutes they heard no signs of pursuit.

But it didn't take the moors long to respond. Groans and shrieks soon echoed all about them.

Drizzt took the lead. Relying on his instincts as much as his vision, he swerved his friends left and right, through the areas of least apparent resistance, while keeping their course generally east. Hoping to play upon the monsters' single fear, they torched anything that would burn as they passed.

They encountered nothing directly as the night wore on, but the groans and sucking footsteps just yards behind them did not relent. They soon began to suspect a collective intelligence working against them, for though they were obviously outdistancing the trolls that were behind them and to their sides, more were always waiting to take up the chase. Something evil permeated the land, as though the Evermoors themselves were the true enemies. Trolls were all about, and that was the immediate danger, but even if all the trolls and other denizens of the moors were slain or driven away, the friends suspected that this would remain a foul place.

Dawn broke, but it brought no relief. "We've angered the moors themselves!" Bruenor cried when he realized that the chase would not end as easily this time. "We be finding no rest until her foul borders are behind us!"

Onward they charged, seeing the lanky forms lurching out at them as they weaved their way, and those running parallel to them or right behind, grimly visible and just waiting for someone to trip up. Heavy fogs closed in on them, preventing them from holding their bearings, further evidence for their fears that the moors themselves had risen against them.

Past all thinking, past all hope, they kept on, pushing themselves beyond their physical and emotional limits for lack of any alternatives.

Barely conscious of his actions, Regis stumbled and went down. His torch rolled away, though he didn't notice—he couldn't even figure how to get back up, or that he was down at all! Hungry mouths descended toward him, a feast assured.

The ravenous monster was foiled, though, as Wulfgar came by and scooped the halfling into his great arms. The huge barbarian slammed into the troll, knocking it aside, but held his own footing and continued past.

Drizzt abandoned all tactics of finesse now, understanding the situation that was fast developing behind him. More than once he had to slow for Bruenor's stumbling and he doubted Wulfgar's ability to continue while carrying the halfling. The exhausted barbarian obviously couldn't hope to raise Aegis-fang to defend himself. Their only chance was straight flight to the border. A wide bog would defeat them, a box gully would entrap them, and even if no natural barriers blocked their way, they had little hope of keeping free of the trolls for much longer. Drizzt feared the difficult decision he saw forthcoming: flee to his own safety, for he alone seemed to have the possibility of escape, or stand beside his doomed friends in a battle they could not win.

They continued on, and made solid progress for another hour, but time itself began to affect them. Drizzt heard Bruenor mumbling behind him, lost in some delusion of his childhood days in Mithril Hall. Wulfgar, with the unconscious halfling, ambled along behind, reciting a prayer to one of his gods, using the rhythm of his chants to keep his feet steadily pumping.

Then Bruenor fell, smacked down by a troll that had veered in on them uncontested.

The fateful decision came easily to Drizzt. He swung back around, scimitars ready. He couldn't possibly carry the stout dwarf, nor could he defeat the horde of trolls that even now closed in. "And so our tale ends, Bruenor Battlehammer!" he cried out. "In battle, as it should!"

Wulfgar, dazed and gasping, did not consciously choose his next move. It was simply a reaction to the scene before him, a maneuver perpetrated by the stubborn instincts of a man who refused to surrender. He stumbled over to the fallen dwarf, who by this time had struggled back to his hands and knees, and scooped him up with his free arm. Two trolls had them trapped.

Drizzt Do'Urden was close by, and the young barbarian's heroic act inspired the drow. Seething flames danced again within his lavender eyes, and his blades whirred into their own dance of death.

The two trolls reached out to claw their helpless prey,

but after a single lightning pass by Drizzt, the monsters had no arms left with which to grab.

"Run on!" Drizzt called, guarding the party's rear and spurring Wulfgar on with a constant stream of rousing words. All weariness flew from the drow in this final burst of battle lust. He leaped all about and shouted challenge to the trolls. Any that came too near found the sting of his blades.

Grunting with every painful step, his eyes burning from his sweat, Wulfgar charged blindly ahead. He didn't think about how long he could keep up the pace with his load. He didn't think about the certain, horrible death that shadowed him on every side, and had probably cut off his route as well. He didn't think about the wrenching pain in his injured back, or about the new sting that he keenly felt on the back of his knee. He concentrated only on putting one heavy boot in front of the other.

They crunched through some brambles, swung down one rise and around another. Their hearts both leaped and fell, for before them loomed the clean forest that Regis had spied, the end of the Evermoors. But between them and the wood waited a solid line of trolls, standing three deep.

The Evermoors' grasp was not so easily broken.

"Keep on," Drizzt said into Wulfgar's ear in a quiet whisper, as though he feared that the moors might be listening. "I have one more trick left to play."

Wulfgar saw the line before him, but even in his present state, his trust in Drizzt overruled any objections of his common sense. Heaving Bruenor and Regis into a more comfortable hold, he put his head low and roared at the beasts, crying out in frenzied rage.

When he had almost reached them, with Drizzt a few steps behind, and the trolls drooling and huddled to stop his momentum, the drow played his final card.

Magical flames sprouted from the barbarian. They had no power to burn, either Wulfgar or the trolls, but to the monsters, the specter of the huge, flame-enshrouded wild man bearing down upon them shot terror into their normally fearless hearts.

Drizzt timed the spell perfectly, allowing the trolls only a split second to react to their imposing foe. Like water before the prow of a high-riding ship they parted, and Wulfgar, nearly overbalancing for his expectations of impact, lumbered through, Drizzt dancing at his heels.

By the time the trolls regrouped to pursue, their prey was already climbing the last rise out of the Evermoors and into the forest—a wood under the protective eye of Lady Alustriel and the gallant Knights of Silver.

Drizzt turned under the boughs of the first tree to watch for signs of pursuit. Heavy fog swirled back down at the moors, as though the foul land had slammed its door behind them. No trolls came through.

The drow sank back against the tree, too drained to smile.

❧ 14 ❧

Star Light, Star Bright

Wulfgar set Regis and Bruenor down on a mossy bed in a small clearing deeper in the wood, then toppled over in pain. Drizzt caught up to him a few minutes later.

"We must camp here," the drow was saying, "though I wish we could put more distance . . . " He stopped when he saw his young friend writhing on the ground and grasping at his injured leg, nearly overcome by the pain. Drizzt rushed over to examine the knee, his eyes widening in shock and disgust.

A troll's hand, probably from one of those he had hacked apart when Wulfgar rescued Bruenor, had latched on to the barbarian as he ran, finding a niche in the back of his knee. One clawed finger had already buried itself deep into the leg, and two others were even now boring in.

"Do not look," Drizzt advised Wulfgar. He reached into his pack for his tinderbox and set a small stick burning, then used it to prod the wretched hand. As soon as the thing began to smoke and wriggle about, Drizzt slid it from the leg and threw it to the ground. It tried to scurry away, but Drizzt sprang upon it, pinning it with one of his scimitars and lighting it fully with the burning stick.

He looked back to Wulfgar, amazed at the sheer determination that had allowed the barbarian to continue with so wicked a wound. But now their flight was ended, and Wulfgar had already succumbed to the pain and the exhaustion. He lay sprawled unconscious on the ground beside Bruenor and Regis.

"Sleep well," Drizzt said softly to the three of them. 'You have earned the right." He moved to each of them to make sure they were not too badly hurt. Then, satisfied that they would all recover, he set to his vigilant watch.

Even the valiant drow, though, had overstepped the bounds of his stamina during the rush through the Evermoors, and soon he too nodded his head and joined his friends in slumber.

Late the next morning Bruenor's grumbling roused them. "Ye forgot me axe!" the dwarf shouted angrily. "I can't be cutting stinkin' trolls without me axe!"

Drizzt stretched out comfortably, somewhat refreshed, but still far from recovered. "I told you to take the axe," he said to Wulfgar, who was similarly shaking off his sound slumber.

"I said it clearly," Drizzt scolded mockingly. "Take the axe and leave the ungrateful dwarf."

"'Twas the nose that confused me," Wulfgar replied. "More akin to an axe-head than to any nose I have ever seen!"

Bruenor unconsciously looked down his long snout. "Bah!" he growled, "I'll find me a club!" and he tromped off into the forest.

"Some quiet, if you will!" Regis snapped as the last hint of his pleasant dreams flitted away. Disgusted at being awakened so early, he rolled back over and covered his head with his cloak.

They could have made Silverymoon that very day, but a single night's rest would not erase the weariness of the days they had spent in the Evermoors, and on a tough road before that. Wulfgar, for one, with his injured leg and back, had to use a walking stick, and the sleep that Drizzt had found the night before had been his first in nearly a week. Unlike the moors, this forest seemed quite wholesome. And though they knew that they were still in the wild lands, they felt safe enough to stretch out the road to the city and enjoy, for the first time since they had left Ten-Towns, a leisurely walk.

They broke out of the forest by noon of the next day and covered the last few miles to Silverymoon. Before sunset, they came over the final climb, and looked down upon the River Rauvin and the countless spires of the enchanted city.

They all felt the sensation of hope and relief when they glanced down upon that magnificent sight, but none felt it more keenly than Drizzt Do'Urden. The drow had hoped from the earliest planning of their adventure that its path would take him through Silverymoon, though he had done nothing to sway Bruenor's decision in choosing a course. Drizzt had heard of Silverymoon after his arrival in Ten-Towns, and were it not for the fact that he had found some measure of tolerance in the rugged frontier community, he would have set back at once for the place. Reknowned for their acceptance of all who came in search of knowledge, regardless of race, the people of Silverymoon offered the renegade black elf a true opportunity to find a home.

Many times he had considered traveling to the place, but something within him, perhaps the fear of false hope and unfulfilled expectations, kept him within the security of Icewind Dale. Thus, when the decision had been made in Longsaddle that Silverymoon would be their next destination, Drizzt had found himself squarely facing the fantasy he had never dared to dream. Looking down now on his one hope for true acceptance in the surface world, he courageously forced his apprehensions away.

"The Moonbridge," Bruenor remarked when a wagon below crossed the Rauvin, seemingly floating in mid-air. Bruenor had heard of the invisible structure as a boy, but had never seen it firsthand.

Wulfgar and Regis watched the spectacle of the flying wagon in blank amazement. The barbarian had overcome many of his fears of magic during his stay in Longsaddle, and he was truly looking forward to exploring this legendary city. Regis had been here once before, but his familiarity with the place did nothing to lessen his excitement.

They approached the guard post on the Rauvin eagerly, despite their weariness, the same post that Entreri's party had passed four days before, with the same guards who had allowed the evil group to enter the city.

"Greetings," Bruenor offered in a tone that could be considered jovial for the dour dwarf. "And know ye that the sight of yer fair city has bringed new life into me weary heart!"

The guards hardly heard him, intent upon the drow, who had pulled back his cowl. They seemed curious, for they had never actually seen a black elf, but they didn't appear too surprised by Drizzt's arrival.

"May we be escorted to the Moonbridge now?" Regis asked after a period of silence that grew increasingly uncomfortable. "You cannot guess how anxious we are to view Silverymoon. So much we have heard!"

Drizzt suspected what was forthcoming. An angry lump welled in his throat.

"Go away," the guard said quietly. "You may not pass."

Bruenor's face reddened in rage, but Regis cut off his explosion. "Surely we have done nothing to cause such a harsh judgement," the halfling protested calmly. "We are simple travelers, seeking no trouble." His hand went to his jacket, and to the hypnotic ruby, but a scowl from Drizzt halted his plan.

"Your reputation seems to outweigh your actions," Wulfgar remarked to the guards.

"I am sorry," replied one, "but I have my duties, and I see them through."

"Us, or the drow?" Bruenor demanded.

"The drow," answered the guard. "The rest of you may go to the city, but the drow may not pass."

Drizzt felt the walls of hope crumbling around him. His hands trembled at his sides. Never before had he experienced such pain, for never before had he come to a place without the expectation of rejection. Still, he managed to sublimate his immediate anger and remind himself that this was Bruenor's quest, not his own, for good or for ill.

"Ye dogs!' Bruenor cried. "Th' elf's worth a dozen of ye, and more! I owe him me life a hundred times, and ye think to say that he's not good enough for yer stinking city! How many trolls be layin' dead for the work of yer sword?"

"Be calm, my friend," Drizzt interrupted, fully in control of himself. "I expect as much. They cannot know Drizzt Do'Urden. Just the reputation of my people. And they cannot be blamed. You go in, then. I will await your return."

"No!" Bruenor declared in a tone that brooked no debate. "If ye can't go in, then none of us will!"

"Think of our goal, stubborn dwarf," Drizzt scolded. "The Vault of Sages is in the city. Perhaps our only hope."

"Bah!" Bruenor snorted. "To the Abyss with this cursed city and all who live here! Sundabar sits less than a week's walking. Helm, the dwarf-friend, will be more inviting, or I'm a bearded gnome!"

"You should enter," Wulfgar said. "Let not our anger defeat our purpose. But I remain with Drizzt. Where he cannot go, Wulfgar, son of Beornegar, refuses to go!"

But the determined stomps of Bruenor's stocky legs were already carrying him down the road back out from the city. Regis shrugged at the other two and started after, as loyal to the drow as any of them.

"Choose your camp as you wish, and without fear," the guard offered, almost apologetically. "The Knights of Silver will not disturb you, nor will they let any monsters near the borders of Silverymoon."

Drizzt nodded, for though the sting of the rejection had not diminished, he understood that the guard had been helpless to change the unfortunate situation. He started slowly away, the disturbing questions that he had avoided for so years already beginning to press in upon him.

Wulfgar was not so forgiving. "You have wronged him," he said to the guard when Drizzt moved away. "Never has he raised sword against any who did not deserve it, and this world, yours and mine, is better off for having Drizzt Do'Urden about!"

The guard looked away, unable to answer the justifiable scolding.

"And I question the honor of one who heeds to unjust commands," Wulfgar declared.

The guard snapped an angry glare on the barbarian. "The Lady's reasons are not asked," he answered, hand on sword hilt. He sympathized with the anger of the travelers, but would accept no criticism of the Lady Alustriel, his beloved leader. "Her commands follow a righteous course, and are beyond the wisdom of me, or you!" he growled.

Wulfgar did not justify the threat with any show of concern. He turned away and started down the road after his friends.

Bruenor purposely positioned their camp just a few hundred yards down the Rauvin, in clear sight of the guard post. He had sensed the guard's discomfort at turning them away and he wanted to play upon that guilt as strongly as he could.

"Sundabar'll show us the way," he kept saying after they had supped, trying to convince himself as much as the others that their failure at Silverymoon would not hurt the quest. "And beyond that lies Citadel Adbar. If any in all the Realms know of Mithril Hall, it be Harbromm and the dwarves of Adbar!"

"A long way," Regis commented. "Summer may run out before we ever reach the fortress of King Harbromm."

"Sundabar," Bruenor reiterated stubbornly. "And Adbar if we must!"

The two went back and forth with the conversation for a while. Wulfgar didn't join in, too intent on the drow, who had moved a short distance away from the camp right after the meal—which Drizzt had hardly touched—

and stood silently staring at the city up the Rauvin.

Presently, Bruenor and Regis settled themselves off to sleep, angry still, but secure enough in the safety of the camp to succumb to their weariness. Wulfgar moved to join the drow.

"We shall find Mithril Hall," he offered in comfort, though he knew that Drizzt's lament did not concern their current objective.

Drizzt nodded, but did not reply.

"Their rejection hurt you," Wulfgar observed. "I thought that you had accepted your fate willingly. Why is this time so different?"

Again the drow made no move to answer.

Wulfgar respected his privacy. "Take heart, Drizzt Do'Urden, noble ranger and trusted friend. Have faith that those who know you would die willingly for you or beside you." He put a hand on Drizzt's shoulder as he turned to leave.

Drizzt said nothing, though he truly appreciated Wulfgar's concern. Their friendship had gone far beyond the need for spoken thanks, though, and Wulfgar only hoped that he had given his friend some comfort as he returned to the camp, leaving Drizzt to his thoughts.

The stars came out and found the drow still standing alone beside the Rauvin. Drizzt had made himself vulnerable for the first time since his initial days on the surface, and the disappointment he now felt triggered the same doubts that he had believed resolved years ago, before he had ever left Menzoberranzan, the city of the black elves. How could he ever hope to find any normalcy in the daylight world of the fair-skinned elves? In Ten-Towns, where murderers and thieves often rose to positions of respect and leadership, he was barely tolerated. In Longsaddle, where prejudice was secondary to the fanatical curiosity of the unsinkable Harpells, he had been placed on display like some mutated farm animal, mentally poked and prodded. And though the wizards meant him no harm, they lacked any compassion or respect for him as anything other than an oddity to be observed.

Now Silverymoon, a city founded and structured on tenets of individuality and fairness, where peoples of all races found welcome if they came in goodwill, had shunned him. All races, it seemed, except for the dark elves.

The inevitability of Drizzt's life as an outcast had never before been so clearly laid out before him. No other city, not even a remote village, in all the Realms could offer him a home, or an existence anywhere but on the fringes of its civilization. The severe limitations of his options, and even moreso, of his future hopes for change, appalled him.

He stood now under the stars, looking up at them with the same profound level of love and awe as any of his surface cousins had ever felt, but sincerely reconsidering his decision to leave the underworld.

Had he gone against a divine plan, crossed the boundaries of some natural order? Perhaps he should have accepted his lot in life and remained in the dark city, among his own kind.

A twinkle in the night sky brought him out of his introspection. A star above him pulsed and grew, already beyond normal proportions. Its light bathed the area around Drizzt in a soft glow, and still the star pulsed.

Then the enchanting light was gone, and standing before Drizzt was a woman, her hair shining silver and her sparkling eyes holding years of experience and wisdom within the luster of eternal youth. She was tall, taller than Drizzt, and straight, wearing a gown of the finest silk and a high crown of gold and gems.

She looked upon him with sincere sympathy, as if she could read his every thought and understood completely the jumble of emotions that he himself had yet to sort through.

"Peace, Drizzt Do'Urden," she said in a voice that

chimed like sweet music. "I am Alustriel, High Lady of Silverymoon."

Drizzt studied her more closely, though her manner and beauty left him no doubts as to her claim. "You know of me?" he asked.

"Many by now have heard of the Companions of the Hall, for that is the name Harkle Harpell has put upon your troupe. A dwarf in search of his ancient home is not so rare in the Realms, but a drow elf walking beside him certainly catches the notice of all those he passes."

She swallowed hard and looked deeply into his lavender eyes. "It was I who denied you passage into the city," she admitted.

"Then why come to me now?" Drizzt asked, more in curiosity than in anger, unable to reconcile that act of rejection with the person who now stood before him. Alustriel's fairness and tolerance were well known throughout the northland, though Drizzt had begun to wonder how exaggerated the stories must be after his encounter at the guard post. But now that he saw the high lady, wearing her honest compassion openly, he could not disbelieve the tales.

"I felt I must explain," she replied.

"You need not justify your decision."

"But I must," said Alustriel. "For myself and my home as much as for you. The rejection has hurt you more than you admit." She moved closer to him.

"It pained me as well," she said softly.

"Then why?" Drizzt demanded, his anger slipping through his calm facade. "If you know of me, then you know as well that I carry no threat to your people."

She ran her cool hand across his cheek. "Perceptions," she explained. "There are elements at work in the north that make perceptions vital at this time, sometimes even overruling what is just. A sacrifice has been forced upon you."

"A sacrifice that has become all too familiar to me."

"I know," Alustriel whispered. "We learned from

Nesme that you had been turned away, a scenario that you commonly face."

"I expect it," Drizzt said coldly.

"But not here," Alustriel retorted. "You did not expect it from Silverymoon, nor should you have."

Her sensitivity touched Drizzt. His anger died away as he awaited her explanation, certain now that the woman had good cause for her actions.

"There are many forces at work here that do not concern you, and should not," she began. "Threats of war and secret alliances; rumors and suspicions that have no basis in fact, nor would make any sense to reasonable people. I am no great friend to the merchants, though they freely pass through Silverymoon. They fear our ideas and ideals as a threat to their structures of power, as well they should. They are very powerful, and would see Silverymoon more akin to their own views.

"But enough of this talk. As I said, it does not concern you. All that I ask you to understand is that, as leader of my city, I am forced at times to act for the overall good, whatever the cost to an individual."

"You fear the lies and suspicions that might befall you if a black elf walks freely in Silverymoon?" Drizzt sighed incredulously. "Simply allowing a drow to walk among your people would implicate you in some devious alliance with the underworld?"

"You are not just any drow elf," Alustriel explained. "You are Drizzt Do'Urden, a name that is destined to be heard throughout the Realms. For now, though, you are a drow who is fast becoming visible to the northern rulers, and, initially at least, they will not understand that you have forsaken your people.

"And this tale gets more complicated, it seems," Alustriel continued. "Know you that I have two sisters?"

Drizzt shook his head.

"Storm, a bard of reknown, and Dove Falconhand, a ranger. Both have taken an interest in the name of Drizzt Do'Urden—Storm as a growing legend in need of proper song, and Dove . . . I have yet to discern her motives. You have become a hero to her, I think, the epitome of those qualities that she, as a fellow ranger, strives to perfect. She came into the city just this morn, and knew of your impending arrival.

"Dove is many years younger than I," Alustriel went on. "And not so wise in the politics of the world."

"She might have sought me out," Drizzt reasoned, seeing the implications that Alustriel feared.

"She will, eventually," the lady answered. "But I cannot allow it now, not in Silverymoon." Alustriel stared at him intently, her gaze hinting at deeper and more personal emotions. "And moreso, I myself would have sought audience with you, as I do now."

The implications of such a meeting within the city seemed obvious to Drizzt in light of the political struggles that Alustriel had hinted at. "Another time, another place perhaps," he queried. "Would it bother you so much?"

She replied with a smile. "Not at all."

Satisfaction and trepidation descended upon Drizzt all at once. He looked back to the stars, wondering if he would ever completely discover the truth about his decision to come to the surface world, or if his life would forever remain a tumult of dangled hope and shattered expectations.

They stood in silence for several moments before Alustriel spoke again.

"You came for the Vault of Sages," she said, "to discover if anything in there spoke of Mithril Hall."

"I urged the dwarf to go in," Drizzt answered. "But he is a stubborn one."

"I assumed as much," laughed Alustriel. "But I did not want my actions to interfere with your most noble quest. I have perused the vault myself. You cannot imagine its size! You would not have known where to begin your search of the thousands of volumes that line the walls. But I know the vault as well as anyone alive. I have learned things that would have taken you and your friends weeks to find. But truthfully, very little has been written about Mithril Hall, and nothing at all that gives more than a passing hint about the general area where it lies."

"Then perhaps we are the better for being turned away."

Alustriel blushed in embarrassment, though Drizzt meant no sarcasm in his observation. "My guards have informed me that you plan to move on to Sundabar," the lady said.

"True," answered Drizzt, "and from there to Citadel Adbar if need be."

"I advise you against this course," said Alustriel. "From everything that I could find in the vault, and from my own knowledge of the legends of the days when treasures flowed from Mithril Hall, my guess is that it lies in the west, not the east."

"We have come from the west, and our trail, seeking those with knowledge of the silvery halls, has led us continually eastward," Drizzt countered. "Beyond Silverymoon, the only hopes we have are Helm and Harbromm, both in the east."

"Helm may have something to tell you," Alustriel agreed. "But you will learn little from King Harbromm and the dwarves of Adbar. They themselves undertook the quest to find the ancient homeland of Bruenor's kin just a few years ago, and they passed through Silverymoon on their journey—heading west. But they never found the place, and returned home convinced that it was either destroyed and buried deep in some unmarked mountain, or that it had never existed and was simply the ruse of southern merchants dealing their goods in the northland."

"You do not offer much hope," Drizzt remarked.

"But I do," Alustriel countered. "To the west of here, less than a day's march, along an unmarked path running north from the Rauvin, lies the Herald's Holdfast, an ancient bastion of accumulated knowledge. The herald,

Old Night, can guide you, if anyone can in this day. I have informed him of your coming and he has agreed to sit with you, though he has not entertained visitors for decades, other than myself and a few select scholars."

"We are in your debt," said Drizzt, bowing low.

"Do not hope for too much," Alustriel warned. "Mithril Hall came and went in the knowledge of this world in the flash of an eye. Barely three generations of dwarves ever mined the place, though I grant you that a dwarven generation is a considerable amount of time, and they were not so open with their trade. Only rarely did they allow anyone to their mines, if the tales are true. They brought out their works in the dark of night and fed them through a secret and intricate chain of dwarven agents to be brought to market."

"They protected themselves well from the greed of the outside world," Drizzt observed.

"But their demise came from within the mines," said Alustriel. "An unknown danger that may lurk there still, you are aware."

Drizzt nodded.

"And still you choose to go?"

"I care not for the treasures, though if they are indeed as splendid as Bruenor describes, then I would wish to look upon them. But this is the dwarf's search, his great adventure, and I would be a sorry friend indeed if I did not help him to see it through."

"Hardly could that label be mantled upon your neck, Drizzt Do'Urden," Alustriel said. She pulled a small vial from a fold in her gown. "Take this with you," she instructed.

"What is it?"

"A potion of remembrance," Alustriel explained. "Give it to the dwarf when the answers to your search seem near at hand. But beware, its powers are strong! Bruenor will walk for a time in the memories of his distant past as well as the experiences of his present.

"And these," she said, producing a small pouch from

the same fold and handing it to Drizzt, "are for all of you. Unguent to help wounds to heal, and biscuits that refresh a weary traveler."

"My thanks and the thanks of my friends," said Drizzt.

"In light of the terrible injustice that I have forced upon you, they are little recompense."

"But the concern of their giver was no small gift," Drizzt replied. He looked straight into her eyes, holding her with his intensity. "You have renewed my hope, Lady of Silverymoon. You have reminded me that there is indeed reward for those who follow the path of conscience, a treasure far greater than the material baubles that too often come to unjust men."

"There is, indeed," she agreed. "And your future will show you many more, proud ranger. But now the night is half gone and you must rest. Fear not, for you are watched this night. Farewell, Drizzt Do'Urden, and may the road before you be swift and clear."

With a wave of her hand, she faded into the starlight, leaving Drizzt to wonder if he had dreamed the whole encounter. But then her final words drifted down to him on the gentle breeze. "Farewell, and keep heart, Drizzt Do'Urden. Your honor and courage do not go unnoticed!"

Drizzt stood silently for a long while. He bent low and picked a wildflower from the riverbank, rolling it over between his fingers and wondering if he and the Lady of Silverymoon might indeed meet again on more accommodating terms. And where such a meeting might lead.

Then he tossed the flower into the Rauvin.

"Let events take their own course," he said resolutely, looking back to the camp and his closest friends. "I need no fantasies to belittle the great treasures that I already possess." He took a deep breath to blow away the remnants of his self-pity.

And with his faith restored, the stoic ranger went to sleep.

☙ 15 ❧

The Golem's Eyes

Drizzt had little trouble convincing Bruenor to reverse their course and head back to the west. While the dwarf was anxious to get to Sundabar and find out what Helm might know, the possibility of valuable information less than a day away set him off and running.

As to how he had come by the information, Drizzt offered little explanation, saying only that he had met up with a lone traveler on the road to Silverymoon during the night. Though the story sounded contrived to them, his friends, respecting his privacy and trusting him fully, did not question him about it. When they ate breakfast, though, Regis hoped that more information would be forthcoming, for the biscuits that this traveler had given to Drizzt were truly delicious and incredibly refreshing. After only a few bites, the halfling felt as if he had spent a week at rest. And the magic salve immediately healed Wulfgar's injured leg and back, and he walked without a cane for the first time since they had left the Evermoors.

Wulfgar suspected that Drizzt's encounter had involved someone of great importance long before the drow revealed the marvelous gifts. For the drow's inner glow of optimism, the knowing sparkle in his eyes that reflected the indomitable spirit that had kept him going through trials that would have crushed most men, had returned, fully and dramatically. The barbarian didn't need to know the identity of the person; he was just glad that his friend had come through the depression.

When they moved out later that morning, they seemed

more a party just beginning an adventure than a road-weary band. Whistling and talking, they followed the flow of the Rauvin on its westerly course. For all of the close calls, they had come through the brutal march relatively unscathed and, it appeared, had made good progress toward their goal. The summer sun shone down upon them and all the pieces of the puzzle of Mithril Hall seemed to be within their grasp.

They could not have guessed that murderous eyes were upon them.

From the foothills north of the Rauvin, high above the travelers, the golem sensed the drow elf's passing. Following the tug of magic spells of seeking that Dendybar had bestowed upon it, Bok soon looked down upon the band as they moved across the trail. Without hesitation the monster obeyed its directives and started out to find Sydney.

Bok tossed aside a boulder that lay in its path, then climbed over another that was too big to move, not understanding the advantages of simply walking around the stones. Bok's path was clearly set and the monster refused to deviate from that course by an inch.

"He is a big one!" chuckled one of the guards at the post on the Rauvin when he saw Bok across the clearing. Even as the words left his mouth, though, the guard realized the impending danger—that this was no ordinary traveler!

Courageously, he rushed out to meet the golem head-on, his sword drawn and his companion close behind.

Transfixed by his goal, Bok paid no heed to their warnings.

"Hold where you are!" the soldier commanded one final time as Bok covered the last few feet between them.

The golem did not know emotion, so it bore no anger toward the guards as they struck. They stood to block the way, though, and Bok swatted them aside without a second thought, the incredible force of its magically strong arms blasting through their parrying defenses and launching them through the air. Without even a pause, the golem continued on to the river and did not slow, disappearing under the rushing waters.

Alarms rang out in the city, for the soldiers at the gate across the river saw the spectacle at the guard post. The huge gates were drawn tight and secured as the Knights of Silver watched the Rauvin for the reappearance of the monster.

Bok kept its line straight across the bottom of the river, plowing through the silt and mud and easily holding its course against the mighty push of the currents. When the monster re-emerged directly across from the guard post, the knights lining the city gate gasped in disbelief but held their stations, grim-faced and weapons ready.

The gate was farther up the Rauvin from the angle of Bok's chosen path. The golem continued on to the city wall, but didn't alter its course to bring it to the gate.

It punched a hole in the wall and walked right through.

Entreri paced anxiously in his room at the Inn of the Wayward Sages, near the center of the city. "They should have come by now," he snapped at Sydney, sitting on the bed and tightening the bonds that held Catti-brie.

Before Sydney could respond, a ball of flame appeared in the center of the room, not a real fire, but the image of flames, illusionary, like something burning in that particular spot on another plane. The fires writhed and transformed into the apparition of a robed man.

"Morkai!" Sydney gasped.

"My greetings," replied the specter. "And the greetings of Dendybar the Mottled."

Entreri slipped back into the corner of the room, wary of the thing. Catti-brie, helpless in her bonds, sat very still.

Sydney, versed in the subtleties of conjuring, knew that the otherworldly being was under Dendybar's control, and she was not afraid. "Why has my master bid you to come here?" she asked boldly.

"I bear news," replied the specter. "The party you seek was turned into the Evermoors a week ago, to the south of Nesme."

Sydney bit her lip in anticipation of the specter's next revelation, but Morkai fell silent and waited as well.

"And where are they now?" Sydney pressed impatiently.

Morkai smiled. "Twice I have been asked, but not yet compelled!" The flames puffed again and the specter was gone.

"The Evermoors," said Entreri. "That would explain their delay."

Sydney nodded her agreement absently, for she had other things on her mind. "Not yet compelled," she whispered to herself, echoing the specter's parting words. Disturbing questions nagged at her. Why had Dendybar waited a week to send Morkai with the news? And why couldn't the wizard have forced the specter to reveal more recent activity of the drow's party? Sydney knew the dangers and limitations of summoning, and understood the tremendous drain of the act on a wizard's power. Dendybar had conjured Morkai at least three times recently—once when the drow's party had first entered Luskan, and at least twice since she and her companions had set out in pursuit. Had Dendybar abandoned all caution in his obsession with the Crystal Shard? Sydney sensed that the mottled wizard's hold over Morkai had lessened greatly, and she hoped that Dendybar would be prudent with any future summonings, at least until he had fully rested.

"Weeks could pass before they arrive!" Entreri spat, considering the news. "If ever they do."

"You may be right," agreed Sydney. "They might have fallen in the moors."

"And if they have?"

"Then we go in after them," Sydney said without hesitation.

Entreri studied her for a few moments. "The prize you

seek must be great indeed," he said.

"I have my duty, and I shall not fail my master," she replied sharply. "Bok will find them even if they lay at the bottom of the deepest bog!"

"We must decide our course soon," Entreri insisted. He turned his evil glare on Catti-brie. "I grow weary of watching this one."

"Nor do I trust her," Sydney agreed. "Although she shall prove useful when we meet with the dwarf. Three more days we will wait. After that we go back to Nesme, and into the Evermoors if we must."

Entreri nodded his reluctant approval of the plan. "Did you hear?" he hissed at Catti-brie. "You have three more days to live, unless your friends arrive. If they are dead in the moors, we have no need of you."

Catti-brie showed no emotion throughout the entire conversation, determined not to let Entreri gain any advantage by learning of her weakness, or strength. She had faith that her friends were not dead. The likes of Bruenor Battlehammer and Drizzt Do'Urden were not destined to die in an unmarked grave in some desolate fen. And Catti-brie would never accept that Wulfgar was dead until the proof was irrefutable. Holding to her faith, her duty to her friends was to maintain a blank facade. She knew that she was winning her personal battle, that the paralyzing fear Entreri held over her lessened every day. She would be ready to act when the time came. She just had to make certain that Entreri and Sydney didn't realize it.

She had noted that the labors of the road, and his new companions, were affecting the assassin. Entreri revealed more emotion, more desperation, every day to get this job over and done. Was it possible that he might make a mistake?

"It has come!" echoed a cry from the hallway, and all three started reflexively, then recognized the voice as Jierdan's, who had been watching the Vault of Sages. A second later, the door burst in and the soldier scrambled into the room, his breathing ragged.

"The dwarf?" Sydney asked, grabbing Jierdan to steady him.

"No!" Jierdan cried. "The golem! Bok has entered Silverymoon! They have it trapped down by the west gate. A wizard was summoned."

"Damn!" Sydney spat and she started from the room. Entreri moved to follow her, grabbing Jierdan's arm and yanking him around, bringing them face to face.

"Stay with the girl," the assassin ordered.

Jierdan glared at him. "She is your problem."

Entreri easily could have killed the soldier right there, Catti-brie noted, hoping that Jierdan had read the assassin's deadly look as clearly as she.

"Do as you are told!" Sydney screamed at Jierdan, ending further argument. She and Entreri left, the assassin slamming the door behind them.

"He would have killed you," Catti-brie told Jierdan when Entreri and Sydney had gone. "You know that."

"Silence," Jierdan growled. "I've had enough of your vile words!" He approached her threateningly, fists clenched at his sides.

"Strike me, then," Catti-brie challenged, knowing that even if he did, his code as a soldier would not allow him to continue such an assault on a helpless foe. "Although in truth I be yer only friend on this cursed road!"

Jierdan stopped his advance. "Friend?" he balked.

"As close as ye'll find out here," Catti-brie replied. "Ye're a prisoner here suren as I be." She recognized the vulnerability of this proud man, who had been reduced to servitude by the arrogance of Sydney and Entreri, and drove her point home hard. "They mean to kill ye, ye know that now, and even if ye escape the blade, ye'll have nowhere to go. Ye've abandoned yer fellows in Luskan, and the wizard in the tower'd put ye to a bad end if ye ever went back there, anyway!"

Jierdan tensed in frustrated rage, but did not lash out.

"Me friends are close by," Catti-brie continued despite

the warning signs. "They be living still, I know, and we'll be meeting them any day. That'll be our time, soldier, to live or to die. For meself, I see a chance. Whether me friends win or I be bargained over, me life'll be me own. But for yerself, the road looks dark indeed! If me friends win, they'll cut ye down, and if yer mates win . . . " She let the grim possibilities hang unspoken for a few moments to let Jierdan weigh them fully.

"When they get what they seek, they'll need ye no more," she said grimly. She noted his trembling, not of fear, but of rage, and pushed him past the edge of control. "They may let ye live," she said, snidely. "Might that they be needin' a lackey!"

He did strike her then, just once, and recoiled.

Catti-brie accepted the blow without complaint, even smiling through the pain, though she was careful to hide her satisfaction. Jierdan's loss of self-restraint proved to her that the continual disrespect Sydney, and especially Entreri, had shown for him had fueled the flames of discontent to the verge of explosion.

She knew, too, that when Entreri returned and saw the bruise Jierdan had given her, those fires would burn even brighter.

Sydney and Entreri rushed through the streets of Silverymoon, following the obvious sounds of commotion. When they reached the wall, they found Bok encapsulated in a sphere of glowing green lights. Riderless horses paced about to the groans of a dozen injured soldiers, and one old man, the wizard, stood before the globe of light, scratching his beard and studying the trapped golem. A Knight of Silver of considerable rank stood impatiently beside him, twitching nervously and clasping the pommel of his sheathed sword tightly.

"Destroy the thing and be done with it," Sydney heard the knight say to the wizard.

"Oh, no!" exclaimed the wizard. "But it is marvelous!"

"Do you mean to hold it here forever?" the knight

snapped back. "Just look around—"

"Your pardon, good sirs," Sydney interrupted. "I am Sydney, of the Hosttower of the Arcane in Luskan. Perhaps I may be of some help."

"Well met," said the wizard. "I am Mizzen of the Second School of Knowledge. Know you the possessor of this magnificent creature?"

"Bok is mine," she admitted.

The knight stared at her, amazed that a woman, or anyone for that matter, controlled the monster that had knocked aside some of his finest warriors and taken down a section of the city wall. "The price shall be high, Sydney of Luskan," he snarled.

"The Hosttower shall make amends," she agreed. "Now would you release the golem to my control?" she asked the wizard. "Bok will obey me."

"Nay!" snapped the knight. "I'll not have the thing turned loose again."

"Calm, Gavin," Mizzen said to him. He turned to Sydney. "I should like to study the golem, if I may. Truly the finest construction I have ever witnessed, with strength beyond the expectations of the books of creation."

"I am sorry," Sydney answered, "but my time is short. I have many roads yet to travel. Name the price of the damage wrought by the golem and I shall relay it to my master, on my word as a member of the Hosttower."

"You'll pay now," argued the guard.

Again Mizzen silenced him. "Excuse Gavin's anger," he said to Sydney. He surveyed the area. "Perhaps we might strike a bargain. None seem to have been seriously injured."

"Three men have been carried away!" Gavin rebutted. "And at least one horse is lame and will have to be destroyed!"

Mizzen waved his hand as if to belittle the claims. "They will heal," he said. "They will heal. And the wall needed repairs anyway." He looked at Sydney and scratched his beard again. "Here is my offer, and a fairer one you'll not hear! Give me the golem for one night, just one, and I shall amend the damage it has wreaked. Just one night."

"And you'll not disassemble Bok," Sydney stated.

"Not even the head?" Mizzen begged.

"Not even the head," Sydney insisted. "And I shall come for the golem at the first light of dawn."

Mizzen scratched his beard again. "A marvellous work," he mumbled, peering into the magical prison. "Agreed!"

"If that monster—" Gavin began angrily.

"Oh, where is your sense of adventure, Gavin?" Mizzen shot back before the knight could even finish his warning. "Remember the precepts of our town, man. We are here to learn. If you only understood the potential of such a creation!"

They started away from Sydney, paying her no more mind, the wizard still rambling into Gavin's ear. Entreri slipped from the shadows of a nearby building to Sydney's side.

"Why did the thing come?" he asked her.

She shook her head. "There can be only one answer."

"The drow?"

"Yes," she said. "Bok must have followed them into the city."

"Unlikely," reasoned Entreri, "though the golem might have seen them. If Bok came crashing through behind the drow and his valiant friends, they would have been down here at the battle, helping to fend it off."

"Then they might be out there still."

"Or perhaps they were leaving the city when Bok saw them," said Entreri. "I will make inquiries with the guards at the gate. Fear not, our prey is close at hand!"

They arrived back at the room a couple of hours later. From the guards at the gate they had learned of the drow's party being turned away and now they were anxious to retrieve Bok and be on their way.

Sydney started a string of instructions to Jierdan concerning their departure in the morning, but what grabbed Entreri's immediate attention was Catti-brie's bruised eye. He moved over to check her bonds and, satisfied that they were intact, spun on Jierdan with his dagger drawn.

Sydney, quickly surmising the situation, cut him off. "Not now!" she demanded. "Our rewards are at hand. We cannot afford this!"

Entreri chuckled evilly and slid the dagger away. "We will yet discuss this," he promised Jierdan with a snarl. "Do not touch the girl again."

Perfect, Catti-brie thought. From Jierdan's perspective, the assassin might as well have said outright that he meant to kill him.

More fuel for the flames.

When she retrieved the golem from Mizzen the next morning, Sydney's suspicions that Bok had seen the drow's party were confirmed. They set out from Silverymoon at once, Bok leading them down the same trail Bruenor and his friends had taken the morning before.

Like the previous party, they, too, were watched.

Alustriel brushed her flowing hair from her fair face, catching the morning sun in her green eyes as she looked down upon the band with growing curiosity. The lady had learned from the gatekeepers that someone had been inquiring about the dark elf.

She couldn't yet figure out what part this new group leaving Silverymoon played in the quest, but she suspected that they were up to no good. Alustriel had sated her own thirst for adventure many years before, but she wished now that she could somehow aid the drow and his friends on their noble mission. Affairs of state pressed in on her, though, and she had no time for such diversions. She considered for a moment dispatching a patrol to capture this second party, so that she could learn its intentions.

Then she turned back to her city, reminding herself that she was just a minor player in the search for Mithril Hall. She could only trust in the abilities of Drizzt Do'Urden and his friends.

❧ BOOK 3: ❧
Trails Anew

❧ 16 ❧

Days of Old

A squat stone tower stood in a small dell against the facing of a steep hill. Because it was ivy covered and overgrown, a casual passer-by would not even have noticed the structure.

But the Companions of the Hall were not casual in their search. This was the Herald's Holdfast, possibly the solution to their entire search.

"Are you certain that this is the place?" Regis asked Drizzt as they peered over a small bluff. Truly the ancient tower appeared more a ruin. Not a thing stirred anywhere nearby, not even animals, as though an eerie, reverent hush surrounded the place.

"I am sure," Drizzt replied. "Feel the age of the tower. It has stood for many centuries. Many centuries."

"And how long has it been empty?" Bruenor asked, thus far disappointed in the place that had been described to him as the brightest promise to his goal.

"It is not empty," Drizzt replied. "Unless the information I received was in err."

Bruenor jumped to his feet and stormed over the bluff. "Probably right," he grumbled. "Some troll or scab yeti's inside the door watching us right now, I'll wager, drooling for us to come in! Let's be on with it, then! Sundabar's a day more away than when we left!"

The dwarf's three friends joined him on the remnants of the overgrown path that had once been a walkway to the tower's door. They approached the ancient stone door cautiously, with weapons drawn.

Moss-covered and worn to a smooth finish by the toll of time, apparently it hadn't been opened in many, many years.

"Use yer arms, boy," Bruenor told Wulfgar. "If any man can get this thing opened, it's yerself!"

Wulfgar leaned Aegis-fang against the wall and moved before the huge door. He set his feet as best he could and ran his hands across the stone in search of a good niche to push against.

But as soon as he applied the slightest pressure to the stone portal, it swung inward, silently and without effort.

A cool breeze wafted out of the still darkness within, carrying a blend of unfamiliar scents and an aura of great age. The friends sensed the place as otherworldly, belonging to a different time, perhaps, and it was not without a degree of trepidation that Drizzt led them in.

They stepped lightly, though their footfalls echoed in the quiet darkness. The daylight beyond the door offered little relief, as though some barrier remained between the inside of the tower and the world beyond.

"We should light a torch—" Regis began, but he stopped abruptly, frightened by the unintentional volume of his whisper.

"The door!" Wulfgar cried suddenly, noticing that the silent portal had begun to close behind them. He leaped to grab it before it shut completely, sinking them into absolute darkness, but even his great strength could not deny the magical force that moved it. It shut without a bang, just a hushed rush of air that resounded like a giant's sigh.

The lightless tomb they all envisioned as the huge door blocked out the final slit of sunlight did not come to pass, for as soon as the door closed, a blue glow lit up the room, the entrance hall to the Herald's Holdfast.

No words could they speak above the profound awe that enveloped them. They stood in view of the history of the race of Man within a bubble of timelessness that denied their own perspectives of age and belonging. In the blink of an eye they had been propelled into the position of removed observers, their own existence suspended in a different time and place, looking in on the passing of the human race as might a god. Intricate tapestries, their once-vivid colors faded and their distinct lines now blurred, swept the friends into a fantastic collage of images that displayed the tales of the race, each one retelling a story again and again; the same tale, it seemed, but subtly altered each time, to present different principles and varied outcomes.

Weapons and armor from every age lined the walls, beneath the standards and crests of a thousand long-forgotten kingdoms. Bas-relief images of heroes and sages, some familiar but most unknown to any but the most studious of scholars, stared down at them from the rafters, their captured visages precise enough to emote the very character of the men they portrayed.

A second door, this one of wood, hung directly across the cylindrical chamber from the first, apparently leading into the hill behind the tower. Only when it began to swing open did the companions manage to break free of the spell of the place.

None went for their weapons, though, understanding that whoever, or whatever, inhabited this tower would be beyond such earthly strength.

An ancient man stepped into the room, older than anyone they had ever seen before. His face had retained its fullness, not hollowed with age, but his skin appeared almost wooden in texture, with lines that seemed more like cracks and a rough edge that defied time as stubbornly as an ancient tree. His walk was more a flow of quiet movement, a floating passing that transcended the definition of steps. He came in close to the friends and waited, his arms, obviously thin even under the folds of his long, satiny robe, peacefully dropped to his sides.

"Are you the herald of the tower?" Drizzt asked.

"Old Night, I am," the man replied in a voice singing

with serenity. "Welcome, Companions of the Hall. The Lady Alustriel informed me of your coming, and of your quest."

Even consumed in the solemn respect of his surroundings, Wulfgar did not miss the reference to Alustriel. He glanced over at Drizzt, meeting the drow's eyes with a knowing smile.

Drizzt turned away and smiled, too.

"This is the Chamber of Man," Old Night proclaimed. "The largest in the Holdfast, except for the library, of course."

He noticed Bruenor's disgruntled scowl. "The tradition of your race runs deep, good dwarf, and deeper yet does the elves'," he explained. "But crises in history are more often measured in generations than in centuries. The short-lived humans might have toppled a thousand kingdoms and built a thousand more in the few centuries that a single dwarven king would rule his people in peace."

"No patience!" Bruenor huffed, apparently appeased.

"Agreed," laughed Old Night. "But come now, let us dine. We have much to do this night."

He led them through the doorway and down a similarly lit hallway. Doors on either side of them identified the various chambers as they passed—one for each of the goodly races, and even a few for the history of orcs and goblins and the giantkind.

The friends and Old Night supped at a huge, round table, its ancient wood as hard as mountain stone. Runes were inscribed all around its edge, many in tongues long lost to the world, that even Old Night could not remember. The food, like everything else, gave the impression of a distant past. Far from stale, though, it was delicious, with a flavor somewhat different from anything the friends had ever eaten before. The drink, a crystalline wine, possessed a rich bouquet surpassing even the legendary elixirs of the elves.

Old Night entertained them as they ate, retelling grand

tales of ancient heroes, and of events that had shaped the Realms into their present state. The companions were an attentive audience, though in all probability substantial clues about Mithril Hall loomed only a door or two away.

When the meal was finished, Old Night rose from his chair and looked around at them with a weird, curious intensity. "The day will come, a millennium from now, perhaps, when I shall entertain again. On that day, I am sure, one of the tales I tell will concern the Companions of the Hall and their glorious quest."

The friends could not reply to the honor that the ancient man had paid them. Even Drizzt, even-keeled and unshakable, sat unblinking for a long, long moment.

"Come," Old Night instructed, "let your road begin anew." He led them through another door, the door to the greatest library in all the North.

Volumes thick and thin covered the walls and lay about in high piles on the many tables positioned throughout the large room. Old Night indicated one particular table, a smaller one off to the side, with a solitary book opened upon it.

"I have done much of your research for you," Old Night explained. "And in all the volumes concerning dwarves, this was the only one I could find that held any reference to Mithril Hall."

Bruenor moved to the book, grasping its edges with trembling hands. It was written in High Dwarven, the language of Dumathoin, Keeper of Secrets Under the Mountain, a script nearly lost in the Realms. But Bruenor could read it. He surveyed the page quickly, then read aloud the passages of concern.

" 'King Elmor and his people profited mightily from the labors of Garumn and the kin of Clan Battlehammer, but the dwarves of the secret mines did not refute Elmor's gains. Settlestone proved a valuable and trustworthy ally whence Garumn could begin the secret trail to market of the mithril works.' " Bruenor looked up at his friends, a gleam of revelation in his eye.

"Settlestone," he whispered. "I know that name." He dove back into the book.

"You shall find little else," Old Night said. "For the words of Mithril Hall are lost to the ages. The book merely states that the flow of mithril soon ceased, to the ultimate demise of Settlestone."

Bruenor wasn't listening. He had to read it for himself, to devour every word penned about his lost heritage, no matter the significance.

"What of this Settlestone?" Wulfgar asked Old Night. "A clue?"

"Perhaps," the old herald replied. "Thus far I have found no reference to the place other than this book, but I am inclined to believe from the work that Settlestone was rather unusual for a dwarven town."

"Above the ground!" Bruenor suddenly cut in.

"Yes," agreed Old Night. "A dwarven community housed in structures above the ground. Rare these days and unheard of back in the time of Mithril Hall. Only two possibilities, to my knowledge."

Regis let out a cry of victory.

"Your enthusiasm may be premature," remarked Old Night. "Even if we discern where Settlestone once lay, the trail to Mithril Hall merely begins there."

Bruenor flipped through a few pages of the book, then replaced it on the table. "So close!" he growled, slamming his fist down on the petrified wood. "And I should know!"

Drizzt moved over to him and pulled a vial out from under his cloak. "A potion," he explained to Bruenor's puzzled look, "that will make you walk again in the days of Mithril Hall."

"A mighty spell," warned Old Night. "And not to be controlled. Consider its use carefully, good dwarf."

Bruenor was already moving, teetering on the verge of a discovery he had to find. He quaffed the liquid in one gulp, then steadied himself on the edge of the table against its potent kick. Sweat beaded on his wrinkled brow and he twitched involuntarily as the potion sent his mind drifting back across the centuries.

Regis and Wulfgar moved over to him, the big man clasping his shoulders and easing him into a seat.

Bruenor's eyes were wide open, but he saw nothing in the room before him. Sweat lathered him now, and the twitch had become a tremble.

"Bruenor," Drizzt called softly, wondering if he had done right in presenting the dwarf with such a tempting opportunity.

"No, me father!" Bruenor screamed. "Not here in the darkness! Come with me, then. What might I do without ye?"

"Bruenor," Drizzt called more emphatically.

"He is not here," Old Night explained, familiar with the potion, for it was often used by long-lived races, particularly elves, when they sought memories of their distant past. Normally the imbibers returned to a more pleasant time, though. Old Night looked on with grave concern, for the potion had returned Bruenor to a wicked day in his past, a memory that his mind had blocked out, or at least blurred, to defend him against powerful emotions. Those emotions would now be laid bare, revealed to the dwarf's conscious mind in all their fury.

"Bring him to the Chamber of the Dwarves," Old Night instructed. Let him bask in the images of his heroes. They will aid in remembering, and give him strength throughout his ordeal."

Wulfgar lifted Bruenor and bore him gently down the passage to the Chamber of the Dwarves, laying him in the center of the circular floor. The friends backed away, leaving the dwarf to his delusions.

Bruenor could only half-see the images around him now, caught between the worlds of the past and present. Images of Moradin, Dumathoin, and all his deities and heroes looked down upon him from their perches in the rafters, adding a small bit of comfort against the waves of tragedy. Dwarven-sized suits of armor and cunningly crafted axes and warhammers surrounded him, and he bathed in the presence of the highest glories of his proud race.

The images, though, could not dispell the horror he now knew again, the falling of his clan, of Mithril Hall, of his father.

"Daylight!" he cried, torn between relief and lament. "Alas for me father, and me father's father! But yea, our escape is at hand! Settlestone . . ." he faded from consciousness for a moment, overcome, " . . . shelter us. The loss, the loss! Shelter us!"

"The price is high," said Wulfgar, pained at the dwarf's torment.

"He is willing to pay," Drizzt replied.

"It will be a sorry payment if we learn nothing," said Regis. "There is no direction to his ramblings. Are we to sit by and hope against hope?"

"His memories have already brought him to Settlestone, with no mention of the trail behind him," Wulfgar observed.

Drizzt drew a scimitar and pulled the cowl of his cloak low over his face.

"What?" Regis started to ask, but the drow was already moving. He rushed to Bruenor's side and put his face close to the dwarf's sweat-lathered cheek.

"I am a friend," he whispered to Bruenor. "Come at the news of the falling of the hall! My allies await! Vengeance will be ours, mighty dwarf of Clan Battlehammer! Show us the way so that we might restore the glories of the hall!"

"Secret," Bruenor gasped, on the edge of consciousness.

Drizzt pressed harder. "Time is short! The darkness is falling!" he shouted. "The way, dwarf, we must know the way!"

Bruenor mumbled some inaudible sounds and all the friends gasped in the knowledge that the drow had broken through the final mental barrier that hindered

Bruenor from finding the hall.

"Louder!" Drizzt insisted.

"Fourthpeak!" Bruenor screamed back. "Up the high run and into Keeper's Dale!"

Drizzt looked over to Old Night, who was nodding in recognition, then turned back to Bruenor. "Rest, mighty dwarf," he said comfortingly. "Your clan shall be avenged!"

"With the description the book gives of Settlestone, Fourthpeak can describe only one place," Old Night explained to Drizzt and Wulfgar when they got back to the library. Regis remained in the Chamber of the Dwarves to watch over Bruenor's fretful sleep.

The herald pulled a scroll tube down from a high shelf and unrolled the ancient parchment it held: a map of the central northland, between Silverymoon and Mirabar.

"The only dwarven settlement in the time of Mithril Hall above ground, and close enough to a mountain range to give a reference to a numbered peak, would be here," he said, marking the southernmost peak on the southernmost spur of the Spine of the World, just north of Nesme and the Evermoors. "The deserted city of stone is simply called "the Ruins" now, and it was commonly known as Dwarvendarrows when the bearded race lived there. But the ramblings of your companion have convinced me that this is indeed the Settlestone that the book speaks of."

"Why, then, would the book not refer to it as Dwarvendarrow?" asked Wulfgar.

"Dwarves are a secretive race," Old Night explained with a knowing chuckle, "especially where treasure is concerned. Garumn of Mithril Hall was determined to keep the location of his trove hidden from the greed of the outside world. He and Elmor of Settlestone no doubt worked out an arrangement that included intricate codes and constructed names to reference their sur-roundings. Anything to throw prying mercenaries off the trail. Names that now appear in disjointed places throughout the tomes of dwarven history. Many scholars have probably even read of Mithril Hall, called by some other name that the readers assumed referred to another of the many ancient dwarven homelands now lost to the world."

The herald paused for a moment to digest everything that had occurred. "You should be away at once," he advised. "Carry the dwarf if you must, but get him to Settlestone before the effects of the potion wear away. Walking in his memories, Bruenor might be able to retrace his steps of two hundred years ago back up the mountains to Keeper's Dale, and to the gate of Mithril Hall."

Drizzt studied the map and the spot that Old Night had marked as the location of Settlestone. "Back to the west," he muttered, echoing Alustriel's suspicions. "Barely two days march from here."

Wulfgar moved in close to view the parchment and added, in a voice that held both anticipation and a measure of sadness, "Our road nears its end."

❧ 17 ❧

The Challenge

They left under stars and did not stop until stars filled the sky once again. Bruenor needed no support. Quite the opposite. It was the dwarf, recovered from his delirium and his eyes focused at last upon a tangible path to his long-sought goal, who drove them, setting the strongest pace since they had come out of Icewind Dale. Glassy-eyed and walking both in past and present, Bruenor's obsession consumed him. For nearly two hundred years he had dreamed of this return, and these last few days on the road seemed longer than the centuries that had come before.

The companions had apparently beaten their worst enemy: time. If their reckoning at the Holdfast was correct, Mithril Hall loomed just a few days away, while the short summer had barely passed its midpoint. With time no longer a pressing issue, Drizzt, Wulfgar, and Regis had anticipated a moderate pace as they prepared to leave the Holdfast. But Bruenor, when he awoke and learned of the discoveries, would hear no arguments about his rush. None were offered, though, for in the excitement, Bruenor's already surly disposition had grown even fouler.

"Keep yer feet moving!" he kept snapping at Regis, whose little legs could not match the dwarf's frantic pace. "Ye should've stayed in Ten-Towns with yer belly hanging over yer belt!" The dwarf would then sink into quiet grumbling, bending even lower over his pumping feet, and driving onward, his ears blocked to any remarks that Regis might shoot back or any comments forthcoming from Wulfgar or Drizzt concerning his behavior.

They angled their path back to the Rauvin, to use its waters as a guide. Drizzt did manage to convince Bruenor to veer back to the northwest as soon as the peaks of the mountain range came into view. The drow had no desire to meet any patrols from Nesme again, certain that it was that city's warning cries that had forced Alustriel to keep him out of Silverymoon.

Bruenor found no relaxation at the camp that night, even though they had obviously covered far more than half the distance to the ruins of Settlestone. He stomped about the camp like a trapped animal, clenching and unclenching his gnarly fists and mumbling to himself about the fateful day when his people had been pushed out of Mithril Hall, and the revenge he would find when he at last returned.

"Is it the potion?" Wulfgar asked Drizzt later that evening as they stood to the side of the camp and watched the dwarf.

"Some of it, perhaps," Drizzt answered, equally concerned about his friend. "The potion has forced Bruenor to live again the most painful experience of his long life. And now, as the memories of that past find their way into his emotions, they keenly edge the vengeance that has festered within him all these years."

"He is afraid," Wulfgar noted.

Drizzt nodded. "This is the trial of his life. His vow to return to Mithril Hall holds within it all the value that he places upon his own existence."

"He pushes too hard," Wulfgar remarked, looking at Regis, who had collapsed, exhausted, right after they had supped. "The halfling cannot keep the pace."

"Less than a day stands before us," Drizzt replied. "Regis will survive this road, as shall we all." He patted the barbarian on the shoulder and Wulfgar, not fully satisfied, but resigned to the fact that he could not sway the dwarf, moved away to find some rest. Drizzt looked back to the pacing dwarf, and his dark face bore a look of deeper concern than he had revealed to the young barbarian.

Drizzt truly wasn't worried about Regis. The halfling always found a way to come through better off than he should. Bruenor, though, troubled the drow. He remembered when the dwarf had crafted Aegis-fang, the mighty warhammer. The weapon had been Bruenor's ultimate creation in a rich career as a craftsman, a weapon worthy of legend. Bruenor could not hope to outdo that accomplishment, nor even equal it. The dwarf had never put hammer to anvil again.

Now the journey to Mithril Hall, Bruenor's lifelong goal. As Aegis-fang had been Bruenor's finest crafting, this journey would be his highest climb. The focus of Drizzt's concern was more subtle, and yet more dangerous, than the success or failure of the search; the dangers of the road affected all of them equally, and they had accepted them willingly before starting out. Whether or not the ancient halls were reclaimed, Bruenor's mountain would be crested. The moment of his glory would be passed.

"Calm yourself, good friend," Drizzt said, moving beside the dwarf.

"It's me home, elf!" Bruenor shot back, but he did seem to compose himself a bit.

"I understand," Drizzt offered. "It seems that we shall indeed look upon Mithril Hall, and that raises a question we must soon answer."

Bruenor looked at him curiously, though he knew well enough what Drizzt was getting at.

"So far we have concerned ourselves only with finding Mithril Hall, and little has been said of our plans beyond the entrance to the place."

"By all that is right, I am King of the Hall," Bruenor growled.

"Agreed," said the drow, "but what of the darkness that

may remain? A force that drove your entire clan from the mines. Are we four to defeat it?"

"It may have gone on its own, elf," Bruenor replied in a surly tone, not wanting to face the possibilities. "For all our knowing, the halls may be clean."

"Perhaps. But what plans have you if the darkness remains?"

Bruenor paused for a moment of thought. "Word'll be sent to Icewind Dale," he answered. "Me kin'll be with us in the spring."

"Barely a hundred strong," Drizzt reminded him.

"Then I'll call to Adbar if more be needed!" Bruenor snapped. "Harbromm'll be glad to help, for a promise of treasure."

Drizzt knew that Bruenor wouldn't be so quick to make such a promise, but he decided to end the stream of disturbing but necessary questions. "Sleep well," he bid the dwarf. "You shall find your answers when you must."

The pace was no less frantic the morning of the next day. Mountains soon towered above them as they ran along, and another change came over the dwarf. He stopped suddenly, dizzied and fighting for his balance. Wulfgar and Drizzt were right beside him, propping him up.

"What is it?" Drizzt asked.

"Dwarvendarrow," Bruenor answered in a voice that seemed far removed. He pointed to an outcropping of rock jutting from the base of the nearest mountain.

"You know the place?"

Bruenor didn't answer. He started off again, stumbling, but rejecting any offers of help. His friends shrugged helplessly and followed.

An hour later, the structures came into view. Like giant houses of cards, great slabs of stone had been cunningly laid together to form dwellings, and though they had been deserted for more than a hundred years, the seasons and the wind had not reclaimed them. Only dwarves could have imbued such strength into the rock, could have laid the stones so perfectly that they would last as the mountains themselves lasted, beyond the generations and the tales of the bards, so that some future race would look upon them in awe and marvel at their construction without the slightest idea of who had created them.

Bruenor remembered. He wandered into the village as he had those many decades ago, a tear rimming his gray eye and his body trembling against the memories of the darkness that had swarmed over his clan.

His friends let him go about for a while, not wanting to interrupt the solemn emotions that had found their way through his thick hide. Finally, as afternoon waned, Drizzt moved over to him.

"Do you know the way?" he asked.

Bruenor looked up at a pass that climbed along the side of the nearest mountain. "Half a day," he replied.

"Camp here?" Drizzt asked.

"It would do me good," said Bruenor. "I've much to think over, elf. I'll not forget the way, fear not." His eyes narrowed in tight focus at the trail he had fled on the day of darkness, and he whispered, "I'll never forget the way again."

*   *   *   *   *

Bruenor's driven pace proved fortunate for the friends, for Bok had easily continued along the drow's trail outside of Silverymoon and had led its group with similar haste. Bypassing the Holdfast altogether—the tower's magical wards would not have let them near it in any case—the golem's party had made up considerable ground.

In a camp not far away, Entreri stood grinning his evil smile and staring at the dark horizon, and at the speck of light he knew to be the campfire of his victim.

Catti-brie saw it, too, and knew that the next day

would bring her greatest challenge. She had spent most of her life with the battle-seasoned dwarves, under the tutelage of Bruenor himself. He had taught her both discipline and confidence. Not a facade of cockiness to hide deeper insecurities, but a true self-belief and measured evaluation of what she could and could not accomplish. Any trouble that she had finding sleep that night was more due to her eagerness to face this challenge than her fear of failure.

They broke camp early and arrived at the ruins just after dawn. No more anxious than Bruenor's party, though, they found only the remnants of the companions' campsite.

"An hour—perhaps two," Entreri observed, bending low to feel the heat of the embers.

"Bok has already found the new trail," said Sydney, pointing to the golem moving off toward the foothills of the closest mountain.

A smile filled Entreri's face as the thrill of the chase swept over him. Catti-brie paid little attention to the assassin, though, more concerned with the revelations painted on Jierdan's face.

The soldier seemed unsure of himself. He took up after them as soon as Sydney and Entreri started behind Bok, but with forced steps. He obviously wasn't looking forward to the pending confrontation, as were Sydney and Entreri.

Catti-brie was pleased.

They charged ahead through the morning, dodging sharp ravines and boulders, and picking their way up the side of the mountains. Then, for the first time since he had begun his search more than two years before, Entreri saw his prey.

The assassin had come over a boulder-strewn mound and was slowing his strides to accommodate a sharp dip into a small dell thick with trees, when Bruenor and his friends broke clear of some brush and made their way across the facing of a steep slope far ahead. Entreri dropped into a crouch and signaled for the others to slow behind him.

"Stop the golem," he called to Sydney, for Bok had already disappeared into the copse below him and would soon come crashing out of the other side and onto another barren mound of stone, in clear sight of the companions.

Sydney rushed up. "Bok, return to me!" she yelled as loudly as she dared, for while the companions were far in the distance, the echoes of noises on the mountainside seemed to carry forever.

Entreri pointed to the specks moving across the facing ahead of them. "We can catch them before they get around the side of the mountain," he told Sydney. He jumped back to meet Jierdan and Catti-brie, and roughly bound Catti-brie's hands behind her back. "If you cry out, you will watch your friends die," he assured her. "And then your own end will be most unpleasant."

Catti-brie painted her most frightened look across her face, all the while pleased that the assassin's latest threat seemed quite hollow to her. She had risen above the level of terror that Entreri had played against her when they had first met back in Ten-Towns. She had convinced herself, against her instinctive revulsion of the passionless killer, that he was, after all, only a man.

Entreri pointed to the steep valley below the facing and the companions. "I will go through the ravine," he explained to Sydney, "and make the first contact. You and the golem continue along the path and close in from behind."

"And what of me?" Jierdan protested.

"Stay with the girl!" Entreri commanded, as absently as if he was speaking to a servant. He spun away and started off, refusing to hear any arguments.

Sydney did not even turn to look at Jierdan as she stood waiting for Bok's return. She had no time for such squabbles and figured that if Jierdan could not speak for himself, he wasn't worth her trouble.

"Act now," Catti-brie whispered to Jierdan, "for yerself and not for me!" He looked at her, more curious than angry, and vulnerable to any suggestions that might help him from this uncomfortable position.

"The mage has thrown all respect for ye, man," Catti-brie continued. "The assassin has replaced ye, and she'd be liken to stand by him above ye. This is yer chance to act, yer last one if me eyes be tellin' me right! Time to show the mage yer worth, Soldier of Luskan!"

Jierdan glanced about nervously. For all of the manipulations he expected from the woman, her words held enough truth to convince him that her assessment was correct.

His pride won over. He spun on Catti-brie and smacked her to the ground, then rushed past Sydney in pursuit of Entreri.

"Where are you going?" Sydney called after him, but Jierdan was no longer interested in pointless talk.

Surprised and confused, Sydney turned to check on the prisoner. Catti-brie had anticipated this and she groaned and rolled on the hard stone as though she had been knocked senseless, though in truth she had turned enough away from Jierdan's blow that he had merely glanced her. Fully conscious and coherent, her movements were calculated to position her where she could slip her tied hands down around her legs and bring them up in front of her.

Catti-brie's act satisfied Sydney enough so that the mage put her attention fully on the coming confrontation between her two comrades. Hearing Jierdan's approach, Entreri had spun on him, his dagger and saber drawn.

"You were told to stay with the girl!" he hissed.

"I did not come on this journey to play guard to your prisoner!" Jierdan retorted, his own sword out.

The characteristic grin made its way onto Entreri's face again. "Go back," he said one last time to Jierdan, though he knew, and was glad, that the proud soldier would not turn away.

Jierdan took another step forward.

Entreri struck.

Jierdan was a seasoned fighter, a veteran of many skirmishes, and if Entreri expected to dispatch him with a single thrust, he was mistaken. Jierdan's sword knocked the blow aside and he returned the thrust.

Recognizing the obvious contempt that Entreri showed to Jierdan, and knowing the level of the soldier's pride, Sydney had feared this confrontation since they had left the Hosttower. She didn't care if one of them died now—she suspected that it would be Jierdan—but she would not tolerate anything that put her mission in jeopardy. After the drow was safely in her hands, Entreri and Jierdan could settle their differences.

"Go to them!" she called to the advancing golem. "Stop this fight!" Bok turned at once and rushed toward the combatants, and Sydney, shaking her head in disgust, believed that the situation would soon be under control and they could resume their hunt.

What she didn't see was Catti-brie rising up behind her.

Catti-brie knew that she had only one chance. She crept up silently and brought her clasped hands down on the back of the mage's neck. Sydney dropped straight to the hard stone and Catti-brie ran by, down into the copse of trees, her blood coursing through her veins. She had to get close enough to her friends to yell a clear warning before her captors overtook her.

Just after Catti-brie slipped into the thick trees, she heard Sydney gasp, "Bok!"

The golem swung back at once, some distance behind Catti-brie, but gaining with each long stride.

Even if they had seen her flight, Jierdan and Entreri were too caught up in their own battle to be concerned with her.

"You shall insult me no more!" Jierdan cried above the clang of steel.

"But I shall!" Entreri hissed. "There are many ways to

defile a corpse, fool, and know that I shall practice every one on your rotting bones." He pressed in harder, his concentration squarely on his foe, his blades gaining deadly momentum in their dance.

Jierdan countered gamely, but the skilled assassin had little trouble in meeting all of his thrusts with deft parries and subtle shifts. Soon the soldier had exhausted his repertoire of feints and strikes, and he hadn't even come close to hitting his mark. He would tire before Entreri—he saw that clearly even this early in the fight.

They exchanged several more blows, Entreri's cuts moving faster and faster, while Jierdan's double-handed swings slowed to a crawl. The soldier had hoped that Sydney would intervene by this point. His weakness of stamina had been clearly revealed to Entreri, and he couldn't understand why the mage had not said anything about the battle. He glanced about, his desperation growing. Then he saw Sydney, lying face down on the stone.

An honorable way out, he thought, still more concerned with himself. "The mage!" he cried to Entreri. "We must help her!" The words fell upon deaf ears.

"And the girl!" Jierdan yelled, hoping to catch the assassin's interest. He tried to break free of the combat, jumping back from Entreri and lowering his sword. "We shall continue this later," he declared in a threatening tone, though he had no intention of engaging the assassin in a fair fight again.

Entreri didn't answer, but lowered his blades accordingly. Jierdan, ever the honorable soldier, turned about to see to Sydney.

A jeweled dagger whistled into his back.

Catti-brie stumbled along, unable to hold her balance with her hands bound together. Loose stone slipped beneath her and more than once she tumbled to the ground. As agile as a cat, she was up quickly.

But Bok was the swifter.

Catti-brie fell again and rolled over a sharp crest of

stone. She started down a dangerous slope of slippery rocks, heard the golem stomping behind her, and knew that she could not possibly outrun the thing. Yet she had no choice. Sweat burned a dozen scrapes and stung her eyes, and all hope had flown from her. Still she ran, her courage denying the obvious end.

Against her despair and terror, she found the strength to search for an option. The slope continued down another twenty feet, and right beside her was the slender and rotting stump of a long-dead tree. A plan came to her then, desperate, but with enough hope for her to try it. She stopped for a moment to survey the root structure of the rotting stump, and to estimate the effect that uprooting the thing might have on the stones.

She backed a few feet up the slope and waited, crouched for her impossible leap. Bok came over the crest and bore down on her, rocks bouncing away from the heavy plodding of its booted feet. It was right behind her, reaching out with horrid arms.

And Catti-brie leaped.

She hooked the rope that bound her hands over the stump as she flew past, throwing all of her weight against the hold of its roots.

Bok lumbered after her, oblivious to her intentions. Even as the stump toppled, and the network of dead roots pulled up from the ground, the golem couldn't understand the danger. As the loose stones shifted and began their descent, Bok kept its focus straight ahead on its prey.

Catti-brie bounced down ahead and to the side of the rockslide. She didn't try to rise, just kept rolling and scrambling in spite of the pain to gain every inch between herself and the crumbling slope. Her determination got her to the thick trunk of an oak, and she rolled around behind it and turned back to look at the slope.

Just in time to see the golem go down under a ton of bouncing stone.

❧ 18 ❧

The Secret of
Keeper's Dale

"Keeper's Dale," Bruenor declared solemnly. The companions stood on a high ledge, looking down hundreds of feet to the broken floor of a deep and rocky gorge.

"How are we to get down there?" Regis gasped, for every side appeared absolutely sheer, as though the canyon had been purposely cut from the stone.

There was a way down, of course, and Bruenor, walking still with the memories of his youth, knew it well. He led his friends around to the eastern rim of the gorge and looked back to the west, to the peaks of the three nearest mountains. "Ye stand upon Fourthpeak," he explained, "named for its place beside th'other three.

"Three peaks to seem as one," the dwarf recited, an ancient line from a longer song that all the young dwarves of Mithril Hall were taught before they were even old enough to venture out of the mines.

> "Three peaks to seem as one,
> Behind ye the morning sun."

Bruenor shifted about to find the exact line of the three western mountains, then moved slowly to the very edge of the gorge and looked over. "We have come to the entrance of the dale," he stated calmly, though his heart was pounding at the discovery.

The other three moved up to join him. Just below the rim they saw a carved step, the first in a long line moving down the face of the cliff, and shaded perfectly by the coloration of the stone to make the entire construction virtually invisible from any other angle.

Regis swooned when he looked over, nearly over-whelmed by the thought of descending hundreds of feet on a narrow stair without even a handhold. "We'll surely fall to our deaths!" he squeaked and backed away.

But again Bruenor wasn't asking for opinions or argu-ments. He started down, and Drizzt and Wulfgar moved to follow, leaving Regis with no choice but to go. Drizzt and Wulfgar sympathized with his distress, though, and they helped him as much as they could, Wulfgar even scooping him up in his arms when the wind began to gust.

The descent was tentative and slow, even with Bruenor in the lead, and it seemed like hours before the stone of the canyon floor had moved any closer to them.

"Five hundred to the left, then a hundred more," Bruenor sang when they finally got to the bottom. The dwarf moved along the wall to the south, counting his measured paces and leading the others past towering pil-lars of stone, great monoliths of another age that had seemed as mere piles of fallen rubble from the rim. Even Bruenor, whose kin had lived here for many centuries, did not know any tales that spoke of the monoliths' crea-tion or purpose. But whatever the reason, they had stood a silent and imposing vigil upon the canyon floor for uncounted centuries, ancient before the dwarves even arrived, casting ominous shadows and belittling mere mortals who had ever walked here.

And the pillars bent the wind into an eerie and mourn-ful cry and gave the entire floor the sensation of some-thing beyond the natural, timeless like the Holdfast, and imposing a realization of mortality upon onlookers, as though the monoliths mocked the living with their age-less existence.

Bruenor, unbothered by the towers, finished his count.

> "Five hundred to the left, then a hundred more,
> The hidden lines of the secret door."

He studied the wall beside him for any marking that would indicate the entrance to the halls.

Drizzt, too, ran his sensitive hands across the smooth stone. "Are you certain?" he asked the dwarf after long minutes of searching, for he had felt no cracks at all.

"I am!" Bruenor declared. "Me people were cunning with their workings and I fear that the door is too well in hiding for an easy find."

Regis moved in to help, while Wulfgar, uncomfortable beneath the shadows of the monoliths, stood guard at their backs.

Just a few seconds later, the barbarian noticed movement from where they'd come, back over by the stone stair. He dipped into a defensive crouch, clutching Aegis-fang as tightly as ever before. "Visitors," he said to his friends, the hiss of his whisper echoing around as though the monoliths were laughing at his attempt at secrecy.

Drizzt sprang out to the nearest pillar and started making his way around, using Wulfgar's frozen squint as a guide. Angered at the interruption, Bruenor pulled a small hatchet from his belt and stood ready beside the barbarian, and Regis behind them.

Then they heard Drizzt call out, "Catti-brie!" and were too relieved and elated to pause and consider what might have possibly brought their friend all the way from Ten-Towns, or how she had ever found them.

Their smiles disappeared when they saw her, bruised and bloodied and stumbling toward them. They rushed to meet her, but the drow, suspecting that someone might be in pursuit, slipped along through the monoliths and took up a lookout.

"What bringed ye?" Bruenor cried, grabbing Catti-brie and hugging her close. "And who was it hurt ye? He'll feel me hands on his neck!"

"And my hammer!" Wulfgar added, enraged at the thought of someone striking Catti-brie.

Regis hung back now, beginning to suspect what had

happened.

"Fender Mallot and Grollo are dead," Catti-brie told Bruenor.

"On the road with ye? But why?" asked the dwarf.

"No, back in Ten-Towns," Catti-brie answered. "A man, a killer, was there, looking for Regis. I chased after him, trying to get to ye to warn ye, but he caught me and dragged me along."

Bruenor spun a glare upon the halfling, who was even farther back now, and hanging his head.

"I knew ye'd found trouble when ye came running up on the road outside the towns!" He scowled. "What is it, then? And no more of yer lying tales!"

"His name is Entreri," Regis admitted. "Artemis Entreri. He came from Calimport, from Pasha Pook." Regis pulled out the ruby pendant. "For this."

"But he is not alone," Catti-brie added. "Wizards from Luskan search for Drizzt."

"For what reason?" Drizzt called from the shadows.

Catti-brie shrugged. "They been taking care not to tell, but me guess is that they seek some answers about Akar Kessell."

Drizzt understood at once. They sought the Crystal Shard, the powerful relic that had been buried beneath the avalanche on Kelvin's Cairn.

"How many?" asked Wulfgar. "And how far behind."

"Three they were," Catti-brie answered. "The assassin, a mage, and a soldier from Luskan. A monster they had with them. A golem, they called it, but I've ne'er seen its likes before."

"Golem," Drizzt echoed softly. He had seen many such creations in the undercity of the dark elves. Monsters of great power and undying loyalty to their creators. These must be mighty foes indeed, to have one along.

"But the thing is gone," Catti-brie continued. "It chased me on me flight, and would have had me, no doubting, but I pulled a trick on it and sent a mountain of rock on its head!"

Bruenor hugged her close again. "Well done, me girl," he whispered.

"And I left the soldier and the assassin in a terrible fight," Catti-brie went on. "One is dead, I guess, and the soldier seems most likely. A pity, it is, for he was a decent sort."

"He'd have found me blade for helping the dogs at all!" Bruenor retorted. "But enough of the tale; there'll be time for telling. Ye're at the hall, girl, do ye know? Ye're to see for yerself the splendors I been telling ye about all these years! So go and rest up." He turned around to tell Wulfgar to see to her, but noticed Regis instead. The half-ling had problems of his own, hanging his head and wondering if he had pushed his friends too far this time.

"Fear not, my friend," said Wulfgar, also seeing Regis's distress. "You acted to survive. There is no shame in that. Though you should have told us the danger!"

"Ah, put yer head up, Rumblebelly!" Bruenor snapped. "We expect as much from ye, ye no-good trickster! Don't ye be thinkin' we're surprised!" Bruenor's rage, an angry possessor somehow growing of its own volition, suddenly mounted as he stood there chastising the halfling.

"How dare ye to put this on us?" he roared at Regis, moving Catti-brie aside and advancing a step. "And with me home right before me!"

Wulfgar was quick to block Bruenor's path to Regis, though he was truly amazed at the sudden shift in the dwarf. He had never seen Bruenor so consumed by emotion. Catti-brie, too, looked on, stunned.

"'Twas not the halfling's fault," she said. "And the wizards would've come anyway!"

Drizzt returned to them then. "No one has made the stair yet," he said, but when he took a better notice of the situation, he realized that his words had not been heard.

A long and uncomfortable silence descended upon them, then Wulfgar took command. "We have come too far along this road to argue and fight among ourselves!" he scolded Bruenor.

Bruenor looked at him blankly, not knowing how to react to the uncharacteristic stand Wulfgar had taken against him. "Bah!" the dwarf said finally, throwing up his hands in frustration. "The fool halfling'll get us killed . . . but not to worry!" he grumbled sarcastically, moving back to the wall to search for the door.

Drizzt looked curiously at the surly dwarf, but was more concerned with Regis at this point. The halfling, thoroughly miserable, had dropped to a sitting position and seemed to have lost all desire to go on. "Take heart," Drizzt said to him. "Bruenor's anger will pass. The essence of his dreams stands before him."

"And about this assassin who seeks your head," Wulfgar said, moving to join the two. "He shall find a mighty welcome when he gets here, if ever he does." Wulfgar patted the head of his warhammer. "Perhaps we can change his mind about this hunt!"

"If we can get into the mines, our trail might be lost to them," Drizzt said to Bruenor, trying to further soothe the dwarf's anger.

"They'll not make the stair," said Catti-brie. "Even watching your climb down, I had trouble finding it!"

"I would rather stand against them now!" Wulfgar declared. "They have much to explain, and they'll not escape my punishment for the way they have treated Catti-brie!"

"Ware the assassin," Catti-brie warned him. "His blades mean death, and no mistaking!"

"And a wizard can be a terrible foe," added Drizzt. "We have a more important task before us—we do not need to take on fights that we can avoid."

"No delays!" said Bruenor, ending any rebuttals from the big barbarian. "Mithril Hall stands before me, and I'm meaning to go in! Let them follow, if they dare." He turned back to the wall to resume his search for the door, calling for Drizzt to join him. "Keep the watch, boy," he ordered Wulfgar. "And see to me girl."

"A word of opening, perhaps?" Drizzt asked when he

stood alone again with Bruenor before the featureless wall.

"Aye," said Bruenor, "there be a word. But the magic that holds to it leaves it after a while, and a new word must be named. None were here to name it!"

"Try the old word, then."

"I have, elf, a dozen times when we first came here." He banged his fist on the stone. "Another way there be, I know," he growled in frustration.

"You will remember," Drizzt assured him. And they set back to inspecting the wall.

Even the stubborn determination of a dwarf does not always pay off, and the night fell and found the friends sitting outside the entrance in the darkness, not daring to light a fire for fear of alerting their pursuers. Of all their trials on the road, the waiting so very close to their goal was possibly the most trying. Bruenor began to second-guess himself, wondering if this was even the correct place for the door. He recited the song he had learned as a child in Mithril Hall over and over, searching for some clues he might have missed.

The others slept uneasily, especially Catti-brie, who knew that the silent death of an assassin's blade stalked them. They would not have slept at all, except that they knew that the keen, ever vigilant eyes of a drow elf watched over them.

* * * * *

A few miles down the trail behind them, a similar camp had been set. Entreri stood quietly, peering to the trails of the eastern mountains for signs of a campfire, though he doubted that the friends would be so careless as to light one if Catti-brie had found and warned them. Behind him, Sydney lay wrapped in a blanket upon the cool stone, resting and recovering from the blow Catti-brie had struck her.

The assassin had considered leaving her—normally he would have without a second thought—but Entreri needed to take some time anyway to regroup his thoughts and figure out his best course of action.

Dawn came and found him standing there still, unmoving and contemplative. Behind him, the mage awoke.

"Jierdan?" she called, dazed. Entreri stepped back and crouched over her.

"Where is Jierdan?" she asked.

"Dead," Entreri answered, no hint of remorse in his voice. "As is the golem."

"Bok?" Sydney gasped.

"A mountain fell on him," Entreri replied.

"And the girl?"

"Gone." Entreri looked back to the east. "When I have seen to your needs, I will go," he said. "Our chase is ended."

"They are close," Sydney argued. "You will give up your hunt?"

Entreri grinned. "The halfling will be mine," he said evenly, and Sydney had no doubt that he spoke the truth. "But our party is disbanded. I will return to my own hunt, and you to yours, though I warn you, if you take what is mine, you will mark yourself as my next prey."

Sydney considered the words carefully. "Where did Bok fall?" she asked on a sudden thought.

Entreri looked along the trail to the east. "In a vale beyond the copse."

"Take me there," Sydney insisted. "There is something that must be done."

Entreri helped her to her feet and led her along the path, figuring that he would part with her when she had put her final business to rest. He had come to respect this young mage and her dedication to her duty, and he trusted that she would not cross him. Sydney was no wizard, and no match for him, and they both knew that his respect for her would not slow his blade if she got in his way.

Sydney surveyed the rocky slope for a moment, then turned on Entreri, a knowing smile upon her face. "You say that our quest together is ended, but you are wrong. We may prove of value to you still, assassin."

"We?"

Sydney turned to the slope. "Bok!" she called loudly and kept her gaze upon the slope.

A puzzled look crossed Entreri's face. He, too, studied the stones, but saw no sign of movement.

"Bok!" Sydney called again, and this time there was indeed a stir. A rumble grew beneath the layer of boulders, and then one shifted and rose into the air, the golem standing beneath it, stretching into the air. Battered and twisted, but apparently feeling no pain, Bok tossed the huge stone aside and moved toward its master.

"A golem is not so easily destroyed," Sydney explained, drawing satisfaction from the amazed expression on Entreri's normally emotionless face. "Bok still has a road to travel, a road it will not so easily forsake."

"A road that will again lead us to the drow," Entreri laughed. "Come, my companion," he said to Sydney, "let us be on with the chase."

* * * * *

The friends still had found no clues when dawn came. Bruenor stood before the wall, shouting a tirade of arcane chants, most of which had nothing to do with words of opening.

Wulfgar took a different approach. Reasoning that a hollow echo would help them ensure that they had come to the correct spot, he moved methodically along with his ear to the wall, tapping with Aegis-fang. The hammer chimed off the solid stone, singing in the perfection of its crafting.

But one blow did not reach its mark. Wulfgar brought the hammer's head in, but just as it reached the stone, it was stopped by a blanket of blue light. Wulfgar jumped back, startled. Creases appeared in the stone, the outline of a door. The rock continued to shift and slide inward, and soon it cleared the wall and slid aside, revealing the entry hall to the dwarven homeland. A gust of air, bottled up within for centuries and carrying the scents of ages past, rushed out upon them.

"A magic weapon!" cried Bruenor. "The only trade me people would accept at the mines!"

"When visitors came here, they entered by tapping the door with a magical weapon?" Drizzt asked.

The dwarf nodded, though his attention was now fixed squarely on the gloom beyond the wall. The chamber directly before them was unlit, except by the daylight shining through the open door, but down a corridor behind the entry hall, they could see the flicker of torches.

"Someone is here," said Regis.

"Not so," replied Bruenor, many of his long-forgotten images of Mithril Hall flooding back to him. "The torches ever burn, for the life of a dwarf and more." He stepped through the portal, kicking dust that had settled untouched for two hundred years.

His friends gave him a moment alone, then solemnly joined him. All around the chamber lay the remains of many dwarves. A battle had been fought here, the final battle of Bruenor's clan before they were expelled from their home.

"By me own eyes, the tales be true," the dwarf muttered. He turned to his friends to explain. "The rumors that came down to Settlestone after me and the younger dwarves arrived there told of a great battle at the entry hall. Some went back to see what truth the rumors held, but they never returned to us."

Bruenor broke off, and on his lead, the companions moved about to inspect the place. Dwarven-sized skeletons lay about in the same poses and places where they had fallen. Mithril armor, dulled by the dust but not rusted, and shining again with the brush of a hand, clearly marked the dead of Clan Battlehammer. Intertwined with those dead were other, similar skeletons in strange-

y crafted mail, as though the fighting had pitted dwarf
against dwarf. It was a riddle beyond the surface-
dwellers' experience, but Drizzt Do'Urden understood.
In the city of the dark elves, he had known the Duergar,
the malicious gray dwarves, as allies. Duergar were the
dwarven equivalent of the drow, and because their surface cousins sometimes delved deep into the earth, and
into their claimed territory, the hatred between the
dwarven races was even more intense than the clash
between the races of elves. The Duergar skeletons
explained much to Drizzt, and to Bruenor, who also recognized the strange armor, and who for the first time
understood what had driven his kin out of Mithril Hall.
If the gray ones were in the mines still, Drizzt knew,
Bruenor would be hard-pressed to reclaim the place.

The magical door slid shut behind them, dimming the
chamber even further. Catti-brie and Wulfgar moved
close together for security, their eyes weak in the dimness, but Regis darted about, searching for the gems and
other treasures that a dwarven skeleton might possess.

Bruenor had also seen something of interest. He
moved over to two skeletons lying back to back. A pile of
gray dwarves had fallen around them, and that alone
told Bruenor who these two were, even before he saw
the foaming mug crest upon their shields.

Drizzt moved behind him, but kept a respectable distance.

"Bangor, me father," Bruenor explained. "And Garumn,
me father's father, King of Mithril Hall. Suren they took
their toll before they fell!"

"As mighty as their next in line," Drizzt remarked.

Bruenor accepted the compliment silently and bent to
dust the dirt from Garumn's helm. "Garumn wears still
the armor and weapons of Bruenor, me namesake and
the hero of me clan. Me guess is that they cursed this
place as they died," he said, "for the gray ones did not
return and loot."

Drizzt agreed with the explanation, aware of the

power of the curse of a king when his homeland has fallen.

Reverently, Bruenor lifted Garumn's remains and bore them into a side chamber. Drizzt did not follow, allowing the dwarf his privacy in this moment. Drizzt returned to Catti-brie and Wulfgar to help them comprehend the importance of the scene around them.

They waited patiently for many minutes, imagining the course of the epic battle that had taken place and their minds hearing clearly the sounds of axe on shield and the brave war cries of Clan Battlehammer.

Then Bruenor returned and even the mighty images the friends' minds had concocted fell short of the sight before them. Regis dropped the few baubles he had found in utter amazement, and in fear that a ghost from the past had returned to thwart him.

Cast aside was Bruenor's battered shield. The dented and one-horned helm was strapped on his backpack. He wore the armor of his namesake, shining mithril, the mug standard on the shield of solid gold, and the helm ringed with a thousand glittering gemstones. "By me owns eyes, I proclaim the legends as true," he shouted boldly, lifting the mithril axe high above him. "Garumn is dead and me father, too. Thus I claim me title: Eighth King of Mithril Hall!"

☙ 19 ☙

Shadows

"Garumn's Gorge," Bruenor said, drawing a line across the rough map he had scratched on the floor. Even though the effects of Alustriel's potion had worn off, simply stepping inside the home of his youth had rekindled a host of memories in the dwarf. The exact location of each of the halls was not clear to him, but he had a general idea of the overall design of the place. The others huddled close to him, straining to see the etchings in the flickers of the torch that Wulfgar had retrieved from the corridor.

"We can get out on the far side," Bruenor continued. "There's a door, opening one way and for leaving only, beyond the bridge."

"Leaving?" Wulfgar asked.

"Our goal was to find Mithril Hall," Drizzt answered, playing the same argument he had used on Bruenor before this meeting. "If the forces that defeated Clan Battlehammer reside here still, we few would find reclaiming it an impossible task. We must take care that the knowledge of the hall's location does not die in here with us."

"I'm meaning to find out what we're to face," Bruenor added. "We mighten be going back out the door we came in; it'd open easy from the inside. Me thinking is to cross the top level and see the place out. I'm needing to know how much is left afore I call on me kin in the dale, and others if I must." He shot Drizzt a sarcastic glance.

Drizzt suspected that Bruenor had more in mind than

"seeing the place out," but he kept quiet, satisfied that he had gotten his concerns through to the dwarf, and that Catti-brie's unexpected presence would temper with caution all of Bruenor's decisions.

"You will come back, then," Wulfgar surmised.

"An army at me heels!" snorted Bruenor. He looked at Catti-brie and a measure of his eagerness left his dark eyes.

She read it at once. "Don't ye be holding back for me!" she scolded. "Fought beside ye before, I have, and held me own, too! I didn't want this road, but it found me and now I'm here with ye to the end!"

After the many years of training her, Bruenor could not now disagree with her decision to follow their chosen path. He looked around at the skeletons in the room. "Get yerself armed and armored then, and let's be off—if we're agreed."

"'Tis your road to choose," said Drizzt. "For 'tis your search. We walk beside you, but do not tell you which way to go."

Bruenor smiled at the irony of the statement. He noted a slight glimmer in the drow's eyes, a hint of their customary sparkle for excitement. Perhaps Drizzt's heart for the adventure was not completely gone.

"I will go," said Wulfgar. "I did not walk those many miles, to return when the door was found!"

Regis said nothing. He knew that he was caught up in the whirlpool of their excitement, whatever his own feelings might be. He patted the little pouch of newly acquired baubles on his belt and thought of the additions he might soon find if these halls were truly as splendid as Bruenor had always said. He honestly felt that he would rather walk the nine hells beside his formidable friends than go back outside and face Artemis Entreri alone.

As soon as Catti-brie was outfitted, Bruenor led them on. He marched proudly in his grandfather's shining armor, the mithril axe swinging beside him, and the crown of the king firmly upon his head. "To Garumn's

Gorge!" he cried as they started from the entry chamber. "From there we'll decide to go out, or down. Oh, the glories that lay before us, me friends. Pray that I be taking ye to them this time through!"

Wulfgar marched beside him, Aegis-fang in one hand and the torch in the other. He wore the same grim but eager expression. Catti-brie and Regis followed, less eager and more tentative, but accepting the road as unavoidable and determined to make the best of it.

Drizzt moved along the side, sometimes ahead of them, sometimes behind, rarely seen and never heard, though the comforting knowledge of his presence made them all step easier down the corridor.

The hallways were not smooth and flat, as was usually the case with dwarven construction. Alcoves jutted out on either side every few feet, some ending inches back, others slipping away into the darkness to join up with other whole networks of corridors. The walls all along the way were chipped and flaked with jutting edges and hollowed depressions, designed to enhance the shadowy effect of the ever-burning torches. This was a place of mystery and secret, where dwarves could craft their finest works in an atmosphere of protective seclusion.

This level was a virtual maze, as well. No outsider could have navigated his way through the endless number of splitting forks, intersections, and multiple passageways. Even Bruenor, aided by scattered images of his childhood and an understanding of the logic that had guided the dwarven miners who had created the place, chose wrong more often than right, and spent as much time backtracking as going forward.

There was one thing that Bruenor did remember, though. "Ware yer step," he warned his friends. "The level ye walk upon is rigged for defending the halls, and a stoneworked trap'd be quick to send ye below!"

For the first stretch of their march that day, they came into wider chambers, mostly unadorned and roughly squared, and showing no signs of habitation. "Guard rooms and guest rooms," Bruenor explained. "Most for Elmor and his kin from Settlestone when they came to collect the works for market."

They moved deeper. A pressing stillness engulfed them, their footfalls and the occasional crackle of a torch the only sounds, and even these seemed stifled in the stagnant air. To Drizzt and Bruenor, the environment only enhanced their memories of their younger days spent under the surface, but for the other three, the closeness and the realization of tons of stone hanging over their heads was a completely foreign experience, and more than a little uncomfortable.

Drizzt slipped from alcove to alcove, taking extra care to test the floor before stepping in. In one shallow depression, he felt a sensation on his leg, and upon closer inspection found a slight draft flowing in through a crack at the base of the wall. He called his friends over.

Bruenor bent low and scratched his beard, knowing at once what the breeze meant, for the air was warm, not cool as an outside draft would be. He removed a glove and felt the stone. "The furnaces," he muttered, as much to himself as to his friends.

"Then someone is below," Drizzt reasoned.

Bruenor didn't answer. It was a subtle vibration in the floor, but to a dwarf, so attuned to the stone, its message came as clear as if the floor had spoken to him; the grating of sliding blocks far below, the machinery of the mines.

Bruenor looked away and tried to realign his thoughts, for he had nearly convinced himself, and had always hoped, that the mines would be empty of any organized group and easy for the taking. But if the furnaces were burning, those hopes were flown.

* * * * *

"Go to them. Show them the stair," Dendybar commanded.

Morkai studied the wizard for a long moment. He

knew that he could break free of Dendybar's weakening hold and disobey the command. Truly, Morkai was amazed that Dendybar had dared to summon him again so soon, for the wizard's strength had obviously not yet returned. The mottled wizard hadn't yet reached the point of exhaustion, upon which Morkai could strike at him, but Dendybar had indeed lost most of his power to compel the specter.

Morkai decided to obey this command. He wanted to keep this game with Dendybar going for as long as possible. Dendybar was obsessed with finding the drow, and would undoubtedly call upon Morkai another time soon. Perhaps then the mottled wizard would be weaker still.

"And how are we to get down?" Entreri asked Sydney. Bok had led them to the rim of Keeper's Dale, but now they faced the sheer drop.

Sydney looked to Bok for the answer, and the golem promptly started over the edge. Had she not stopped it, it would have dropped off the cliff. The young mage looked at Entreri with a helpless shrug.

They then saw a shimmering blur of fire, and the specter, Morkai, stood before them once again. "Come," he said to them. "I am bid to show you the way."

Without another word, Morkai led them to the secret stair, then faded back into flames and was gone.

"Your master proves to be of much assistance," Entreri remarked as he took the first step down.

Sydney smiled, masking her fears. "Four times, at least," she whispered to herself, figuring the instances when Dendybar had summoned the specter. Each time Morkai had seemed more relaxed in carrying out his appointed mission. Each time Morkai had seemed more powerful. Sydney moved to the stair behind Entreri. She hoped that Dendybar would not call upon the specter again—for all their sakes.

When they had descended to the gorge's floor, Bok led them right to the wall and the secret door. As if realizing the barrier that it faced, it stood patiently out of the way, awaiting further instructions from the mage.

Entreri ran his fingers across the smooth rock, his face close against it as he tried to discern any substantial crack in it.

"You waste your time," Sydney remarked. "The door is dwarven crafted and will not be found by such inspection."

"If there is a door," replied the assassin.

"There is," Sydney assured him. "Bok followed the drow's trail to this spot, and knows that it continues through the wall. There is no way that they could have diverted the golem from the path."

"Then open your door," Entreri sneered. "They move farther from us with each moment!"

Sydney took a steadying breath and rubbed her hands together nervously. This was the first time since she had left the Hosttower that she had found opportunity to use her magical powers, and the extra spell energy tingled within her, seeking release.

She moved through a string of distinct and precise gestures, mumbled several lines of arcane words, then commanded, "*Bausin saumine!*" and threw her hands out in front of her, toward the door.

Entreri's belt immediately unhitched, dropping his saber and dagger to the ground.

"Well done," he remarked sarcastically, retrieving his weapons.

Sydney looked at the door, perplexed. "It resisted my spell," she said, observing the obvious. "Not unexpected from a door of dwarven crafting. The dwarves use little magic themselves, but their ability to resist the spellcastings of others is considerable."

"Where do we turn?" hissed Entreri. "There is another entrance, perhaps?"

"This is our door," Sydney insisted. She turned to Bok and snarled, "Break it down!" Entreri jumped far aside when the golem moved to the wall.

Its great hands pounding like battering rams, Bok slammed the wall, again and again, heedless of the damage to its own flesh. For many seconds, nothing happened, just the dull thud of the fists punching the stone.

Sydney was patient. She silenced Entreri's attempt to argue their course and watched the relentless golem at work. A crack appeared in the stone, and then another. Bok knew no weariness; its tempo did not slow.

More cracks showed, then the clear outline of the door. Entreri squinted his eyes in anticipation.

With one final punch, Bok drove its hand through the door, splitting it asunder and reducing it to a pile of rubble.

For the second time that day, the second time in nearly two hundred years, the entry chamber of Mithril Hall was bathed in daylight.

* * * * *

"What was that?" Regis whispered after the echoes of the banging had finally ended.

Drizzt could guess easily enough, though with the sound bouncing at them from the bare rock walls in every direction, it was impossible to discern the direction of its source.

Catti-brie had her suspicions, too, remembering well the broken wall in Silverymoon.

None of them said anything more about it. In their situation of ever-present danger, echoes of a potential threat in the distance did not spur them to action. They continued on as though they had heard nothing, except that they walked even more cautiously, and the drow kept himself more to the rear of the party.

Somewhere in the back of his mind, Bruenor sensed danger huddling in around them, watching them, poised to strike. He could not be certain if his fears were justified, or if they were merely a reaction to his knowledge that the mines were occupied and to his rekindled memories of the horrible day when his clan had been driven out.

He forged ahead, for this was his homeland, and he would not surrender it again.

At a jagged section of the passageway, the shadows lengthened into a deeper, shifting gloom.

One of them reached out and grabbed Wulfgar.

A sting of deathly chill shivered into the barbarian. Behind him, Regis screamed, and suddenly moving blots of darkness danced all around the four.

Wulfgar, too stunned to react, was hit again. Catti-brie charged to his side, striking into the blackness with the short sword she had picked up in the entry hall. She felt a slight bite as the blade knifed through the darkness, as though she had hit something that was somehow not completely there. She had no time to ponder the nature of her weird foe, and she kept flailing away.

Across the corridor, Bruenor's attacks were even more desperate. Several black arms stretched out to strike the dwarf at once, and his furious parries could not connect solidly enough to push them away. Again and again he felt the stinging coldness as the darkness grasped him.

Wulfgar's first instinct when he had recovered was to strike with Aegis-fang, but recognizing this, Catti-brie stopped him with a yell. "The torch!" she cried. "Put the light into the darkness!"

Wulfgar thrust the flame into the shadows' midst. Dark shapes recoiled at once, slipping away from the revealing brightness. Wulfgar moved to pursue and drive them even farther away, but he tripped over the halfling, who was huddled in fear, and fell to the stone.

Catti-brie scooped up the torch and waved it wildly to keep the monsters at bay.

Drizzt knew these monsters. Such things were commonplace in the realms of the drow, sometimes even allied with his people. Calling again on the powers of his heritage, he conjured magical flames to outline the dark shapes, then charged in to join the fight.

The monsters appeared humanoid, as the shadows of

men might appear, though their boundaries constantly shifted and melded with the gloom about them. They outnumbered the companions, but their greatest ally, the concealment of darkness, had been stolen by the drow's flames. Without the disguise, the living shadows had little defense against the party's attacks and they quickly slipped away through nearby cracks in the stone.

The companions wasted no more time in the area either. Wulfgar hoisted Regis from the ground and followed Bruenor and Catti-brie as they sped down the passageway, Drizzt lingering behind to cover their retreat.

They had put many turns and halls behind them before Bruenor dared to slow the pace. Disturbing questions again hovered about the dwarf's thoughts, concerns about his entire fantasy of reclaiming Mithril Hall, and even about the wisdom in bringing his dearest friends into the place. He looked at every shadow with dread now, expecting a monster at each turn.

Even more subtle was the emotional shift that the dwarf had experienced. It had been festering within his subconscious since he had felt the vibrations on the floor, and now the fight with the monsters of darkness had pushed it to completion. Bruenor accepted the fact that he no longer felt as though he had returned home, despite his earlier boastings. His memories of the place, good memories of the prosperity of his people in the early days, seemed far removed from the dreadful aura that surrounded the fortress now. So much had been despoiled, not the least of which were the shadows of the ever-burning torches. Once representative of his god, Dumathoin, the Keeper of Secrets, the shadows now merely sheltered the denizens of darkness.

All of Bruenor's companions sensed the disappointment and frustration that he felt. Wulfgar and Drizzt, expecting as much before they had ever entered the place, understood better than the others and were now even more concerned. If, like the crafting of Aegis-fang, the return to Mithril Hall represented a pinnacle in Bruenor's life—and they had worried about his reaction assuming the success of their quest—how crushing would be the blow if the journey proved disastrous?

Bruenor pushed onward, his vision narrowed upon the path to Garumn's Gorge and the exit. On the road these long weeks, and when he had first entered the halls, the dwarf had every intention of staying until he had taken back all that was rightfully his, but now all of his senses cried to him to flee the place and not return.

He felt that he must at least cross the top level, out of respect for his long dead kin, and for his friends, who had risked so much in accompanying him this far. And he hoped that the revulsion he felt for his former home would pass, or at least that he might find some glimmer of light in the dark shroud that encompassed the halls. Feeling the axe and shield of his heroic namesake warm in his grasp, he steeled his bearded chin and moved on.

The passageway sloped down, with fewer halls and side corridors. Hot drafts rose up all through this section, a constant torment to the dwarf, reminding him of what lay below. The shadows were less imposing here, though, for the walls were carved smoother and squared. Around a sharp turn, they came to a great stone door, its singular slab blocking the entire corridor.

"A chamber?" Wulfgar asked, grasping the heavy pull ring.

Bruenor shook his head, not certain of what lay beyond. Wulfgar pulled the door open, revealing another empty stretch of corridor that ended in a similarly unmarked door.

"Ten doors," Bruenor remarked, remembering the place again. "Ten doors on the down slope," he explained. "Each with a locking bar behind it." He reached inside the portal and pulled down a heavy metal rod, hinged on one end so that it could be easily dropped across the locking latches on the door. "And beyond the ten, ten more going up, and each with a bar on th'other side."

"So if ye fled a foe, either way, ye'd lock the doors behind ye," reasoned Catti-brie. "Meeting in the middle with yer kin from the other side."

"And between the center doors, a passage to the lower levels," added Drizzt, seeing the simple but effective logic behind the defensive structure.

"The floor's holding a trap door," Bruenor confirmed.

"A place to rest, perhaps," said the drow.

Bruenor nodded and started on again. His recollections proved accurate, and a few minutes later, they passed through the tenth door and into a small, oval-shaped room, facing a door with the locking bar on their side. In the very center of the room was a trap door, closed for many years, it seemed, and also with a bar to lock it shut. All along the room's perimeter loomed the familiar darkened alcoves.

After a quick search to ensure that the room was safe, they secured the exits and began stripping away some of their heavy gear, for the heat had become oppressive and the stuffiness of the unmoving air weighed in upon them.

"We have come to the center of the top level," Bruenor said absently. "Tomorrow we're to be finding the gorge."

"Then where?" Wulfgar asked, the adventurous spirit within him still hoping for a deeper plunge into the mines.

"Out, or down," Drizzt answered, emphasizing the first choice enough to make the barbarian understand that the second was unlikely. "We shall know when we arrive."

Wulfgar studied his dark friend for some hint of the adventurous spirit he had come to know, but Drizzt seemed nearly as resigned to leaving as Bruenor. Something about this place had diffused the drow's normally unstoppable verve. Wulfgar could only guess that Drizzt, too, battled unpleasant memories of his past in a similarly dark place.

The perceptive young barbarian was correct. The

drow's memories of his life in the underworld had indeed fostered his hopes that they might soon leave Mithril Hall, but not because of any emotional upheaval he was experiencing upon his return to his childhood realm. What Drizzt now remembered keenly about Menzoberranzan were the dark things that lived in dark holes under the earth. He felt their presence here in the ancient dwarven halls, horrors beyond the surface dwellers' imagination. He didn't worry for himself. With his drow heritage, he could face these monsters on their own terms. But his friends, except perhaps the experienced dwarf, would be at a sorry disadvantage in such fighting, ill-equipped to battle the monsters they would surely face if they remained in the mines.

And Drizzt knew that eyes were upon them.

Entreri crept up and put his ear against the door, as he had nine times before. This time, the clang of a shield being dropped to the stone brought a smile to his face. He turned back to Sydney and Bok and nodded.

He had at last caught his prey.

The door they had entered shuddered from the weight of an incredible blow. The companions, just settled in after their long march, looked back in amazement and horror just as the second blow fell and the heavy stone splintered and broke away. The golem crashed into the oval room, kicking Regis and Catti-brie aside before they could even reach for their weapons.

The monster could have squashed both of them right there, but its target, the goal that pulled at all of its senses, was Drizzt Do'Urden. It rushed by the two into the middle of the room to locate the drow.

Drizzt hadn't been so surprised, slipping into the shadows on the side of the room and now making his way toward the broken door to secure it against further entry. He couldn't hide from the magical detections that Dendybar had bestowed upon the golem, though, and

Bok turned toward him almost immediately.

Wulfgar and Bruenor met the monster head on.

Entreri entered the chamber right after Bok, using the commotion caused by the golem to slip unnoticed through the door and off into the shadows in a manner strikingly similar to the drow. As they approached the midpoint of the oval room's wall, each was met by a shadow so akin to his own that he had to stop and take measure of it before he engaged.

"So at last I meet Drizzt Do'Urden," Entreri hissed.

"The advantage is yours," replied Drizzt, "for I know naught of you."

"Ah, but you will, black elf!" the assassin said, laughing. In a blur, they came together, Entreri's cruel saber and jeweled dagger matching the speed of Drizzt's whirring scimitars.

Wulfgar pounded his hammer into the golem with all his might, the monster, distracted by its pursuit of the drow, not even raising a pretense of defense. Aegis-fang knocked it back, but it seemed not to notice, and started again toward its prey. Bruenor and Wulfgar looked at each other in disbelief and drove in on it again, hammer and axe flailing.

Regis lay unmoving against the wall, stunned by the kick of Bok's heavy foot. Catti-brie, though, was back up on one knee, her sword in hand. The spectacle of grace and skill of the combatants along the wall held her in check for a moment.

Sydney, just outside the doorway, was likewise distracted, for the battle between the dark elf and Entreri was unlike anything she had ever seen, two master swordsmen weaving and parrying in absolute harmony.

Each anticipated the other's movements exactly, countering the other's counter, back and forth in a battle that seemed as though it could know no victor. One appeared the reflection of the other, and the only thing that kept the onlookers aware of the reality of the struggle was the constant clang of steel against steel as scimitar and saber came ringing together. They moved in and out of the shadows, seeking some small advantage in a fight of equals. Then they slipped into the darkness of one of the alcoves.

As soon as they disappeared from sight, Sydney remembered her part in the battle. Without further delay, she drew a thin wand from her belt and took aim on the barbarian and the dwarf. As much as she would have liked to see the battle between Entreri and the dark elf played out to its end, her duty told her to free up the golem and let it take the drow quickly.

Wulfgar and Bruenor dropped Bok to the stone, Bruenor ducking between the monster's legs while Wulfgar slammed his hammer home, toppling Bok over the dwarf.

Their advantage was short-lived. Sydney's bolt of energy sliced into them, its force hurling Wulfgar backward into the air. He rolled to his feet near the opposite door, his leather jerkin scorched and smoking, and his entire body tingling in the aftermath of the jolt.

Bruenor was slammed straight down to the floor and he lay there for a long moment. He wasn't too hurt—dwarves are as tough as mountain stone and especially resistant to magic—but a specific rumble that he heard while his ear was against the floor demanded his attention. He remembered that sound vaguely from his childhood, but couldn't pinpoint its exact source.

He did know, though, that it foretold doom.

The tremor grew around them, shaking the chamber, even as Bruenor lifted his head. The dwarf understood. He looked helplessly to Drizzt and yelled, "Ware elf!" the second before the trap sprang and part of the alcove's floor fell away.

Only dust emerged from where the drow and the assassin had been. Time seemed to freeze for Bruenor, who was fixated upon that one horrible moment. A heavy block dropped from the ceiling in the alcove, stealing the very last of the dwarf's futile hopes.

The execution of the stonework trap only multiplied the violent tremors in the chamber. Walls cracked apart, chunks of stone shook loose from the ceiling. From one doorway, Sydney cried for Bok, while at the other, Wulfgar threw the locking bar aside and yelled for his friends.

Catti-brie leaped to her feet and rushed to the fallen halfling. She dragged him by the ankles toward the far door, calling for Bruenor to help.

But the dwarf was lost in the moment, staring vacantly at the ruins of the alcove.

A wide crack split the floor of the chamber, threatening to cut off their escape. Catti-brie gritted her teeth in determination and charged ahead, making the safety of the hallway. Wulfgar screamed for the dwarf, and even started back for him.

Then Bruenor rose and moved toward them—slowly, his head down, almost hoping in his despair that a crack would open beneath him and drop him into a dark hole.

And put an end to his intolerable grief.

❧ 20 ❧

End of a Dream

When the last tremors of the cave-in had finally died away, the four remaining friends picked their way through the rubble and the veil of dust back to the oval chamber. Heedless of the piles of broken stone and the great cracks in the floor that threatened to swallow them up, Bruenor scrambled into the alcove, the others close on his heels.

No blood or any other sign of the two master swordsmen was anywhere to be found, just the mound of rubble covering the hole of the stonework trap. Bruenor could see the edgings of darkness beneath the pile, and he called out to Drizzt. His reason told him, against his heart and hopes, that the drow could not hear, that the trap had taken Drizzt from him.

The tear that rimmed his eye dropped to his cheek when he spotted the lone scimitar, the magical blade that Drizzt had plundered from a dragon's lair, resting against the ruins of the alcove. Solemnly, he picked it up and slid it into his belt.

"Alas for ye, elf," he cried into the destruction. "Ye deserved a better end." If the others had not been so caught up in their own reflections at that moment, they would have noticed the angry undertone to Bruenor's mourning. In the face of the loss of his dearest and most trusted friend, and already questioning the wisdom of continuing through the halls before the tragedy, Bruenor found his grief muddled with even stronger feelings of guilt. He could not escape the part he had played in bringing about the dark elf's fall. He remembered bitterly how he had tricked Drizzt into joining the quest, feigning his own death and promising an adventure the likes of which none of them had ever seen.

He stood now, quietly, and accepted his inner torment.

Wulfgar's grief was equally deep, and uncomplicated by other feelings. The barbarian had lost one of his mentors, the warrior who had transformed him from a savage, brutish warrior to a calculating and cunning fighter.

He had lost one of his truest friends. He would have followed Drizzt to the bowels of the Abyss in search of adventure. He firmly believed that the drow would one day get them into a predicament from which they could not escape, but when he was fighting beside Drizzt, or competing against his teacher, the master, he felt alive, existing on the very dangerous edge of his limits. Often Wulfgar had envisioned his own death beside the drow, a glorious finish that the bards would write and sing about long after the enemies who had slain the two friends had turned to dust in unmarked graves.

That was an end the young barbarian did not fear.

"Ye've found yer peace now, me friend," Catti-brie said softly, understanding the drow's tormented existence better than anyone. Catti-brie's perceptions of the world were more attuned to Drizzt's sensitive side, the private aspect of his character that his other friends could not see beneath his stoic features. It was the part of Drizzt Do'Urden that had demanded he leave Menzoberranzan and his evil race, and had forced him into a role as an outcast. Catti-brie knew the joy of the drow's spirit, and the unavoidable pain he had suffered at the snubbings of those who could not see that spirit for the color of his skin.

She realized, too, that both the causes of good and evil had lost a champion this day, for in Entreri Catti-brie saw the mirror-image of Drizzt. The world would be better for the loss of the assassin.

But the price was too high.

Any relief that Regis might have felt at the demise of Entreri was lost in the swirling mire of his anger and sorrow. A part of the halfling had died in that alcove. No longer would he have to run—Pasha Pook would pursue him no more—but for the first time in his entire life Regis had to accept some consequences for his actions. He had joined up with Bruenor's party knowing that Entreri would be close behind, and understanding the potential danger to his friends.

Ever the confident gambler, the thought of losing this challenge had never entered his head. Life was a game that he played hard and to the edge, and never before had he been expected to pay for his risks. If anything in the world could temper the halfling's obsession with chance, it was this, the loss of one of his few true friends because of a risk he had chosen to take.

"Farewell, my friend," he whispered into the rubble. Turning to Bruenor, he then said, "Where do we go? How do we get out of this terrible place?"

Regis hadn't meant the remark as an accusation, but forced into a defensive posture by the mire of his own guilt, Bruenor took it as such and struck back. "Ye did it yerself!" he snarled at Regis. "Ye bringed the killer after us!" Bruenor took a threatening step forward, his face contorted by mounting rage and his hands whitened by the intensity of their clench.

Wulfgar, confused by this sudden pulse of anger, moved a step closer to Regis. The halfling did not back away, but made no move to defend himself, still not believing that Bruenor's anger could be so consuming.

"Ye thief!" Bruenor roared. "Ye go along picking yer way with no concern for what yer leaving behind—and yer friends pay for it!" His anger swelled with each word, again almost a separate entity from the dwarf, gaining its own momentum and strength.

His next step would have brought him right up to Regis, and his motion showed them all clearly that he meant to strike, but Wulfgar stepped between the two and halted Bruenor with an unmistakable glare.

Broken from his angry trance by the barbarian's stern posture, Bruenor realized then what he was about to do. More than a little embarrassed, he covered his anger beneath his concern for their immediate survival and turned away to survey the remains of the room. Few, if any, of their supplies had survived the destruction. "Leave the stuff; no time for wasting!" Bruenor told the others, clearing the choked growls from his throat. "We're to be putting this foul place far behind us!"

Wulfgar and Catti-brie scanned the rubble, searching for something that could be salvaged and not so ready to agree with Bruenor's demands that they press on without any supplies. They quickly came to the same conclusion as the dwarf, though, and with a final salute to the ruins of the alcove, they followed Bruenor back into the corridor.

"I'm meaning to make Garumn's Gorge afore the next rest," Bruenor exclaimed. "So ready yerselves for a long walk."

"And then where?" Wulfgar asked, guessing, but not liking, the answer.

"Out!" Bruenor roared. "Quick as we can!" He glared at the barbarian, daring him to argue.

"To return with the rest of your kin beside us?" Wulfgar pressed.

"Not to return," said Bruenor. "Never to return!"

"Then Drizzt has died in vain!" Wulfgar stated bluntly. "He sacrificed his life for a vision that will never be fulfilled."

Bruenor paused to steady himself in the face of Wulfgar's sharp perception. He hadn't looked at the tragedy in that cynical light, and he didn't like the implications. "Not for nothing!" he growled at the barbarian. "A warning it is to us all to be gone from the place. Evil's here, thick as orcs on mutton! Don't ye smell it, boy? Don't yer eyes and nose tell ye to be gone from here?"

"My eyes tell me of the danger," Wulfgar replied evenly.

"As often they have before. But I am a warrior and pay little heed to such warnings!"

"Then ye're sure to be a dead warrior," Catti-brie put in.

Wulfgar glared at her. "Drizzt came to help take back Mithril Hall, and I shall see the deed done!"

"Ye'll die trying," muttered Bruenor, the anger off his voice now. "We came to find me home, boy, but this is not the place. Me people once lived here, 'tis true, but the darkness that creeped into Mithril Hall has put an end to me claim on it. I've no wish to return once I'm clear of the stench of the place, know that in yer stubborn head. It's for the shadows now, and the gray ones, and may the whole stinkin' place fall in on their stinkin' heads!"

Bruenor had said enough. He turned abruptly on his heel and stamped off down the corridor, his heavy boots pounding into the stone with uncompromising determination.

Regis and Catti-brie followed closely, and Wulfgar, after a moment to consider the dwarf's resolve, trotted to catch up with them.

Sydney and Bok returned to the oval chamber as soon as the mage was certain the companions had left. Like the friends before her, she made her way to the ruined alcove and stood for a moment reflecting on the effect this sudden turn of events would have on her mission. She was amazed at the depth of her sorrow for the loss of Entreri, for though she didn't fully trust the assassin and suspected that he might actually be searching for the same powerful artifact she and Dendybar sought, she had come to respect him. Could there have been a better ally when the fighting started?

Sydney didn't have a lot of time to mourn for Entreri, for the loss of Drizzt Do'Urden conjured more immediate concerns for her own safety. Dendybar wasn't likely to take the news lightly, and the mottled wizard's talent at punishment was widely acknowledged in the Hosttower of the Arcane.

Bok waited for a moment, expecting some command from the mage, but when none was forthcoming, the golem stepped into the alcove and began removing the mound of rubble.

"Stop," Sydney ordered.

Bok kept on with its chore, driven by its directive to continue its pursuit of the drow.

"Stop!" Sydney said again, this time with more conviction. "The drow is dead, you stupid thing!" The blunt statement forced her own acceptance of the fact and set her thoughts into motion. Bok did stop and turn to her, and she waited a moment to sort out the best course of action.

"We will go after the others," she said offhandedly, as much trying to enlighten her own thoughts with the statement as to redirect the golem. "Yes, perhaps if we deliver the dwarf and the other companions to Dendybar he will forgive our stupidity in allowing the drow to die."

She looked to the golem, but of course its expression had not changed to offer any encouragement.

"It should have been you in the alcove," Sydney muttered, her sarcasm wasted on the thing. "Entreri could at least offer some suggestions. But no matter, I have decided. We shall follow the others and find the time when we might take them. They will tell us what we need to know about the Crystal Shard!"

Bok remained motionless, awaiting her signal. Even with its most basic of thought patterns, the golem understood that Sydney best knew how they could complete their mission.

The companions moved through huge caverns, more natural formations than dwarf-carved stone. High ceilings and walls stretched out into the blackness, beyond the glow of the torches, leaving the friends dreadfully aware of their vulnerability. They kept close together as they marched, imagining a host of gray dwarves watching them from the unlit reaches of the caverns, or expecting some horrid creature to swoop down upon them from the darkness above.

The ever-present sound of dripping water paced them with its rhythm, its "plip, plop" echoing through every hall, accentuating the emptiness of the place.

Bruenor remembered this section of the complex well, and found himself once again deluged by long-forgotten images of his past. These were the Halls of Gathering, where all of Clan Battlehammer would come together to hear the words of King Garumn, or to meet with important visitors. Battle plans were laid here, and strategies set for commerce with the outside world. Even the youngest dwarves were present at the meetings, and Bruenor recalled fondly the many times he had sat beside his father, Bangor, behind his grandfather, King Garumn, with Bangor pointing out the king's techniques for capturing the audience, and instructing the young Bruenor in the arts of leadership that he would one day need.

The day he became King of Mithril Hall.

The solitude of the caverns weighed heavily on the dwarf, who had heard them ring out in the common cheering and chanting of ten-thousand dwarves. Even if he were to return with all of the remaining members of the clan, they would fill only a tiny corner of one chamber.

"Too many gone," Bruenor said into the emptiness, his soft whisper louder than he had intended in the echoing stillness. Catti-brie and Wulfgar, concerned for the dwarf and scrutinizing his every action, noted the remark and could easily enough guess the memories and emotions that had prompted it. They looked to each other and Catti-brie could see that the edge of Wulfgar's anger at the dwarf had dissipated in a rush of sympathy.

Hall after great hall loomed up with only short corridors connecting them. Turns and side exits broke off every few feet, but Bruenor felt confident that he knew the way to the gorge. He knew, too, that anyone below would have heard the crashing of the stonework trap and would be coming to investigate. This section of the upper level, unlike the areas they had left behind, had many connecting passages to the lower levels. Wulfgar doused the torch and Bruenor led them on under the protective dimness of the gloom.

Their caution soon proved prudent, for as they entered yet another immense cavern, Regis grabbed Bruenor by the shoulder, stopping him, and motioned for all of them to be silent. Bruenor almost burst out in rage, but saw at once the sincere look of dread on Regis's face.

His hearing sharpened by years of listening for the click of a lock's tumblers, the halfling had picked out a sound in the distance other than the dripping of water. A moment later, the others caught it, too, and soon they identified it as the marching steps of many booted feet. Bruenor took them into a dark recess where they watched and waited.

They never saw the passing host clearly enough to count its numbers or identify its members, but they could tell by the number of torches crossing the far end of the cavern that they were outnumbered by at least ten to one, and they could guess the nature of the marchers.

"Gray ones, or me mother's a friend of orcs," Bruenor grumbled. He looked at Wulfgar to see if the barbarian had any further complaints about his decision to leave Mithril Hall.

Wulfgar accepted the stare with a conceding nod. "How far to Garumn's Gorge?" he asked, fast becoming as resigned to leaving as the others. He still felt as though he was deserting Drizzt, but he understood the wisdom of Bruenor's choice. It grew obvious now that if they remained, Drizzt Do'Urden would not be the only one of them to die in Mithril Hall.

"An hour to the last passage," Bruenor answered. "Another hour, no more, from there."

The host of gray dwarves soon cleared the cavern and the companions started off again, using even more caution and dreading each shuffling footfall that thumped the floor harder than intended.

His memories coming clearer with each passing step, Bruenor knew exactly where they were, and made for the most direct path to the gorge, meaning to be out of the halls as quickly as possible. After many minutes of walking, though, he came across a side passage that he simply could not pass by. Every delay was a risk, he knew, but the temptation emanating from the room at the end of this short corridor was too great for him to ignore. He had to discover how far the despoilment of Mithril Hall had gone; he had to learn if the most treasured room of the upper level had survived.

The friends followed him without question and soon found themselves standing before a tall, ornate metal door inscribed with the hammer of Moradin, the greatest of the dwarven gods, and a series of runes beneath it. Bruenor's heavy breathing belied his calmness.

"Herein lie the gifts of our friends," Bruenor read solemnly, "and the craftings of our kin. Know ye as ye enter this hallowed hall that ye look upon the heritage of Clan Battlehammer. Friends be welcome, thieves beware!" Bruenor turned to his companions, beads of nervous sweat on his brow. "The Hall of Dumathoin," he explained.

"Two hundred years of your enemies in the halls," Wulfgar reasoned. "Surely it has been pillaged."

"Not so," said Bruenor. "The door is magicked and would not open for enemies of the clan. A hundred traps are inside to take the skin from a gray one who was to get through!" He glared at Regis, his gray eyes narrowed in a stern warning. "Watch to yer own hands, Rumblebelly. Mighten be that a trap won't know ye to be a friendly thief!"

The advice seemed sound enough for Regis to ignore the dwarf's biting sarcasm. Unconsciously admitting the truth of Bruenor's words, the halfling slipped his hands into his pockets.

"Fetch a torch from the wall," Bruenor told Wulfgar. "Me thoughts tell me that no lights burn within."

Before Wulfgar even returned to them, Bruenor began opening the huge door. It swung easily under the push of the hands of a friend, swinging wide into a short corridor that ended in a heavy black curtain. A pendulum blade hung ominously in the center of the passage, a pile of bones beneath it.

"Thieving dog," Bruenor chuckled with grim satisfaction. He stepped by the blade and moved to the curtain, waiting for all of his friends to join him before he entered the chamber.

Bruenor paused, mustering the courage to open the last barrier to the hall, sweat glistening on all the friends' faces now as the dwarf's anxiety swept through them.

With a determined grunt, Bruenor pulled the curtain aside. "Behold the Hall of Duma—" he began, but the words stuck in his throat as soon as he looked beyond the opening. Of all the destruction they had witnessed in the halls, none was more complete than this. Mounds of stone littered the floor. Pedestals that had once held the finest works of the clan lay broken apart, and others had been trampled into dust.

Bruenor stumbled in blindly, his hands shaking and a great scream of outrage lumped in his throat. He knew before he even looked upon the entirety of the chamber that the destruction was complete.

"How?" Bruenor gasped. Even as he asked, though, he saw the huge hole in the wall. Not a tunnel carved around the blocking door, but a gash in the stone, as though some incredible ram had blasted through.

"What power could have done such a thing?" Wulfgar asked, following the line of the dwarf's stare to the hole.

Bruenor moved over, searching for some clue, Cattibrie and Wulfgar with him. Regis headed the other way, just to see if anything of value remained.

Catti-brie caught a rainbowlike glitter on the floor and moved to what she thought was a puddle of some dark liquid. Bending close, though, she realized that it wasn't liquid at all, but a scale, blacker than the blackest night and nearly the size of a man. Wulfgar and Bruenor rushed to her side at the sound of her gasp.

"Dragon!" Wulfgar blurted, recognizing the distinctive shape. He grasped the thing by its edge and hoisted it upright to better inspect it. Then he and Catti-brie turned to Bruenor to see if he had any knowledge of such a monster.

The dwarf's wide-eyed, terror-stricken stare answered their question before it was asked.

"Blacker than the black," Bruenor whispered, speaking again the most common words of that fateful day those two hundred years ago. "Me father told me of the thing," he explained to Wulfgar and Catti-brie. "A demon-spawned dragon, he called it, a darkness blacker than the black. 'Twas not the gray ones that routed us—we would've fought them head on to the last. The dragon of darkness took our numbers and drove us from the halls. Not one in ten remained to stand against its foul hordes in the smaller halls at th'other end."

A hot draft of air from the hole reminded them that it probably connected to the lower halls, and the dragon's lair.

"Let's be leaving," Catti-brie suggested, "afore the beast gets a notion that we're here."

Regis then cried out from the other side of the chamber. The friends rushed to him, not knowing if he had stumbled upon treasure or danger.

They found him crouched beside a pile of stone, peering into a gap in the blocks.

He held up a silver-shafted arrow. "I found it in there," he explained. "And there's something more—a bow, I think."

Wulfgar moved the torch closer to the gap and they all saw clearly the curving arc that could only be the wood of a longbow, and the silvery shine of a bowstring. Wulfgar grasped the wood and tugged lightly, expecting it to break apart in his hands under the enormous weight of the stone.

But it held firmly, even against a pull of all his strength. He looked around at the stones, seeking the best course to free the weapon.

Regis, meanwhile, had found something more, a golden plaque wedged in another crack in the pile. He managed to slip it free and brought it into the torchlight to read its carved runes.

" 'Taulmaril the Heartseeker,' " he read. " 'Gift of—' "

"Anariel, Sister of Faerun," Bruenor finished without even looking at the plaque. He nodded in recognition to Catti-brie's questioning glance.

"Free the bow, boy," he told Wulfgar. "Suren it might be put to a better use than this."

Wulfgar had already discerned the structure of the pile and started lifting away specific blocks at once. Soon Catti-brie was able to wiggle the longbow free, but she saw something else beyond its nook in the pile and asked Wulfgar to keep digging.

While the muscled barbarian pushed aside more stones, the others marveled at the beauty of the bow. Its wood hadn't even been scratched by the stones and the deep finish of its polish returned with a single brush of the hand. Catti-brie strung it easily and held it up, feeling its solid and even draw.

"Test it," Regis offered, handing her the silver arrow.

Catti-brie couldn't resist. She fitted the arrow to the silvery string and drew it back, meaning only to try its fit and not intending to fire.

"A quiver!" Wulfgar called, lifting the last of the stones. "And more of the silver arrows."

Bruenor pointed into the blackness and nodded. Catti-brie didn't hesitate.

A streaking tail of silver followed the whistling missile as it soared into the darkness, ending its flight abruptly with a crack. They all rushed after it, sensing something beyond the ordinary. They found the arrow easily, for it was buried halfway to its fletches in the wall!

All about its point of entry, the stone had been scorched, and even tugging with all of his might, Wulfgar couldn't budge the arrow an inch.

"Not to fret," said Regis, counting the arrows in the quiver that Wulfgar held. "There are nineteen . . . twenty more!" He backed away, stunned. The others looked at him in confusion.

"Nineteen, there were," Regis explained. "My count was true."

Wulfgar, not understanding, quickly counted the arrows. "Twenty," he said.

"Twenty now," Regis answered. "But nineteen when I first counted."

"So the quiver holds some magic, too," Catti-brie surmised. "A mighty gift, indeed, the Lady Anariel gave to the clan!"

"What more might we find in the ruins of this place?" Regis asked, rubbing his hands together.

"No more," Bruenor answered gruffly. "We're for leaving, and not a word of arguin' from ye!"

Regis knew with a look at the other two that he had no support against the dwarf, so he shrugged helplessly and followed them back through the curtain and into the corridor.

"The gorge!" Bruenor declared, starting them off again.

"Hold, Bok," Sydney whispered when the companions' torchlight re-entered the corridor a short distance ahead of them.

"Not yet," she said, an anticipating smile widening across her dust-streaked face. "We shall find a better time!"

♠ 21 ♠

Silver in the Shadows

Suddenly, he found a focus in the blur of gray haze, something tangible amid the swirl of nothingness. It hovered before him and turned over slowly.

Its edges doubled and rolled apart, then rushed together again. He fought the dull ache in his head, the inner blackness that had consumed him and now fought to keep him in its hold. Gradually, he became aware of his arms and legs, who he was, and how he had come to be here.

In his startled awareness, the image sharpened to a crystalline focus. The tip of a jeweled dagger.

Entreri loomed above him, a dark silhouette against the backdrop of a single torch set into the wall a few yards beyond, his blade poised to strike at the first sign of resistance. Drizzt could see that the assassin, too, had been hurt in the fall, though he had obviously been the quicker to recover.

"Can you walk?" Entreri asked, and Drizzt was smart enough to know what would happen if he could not.

He nodded and moved to rise, but the dagger shot in closer.

"Not yet," Entreri snarled. "We must first determine where we are, and where we are to go."

Drizzt turned his concentration away from the assassin then and studied their surroundings, confident that Entreri would have already killed him if that was the assassin's intent. They were in the mines, that much was apparent, for the walls were roughly carved stone supported by wooden columns every twenty feet or so.

"How far did we fall?" he asked the assassin, his senses telling him that they were much deeper than the room they had fought in.

Entreri shrugged. "I remember landing on hard stone after a short drop, and then sliding down a steep and twisting chute. It seemed like many moments before we finally dropped in here." He pointed to an opening at the corner of the ceiling, where they had fallen through. "But the flow of time is different for a man thinking he is about to die, and the whole thing may have been over much more quickly than I remember."

"Trust in your first reaction," Drizzt suggested, "for my own perceptions tell me that we have descended a long way indeed."

"How can we get out?"

Drizzt studied the slight grade in the floor and pointed to his right. "The slope is up to that direction," he said.

"Then on your feet," Entreri said, extending a hand to help the drow.

Drizzt accepted the assistance and rose cautiously and without giving any sign of a threat. He knew that Entreri's dagger would cut him open long before he could strike a blow of his own.

Entreri knew it, too, but didn't expect any trouble from Drizzt in their present predicament. They had shared more than an exchange of swordplay up in the alcove, and both looked upon the other with grudging respect.

"I need your eyes," Entreri explained, though Drizzt had already figured as much. "I have found but one torch, and that will not last long enough to get me out of here. Your eyes, black elf, can find their way in the darkness. I will be close enough to feel your every move, close enough to kill you with a single thrust!" He turned the dagger over again to emphasize his point, but Drizzt understood him well enough without the visual aid.

When he got to his feet, Drizzt found that he wasn't a

adly injured as he had feared. He had twisted his ankle
nd knee on one leg and knew as soon as he put any
eight upon it that every step would be painful. He
ouldn't let on to Entreri, though. He wouldn't be much
f an asset to the assassin if he couldn't keep up.

Entreri turned to retrieve the torch and Drizzt took a
uick look at his equipment. He had seen one of his scimi-
rs tucked into Entreri's belt, but the other, the magical
lade, was nowhere around. He felt one of his daggers
till tucked into a hidden sheath in his boot, though he
vasn't sure how much it would help him against the
aber and dagger of his skilled enemy. Facing Entreri
vith any kind of a disadvantage was a prospect reserved
nly for the most desperate situation.

Then, in sudden shock, Drizzt grabbed at his belt
ouch, his fear intensifying when he saw that its ties
vere undone. Even before he had slipped his hand
nside, he knew that Guenhwyvar was gone. He looked
bout frantically, and saw only the fallen rubble.

Noting his distress, Entreri smirked evilly under the
owl of his cloak. "We go," he told the drow.

Drizzt had no choice. He certainly couldn't tell Entreri
f the magical statue and take the risk that Guenhwyvar
vould once again fall into the possession of an evil mas-
er. Drizzt had rescued the great panther from that fate
nce, and would rather that it remained forever buried
nder the tons of stone than return to an unworthy mas-
er's hands. A final mourning glance at the rubble, and
e stoically accepted the loss, taking comfort that the cat
ved, quite unharmed, on its own plane of existence.

The tunnel supports drifted past them with disturbing
egularity, as though they were passing the same spot
gain and again. Drizzt sensed that the tunnel was arcing
round in a wide circle as it slightly climbed. This made
im even more nervous. He knew the prowess of
warves in tunneling, especially where precious gems or
etals were concerned, and he began to wonder how
any miles they might have to walk before they even

reached the next highest level.

Although he had less keen underground perceptio
and was unfamiliar with dwarven ways, Entreri share
the same uneasy feelings. An hour became two and sti
the line of wooden supports stretched away into th
blackness.

"The torch burns low," Entreri said, breaking th
silence that had surrounded them since they had starte
Even their footfalls, the practiced steps of stealthy wa
riors, died away in the closeness of the low passage. "Pe
haps the advantage will shift to you, black elf."

Drizzt knew better. Entreri was a creature of the nigh
as much as he, with heightened reflexes and ample expe
rience to more than compensate for his lack of vision i
the blackness. Assassins did not work under the light o
the midday sun.

Without answering, Drizzt turned back to the pat
ahead, but as he was looking around, a sudden reflectio
of the torch caught his eye. He moved to the corrido
wall, ignoring Entreri's uneasy shuffle behind him, an
started feeling the surface's texture, and peered intentl
at it in hopes of seeing another flash. It came for just
second as Entreri shifted behind him, a flicker of silve
along the wall.

"Where silver rivers run," he muttered in disbelief.

"What?" demanded Entreri.

"Bring the torch," was Drizzt's only reply. He moved h
hands eagerly over the wall now, seeking the evidenc
that would overcome his own stubborn logic and vind
cate Bruenor from his suspicions that the dwarf ha
exaggerated the tales of Mithril Hall.

Entreri was soon beside him, curious. The torc
showed it clearly: a stream of silver running along th
wall, as thick as Drizzt's forearm and shining brightly i
its purity.

"Mithril," Entreri said, gawking. "A king's hoard!"

"But of little use to us," Drizzt said to diffuse the
excitement. He started again down the hall, as thoug

the lode of mithril did not impress him. Somehow he felt that Entreri should not look upon this place, that the assassin's mere presence fouled the riches of Clan Battle-hammer. Drizzt did not want to give the assassin any reason to seek these halls again. Entreri shrugged and followed.

The grade in the passageway became more apparent as they went along, and the silvery reflections of the mithril veins reappeared with enough regularity to make Drizzt wonder if Bruenor may have even under-stated the prosperity of his clan.

Entreri, always no more than a step behind the drow, was too intent upon watching his prisoner to take much notice of the precious metal, but he understood well the potential that surrounded him. He didn't care much for such ventures himself, but knew that the information would prove valuable and might serve him well in future bargaining.

Before long the torch died away, but the two found that they could still see, for a dim light source was some-where up ahead, beyond the turns of the tunnel. Even so, the assassin closed the gap between he and Drizzt, putting the dagger tip against Drizzt's back and taking no chances of losing his only hope of escape if the light faded completely.

The glow only brightened, for its source was great indeed. The air grew warmer around them and soon they heard the grinding of distant machinery echoing down the tunnel. Entreri tightened his reins even fur-ther, grasping Drizzt's cloak and pulling himself closer. "You are as much an intruder here as I," he whispered. "Avoidance is ally to both of us."

"Could the miners prove worse than the fate you offer?" Drizzt asked with a sarcastic sigh.

Entreri released the cloak and backed away. "It seems I must offer you something more to ensure your agree-ment," he said.

Drizzt studied him closely, not knowing what to

expect. "Every advantage is yours," he said.

"Not so," replied the assassin. Drizzt stood perplexed as Entreri slid his dagger back into its sheath. "I could kill you, I agree, but to what gain? I take no pleasure in killing."

"But murder does not displease you," Drizzt retorted.

"I do as I must," Entreri said, dismissing the biting comment under a veil of laughter.

Drizzt recognized this man all too well. Passionless and pragmatic, and undeniably skilled in the ways of dealing death. Looking at Entreri, Drizzt saw what he himself might have become if he had remained in Menzoberranzan among his similarly amoral people. Entreri epitomized the tenets of drow society, the selfish heartlessness that had driven Drizzt from the bowels of the world in outrage. He eyed the assassin squarely, detesting every inch of the man, but somehow unable to detach himself from the empathy he felt.

He had to make a stand for his principles now, he decided, just as he had those years ago in the dark city. "You do as you must," he spat in disgust, disregarding the possible consequences. "No matter the cost."

"No matter the cost," Entreri echoed evenly, his self-satisfying smile distorting the insult into a compliment. "Be glad that I am so practical, Drizzt Do'Urden, else you would never have awakened from your fall.

"But enough of this worthless arguing. I have a deal to offer you that might prove of great benefit to us both." Drizzt remained silent and gave no hints to the level of his interest.

"Do you know why I am here?" Entreri asked.

"You have come for the halfling."

"You are in error," replied Entreri. "Not for the halfling, but for the halfling's pendant. He stole it from my master, though I doubt that he would have admitted as much to you."

"I guess more than I am told," Drizzt said, ironically leading into his next suspicion. "Your master seeks engeance as well, does he not?"

"Perhaps," said Entreri without a pause. "But the return of the pendant is paramount. So I offer this to you: We shall work together to find the road back to your friends. I offer my assistance on the journey and your life in exchange for the pendant. Once we are there, persuade the halfling to surrender it to me and I shall go on my way and not return. My master retrieves his treasure and your little friend lives out the rest of his life without looking over his shoulder."

"On your word?" Drizzt balked.

"On my actions," Entreri retorted. He pulled the scimitar from his belt and tossed it to Drizzt. "I have no intentions of dying in these forsaken mines, drow, nor do you, I would hope."

"How do you know I will go along with my part when we rejoin my companions?" asked Drizzt, holding the blade out before him in inspection, hardly believing the turn of events.

Entreri laughed again. "You are too honorable to put such doubts in my mind, dark elf. You will do as you agree, of that I am certain! A bargain, then?"

Drizzt had to admit the wisdom of Entreri's words. Together, they stood a fair chance of escaping from the lower levels. Drizzt wasn't about to pass up the opportunity to find his friends, not for the price of a pendant that usually got Regis into more trouble than it was worth. "Agreed," he said.

The passageway continued to brighten at each turn, not with flickering light, as with torches, but in a continuous glow. The noise of machinery increased proportionately and the two had to shout to each other to be understood.

Around a final bend, they came to the abrupt end of the mine, its last supports opening into a huge cavern. They moved tentatively through the supports and onto a small ledge that ran along the side of a wide gorge—the great undercity of Clan Battlehammer.

Luckily they were on the top level of the chasm, for both walls had been cut into huge steps right down to the floor, each one holding rows of the decorated doorways that had once marked the entrances to the houses of Bruenor's kin. The steps were mostly empty now, but Drizzt, with the countless tales Bruenor had told to him, could well imagine the past glory of the place. Ten thousand dwarves, untiring in their passion for their beloved work, hammering at the mithril and singing praises to their gods.

What a sight that must have been! Dwarves scrambling from level to level to show off their latest work, a mithril item of incredible beauty and value. And yet, judging from what Drizzt knew of the dwarves in Icewind Dale, even the slightest imperfection would send the artisans scurrying back to their anvils, begging their gods for forgiveness and the gift of skill sufficient to craft a finer piece. No race in all the Realms could claim such pride in their work as the dwarves, and the folk of Clan Battlehammer were particular even by the standards of the bearded people.

Now only the very floor of the chasm bustled in activity, for, hundreds of feet below them and stretching off in either direction, loomed the central forges of Mithril Hall, furnaces hot enough to melt the hard metal from the mined stone. Even at this height Drizzt and Entreri felt the searing heat, and the intensity of the light made them squint. Scores of squat workers darted about, pushing barrows of ore or fuel for the fires. Duergar, Drizzt assumed, though he couldn't see them clearly in the glare from this height.

Just a few feet to the right of the tunnel exit, a wide, gently arching ramp spiraled down to the next lower step. To the left, the ledge moved on along the wall, narrow and not designed for casual passage, but farther down its course, Drizzt could see the black silhouette of a bridge arching across the chasm.

Entreri motioned him back into the tunnel. "The

bridge seems our best route," the assassin said. "But I am wary of moving out across the ledge with so many about."

"We have little choice," Drizzt reasoned. "We could backtrack and search for some of the side corridors that we passed, but I believe them to be no more than extensions of the mine complex and I doubt that they would lead us back even this far."

"We must go on," Entreri agreed. "Perhaps the noise and glare will provide us ample cover." Without further delay, he slipped out onto the ledge and began making his way to the dark outline of the chasm bridge, Drizzt right behind.

Although the ledge was no more than two feet wide at any point and much narrower than that at most, the nimble fighters had no trouble navigating it. Soon they stood before the bridge, a narrow walk of stone arching over the bustle below.

Creeping low, they moved out easily. When they crossed the midpoint and began the descent down the back half of the arch, they saw a wider ledge running along the chasm's other wall. At the end of the bridge loomed a tunnel, torchlit like the ones they had left on the upper level. To the left of the entrance, several small shapes, Duergar, stood huddled in conversation, taking no notice of the area. Entreri looked back at Drizzt with a sneaky smile and pointed to the tunnel.

As silent as cats and invisible in the shadows, they crossed into the tunnel, the group of Duergar oblivious to their passing.

Wooden supports rolled past the two easily now as they took up a swift gait, leaving the undercity far behind. Roughhewn walls gave them plenty of shadowy protection in the torchlight, and as the noise of the workers behind them dimmed to a distant murmur they relaxed a bit and began looking ahead to the prospect of meeting back up with the others.

They turned a bend in the tunnel and nearly ran over a

lone Duergar sentry.

"What're yer fer?" the sentry barked, mithril broadsword gleaming with each flicker of the torchlight. His armor, too, chain mail, helm, and shining shield, were of the precious metal, a king's treasure to outfit a single soldier!

Drizzt passed his companion and motioned for Entreri to hold back. He didn't want a trail of bodies to follow their escape route. The assassin understood that the black elf might have some luck in dealing with this other denizen of the underworld. Not wanting to let on that he was human, and possibly hinder the credibility of whatever story Drizzt had concocted, he hitched his cloak up over his face.

The sentry jumped back a step, his eyes wide in amazement when he recognized Drizzt as a drow. Drizzt scowled at him and did not reply.

"Er . . . what might ye be doin' in the mines?" the Duergar asked, rephrasing both his question and tone politely.

"Walking," Drizzt replied coldly, still feigning anger at the gruff greeting he had initially received.

"And . . . uh . . . who might ye be?" stuttered the guard.

Entreri studied the gray dwarf's obvious terror of Drizzt. It appeared that the drow carried even more fearful respect among the races of the underworld than among the surface dwellers. The assassin made a mental note of this, determined to deal with Drizzt even more cautiously in the future.

"I am Drizzt Do'Urden, of the house of Daermon N'a'shezbaernon, ninth family of the throne to Menzoberranzan," Drizzt said, seeing no reason to lie.

"Greetings!" cried the sentry, overly anxious to gain the favor of the stranger. "Mucknuggle, I be, of Clan Bukbukken." He bowed low, his gray beard sweeping the floor. "Not often do we greet guests in the mines. Be it someone ye seek? Or something that I could be helpin' ye with?"

Drizzt thought for a moment. If his friends had survived the cave-in, and he had to go on his hopes that they had, they would be making for Garumn's Gorge. "My business here is complete," he told the Duergar. "I am satisfied."

Mucknuggle looked at him curiously. "Satisfied?"

"Your people have delved too deep," Drizzt explained. "You have disturbed one of our tunnels with your digging. Thus we have come to investigate this complex, to ensure that it is not again inhabited by enemies of the drow. I have seen your forges, gray one, you should be proud."

The sentry straightened his belt and sucked in his belly. Clan Bukbukken was indeed proud of its setup, though they had in truth stolen the entire operation from Clan Battlehammer. "And ye're satisfied, ye say. Then where might ye be headin' now, Drizzt Do'Urden? T'see the boss?"

"Who would I seek if I were?"

"Ain't ye not heared o' Shimmergloom?" answered Mucknuggle with a knowing chuckle. "The Drake o' Darkness, he be, black as black and fiercer than a pin-stuck demon! Don't know 'ow he'll take to drow elves in his mines, but we'll be seein'!"

"I think not," replied Drizzt. "I have learned all that I came to learn, and now my trail leads home. I shan't disturb Shimmergloom, nor any of your hospitable clan again."

"Me thinkin's that ye're goin' to the boss," said Mucknuggle, drawing more courage from Drizzt's politeness and from the mention of his mighty leader's name. He folded his gnarly arms across his chest, the mithril sword resting most visibly on the shining shield.

Drizzt resumed his scowl and poked a finger into the fabric under his cloak, pointing in the Duergar's direction. Mucknuggle noted the move, as did Entreri, and the assassin nearly fell back in confusion at the reaction of the Duergar. A noticeable ashen pall came over Mucknuggle's already gray features and he stood perfectly still, not even daring to draw breath.

"My trail leads home," Drizzt said again.

"Home, it do!" cried Mucknuggle. "Mighten I be of some help in findin' the way? The tunnels get rightly mixed up back that way."

Why not? Drizzt thought, figuring their chances would be better if they at least knew the quickest route. "A chasm," he told Mucknuggle. "In the time before Clan Bukbukken, we heard it named as Garumn's Gorge."

"Shimmergloom's Run it is now," Mucknuggle corrected. "The left tunnel at the next fork," he offered, pointing down the hallway. "And a straight run from there."

Drizzt didn't like the sound of the gorge's new name. He wondered what monster his friends might find waiting for them if they reached the gorge. Not wanting to waste any more time, he nodded to Mucknuggle and walked past. The Duergar was all too willing to let him by without further conversation, stepping as far aside as he could.

Entreri looked back at Mucknuggle as they passed and saw him wiping nervous sweat from his brow. "We should have killed him," he told Drizzt when they were safely away. "He will bring his kin after us."

"No faster than a dead body, or a missing sentry would have set off a general alarm," replied Drizzt. "Perhaps a few will come to confirm his tale, but at least we now know the way out. He would not have dared to lie to me, in fear that my inquiry was just a test of the truth of his words. My people have been known to kill for such lies."

"What did you do to him?" Entreri asked.

Drizzt couldn't help but chuckle at the ironic benefits of his people's sinister reputation. He poked the finger under the fabric of his cloak again. "Envision a crossbow small enough to fit into your pocket," he explained. "Would it not make such an impression when pointed at a target? The drow are well known for such crossbows."

"But how deadly could so small a bolt prove against a suit of mithril?" Entreri asked, still not understanding why the threat had been so effective.

"Ah, but the poison," Drizzt smirked, moving away down the corridor.

Entreri stopped and grinned at the obvious logic. How devious and merciless the drow must be to command so powerful a reaction to so simple a threat! It seemed that their deadly reputation was not an exaggeration.

Entreri found that he was beginning to admire these black elves.

The pursuit came faster than they had expected, despite their swift pace. The stamp of boots sounded loudly and then disappeared, only to reappear at the next turn even closer than before. Side-passages, Drizzt and Entreri both understood, cursing every turn in their own twisting tunnel. Finally, when their pursuers were nearly upon them, Drizzt stopped the assassin.

"Just a few," he said, picking out each individual footfall.

"The group from the ledge," Entreri surmised. "Let us make a stand. But be quick, there are more behind them, no doubt!" The excited light that came into the assassin's eyes seemed dreadfully familiar to Drizzt.

He didn't have time to ponder the unpleasant implications. He shook them from his head, regaining full concentration for the business at hand, then pulled the hidden dagger out of his boot—no time for secrets from Entreri now—and found a shadowed recess on the tunnel wall. Entreri did likewise, positioning himself a few feet farther down from the drow and across the corridor.

Seconds passed slowly with only the faint shuffle of boots. Both companions held their breath and waited patiently, knowing that they had not been passed by.

Suddenly the sound multiplied as the Duergar came rushing out of a secret door and into the main tunnel.

"Can't be far now!" Drizzt and Entreri heard one of

them say.

"The drake'll be feedin' us well fer this catch!" hooted another.

All clad in shining mail and wielding mithril weapons, they rounded the last bend and came into sight of the hidden companions.

Drizzt looked at the dull steel of his scimitar and considered how precise his strikes must be against armor of mithril. A resigned sigh escaped him as he wished that he now held his magical weapon.

Entreri saw the problem, too, and knew that they had to somehow balance the odds. Quickly he pulled a pouch of coins from his belt and hurled it farther down the corridor. It sailed through the gloom and clunked into the wall where the tunnel twisted again.

The Duergar band straightened as one. "Just ahead!" one of them cried, and they bent low to the stone and charged for the next bend. Between the waiting drow and assassin.

The shadows exploded into movement and fell over the stunned gray dwarves. Drizzt and Entreri struck together, seizing the moment of best advantage, when the first of the band had reached the assassin and the last was passing Drizzt.

The Duergar shrieked in surprised horror. Daggers, saber, and scimitar danced all about them in a flurry of flashing death, poking at the seams of their armor, seeking an opening through the unyielding metal. When they found one, they drove the point home with merciless efficiency.

By the time the Duergar recovered from the initial shock of the attack, two lay dead at the drow's feet, a third at Entreri's, and yet another stumbled away, holding his belly in with a blood-soaked hand.

"Back to back!" Entreri shouted, and Drizzt, thinking the same strategy, had already begun quick-stepping his way through the disorganized dwarves. Entreri took another one down just as they came together, the unfortunate Duergar looking over its shoulder at the approaching drow just long enough for the jeweled dagger to slip through the seam at the base of its helmet.

Then they were together, back against back, twirling in the wake of each other's cloak and maneuvering their weapons in blurred movements so similar that the three remaining Duergar hesitated before their attack to sort out where one enemy ended and the other began.

With cries to Shimmergloom, their godlike ruler, they came on anyway.

Drizzt scored a series of hits at once that should have felled his opponent, but the armor was of tougher stuff than the steel scimitar and his thrusts were turned aside. Entreri, too, had trouble finding an opening to poke through against the mithril mail and shields.

Drizzt turned one shoulder in and let the other fall away from his companion. Entreri understood and followed the drow's lead, dipping around right behind him.

Gradually their circling gained momentum, as synchronous as practiced dancers, and the Duergar did not even try to keep up. Opponents changed continually, the drow and Entreri coming around to parry away the sword or axe that the other had blocked on the last swing. They let the rhythm hold for a few turns, allowed the Duergar to fall into the patterns of their dance, and then, Drizzt still leading, stuttered their steps, and even reversed the flow.

The three Duergar, evenly spaced about the pair, did not know which direction would bring the next attack.

Entreri, practically reading the drow's every thought by this point, saw the possibilities. As he moved away from one particularly confused dwarf, he feigned a reversed attack, freezing the Duergar just long enough for Drizzt, coming in from the other side, to find an opening.

"Take him!" the assassin cried in victory.

The scimitar did its work.

Now they were two against two. They stopped the

dance and faced off evenly.

Drizzt swooped about his smaller foe with a sudden leap and shuffle along the wall. The Duergar, intent on the killing blades of the drow, hadn't noticed Drizzt's third weapon join the fray.

The gray dwarf's surprise was only surmounted by his anticipation of the coming fatal blow when Drizzt's trailing cloak floated in and fell over him, enshrouding him in a blackness that would only deepen into the void of death.

Contrary to Drizzt's graceful technique, Entreri worked with sudden fury, tying up his dwarf with undercuts and lightning-fast counters, always aimed at the weapon hand. The gray dwarf understood the tactic as his fingers began to numb under the nicks of several minor hits.

The Duergar overcompensated, turning his shield in to protect the vulnerable hand.

Exactly as Entreri had expected. He rolled around opposite the movement of his opponent, finding the back of the shield, and a seam in the mithril armor just beneath the shoulder. The assassin's dagger drove in furiously, taking a lung and hurling the Duergar to the stone floor. The gray dwarf lay there, hunched up on one elbow, and gasped out his final breaths.

Drizzt approached the final dwarf, the one who had been wounded in the initial attack, leaning against the wall only a few yards away, torchlight reflecting grotesque red off the pool of blood below him. The dwarf still had fight in him. He raised his broadsword to meet the drow.

It was Mucknuggle, Drizzt saw, and a silent plea of mercy came into the drow's mind and took the fiery glow from his eyes.

A shiny object, glittering in the hues of a dozen distinct gemstones, spun by Drizzt and ended his internal debate.

Entreri's dagger buried deep into Mucknuggle's eye.

The dwarf didn't even fall, so clean was the blow. He just held his position, leaning against the stone. But now the blood pool was fed from two wounds.

Drizzt stopped himself cold in rage and did not even flinch as the assassin walked coolly by to retrieve the weapon.

Entreri pulled the dagger out roughly then turned to face Drizzt as Mucknuggle tumbled down to splash in the blood.

"Four to four," the assassin growled. "You did not believe that I would let you get the upper count?"

Drizzt did not reply, nor blink.

Both felt the sweat in their palms as they clutched their weapons, a pull upon them to complete what they had started in the alcove above.

So alike, yet so dramatically different.

The rage at Mucknuggle's death did not play upon Drizzt at that moment, no more than to further confirm his feelings about his vile companion. The longing he held to kill Entreri went far deeper than the anger he might hold for any of the assassin's foul deeds. Killing Entreri would mean killing the darker side of himself, Drizzt believed, for he could have been as this man. This was the test of his worth, a confrontation against what he might have become. If he had remained among his kin, and often were the times that he considered his decision to leave their ways and their dark city a feeble attempt to distort the very order of nature, his own dagger would have found Mucknuggle's eye.

Entreri looked upon Drizzt with equal disdain. What potential he saw in the drow! But tempered by an intolerable weakness. Perhaps in his heart the assassin was actually envious for the capacity for love and compassion that he recognized in Drizzt. So much akin to him, Drizzt only accentuated the reality of his own emotional void.

Even if those feelings were truly within, they would never gain a perch high enough to influence Artemis

Entreri. He had spent his life building himself into an instrument for killing, and no shred of light could ever cut through that callous barrier of darkness. He meant to prove, to himself and to the drow, that the true fighter has no place for weakness.

They were closer now, though neither of them knew which one had moved, as if unseen forces were acting upon them. Weapons twitched in anticipation, each waiting for the other to show his hand.

Each wanting the other to be the first to yield to their common desire, the ultimate challenge of the tenets of their existence.

The stamp of booted feet broke the spell.

❦ 22 ❦

The Dragon of Darkness

At the heart of the lower levels, in an immense cavern of uneven and twisting walls pocketed with deep shadows, and a ceiling too high for the light of the brightest fire to find, rested the present ruler of Mithril Hall, perched upon a solid pedestal of the purest mithril that rose from a high and wide mound of coins and jewelry, goblets and weapons, and countless other items pounded from the rough blocks of mithril by the skilled hands of dwarven craftsmen.

Dark shapes surrounded the beast, huge dogs from its own world, obedient, long-lived, and hungry for the meat of human or elf, or anything else that would give them the pleasure of their gory sport before the kill.

Shimmergloom was not now amused. Rumblings from above foretold of intruders, and a band of Duergar spoke of murdered kin in the tunnels and whispered rumors that a drow elf had been seen.

The dragon was not of this world. It had come from the Plane of Shadows, a dark image of the lighted world, unknown to the dwellers here except in the less substantial stuff of their blackest nightmares. Shimmergloom had been of considerable standing there, old even then, and in high regard among its dragon kin that ruled the plane. But when the foolish and greedy dwarves that once inhabited these mines had delved into deep holes of sufficient darkness to open a gate to its plane, the dragon had been quick to come through. Now possessing a treasure tenfold beyond the greatest of its own plane, Shimmergloom had no intentions of returning.

It would deal with the intruders.

For the first time since the routing of Clan Battlehammer, the baying of the shadow hounds filled the tunnels,
striking dread even into the hearts of their gray dwarf
handlers. The dragon sent them west on their mission,
up toward the tunnels around the entry hall in Keeper's
Dale, where the companions had first entered the complex. With their powerful maws and incredible stealth,
the hounds were indeed a deadly force, but their mission
now was not to catch and kill—only to herd.

In the first fight for Mithril Hall, Shimmergloom alone
had routed the miners in the lower caverns and in some
of the huge chambers on the eastern end of the upper
level. But final victory had escaped the dragon, for the
end had come in the western corridors, too tight for its
scaly bulk.

The beast would not miss the glory again. It set its minions in motion, to drive whoever or whatever had come
into the halls toward the only entrance that it had to the
upper levels: Garumn's Gorge.

Shimmergloom stretched to the limit of its height and
unfolded its leathery wings for the first time in nearly
two hundred years, blackness flowing out under them as
they extended to the sides. Those Duergar who had
remained in the throne room fell to their knees at the
sight of their rising lord, partly in respect, but mostly in
fear.

The dragon was gone, gliding down a secret tunnel at
the back of the chamber, to where it had once known glory, the place its minions had named Shimmergloom's Run
in praise of their lord.

A blur of indistinguishable darkness, it moved as silently as the cloud of blackness that followed.

* * * * *

Wulfgar worried just how low he would be crouching
by the time they reached Garumn's Gorge, for the tun-

nels became dwarven sized as they neared the eastern end of the upper level. Bruenor knew this as a good sign, the only tunnels in the complex with ceilings below the six foot mark were those of the deepest mines and those crafted for defense of the gorge.

Faster than Bruenor had hoped, they came upon the secret door to a smaller tunnel breaking off to the left, a spot familiar to the dwarf even after his two-century absence. He ran his hand across the unremarkable wall beneath the torch and its telltale red sconce, searching for the brailed pattern that would lead his fingers to the precise spot. He found one triangle, then another, and followed their lines to the central point, the bottommost point in the valley between the peaks of the twin mountains that they signified, the symbol of Dumathoin, the Keeper of Secrets Under the Mountain. Bruenor pushed with a single finger, and the wall fell away, opening yet another low tunnel. No light came from this one, but a hollow sound, like the wind across a rock face, greeted them.

Bruenor winked at them knowingly and started right in, but slowed when he saw the runes and sculpted reliefs carved into the walls. All along the passage, on every surface, dwarven artisans had left their mark. Bruenor swelled with pride, despite his depression, when he saw the admiring expressions upon his friends' faces.

A few turns later they came upon a portcullis, lowered and rusted, and beyond it saw the wideness of another huge cavern.

"Garumn's Gorge," Bruenor proclaimed, moving up to the iron bars. "'Tis said ye can throw a torch off the rim and it'll burn out afore ever it hits."

Four sets of eyes looked through the gate in wonder. If the journey through Mithril Hall had been a disappointment to them, for they had not yet seen the grander sights Bruenor had often told them of, the sight before them now made up for it. They had reached Garumn's

Gorge, though it seemed more a full-sized canyon than a gorge, spanning hundreds of feet across and stretching beyond the limits of their sight. They were above the floor of the chamber, with a stairway running down to the right on the other side of the portcullis. Straining to poke as much of their heads as they could through the bars, they could see the light of another room at the base of the stairs, and hear clearly the ruckus of several Duergar.

To the left, the wall arced around to the edge, though the chasm continued on beyond the bordering wall of the cavern. A single bridge spanned the break, an ancient work of stone fitted so perfectly that its slight arch could still support an army of the hugest mountain giants.

Bruenor studied the bridge carefully, noting that something about its understructure did not seem quite right. He followed the line of a cable across the chasm, figuring it to continue under the stone flooring and connect to a large lever sticking up from a more recently constructed platform across the way. Two Duergar sentries milled about the lever, though their lax attitude spoke of countless days of boredom.

"They've rigged the thing to fall!" Bruenor snorted.

The others immediately understood what he was talking about. "Is there another way across, then?" Catti-brie asked.

"Aye," replied the dwarf. "A ledge to the south end of the gorge. But hours o' walking, and the only way to it is through this cavern!"

Wulfgar grasped the iron bars of the portcullis and tested them. They held fast, as he suspected. "We could not get through these bars, anyway," he put in. "Unless you know where we might find their crank."

"Half a day's walking," Bruenor replied, as though the answer, perfectly logical to the mindset of a dwarf protecting his treasures, should have been obvious. "The other way."

"Fretful folk," Regis said under his breath.

Catching the remark, Bruenor growled and grabbed Regis by the collar, hoisting him from the ground and pressing their faces together. "Me people are a careful lot," he snarled, his own frustration and confusion boiling out again in his misdirected rage. "We like to keep what's our own to keep, especially from little thieves with little fingers and big mouths."

"Suren there's another way in," Catti-brie reasoned, quick to diffuse the confrontation.

Bruenor dropped the halfling to the floor. "We can get to that room," he replied, indicating the lighted area at the base of the stairs.

"Then let's be quick," Catti-brie demanded. "If the noise of the cave-in called out alarms, the word might not have reached this far."

Bruenor led them back down the small tunnel swiftly, and back to the corridor behind the secret door.

Around the next bend in the main corridor, its walls, too, showing the runes and sculpted reliefs of the dwarven craftsmen, Bruenor was again engulfed in the wonder of his heritage and quickly lost all thoughts of anger at Regis. He heard again in his mind the ringing of hammers in Garumn's day, and the singing of common gatherings. If the foulness that they had found here, and the loss of Drizzt, had tempered his fervent desire to reclaim Mithril Hall, the vivid recollections that assaulted him as he moved along this corridor worked to refuel those fires.

Perhaps he would return with his army, he thought. Perhaps the mithril would again ring out in the smithies of Clan Battlehammer.

Thoughts of regaining his people's glory suddenly rekindled, Bruenor looked around to his friends, tired, hungry, and grieving for the drow, and reminded himself that the mission before him now was to escape the complex and get them back to safety.

A more intense glow ahead signaled the end of the

tunnel. Bruenor slowed their pace and crept along to the exit cautiously. Again the companions found themselves on a stone balcony, overlooking yet another corridor, a huge passageway, nearly a chamber in itself, with a high ceiling and decorated walls. Torches burned every few feet along both sides, running parallel below them.

A lump welled in Bruenor's throat when he looked upon the carvings lining the opposite wall across the way, great sculpted bas reliefs of Garumn and Bangor and of all the patriarchs of Clan Battlehammer. He wondered, and not for the first time, if his own bust would ever take its place alongside his ancestors'.

"Half-a-dozen to ten, I make them," Catti-brie whispered, more intent on the clamor rolling out of a partly opened door down to the left, the room they had seen from their perch in the chamber of the gorge. The companions were fully twenty feet above the floor of the larger corridor. To the right, a stairway descended to the floor, and beyond it the tunnel wound its way back into the great halls.

"Side rooms where others might be hiding?" Wulfgar asked Bruenor.

The dwarf shook his head. "One anteroom there be and only one," he answered. "But more rooms lay within the cavern of Garumn's Gorge. Whether they be filled with gray ones or no, we cannot know. But no mind to them; we're to get through this room, and through the door across its way to come to the gorge."

Wulfgar slapped his hammer into a fighting grip. "Then let us go," he growled, starting for the stair.

"What about the two in the cavern beyond?" asked Regis, staying the anxious warrior with his hand.

"They'll drop the bridge afore we ever make the gorge," added Catti-brie.

Bruenor scratched his beard, then looked to his daughter. "How well do ye shoot?" he asked her.

Catti-brie held the magical bow out before her. "Well

enough to take the likes of two sentries!" she answered.

"Back to th'other tunnel with ye," said Bruenor. "At first sound of battle, take 'em out. And be fast, girl; the cowardly scum're likely to drop the bridge at the first signs of trouble!"

With a nod, she was gone. Wulfgar watched her disappear back down the corridor, not so determined to have this fight now, without knowing that Catti-brie would be safe behind him. "What if the gray ones have reinforcements near?" he asked Bruenor. "What of Catti-brie? She will be blocked from returning to us."

"No whinin', boy!" Bruenor snapped, also uncomfortable with his decision to separate. "Yer heart's for her is me guess, though ye aren't to admit it to yerself. Keep in yer head that Cat's a fighter, trained by meself. The other tunnel's safe enough, still secret from the gray ones by all the signs I could find. The girl's battle-smart to taking care of herself! So put yer thoughts to the fight before ye. The best ye can do for her is to finish these gray-bearded dogs too quick for their kin to come!"

It took some effort, but Wulfgar tore his eyes away from the corridor and refocused his gaze on the open door below, readying himself for the task at hand.

Alone now, Catti-brie quietly trotted back the short distance down the corridor and disappeared through the secret door.

"Hold!" Sydney commanded Bok, and she, too, froze in her tracks, sensing that someone was just ahead. She crept forward, the golem on her heel, and peeked around the next turn in the tunnel, expecting that she had come up on the companions. There was only empty corridor in front of her.

The secret door had closed.

Wulfgar took a deep breath and measured the odds. If Catti-brie's estimate was correct, he and Bruenor would be outnumbered several times when they burst through the door. He knew that they had no options open before them. With another breath to steady himself, he started again down the stairs, Bruenor moving on his cue and Regis following tentatively behind.

The barbarian never slowed his long strides, or turned from the straightest path to the door, yet the first sounds that they all heard were not the thumps of Aegis-fang or the barbarian's customary war cry to Tempus, but the battle song of Bruenor Battlehammer.

This was his homeland and his fight, and the dwarf placed the responsibility for the safety of his companions squarely upon his own shoulders. He dashed by Wulfgar when they reached the bottom of the stairs and crashed through the door, the mithril axe of his heroic namesake raised before him.

"This one's for me father!" he cried, splitting the shining helm of the closest Duergar with a single stroke. "This one's for me father's father!" he yelled, felling the second. "And this one's for me father's father's father!"

Bruenor's ancestral line was long indeed. The gray dwarves never had a chance.

Wulfgar had started his charge right after he realized Bruenor was rushing by him, but by the time he got into the room, three Duergar lay dead and the furious Bruenor was about to drop the fourth. Six others scrambled around trying to recover from the savage assault, and mostly trying to get out the other door and into the cavern of the gorge where they could regroup. Wulfgar hurled Aegis-fang and took another, and Bruenor pounced upon his fifth victim before the gray dwarf got through the portal.

Across the gorge, the two sentries heard the start of battle at the same time as Catti-brie, but not understanding what was happening, they hesitated.

Catti-brie didn't.

A streak of silver flashed across the chasm, exploding into the chest of one of the sentries, its powerful magic blasting through his mithril armor and hurling him backward into death.

The second lunged immediately for the lever, but Catti-brie coolly completed her business. The second streaking arrow took him in the eye.

The routed dwarves in the room below poured out into the cavern below her, and others from rooms beyond the first charged out to join them. Wulfgar and Bruenor would come through soon, too, Catti-brie knew, right into the midst of a ready host!

Bruenor's evaluation of Catti-brie had been on target. A fighter she was, and as willing to stand against the odds as any warrior alive. She buried any fears that she might have had for her friends and positioned herself to be of greatest assistance to them. Eyes and jaw steeled in determination, she took up Taulmaril and launched a barrage of death at the assembling host that put them into chaos and sent many of them scrambling for cover.

Bruenor roared out, blood-spattered, his mithril axe red from kills, and still with a hundred great-great ancestors as yet unavenged. Wulfgar was right behind, consumed by the blood lust, singing to his war god, and swatting aside his smaller enemies as easily as he would part ferns on a forest path.

Catti-brie's barrage did not relent, arrow after streaking arrow finding its deadly mark. The warrior within her possessed her fully and her actions stayed on the edges of her conscious thoughts. Methodically, she called for another arrow, and the magical quiver of Anariel obliged. Taulmaril played its own song, and in the wake of its notes lay the scorched and blasted bodies of many Duergar.

Regis hung back throughout the fight, knowing that he would be more trouble than use to his friends in the main fray, just adding one more body for them to protect when they already had all they could handle in looking out for themselves. He saw that Bruenor and Wulfgar had gained enough of an early advantage to claim victory, even against the many enemies that had come into the

cavern to face them, so Regis worked to make sure their
fallen opponents in the room were truly down and
would not come sneaking up behind.

Also, though, to make sure that any valuables these
gray ones possessed were not wasted on corpses.

He heard the heavy thump of a boot behind him. He
dove aside and rolled to the corner just as Bok crashed
through the doorway, oblivious to his presence. When
Regis recovered his voice, he moved to yell a warning to
his friends.

But then Sydney entered the room.

Two at a time fell before the sweeps of Wulfgar's warhammer. Spurred by the snatches that he caught of the
enraged dwarf's battle cries, " . . . for me father's father's
father's father's father's father's . . . " Wulfgar wore a
grim smile as he moved through the Duergar's disorganized ranks. Arrows burned lines of silver right beside
him as they sought their victims, but he trusted enough
in Catti-brie not to fear a stray shot. His muscles flexed in
another crushing blow, even the Duergar's shining
armor offering no protection against his brute strength.

But then arms stronger than his own caught him from
behind.

The few Duergar that remained before him did not
recognize Bok as an ally. They fled in terror to the chasm
bridge, hoping to cross and destroy the route of any pursuit behind them.

Catti-brie cut them down.

Regis didn't make any sudden moves, knowing Sydney's power from the encounter back in the oval room.
Her bolt of energy had flattened both Bruenor and
Wulfgar; the halfling shuddered to think what it could do
to him.

His only chance was the ruby pendant, he thought. If
he could get Sydney caught in its hypnotizing spell, he
might hold her long enough for his friends to return.

Slowly, he moved his hand under his jacket, his eyes trained upon the mage, wary for the beginnings of any killing bolt.

Sydney's wand remained tucked into her belt. She had a trick of her own planned for the little one. She muttered a quick chant, then rolled her hand open to Regis and puffed gently, launching a filmy string in his direction.

Regis understood the spell's nature when the air around him was suddenly saturated with floating webs—sticky spiders' webs. They clung to every part of him, slowing his movements, and filled the area around him. He had his hand around the magical pendant, but the web had him fully within its own grip.

Pleased in the exercising of her power, Sydney turned to the door and the battle beyond. She preferred calling upon the powers within her, but understood the strength of these other enemies, and drew her wand.

Bruenor finished the last of the gray dwarves facing him. He had taken many hits, some serious, and much of the blood covering him was his own. The rage within him that he had built over the course of centuries, though, blinded him to the pain. His blood lust was sated now, but only until he turned back toward the anteroom and saw Bok lifting Wulfgar high into the air and crushing the life out of him.

Catti-brie saw it, too. Horrified, she tried to get a clear shot at the golem, but with Wulfgar's desperate struggling, the combatants stumbled about too often for her to dare. "Help him!" she begged to Bruenor under her breath, as all that she could do was watch.

Half of Wulfgar's body was numbed under the incredible force of Bok's magically strengthened arms. He did manage to squirm around and face his foe, though, and he put a hand in the golem's eye and pushed with all his strength, trying to divert some of the monster's energy from the attack.

Bok seemed not to notice.

Wulfgar slammed Aegis-fang into the monster's face with all the force he could muster under the tight circumstances, still a blow that would have felled a giant.

Again Bok seemed not to notice.

The arms closed relentlessly. A wave of dizziness swept through the barbarian. His fingers tingled with numbness. His hammer dropped to the ground.

Bruenor was almost there, axe poised and ready to begin chopping. But as the dwarf passed the open door to the anteroom, a blinding flash of energy shot out at him. It struck his shield, luckily, and deflected up to the cavern ceiling, but the sheer force of it hurled Bruenor from his feet. He shook his head in disbelief and struggled to a sitting position.

Catti-brie saw the bolt and remembered the similar blast that had dropped both Bruenor and Wulfgar back in the oval room. Instinctively, without the slightest hesitation or concern for her own safety, she was off, running back down the passageway, driven by the knowledge that if she couldn't get to the mage, her friends didn't have a chance.

Bruenor was more prepared for the second bolt. He saw Sydney inside the anteroom lift the wand at him. He dove on his belly and threw his shield above his head, facing the mage. It held again against the blast, deflecting the energy harmlessly away, but Bruenor felt it weaken under the impact and knew that it would not withstand another.

The stubborn survival instincts of the barbarian brought his drifting mind from the swoon and back into focus on the battle. He didn't call for his hammer, knowing it to be of little use against the golem and doubting that he could have clasped it anyway. He summoned his own strength, wrapping his huge arms around Bok's neck. His corded muscles tensed to their limits and ripped beyond as he struggled. No breath would come to him; Bruenor would not get there in time. He growled away the pain and the fear, grimaced through the sensations of numbness.

And twisted with all his might.

Regis at last managed to get his hand and the pendant out from under his jacket. "Wait, mage!" he cried at Sydney, not expecting her to listen, but only hoping to divert her attention long enough for her to glimpse the gemstone, and praying that Entreri had not informed her of its hypnotizing powers.

Again the mistrust and secrecy of the evil party worked against them. Oblivious to the dangers of the halfling's ruby, Sydney glanced at him out of the corner of her eye, more to ensure that her web still held him tightly than to listen to any words he might have to say.

A sparkle of red light caught her attention more fully than she had intended, and long moments passed before she would look away.

In the main passage, Catti-brie crouched low and sped along as swiftly as she could. Then she heard the baying.

The hunting shadow hounds filled the corridors with their excited cries, and filled Catti-brie with dread. The hounds were far behind, but her knees went weak as the unearthly sound descended upon her, echoing from wall to wall and encasing her in a dizzying jumble. She gritted her teeth against the assault and pressed on. Bruenor needed her, Wulfgar needed her. She would not fail them.

She made the balcony and sprinted down the stairs, finding the door to the anteroom closed. Cursing the luck, for she had hoped to get a shot at the mage from a distance, she slung Taulmaril over her shoulder, drew her sword, and boldly, blindly, charged through.

Locked in a killing embrace, Wulfgar and Bok stumbled around the cavern, sometimes dangerously close to the gorge. The barbarian matched his muscle against Dendybar's magical work; never before had he faced such a foe. Wildly, he jerked Bok's massive head back and forth, breaking the monster's ability to resist. Then he began turning it in one direction, driving on with every ounce of power that he had left to give. He couldn't remember the last time he had found a breath; he no longer knew who he was, or where he was.

His sheer stubbornness refused to yield.

He heard the snap of bone, and couldn't be sure if it had been his own spine or the golem's neck. Bok never flinched, nor loosened its vicelike grip. The head turned easily now, and Wulfgar, driven on by the final darkness that began its descent upon him, tugged and turned in a final flurry of defiance.

Skin ripped away. The blood-stuff of the wizard's creation poured onto Wulfgar's arms and chest, and the head tore free. Wulfgar, to his own amazement, thought that he had won.

Bok seemed not to notice.

The beginnings of the ruby pendant's hypnotizing spell shattered when the door crashed in, but Regis had played his part. By the time Sydney recognized the coming danger, Catti-brie was too close for her to cast her spells.

Sydney's gaze locked into a stunned, wide-eyed stare of confused protest. All of her dreams and future plans fell before her in that one instant. She tried to scream out a denial, certain that the gods of fate had a more important role planned for her in their scheme of the universe, convinced that they would not allow the shining star of her budding power to be extinguished before it ever came to its potential.

But a thin, wooden wand is of little use in parrying a metal blade.

Catti-brie saw nothing but her target, felt nothing in that instant but the necessity of her duty. Her sword snapped through the feeble wand and plunged home.

She looked at Sydney's face for the first time. Time itself seemed to halt.

Sydney's expression had not changed, her eyes and mouth still open in denial of this possibility.

Catti-brie watched in helpless horror as the last flickers of hope and ambition faded from Sydney's eyes. Warm blood gushed over Catti-brie's arm. Sydney's final gasp of breath seemed impossibly loud.

And Sydney slid, ever so slowly, from the blade and into the realm of death.

A single, vicious cut from the mithril axe severed one of Bok's arms, and Wulfgar fell free. He landed on one knee, barely on the edge of consciousness. His huge lungs reflexively sucked in a volume of revitalizing oxygen.

Sensing the dwarf's presence clearly, but without eyes to focus upon its target, the headless golem lunged confusedly at Bruenor and missed badly.

Bruenor had no understanding of the magical forces that guided the monster, or kept it alive, and he had little desire to test his fighting skills against it. He saw another way. "Come on, ye filthy mold of orc-dung," he teased, moving toward the gorge. In a more serious tone, he called to Wulfgar, "Get yer hammer ready, boy."

Bruenor had to repeat the request over and over, and by the time Wulfgar began to hear it, Bok had backed the dwarf right up to the ledge.

Only half aware of his actions, Wulfgar found the warhammer returned to his hand.

Bruenor stopped, his heels clear of the stone floor, a smile on his face that accepted death. The golem paused, too, somehow understanding that Bruenor had nowhere left to run.

Bruenor dropped to the floor as Bok lunged forward. Aegis-fang slammed into its back, pushing it over the dwarf. The monster fell silently, with no ears to hear the sound of the air rushing past.

Catti-brie was still standing motionless over the mage's body when Wulfgar and Bruenor entered the anteroom. Sydney's eyes and mouth remained open in silent denial, a futile attempt to belie the pool of blood that deepened around her body.

Lines of tears wetted Catti-brie's face. She had felle goblinoids and gray dwarves, once an ogre and a tundr yeti, but never before had she killed a human. Neve before had she looked into eyes akin to her own an watched the light leave them. Never before had sh understood the complexity of her victim, or even tha the life she had taken existed outside the present field o battle.

Wulfgar moved to her and embraced her in full sympa thy while Bruenor cut the halfling free of the remainin strands of webbing.

The dwarf had trained Catti-brie to fight and had reve ed in her victories against orcs and the like, foul beast that deserved death by all accounts. He had alway hoped, though, that his beloved Catti-brie would b spared this experience.

Again Mithril Hall loomed as the source of his friend suffering.

Distant howls echoed from beyond the open doo behind them. Catti-brie slid the sword into its sheath, no even thinking to wipe the blood from it, and steadie herself. "The pursuit is not ended," she stated flatly. "It i past time we leave."

She led them from the room then, but left a part of her self, the pedestal of her innocence, behind.

♥ 23 ♥

The Broken Helm

Air rolled across its black wings like the continuous rumble of distant thunder as the dragon swept out of the passageway and into Garumn's Gorge, using the same exit that Drizzt and Entreri had passed just a few moments before. The two, a few dozen yards higher on the wall, held perfectly still, not even daring to breathe. They knew that the dark lord of Mithril Hall had come.

The black cloud that was Shimmergloom rushed by them, unnoticing, and soared down the length of the chasm. Drizzt, in the lead, scrambled up the side of the gorge, clawing at the stone to find whatever holds he could and trusting to them fully in his desperation. He had heard the sounds of battle far above him when he first entered the chasm, and knew that even if his friends had been victorious thus far, they would soon be met by a foe mightier than anything they had ever faced.

Drizzt was determined to stand beside them.

Entreri matched the drow's pace, wanting to keep close to him, though he hadn't yet formulated his exact plan of action.

Wulfgar and Catti-brie supported each other as they walked. Regis kept beside Bruenor, concerned for the dwarf's wounds, even if the dwarf was not. "Keep yer worries for yer own hide, Rumblebelly," he kept snapping at the halfling, though Regis could see that the depth of Bruenor's gruffness had diminished. The dwarf seemed somewhat embarrassed for the way he had act-

ed earlier. "Me wounds'll heal; don't ye be thinking ye'v
gotten rid of me so easy! There'll be time for looking t
them once we've put this place behind us."

Regis had stopped walking, a puzzled expression on hi
face. Bruenor looked back at him, confused, too, an
wondered if he had somehow offended the halflin
again. Wulfgar and Catti-brie stopped behind Regis an
waited for some indication of the trouble, not knowin
what had been said between him and the dwarf.

"What's yer grief?" Bruenor demanded.

Regis was not bothered by anything Bruenor had saic
nor with the dwarf at all at that moment. It was Shim
mergloom that he had sensed, a sudden coldness tha
had entered the cavern, a foulness that insulted the com
panions' caring bond with its mere presence.

Bruenor was about to speak again, when he, too, fel
the coming of the dragon of darkness. He looked to th
gorge just as the tip of the black cloud broke the chasm'
rim, far down to the left beyond the bridge, but speedin
toward them.

Catti-brie steered Wulfgar to the side, then he was pull
ing her with all his speed. Regis scurried back toward th
anteroom.

Bruenor remembered.

The dragon of darkness, the ultimately foul monste
that had decimated his kin and sent them fleeing for th
smaller corridors of the upper level. His mithril ax
raised, his feet frozen to the stone below them, he wait
ed.

The blackness dipped under the arch of the ston
bridge, then rose to the ledge. Spearlike talons grippe
the rim of the gorge, and Shimmergloom reared u
before Bruenor in all its horrid splendor, the usurpin
worm facing the rightful King of Mithril Hall.

"Bruenor!" Regis cried, drawing his little mace and
turning back to the cavern, knowing that the best h
could do would be to die beside his doomed friend.

Wulfgar threw Catti-brie behind him and spun back o

the dragon.

The worm, eyes locked with the dwarf's unyielding stare, did not even notice Aegis-fang spinning toward it, nor the fearless charge of the huge barbarian.

The mighty warhammer struck home against the raven black scales, but was harmlessly turned away. Infuriated that someone had interrupted the moment of its victory, Shimmergloom snapped its glare at Wulfgar.

And it breathed.

Absolute blackness enveloped Wulfgar and sapped the strength from his bones. He felt himself falling, forever falling, though there seemed to be no stone to catch him.

Catti-brie screamed and rushed to him, oblivious to her own danger as she plunged into the black cloud of Shimmergloom's breath.

Bruenor trembled in outrage, for his long-dead kin and for his friend. "Get yerself from me home!" he roared at Shimmergloom, then charged head-on and dove into the dragon, his axe flailing wildly, trying to drive the beast over the edge. The mithril weapon's razored edge had more effect on the scales than the warhammer, but the dragon fought back.

A heavy foot knocked Bruenor back to the ground, and before he could rise, the whiplike neck snapped down upon him and he was lifted in the dragon's maw.

Regis fell back again, shaking with fear. "Bruenor!" he cried again, this time his words coming out as no more than a whisper.

The black cloud dissipated around Catti-brie and Wulfgar, but the barbarian had taken the full force of Shimmergloom's insidious venom. He wanted to flee, even if the only route of escape meant plunging headlong over the side of the gorge. The shadow hounds' baying, though it was still many minutes behind them, closed in upon him. All of his wounds, the crushing of the golem, the nicks the gray dwarves had put into him, hurt him vividly, making him flinch with every step, though his adrenaline of battle had many times before dismissed far more serious and painful injuries.

The dragon seemed ten times mightier to Wulfgar, and he couldn't even have brought himself to raise a weapon against it, for he believed in his heart that Shimmergloom could not be defeated.

Despair had stopped him where fire and steel had not. He stumbled back with Catti-brie toward another room, having no strength to resist her pull.

Bruenor felt his breath blasted out, as the terrible maw crunched into him. He stubbornly held onto the axe, and even managed a swing or two.

Catti-brie pushed Wulfgar through the doorway and into the shelter of the small room, then turned back to the fight in the cavern. "Ye bastard son of a demon lizard!" she spat, as she set Taulmaril into motion. Silver-streaking arrows blasted holes into Shimmergloom's black armor. When Catti-brie understood the measure of the effectiveness of her weapon, she grasped at a desperate plan. Aiming her next shots at the monster's feet, she sought to drive it from the ledge.

Shimmergloom hopped in pain and confusion as the stinging bolts whistled in. The seething hatred of the dragon's narrowed eyes bore down upon the brave young woman. It spat Bruenor's broken form across the floor and roared, "Know fear, foolish girl! Taste of my breath and know you are doomed!" The black lungs expanded, perverting the intaken air into the foul cloud of despair.

Then the stone at the edge of the gorge broke away.

Little joy came to Regis when the dragon fell. He managed to drag Bruenor back into the anteroom, but had no idea of what to do next. Behind him, the relentless pursuit of the shadow hounds drew closer, he was separated from Wulfgar and Catti-brie, and he didn't dare cross the cavern without knowing if the dragon was truly gone. He looked down at the battered and blood-covered form of his oldest friend, having not the slightest notion of how he might begin to help him, or even if Bruenor was still alive.

Only surprise delayed Regis's immediate squeals of joy when Bruenor opened his gray eyes and winked.

Drizzt and Entreri flattened themselves against the wall as the rockslide from the broken ledge tumbled dangerously close. It was over in a moment and Drizzt started up at once, desperate to get to his friends.

He had to stop again, though, and wait nervously as the black form of the dragon dropped past him, then recovered quickly and moved back up toward the rim.

"How?" Regis asked, gawking at the dwarf.

Bruenor shifted uncomfortably and struggled to his feet. The mithril mail had held against the dragon's bite, though Bruenor had been squeezed terribly and bore rows of deep bruises, and probably a host of broken ribs, for the experience. The tough dwarf was still very much alive and alert, though, dismissing his considerable pain for the more important matter before him—the safety of his friends.

"Where's the boy, and Catti-brie?" he pressed immediately, the background howls of the shadow hounds accentuating the desperation of his tone.

"Another room," Regis answered, indicating the area to the right beyond the door to the cavern.

"Cat!" Bruenor shouted. "How do ye fare?"

After a stunned pause, for Catti-brie, too, had not expected to hear Bruenor's voice again, she called back, "Wulfgar's gone for the fight, I fear! A dragon's spell, for all I can make it! But for meself, I'm for leaving! The dogs'll be here sooner than I like!"

"Aye!" agreed Bruenor, clutching at a twinge of pain in his side when he yelled. "But have ye seen the worm?"

"No, nor heared the beast!" came the uncertain reply.

Bruenor looked to Regis.

"It fell, and has been gone since," the halfling answered the questioning stare, equally unconvinced that Shimmergloom had been defeated so easily.

"Not a choice to us, then!" Bruenor called out. "We're to make the bridge! Can ye bring the boy?"

"It's his heart for fightin' that's been bruised, no more!" replied Catti-brie. "We'll be along!"

Bruenor clasped Regis's shoulder, lending support to his nervous friend. "Let's be going, then!" he roared in his familiar voice of confidence.

Regis smiled in spite of his dread at the sight of the old Bruenor again. Without further coaxing, he walked beside the dwarf out of the room.

Even as they took the first step toward the gorge, the black cloud that was Shimmergloom again crested the rim.

"Ye see it?" cried Catti-brie.

Bruenor fell back into the room, viewing the dragon all too clearly. Doom closed in all around him, insistent and inescapable. Despair denied his determination, not for himself, for he knew that he had followed the logical course of his fate in coming back to Mithril Hall—a destiny that had been engraved upon the fabric of his very being from the day his kin had been slaughtered—but his friends should not perish this way. Not the halfling, who always before could find an escape from every trap. Not the boy, with so many glorious adventures left before him upon his road.

And not his girl. Catti-brie, his own beloved daughter. The only light that had truly shone in the mines of Clan Battlehammer in Icewind Dale.

The fall of the drow alone, willing companion and dearest friend, had been too high a price for his selfish daring. The loss that faced him now was simply too much for him to bear.

His eyes darted around the small room. There had to be an option. If ever he had been faithful to the gods of the dwarves, he asked them now to grant him this one thing. Give him an option.

There was a small curtain against one of the room's

valls. Bruenor looked curiously at Regis.

The halfling shrugged. "A storage area," he said. "Nothing of value. Not even a weapon."

Bruenor wouldn't accept the answer. He dashed through the curtain and started tearing through the crates and sacks that lay within. Dried food. Pieces of wood. An extra cloak. A skin of water.

A keg of oil.

Shimmergloom swooped back and forth along the length of the gorge, waiting to meet the intruders on its own terms in the open cavern and confident that the shadow hounds would flush them out.

Drizzt had nearly reached the level of the dragon, pressing on in the face of peril with no other concerns than those he felt for his friends.

"Hold!" Entreri called to him from a short distance below. "Are you so determined to get yourself killed?"

"Damn the dragon!" Drizzt hissed back. "I'll not cower in the shadows and watch my friends be destroyed."

"There is value in dying with them?" came the sarcastic reply. "You are a fool, drow. Your worth outweighs that of all your pitiful friends!"

"Pitiful?" Drizzt echoed incredulously. "It is you that I pity, assassin."

The drow's disapproval stung Entreri more than he would have expected. "Then pity yourself!" he shot back angrily. "For you are more akin to me than you care to believe!"

"If I do not go to them, your words will hold the truth," Drizzt continued, more calmly now. "For then my life will be of no value, less even than your own! Beyond my embrace of the heartless emptiness that rules your world, my entire life would then be no more than a lie." He started up again, fully expecting to die, but secure in his realization that he was indeed very different from the murderer that followed him.

Secure, too, in the knowledge that he had escaped his

own heritage.

Bruenor came back through the curtain, a wild smir
upon his face, an oil-soaked cloak slung over his shou
der, and the keg tied to his back. Regis looked upon hir
in complete confusion, though he could guess enough o
what the dwarf had in mind to be worried for his frienc

"What are ye lookin' at?" Bruenor said with a wink.

"You are crazy," Regis replied, Bruenor's plan comin
into clearer focus the longer he studied the dwarf.

"Aye, we agreed on that afore our road e'er began'
snorted Bruenor. He calmed suddenly, the wild glimme
mellowing to a caring concern for his little friend. "Y
deserve better'n what I've given ye, Rumblebelly," h
said, more comfortable than he had ever been in apo
ogy.

"Never have I known a more loyal friend than Brueno
Battlehammer," Regis replied.

Bruenor pulled the gem-studded helmet from his hea
and tossed it to the halfling, confusing Regis even more
He reached around to his back and loosened a strap fas
tened between his pack and his belt and took out his ol
helm. He ran a finger over the broken horn, smiling i
remembrance of the wild adventures that had given thi
helm such a battering. Even the dent where Wulfgar ha
hit him, those years ago, when first they met as enemie:

Bruenor put the helm on, more comfortable with it
fit, and Regis saw him in the light of old friend.

"Keep the helm safe," Bruenor told Regis. "It's th
crown of the King of Mithril Hall!"

"Then it is yours," Regis argued, holding the crow
back out to Bruenor.

"Nay, not by me right or me choice. Mithril Hall is n
more, Rumble—Regis. Bruenor of Icewind Dale, I am
and have been for two hundred years, though me head'
too thick to know it!

"Forgive me old bones," he said. "Suren me thoughts'v
been walking in me past and me future."

Regis nodded and said with genuine concern, "What are you going to do?"

"Mind to yer own part in this!" Bruenor snorted, suddenly the snarling leader once more. "Ye'll have enough gettin' yerself from these cursed halls when I'm through!" He growled threateningly at the halfling to keep him back, then moved swiftly, pulling a torch from the wall and dashing through the door to the cavern before Regis could even make a move to stop him.

The dragon's black form skimmed the rim of the gorge, dipping low beneath the bridge and returning to its patrolling level. Bruenor watched it for a few moments to get a feel for the rhythm of its course.

"Yer mine, worm!" he snarled under his breath, and then he charged. "Here's one from yer tricks, boy!" he cried at the room holding Wulfgar and Catti-brie. "But when me mind's to jumping on the back of a worm, I ain't about to miss!"

"Bruenor!" Catti-brie screamed when she saw him running out toward the gorge.

It was too late. Bruenor put the torch to the oil-soaked cloak and raised his mithril axe high before him. The dragon heard him coming and swerved in closer to the rim to investigate—and was as amazed as the dwarf's friends when Bruenor, his shoulder and back aflame, leaped from the edge and streaked down upon it.

Impossibly strong, as though all of the ghosts of Clan Battlehammer had joined their hands with Bruenor's upon the weapon handle and lent him their strength, the dwarf's initial blow drove the mithril axe deep into Shimmergloom's back. Bruenor crashed down behind, but held fast to the embedded weapon, even though the keg of oil broke apart with the impact and spewed flames all across the monster's back.

Shimmergloom shrieked in outrage and swerved wildly, even crashing into the stone wall of the gorge.

Bruenor would not be thrown. Savagely, he grasped the handle, waiting for the opportunity to tear the weapon free and drive it home again.

Catti-brie and Regis rushed to the edge of the gorge, helplessly calling out to their doomed friend. Wulfgar, too, managed to drag himself over, still fighting the black depths of despair.

When the barbarian looked upon Bruenor, sprawled amid the flames, he roared away the dragon's spell and, without the slightest hesitation, launched Aegis-fang. The hammer caught Shimmergloom on the side of its head and the dragon swerved again in its surprise, clipping the other wall of the gorge.

"Are ye mad?" Catti-brie yelled at Wulfgar.

"Take up your bow," Wulfgar told her. "If a true friend of Bruenor's you be, then let him not fall in vain!" Aegis-fang returned to his grasp and he launched it again, scoring a second hit.

Catti-brie had to accept the reality. She could not save Bruenor from the fate he had chosen. Wulfgar was right—she could aid the dwarf in gaining his desired end. Blinking away the tears that came to her, she took Taulmaril in hand and sent the silver bolts at the dragon.

Both Drizzt and Entreri watched Bruenor's leap in utter amazement. Cursing his helpless position, Drizzt surged ahead, nearly to the rim. He shouted out for his remaining friends, but in the commotion, and with the roaring of the dragon, they could not hear.

Entreri was directly below him. The assassin knew that his last chance was upon him, though he risked losing the only challenge he had ever found in this life. As Drizzt scrambled for his next hold, Entreri grabbed his ankle and pulled him down.

Oil found its way in through the seams in Shimmergloom's scales, carrying the fire to the dragon flesh. The dragon cried out from a pain it never believed it could know.

The thud of the warhammer! The constant sting of

those streaking lines of silver! And the dwarf! Relentless
in his attacks, somehow oblivious to the fires.

Shimmergloom tore along the length of the gorge, dipping suddenly, then swooping back up and rolling over
and about. Catti-brie's arrows found it at every turn. And
Wulfgar, wiser with each of his strikes, sought the best
opportunities to throw the warhammer, waiting for the
dragon to cut by a rocky outcropping in the wall, then
driving the monster into the stone with the force of his
throw.

Flames, stone, and dust flew wildly with each thunderous impact.

Bruenor held on. Singing out to his father and his kin
beyond that, the dwarf absolved himself of his guilt, content that he had satisfied the ghosts of his past and given
his friends a chance for survival. He didn't feel the bite of
the fire, nor the bump of stone. All he felt was the quivering of the dragon flesh below his blade, and the rever-
berations of Shimmergloom's agonized cries.

Drizzt tumbled down the face of the gorge, desperately scrambling for some hold. He slammed onto a ledge
twenty feet below the assassin and managed to stop his
descent.

Entreri nodded his approval and his aim, for the drow
had landed just where he had hoped. "Farewell, trusting
fool!" he called down to Drizzt and he started up the
wall.

Drizzt never had trusted in the assassin's honor, but he
had believed in Entreri's pragmatism. This attack made
no practical sense. "Why?" he called back to Entreri. "You
could have had the pendant without recourse!"

"The gem is mine," Entreri replied.

"But not without a price!" Drizzt declared. "You know
that I will come after you, assassin!"

Entreri looked down at him with an amused grin. "Do
you not understand, Drizzt Do'Urden? That is exactly
the purpose!"

The assassin quickly reached the rim, and peered above it. To his left, Wulfgar and Catti-brie continued their assault on the dragon. To his right, Regis stood enamored of the scene, completely unaware.

The halfling's surprise was complete, his face blanching in terror, when his worst nightmare rose up before him. Regis dropped the gem-studded helm and went limp with fear as Entreri silently picked him up and started for the bridge.

Exhausted, the dragon tried to find another method of defense. Its rage and pain had carried it too far into the battle, though. It had taken too many hits, and still the silver streaks bit into it again and again.

Still the tireless dwarf twisted and pounded the axe into its back.

One last time the dragon cut back in mid-flight, trying to snake its neck around so that it could at least take vengeance upon the cruel dwarf. It hung motionless for just a split second, and Aegis-fang took it in the eye.

The dragon rolled over in blinded rage, lost in a dizzying swirl of pain, headlong into a jutting portion of the wall.

The explosion rocked the very foundations of the cavern, nearly knocking Catti-brie from her feet and Drizzt from his precarious perch.

One final image came to Bruenor, a sight that made his heart leap one more time in victory: the piercing gaze of Drizzt Do'Urden's lavender eyes bidding him farewell from the darkness of the wall.

Broken and beaten, the flames consuming it, the dragon of darkness glided and spun, descending into the deepest blackness it would ever know, a blackness from which there could be no return. The depths of Garumn's Gorge.

And bearing with it the rightful King of Mithril Hall.

❧ 24 ❧

Eulogy for Mithril Hall

The burning dragon drifted lower and lower, the light of the flames slowly diminishing to a mere speck at the bottom of Garumn's Gorge.

Drizzt scrambled up over the ledge and came up beside Catti-brie and Wulfgar, Catti-brie holding the gem-studded helm, and both of them staring helplessly across the chasm. The two of them nearly fell over in surprise when they turned to see their drow friend returned from the grave. Even the appearance of Artemis Entreri had not prepared Wulfgar and Catti-brie for the sight of Drizzt.

"How?" Wulfgar gasped, but Drizzt cut him short. The time for explanations would come later; they had more urgent business at hand.

Across the gorge, right next to the lever hooked to the bridge, stood Artemis Entreri, holding Regis by the throat before him and grinning wickedly. The ruby pendant now hung around the assassin's neck.

"Let him go," Drizzt said evenly. "As we agreed. You have the gem."

Entreri laughed and pulled the lever. The stone bridge shuddered, then broke apart, tumbling into the darkness below.

Drizzt had thought that he was beginning to understand the assassin's motivations for this treachery, reasoning now that Entreri had taken Regis to ensure pursuit, continuing his own personal challenge with Drizzt. But now with the bridge gone and no apparent escape open before Drizzt and his friends, and the incessant baying of the shadow hounds growing closer at their backs, the drow's theories didn't seem to hold up. Angered by his confusion, he reacted quickly. Having lost his own bow back in the alcove, Drizzt grabbed Taulmaril from Catti-brie and fitted an arrow.

Entreri moved just as fast. He rushed to the ledge, scooped Regis up by an ankle, and held him by one hand over the edge. Wulfgar and Catti-brie sensed the strange bond between Drizzt and the assassin and knew that Drizzt was better able to deal with this situation. They moved back a step and held each other close.

Drizzt kept the bow steady and cocked, his eyes unblinking as he searched for the one lapse in Entreri's defenses.

Entreri shook Regis dangerously and laughed again. "The road to Calimport is long indeed, drow. You shall have your chance to catch up with me."

"You have blocked our escape," Drizzt retorted.

"A necessary inconvenience," explained Entreri. "Surely you will find your way through this, even if your other friends do not. And I will be waiting!"

"I will come," Drizzt promised. "You do not need the halfling to make me want to hunt you down, foul assassin."

"'Tis true," said Entreri. He reached into his pouch, pulled out a small item, and tossed it into the air. It twirled up above him then dropped. He caught it just before it passed beyond his reach and would have fallen into the gorge. He tossed it again. Something small, something black.

Entreri tossed it a third time, teasingly, the smile widening across his face as Drizzt lowered the bow.

Guenhwyvar.

"I do not need the halfling," Entreri stated flatly and he held Regis farther out over the chasm.

Drizzt dropped the magical bow behind him, but kept his glare locked upon the assassin.

Entreri pulled Regis back in to the ledge. "But my master demands the right to kill this little thief. Lay your plans, drow, for the hounds draw near. Alone, you stand a better chance. Leave those two, and live!

"Then come, drow. Finish our business." He laughed one more time and spun away into the darkness of the final tunnel.

"He's out, then," said Catti-brie. "Bruenor named that passage as a straight run to a door out of the halls."

Drizzt looked all around, trying to find some means to get them across the chasm.

"By Bruenor's own words, there is another way," Catti-brie offered. She pointed down to her right, toward the south end of the cavern. "A ledge," she said, "but hours of walking."

"Then run," replied Drizzt, his eyes still fixed upon the tunnel across the gorge.

By the time the three companions reached the ledge, the echoes of howls and specks of light far to the north told them that Duergar and shadow hounds had entered the cavern. Drizzt led them across the narrow walkway, his back pressed against the wall as he inched his way toward the other side. All the gorge lay open before him, and the fires still burned below, a grim reminder of the fate of his bearded friend. Perhaps it was fitting that Bruenor died here, in the home of his ancestors, he thought. Perhaps the dwarf had finally satisfied the yearning that had dictated so much of his life.

The loss remained intolerable to Drizzt, though. His years with Bruenor had shown him a compassionate and respected friend, a friend he could rely upon at any time, in any circumstance. Drizzt could tell himself over and over that Bruenor was satisfied, that the dwarf had climbed his mountain and won his personal battle, but in the terrible immediacy of his death, those thoughts did little to dispel the drow's grief.

Catti-brie blinked away more tears, and Wulfgar's sigh belied his stoicism when they moved out across the gorge that had become Bruenor's grave. To Catti-brie, Bruenor was father and friend, who taught her toughness and touched her with tenderness. All of the constants of her world, her family and home, lay burning far below, on the back of a hell-spawned dragon.

A numbness descended over Wulfgar, the cold chill of mortality and the realization of how fragile life could be. Drizzt had returned to him, but now Bruenor was gone. Above any emotions of joy or grief came a wave of instability, a tragic rewriting of heroic images and bard-sung legends that he had not expected. Bruenor had died with courage and strength, and the story of his fiery leap would be told and retold a thousand times. But it would never fill the void that Wulfgar felt at that moment.

They made their way across to the chasm's other side and raced back to the north to get to the final tunnel and be free of the shadows of Mithril Hall. When they came again into the wide end of the cavern, they were spotted. Duergar shouted and cursed at them; the great black shadow hounds roared their threats and scratched at the lip of the other side of the gorge. But their enemies had no way to get at them, short of going all the way around to the ledge, and Drizzt stepped unopposed into the tunnel that Entreri had entered a few hours earlier.

Wulfgar followed, but Catti-brie paused at the entrance and looked back across the gorge at the gathered host of gray dwarves.

"Come," Drizzt said to her. "There is nothing that we can do here, and Regis needs our help."

Catti-brie's eyes narrowed and the muscles in her jaw clenched tightly as she fitted an arrow to her bow and fired. The silver streak whistled into the crowd of Duergar and blasted one from life, sending the others scurrying for cover. "Nothing now," Catti-brie replied grimly, "but I'll be comin' back! Let the gray dogs know it for truth.

"I'll be back!"

Epilogue

Drizzt, Wulfgar, and Catti-brie came into Longsaddle a few days later, road weary and still wrapped in a shroud of grief. Harkle and his kin greeted them warmly and invited them to stay at the Ivy Mansion for as long as they desired. But though all three of them would have welcomed the opportunity to relax and recover from their trials, other roads summoned them.

Drizzt and Wulfgar stood at the exit of Longsaddle the very next morning, with fresh horses provided by the Harpells. Catti-brie walked down to them slowly, Harkle holding back a few steps behind her.

"Will you come?" Drizzt asked, but guessed by her expression that she would not.

"Would that I could," Catti-brie replied. "Ye'll get to the halfling, I don't fear. I've another vow to fulfill."

"When?" Wulfgar asked.

"In the spring, by me guess," said Catti-brie. "The magic of the Harpells has set the thing to going; already they've called out to the clan in the dale, and to Harbromm in Citadel Adbar. Bruenor's kin'll be marchin' out afore the week's end, with many allies from Ten-Towns. Harbromm promises eight thousand, and some of the Harpells have pledged their help."

Drizzt thought of the undercity he had viewed in his passage of the lower levels, and of the bustle of thousands of gray dwarves, all outfitted in shining mithril. Even with all of Clan Battlehammer and their friends from the dale, eight thousand battle-seasoned dwarves from Adbar, and the magical powers of the Harpells, the victory would be hard won if won at all.

Wulfgar also understood the enormity of the task that Catti-brie would face, and doubt came to him about his decision to set out with Drizzt. Regis needed him, but he could not turn away from Catti-brie in her need.

Catti-brie sensed his torment. She walked up to him and kissed him suddenly, passionately, then jumped back. "Get yer business done and over, Wulfgar, son of Beornegar," she said. "And get ye back to me!"

"I, too, was Bruenor's friend," Wulfgar argued. "I, too, shared in his vision of Mithril Hall. I should be beside you when you go to honor him."

"Ye've a friend alive that needs ye now," Catti-brie snapped at him. "I can set the plans to going. Ye get yerself after Regis! Pay Entreri all he's got coming, and be quick. Mighten be that ye'll get back in time to march to the halls."

She turned to Drizzt, a most-trusted hero. "Keep him safe for me," she pleaded. "Show him a straight road, and show him the way back!"

On Drizzt's nod, she spun and ran back up to Harkle and toward the Ivy Mansion. Wulfgar did not follow. He trusted in Catti-brie.

"For the halfling and the cat," he said to Drizzt, clasping Aegis-fang and surveying the road before them.

Sudden fires glowed in the drow's lavender eyes, and Wulfgar took an involuntary step back. "And for other reasons," Drizzt said grimly, looking out over the wide southland that held the monster he might have become. It was his destiny to meet Entreri in battle again, he knew, the test of his own worth to defeat the killer.

"For other reasons."

*　*　*　*　*

Dendybar's breath came hard to him as he viewed the scene—Sydney's corpse stuffed into a corner of a dark room.

The specter, Morkai, waved his arm and the image was replaced by a view of the bottom of Garumn's Gorge.

"No!" Dendybar screamed when he saw the remains of the golem, headless and lying among the rubble. The mottled wizard shook visibly. "Where is the drow?" he demanded of the specter.

Morkai waved the image away and stood silent, pleased at Dendybar's distress.

"Where is the drow?" Dendybar repeated, more loudly.

Morkai laughed at him. "Find your own answers, foolish mage. My service to you is ended!" The apparition puffed into fire and was gone.

Dendybar leaped wildly from his magic circle and kicked the burning brazier over. "I shall torment you a thousand times for your insolence!" he yelled into the emptiness of the room. His mind spun with the possibilities. Sydney dead. Bok dead. Entreri? The drow and his friends? Dendybar needed answers. He could not forsake his search for the Crystal Shard, could not be denied the power he sought.

Deep breaths steadied him as he concentrated on the beginnings of a spell. He saw the bottom of the gorge again, brought the image into sharp focus within his mind. As he chanted through the ritual, the scene became more real, more tangible. Dendybar experienced it fully; the darkness, the hollow emptiness of the shadowy walls and the almost imperceptible swish of air running through the ravine, the jagged hardness of the broken stone under his feet.

He stepped out of his thoughts and into Garumn's Gorge.

"Bok," he whispered as he stared down at the twisted and broken form of his creation, his greatest achievement.

The thing stirred. A rock rolled away from it as it shifted and struggled to rise before its creator. Dendybar watched in disbelief, amazed that the magical strength he had imbued upon the golem was so resilient as to survive such a drop, and such mutilation.

Bok stood in front of him, waiting.

Dendybar studied the thing for a long moment, pondering how he might begin to restore it. "Bok!" he greeted it emphatically, a hopeful grin coming to him. "Come, my pet. I shall take you back home and mend your wounds."

Bok took a step forward, crowding Dendybar against the wall. The wizard, still not understanding, started to order the golem away.

But Bok's remaining arm shot up and grasped Dendybar by the throat, lifting him into the air and choking off any further commands. Dendybar grabbed and flailed at the arm, helpless and confused.

A familiar laugh came to his ears. A ball of fire appeared above the torn stump of the golem's neck, transforming into a familiar face.

Morkai.

Dendybar's eyes bulged in terror. He realized that he had overstepped his limits, had summoned the specter too many times. He had never truly dismissed Morkai from this last encounter, and suspected rightly that he probably wouldn't have been strong enough to push the specter from the material plane even if he had tried. Now, outside of his magic circle of protection, he was at the mercy of his nemesis.

"Come, Dendybar," Morkai grinned, his dominating will twisting the golem's arm. "Join me in the realm of death where we might discuss your treachery!"

A snap of bone echoed across the stones, the ball of fire puffed away, and wizard and golem tumbled down, lifeless.

Farther down the gorge, half buried in a pile of debris, the fires of the burning dragon had died to a smoky smolder.

Another rock shifted and rolled away.

THE AUTHOR

Born in Massachusetts in 1959, Bob Salvatore lives there still with his wife, Diane, and their three children. His love affair with fantasy, and with literature in general, began during his sophomore year of college when he was given a copy of J.R.R. Tolkien's *The Lord of the Rings* as a Christmas gift. He promptly changed his major from computer science to journalism and was awarded a bachelor of science degree in Communications/Media from Fitchburg State College in 1981. He has continued his studies part-time since and is nearing completion of his bachelor of arts degree in English.

During the day, he works as a financial specialist for a manufacturer of automatic test equipment. He spends his evenings at his word processor, after the kids are tucked away in bed.

He has written two novels in the Icewind Dale Trilogy, *The Crystal Shard* and *Streams of Silver*, set in TSR, Inc.'s FORGOTTEN REALMS™ fantasy setting.

BUCK ROGERS™

ADVENTURE BOOKS

ARRIVAL

Stories By Today's Hottest Science Fiction Writers!

Flint Dille

Augustine Funnell

S.N. Lewitt

M.S. Murdock

Jerry Oltion

Robert Sheckley

A.D. 1995: An American pilot flies a suicide mission against an enemy Space Defense Platform to save the world from nuclear war. Buck Rogers blasts his target and vanishes in a fiery blaze.

A.D. 2456: In the midst of this 25th century battlefield an artifact is discovered--one that is valuable enough to ignite a revolution. This artifact is none other than the perfectly preserved body of the 20th century hero, Buck Rogers.

FANTASY ADVENTURE

THE MOONSHAE TRILOGY
Douglas Niles

The conclusion!

Darkwell

The ultimate struggle of good and evil.... At stake, the survival of the Moonshae Isles. Tristan must forge a lasting alliance between the divergent people of the Isles. Robyn must confront an evil that has infested the land itself. Together they must decide if they will face the future together as king and queen--or as enemies, forever separated by failure and mistrust. Available in March 1989.

1987: *Darkwalker on Moonshae*

Tristan Kendrick must rally the diverse people of the Isles of Moonshae to halt the spread of a relentless army of firbolgs and dread Bloodriders.

1988: *Black Wizards*

An army of ogres and zombies guided by Bhaal threatens the gentle Ffolk while the puppet king acquiesces.

Wondrous New TSR™ Books

Illegal Aliens
Nick Pollotta
Phil Foglio
Hugo award-winning illustrator

A New York City street gang becomes guinea pigs for a group of weirdo aliens. Available in February 1989.

The Jewels of Elvish
Nancy V. Berberick Author of best -selling *Stormblade*

A tenuous alliance is threatened when a powerful ruby is stolen. Available in April 1989.

Monkey Station
Ardath Mayhar
Ron Fortier

A deadly plague sweeps the globe, causing the Macaques in the rain forests of South America to evolve faster. Available in June 1989.